Greed

VERSUS

Goodness

Rod Plotnik

authorHOUSE®

AuthorHouse™
1663 Liberty Drive
Bloomington, IN 47403
www.authorhouse.com
Phone: 1-800-839-8640

Published by AuthorHouse 1/4/2013

ISBN: 978-1-4817-0444-1 (sc)
ISBN: 978-1-4817-0443-4 (hc)
ISBN: 978-1-4817-0442-7 (e)

Cover illustration by Tim Jacobus tjacobus@optoline.net

Library of Congress Control Number: 2012924383

This book is printed on acid-free paper.

CHAPTER 1

▬ ▬ ▬

On Tuesday morning, the following bold headline appeared across the front page of the San Diego Union-Tribune:

BALDNESS CURE — 100 MILLION-DOLLAR HOAX

Little did anyone know this headline would set off an improbable series of events that would eventually include false tips to police, blackmail, a hundred lies, three murder attempts, a national manhunt, an Abbot accused of growing marijuana, a lecture on exorcism, bass fishing in Florida, two planned kidnappings, an ancient forest inhabited by red-eyed devils, and finally, an immoral but pleasurable act committed in a church confessional.

The person responsible for setting off the unusual series of events was Herbert Hallmore, a pudgy, God-fearing man, who rose at five o'clock every morning, brought in the morning paper, and read it front to back as he drank two cups of coffee with half and half and ate two jelly donuts.

"Thank you Jesus," Herbert said out loud after he had read and reread the hoax article. Herbert was a religious man who loved God and money in almost equal amounts. He regularly thanked God for helping him become Chief Financial Officer of the Money Bank in San Diego, which gave him endless opportunities to handle and accumulate the lovely green stuff. Of course, Herbert denied having a greedy nature, saying his interest in money was simply part of his job as Chief Financial Officer.

After Herbert read the hoax-article in the morning paper, his greedy desires surfaced and dollar signs began flashing in his brain like a marquee advertising the latest 3-D movie. Herbert put the newspaper down on his table, folded his hands in prayer, looked up at the ceiling of his humble kitchen, and thanked God for presenting him with a very advantageous financial opportunity.

Later that same morning, Randolph Stranger, senior partner of the prestigious law firm Stranger, Foremore, and Long, had read the same hoax article. Randolph would be the second person involved in setting off the implausible sequence of events.

Randolph looked again at the headline and thought, *how could it have been a hoax? I saw at least a fifty bald rats growing new, healthy hair. I held one in my hands. I even tugged the hair to make sure it was real. I was guaranteed my initial investment of two million would in a few years turn into fifty million.*

Randolph knew this hoax would cause serious financial problems, but he was not particularly worried because he was a genius at weathering problems and coming out a winner. Randolph could lie so convincingly that not even the pope would doubt his word. He sometimes looked in the mirror and said, *I'm looking at the best liar God ever created.* He could assume whatever personality the situation demanded. He had been kind, sympathetic, and supportive in his courting of his wife, Marjorie Whatting, who had inherited a considerable fortune from her deceased father. He had been controlling, assertive, and hard-nosed when raising Bart, his stepson, who needed to develop toughness to compete in today's world. He had been clever, cunning, and convincing when persuading Marjorie to transfer her inheritance to another bank, the Money Bank, under the guise of getting higher returns, which was a very believable lie. The truth was her current financial planner was much too suspicious and nixed all his schemes to gain access to Marjorie's millions. The new Chief Financial Officer at the Money Bank, one Herbert Hallmore, had agreed to be his silent and cooperative partner in various shady deals as long as he received a percentage of the profits.

Randolph's secretary buzzed and said, "Herbert Hallmore is on the line."

"Hello, Herbert. I thought you might be calling," Randolph said, sounding upbeat and not the least bit worried.

"You sound very cherry for having just lost two million dollars. If you remember, I repeatedly warned you against investing in a Chinese company claiming to have cured baldness with injections of stem cells. I repeatedly told you to check out their claim, and you assured me you had. Apparently you hadn't done due diligence because your two million is gone. The question is how will you now repay the loan?" Herbert asked, his voice rising to emphasize the hopelessness of his question.

But Herbert wasn't hopeless or even the least bit worried that his bank might have to write off Randolph's loan. Herbert had approved Randolph's unusually large personal loan only after Marjorie had acted as cosigner,

2

pledging her large fortune as collateral. And best of all, after the loan documents were signed, Randolph had sent a black leather briefcase containing thirty thousand dollars in used bills as a thank you. The lovely briefcase had made Herbert's day and he looked forward to many more such briefcases.

"Herbert, please calm down or you will have another one of your gastric attacks," Randolph said, knowing Herbert practically lived on Maalox and jelly donuts.

"Calm down? How can I?" Herbert said in an exaggerated tone, still acting like an anguished banker. "My signature is on the loan documents, and my reputation is at stake. How could you have been so completely fooled? How could you —"

"Herbert," Randolph interrupted, "you do not need to tell me what I already know. I not only read the newspaper article but had personally taken a tour of the Chinese laboratory before I decided to invest my money."

Randolph sounded testy and wanted to move on to the real purpose of Herbert's call.

"Just let me finish! When you took the tour did the Chinese so-called scientists explain the rats they were using were expensive because they were specially bred to be hairless?" Herbert asked, taking pleasure in rubbing Randolph's nose is his dumb decision.

"Yes, they explained all the rats had been specially bred to be hairless and were often used in various kinds of research," Randolph said, knowing there was no stopping Herbert now.

"Did the Chinese scientists ask you to randomly select one of the treated rats from rows of cages to prove there were no fake or planted rats?" Herbert asked.

"Yes they did, and I randomly selected a treated rat for inspection," Randolph said.

"And when you looked at the rat, was its right side hairless? Just pink skin?" Herbert asked.

"Of course the rat's right side was nothing but pink skin because it was bred to be hairless," Randolph said, trying not to show his impatience.

"And when you looked at the rat's left side, which was supposedly injected with modified stem cells, was it fully covered in thick, healthy hair?"

"Yes," Randolph said.

"And to prove the hair was not glued on like a fancy wig, did they ask you to tug the hair as hard as you wanted?" Herbert asked.

"Yes, the rat's left side was covered in healthy hair, and I did tug and pull, and it was real hair," Randolph said.

3

He remembered seeing the amazing contrast between the rat's natural, pink-skinned right side and its healthy, thick-haired, treated left side. The contrast had been so astonishing that it completely convinced him the Chinese company had found a stem cell cure for baldness.

"And do you know the saying, if something appears to be to good to be true, it—"

"Yes, Herbert," Randolph again interrupted, "I know the saying. So what is your point?"

"My point is all the rats you saw were actually normal, healthy, hairy rats, not a single one bred to be hairless. The Chinese so-called scientists were not skilled researchers but only very skilled barbers. They regularly shaved the rats' right sides to expose their pink skin, making them appear hairless. They said they had injected the rats' left sides with stem cells, which resulted in the rats growing new, healthy hair. But, in fact, nothing had been done to the rats' left sides. They were simply covered in their normal, healthy hair. It was a such a clever hoax that it might make a great movie," Herbert said, sounding much too sarcastic.

Randolph did not like sarcasm and did not reply.

"Are you still there?" Herbert asked.

"Yes," Randolph said, knowing Herbert would not stop until he had regurgitated the entire article.

"I'm almost finished," Herbert said. "According to the article, each potential backer was told two million dollars was the minimum initial investment, but when the company went public in six to twelve months, the shares would skyrocket since finding a cure for baldness was the holy grail of research. But then, *poof*, the Chinese vanish, it's all a hoax, and you're out two million dollars."

Herbert almost started singing his favorite hymn, "God is so Good," because some very easy money was about to come his way.

Randolph knew he had been duped as badly as someone writing a two million dollar check to buy the Brooklyn Bridge. For one of the few times in his entire life, he had acted rashly, motivated by his chance to make millions, be truly rich in his own right, and end the ugly gossip about how he was living on Marjorie's money.

"Because your personal loan was exceptionally large there was a condition if anything went amiss with your investment, the bank could call in the loan and you have ninety days to repay the two million dollars, plus accrued interest. Obviously, something went amiss since the investment was a hoax. Now the bank has no choice but to call in your loan," Herbert finished as if he were a hangman ready to put on the noose.

Herbert had no way to know Marjorie had not actually cosigned

4

the loan. Randolph had forged her signature because he had deemed the baldness cure a chance in a lifetime to make a fortune. Marjorie was not a risky investor and would never have invested in a questionable Chinese company. But without Marjorie as cosigner, Herbert's bank would never have approved such a large person loan. Randolph was on dangerous ground because if his forgery of Marjorie's signature ever came to light, he would certainly be disbarred and might even face jail time.

Herbert made a suggestion he had thought about before calling Randolph. "I think the bank would consider giving you a year to pay off your loan provided you agreed to a slightly higher interest rate." Herbert smiled to himself as he would receive an extra large year-end bonus for renegotiating Randolph's loan at higher interest.

"I think that is a reasonable suggestion," Randolph said, knowing he didn't have a choice.

"I'll draw up the new loan documents and have them sent over for you and Marjorie to sign," Herbert said and quickly added, "By the way, my black briefcase has disappeared, so I'll be needing a new one."

"All right," was all Randolph said, knowing Herbert expected his usual pay off of thirty thousand dollars. Randolph would have to forge Marjorie's signature yet again, something he could do very well.

Herbert put down his phone, already calculating the bonus he would receive and looking forward to a new, black briefcase filled with thirty thousand dollars. Herbert glanced up at the ceiling and mouthed, *Thank you Jesus for my good fortune.*

Randolph stared at the phone and thought, *I must come up with two million dollars in a year. Difficult but not impossible since I know where a little over two million dollars is waiting with my name on it. Taking it might cause tears but they won't be mine.*

Chapter 2

— — —

Norman Bestsome, Marjorie's father, thought Randolph was another one of the slick suitors who had their eyes on the fortune she would inherit when he died. He had asked Marjorie to stop by, and they were now sitting in his living room. Norman was a shrewd, straightforward kind of person, did not like small talk, and got right to what needed to be said.

"I know you are getting serious about Randolph, so I did some checking and discovered some disturbing things. It turns out he is a successful lawyer, but some of his wealthy clients are suspect and maybe connected to a drug cartel in Tijuana," Norman said.

"His clients don't concern me," Marjorie said, her face turning red with anger. "Randolph has been very loving and supportive. And he's always treated me with complete respect. Never once did he talk about money or ask about my inheritance."

That didn't surprise Norman, who figured Randolph was much too clever to talk about money. He switched to another topic.

"I also asked several of my colleagues how Randolph made full partner in two years, when it usually takes at least five or more years. They said the talk on the street was Randolph had threatened to reveal some very damning personal information about the two senior partners. In other words, Randolph became full partner by using blackmail, which certainly raises questions about his character. I would advise you think long and hard before agreeing to marry him."

"I'm sure those accusations are nothing but rumors, spread by people who are jealous and envious of Randolph's talents. I love him and intend to marry him," Marjorie said in an angry tone, her face turning red hot.

Norman was a crusty old man and not accustomed to people rejecting his good advice, especially not his own daughter. He looked at her through eyes partially cloudy from cataracts and tried to keep his voice calm.

"Marjorie, from what I have just told you, how can you possibly trust him? However, if you insist on marrying him, will you at least take my advice and protect your inheritance by asking him to sign a prenuptial agreement?"

Marjorie loved her father and did not want to argue because stress was bad for his failing heart.

Norman had drawn up a prenuptial agreement that prevented Randolph from ever getting any monies from Marjorie's inheritance. But Randolph was determined to marry her anyway. He knew he had years to figure out a way to work around the terms of the prenuptial agreement.

Norman's health continued to fail, and he was confined to his sick bed. One day when Marjorie came to visit, Norman had said, "I do not have much time left and would like to give Randolph some last good advice."

She had agreed and had brought Randolph to Norman's sick bed. She remembered Randolph bending down and putting his ear close to Norman's mouth to hear what he was saying. After leaving Norman's sick bed, Marjorie asked Randolph what advice Norman had given him.

Randolph had kept his face neutral and said in a calm voice, "Norman said I must promise to always love and protect you."

But that was another of Randolph convenient lies.

What Norman had actually whispered into Randolph's ear was, "Make your own money, you bastard. You'll never get any of Marjorie's."

Randolph had been so angry he would have reached out and strangled the old man's wrinkled neck if Marjorie had not been there.

During his final days, Norman had added another stipulation to Marjorie's prenuptial agreement. He decided not to inform Marjorie, because it would be too upsetting. But he decided to tell Carol about the stipulation so she could look out for and have the legal means to protect her mother. The stipulation read: if at any time Randolph were ever found to be unfaithful, such behavior would trigger immediate divorce proceedings.

With his health failing, Norman began to set up trust funds for Marjorie's two children, Bart and Carol. Norman had been well enough to carefully check Carol's trust documents, but he took a turn for the worse before he could do the same for Bart's. Norman had asked Marjorie to check Bart's documents, but she was too worried about Norman's health and instead asked Randolph to do the checking. Randolph saw his chance to get some revenge for Norman forcing him to sign the prenuptial agreement. Randolph had cleverly inserted a malfeasance clause among four pages of single-spaced trust documents. In everyday terms, the malfeasance clause said if Bart were arrested or convicted of any criminal action before the age of thirty, the management of his trust fund would automatically come under the sole discretionary control of Randolph. A few weeks later Marjorie had married Randolph and a month later Norman died.

7

* * * *

Randolph was now sitting is his office, thinking of ways to raid Bart's trust fund, which he knew held about two million. *I'll first try the honey approach, which is quick and easy. If it doesn't work, I switch to the vinegar approach, which is underhanded, cause some tears but guaranteed to work.*

If he used the honey approach, he would tell Bart he could double his money if he transferred his trust to Herbert's bank. Bart would need to sign several pages of single-spaced legalese documents, which like most people, he wouldn't bother to read. Buried in the documents, Randolph would insert a clause that essentially gave him alone complete control over Bart's trust, no longer needing approval of a bank officer. Once Bart signed the documents, Randolph could gradually start withdrawing money to pay off his loan.

Randolph sat back in his chair and figured if the honey approach didn't work, he'd switch to the vinegar approach. That would involve asking a retired police officer and former client to arrange for Bart to be arrested for something, probably using illegal drugs. As long as Bart were arrested for something, even if never convicted, the malfeasance clause Randolph had inserted into Bart's original trust documents would be triggered and sole control of the trust would be automatically transferred to him.

The only reason Randolph decided to first try the honey approach was he owed his stepson some consideration. Besides, the vinegar approach makes Marjorie and Carol very unhappy but he would deal with their tears when the time came.

Randolph thought, *I'm sure the dearly-departed Norman would turn over in his expensive, Heavenly White, lead-sealed casket if he knew I was planning to raid his grandson's seemingly secure, multimillion-dollar trust fund.*

Randolph did have one rather large problem. He and Bart were not on the best of terms. When Bart was growing up, Randolph had given Bart a hard time because he wanted Bart to develop a backbone and learn how to deal with adversity. But the real underlying reasons were Randolph wanted to be top-dog and hated when Bart stood up and talked back. Because of their combative relationship, Randolph needed some reason for Bart to come to his office and sign the transfer documents. *The two things Bart enjoys most in the world are surfing and baseball. I'll propose taking him to a Padres game. He'll jump at the chance, especially if a promise to get the best seats. The Padres' tickets will be the honey. I'll need to call Marjorie so she can encourage Bart to come. He would never disappoint his mother.*

Randolph picked up his phone and dialed Marjorie's number.

"Hello," came Marjorie's sweet voice.

"How are you feeling?" Randolph asked.

"Much better. I was working in the garden, and that always cheers me up," Marjorie said.

"I'm glad to hear that," Randolph said, but at the moment he wasn't particularly interested in flowers or Marjorie's health.

"I was reading the local paper and noticed the Padres were playing on Sunday. I know how much Bart likes baseball, and I wanted to call and invite him to Sunday's game," Randolph said.

He heard only silence on Marjorie's end so he quickly added, "I know I haven't spent much time with Bart, but I would like to change that and be a better father. I only hope it is not too late to start."

Randolph's saying he wanted to start spending time with Bart left Marjorie totally dumfounded and speechless. She did not know what had prompted Randolph's change of heart, but it was something she had hoped and prayed for all these years. She would do anything and everything in her power to foster a caring father/son relationship.

"Oh, that's wonderful," was all Marjorie could say as tears of joy filled her eyes.

"I wanted to call Bart and invite him to a Padre game, but I misplaced his new cell number. Could you call him for me and ask if he could drop by tomorrow, around one o'clock, so we could make plans. Lately I have been very busy and have not been able to spend as much time with Bart as I like."

"Oh yes. Of course," Marjorie said, trying to hold back her tears. "It's so wonderful you're doing this. I'm sure Bart will be really pleased."

"Remember, have him come by this Wednesday, about one. Please remind him to dress professionally and try not to be late," Randolph added.

"I'll call Bart as soon as we finish talking. I'm so very pleased you are reaching out to him," Marjorie said, holding her hand over her pounding heart, feeling it beat with happiness.

Wiping the tears from her cheeks, she sat down for a minute, and thought how Randolph had always been kinder to Carol, the older of her two children but now he was finally reaching out to Bart. *How wonderful it would be if they could finally be one happy family.* She speed dialed Bart's number and couldn't wait to tell him the good news.

"Hello," Bart said.

"Hi, it's mom. I've got some really good news. Randolph just called to say he wanted to take you to a Padre game because he knows you love baseball. He wondered if you could stop by Wednesday, about one o'clock, and make plans to go to a game. I assured him you would be delighted to do that," Marjorie said.

Bart was so stunned he dropped the peanut butter and strawberry jelly toast he had been holding and watched it land on its jelly side. He stared dumbly at the dropped toast and wondered if the world were coming to an end.

Finally he managed to say, "Mom, you know I love baseball, but I know Randolph hates it. He's never offered to take me to a game. What's come over him?" Bart asked.

"He said that he's been very busy and now wants to make it up to you. He hopes you'll be understanding and give him a chance to make a fresh start," Marjorie said, embellishing Randolph's words and adding in some of her own hopes and dreams.

"I think it might be a little late," Bart said.

"It's never too late when it comes to family matters. Please, just do this one thing for me. Give him a chance. I know it will work out. Promise me you'll go Wednesday and see him," Marjorie pleaded.

"OK," Bart said, knowing he would do anything to please his loving mother, even go to Randolph's office, which would be as much fun as going into a dragon's liar.

"Oh, that's wonderful. It makes me so happy to think you two might become friends at last. And please, wear your nice suit and tie so you'll make a good impression. You know how he likes to see you all dressed up. Remember, just give him a chance."

"OK. I'll give him a chance," Bart said and made a face like he had just swallowed a big, green, ugly bug.

"And will you promise to wear a suit and tie?" his mother begged.

"Yes," Bart said, unconsciously crossing his fingers behind his back.

Chapter 3

— — —

On Wednesday morning Bart had three cups of coffee, needing the caffeine to keep him bright and alert. He had his doubts about Randolph wanting to make a fresh start, but he had promised his mom to give Randolph a chance. But down deep he knew Randolph was a first-class operator and might be up to one of his devious tricks.

He carefully selected his clothes, checked his appearance in the mirror, and adjusted his baseball cap.

"That's about right," he said.

Just before he went out the door, he texted Carol.

I'm going to see Randy-Dandy. Wish me luck.

Bart only referred to his stepfather as Randy-Dandy when privately talking to Carol. After the marriage vows were read, his stepfather had preferred being called Randolph, and not friendly names like *father*, *dad*, or *daddy*.

It was about twelve-thirty when Bart finally left his small, rented house in Ocean Beach (or as the natives said, "OB"). He liked living in OB because it was a small community with no high-rises, boarded the ocean, had excellent surfing spots, and was populated by a great mix of people trying to keep the planet green. OB was only twenty minutes away from UCSD, which was short for University of California, San Diego. He was a junior, majoring in computer science and hoping one day to start his own hi-tech company.

Starting his rusting but reliable, topless jeep, Bart drove to downtown San Diego, which took about twenty minutes. He parked in a cheapo lot, walked six blocks, and entered the lobby of an impressive, fifty-two-storied skyscraper on the corner of Fourth and Broadway. He went through the crowded lobby, whose signature piece was an eye-catching, twenty-foot long aquarium filled with every kind of colorful tropical fish.

Bart got on the express elevator and rode to the top floor. When the elevator's doors opened on the fifty-second floor, he got off and started walking down the maroon carpeted hallway. He stopped in front of two frosted, double glass doors with large gold lettering that read:

Stranger, Foremore, and Long, Attorneys at Law

He pushed open both doors, held his shoulders high, and walked though as is he were a celebrity going to the Academy Awards.

He went up to the secretary's ebony and chrome-trimmed desk, stopped a few feet away, and smiled.

"Hi, I'm Bart," he said. "Here to see Randolph for a one o'clock appointment."

"I'll tell Mr. Stranger you are here," the secretary said and smiled back. She was attractive and wore a sleek dark blue pant suit and a light blue silk blouse, with a single strand of white pearls around her neck and matching, dangling pearl earrings.

Bart had kept one promise to his mother, which was to go to Randolph's office. But he simply couldn't keep the second promise, which was to make a good impression by wearing a suit and tie. Instead, he had chosen his favorite, worn-but-clean Levis and an oversized Padre jersey bearing the name and number of his favorite player and Hall-of-Famer, Tony Gwynn. And for good measure, he wore a Padres cap, turned backwards.

Bart walked over and sat down in one the very classy, black leather chairs trimmed in chrome. Bart thought, *if Randolph really wanted to make a fresh start, he can start by accepting how I'm dressed.*

As Bart waited, he couldn't help remembering how nice Randolph had been when he first started dating his mom. She had always been strong and confident but became hesitant and depressed after his real father had suddenly and expectedly died from an undiagnosed, congenital heart problem.

Marjorie had desperately needed someone to love, support, and care for her, plus help raise two freewheeling kids. Along had come handsome, charming Randolph, who was everything she needed and wanted. He was like a shining knight coming to the rescue of a grieving maiden. And while they were dating, Randolph had been very nice to Bart and Carol. He had bought them presents, taken them to the zoo, and acted like a caring stepfather. But after the sound of the wedding bells had faded, Randolph changed and became less fatherly, more controlling, and tolerated no disagreements. Bart didn't take to Randolph being such a big wheel, know-it-all, and he often talked back. Thankfully, his older sister Carol was around to help get him out of trouble.

He was thinking of the time when—

"Mr. Stranger will see you now," came the secretary's voice. "Mr. Randolph's office is at the end of this hallway."

Bart walked down the hallway until he reached a door with a large, silver nameplate that read:

Mr. Randolph Stranger, Senior Partner

He squared his shoulders and knocked on Randolph's door.

"Come in," Randolph said in his professional voice.

Bart opened the door and walked into Randolph's corner office, which had thick grey carpeting, fifteen-foot, floor-to-ceiling windows, and an amazing wide-angle view of the San Diego harbor.

Randolph stood up and came out from behind his desk. Wanting to foster a friendly feeling, he shook Bart's hand.

Standing over six feet tall, Randolph made an impressive image. He was wearing a charcoal mohair suit with thin, ivory pinstripes, a light grey, silk shirt, a dark burgundy, Hermès tie, and a matching Hermès pocket square. Believing clothes made the man, Randolph dressed and acted like he ranked a little below God but well above Moses.

Randolph smiled and said in a friendly tone, "Glad you could make it. I like your baseball attire. Very appropriate dress for our discussion about going to a Padres game."

"Thanks," Bart said and then sat down.

Randolph immediately began to pour on the honey. "I pulled a few strings and succeeded in getting seats in the Padres' owner's box."

Of course it was a lie, but Randolph could see from Bart's pleased expression it was a perfect lie.

"That's incredible. Those seats are impossible to get unless you are a friend of the owners, a famous ex-player, or big celebrity."

"I thought you'd appreciate sitting in the owners' box," Randolph said, knowing the honey bait had worked and now it was time for the switch.

Randolph said, "Oh, I almost forgot. Before we discuss which Padres game to attend, there was something your mother asked me to tell you about. I had recently recommended she transfer all her financial assets to Money bank, which offered a much higher rate of return. She agreed, and was so pleased with the move she told me to give you the same opportunity. My best estimate is you will double or triple your returns compared to those you are currently receiving."

"Sounds like a great idea," Bart said, remembering his mother had said Randolph was a genius when it came to managing money.

Bart liked the idea of getting better returns but wondered why was Randolph talking about transferring his trust when they were supposed to be talking about going to a Padres' game. *I hope this meeting isn't going to turn out to be the old bait and switch ploy.*

"I was so sure you would agree with your mother's suggestion I had the necessary papers drawn up. They only need to be signed and notarized," Randolph said in a convincing voice.

"As soon as you sign these standard transfer documents, we will go over the Padres schedule so you can select one we can watch from seats in the owners' box," Randolph said.

Randolph pushed six pages across the desk and said, "Just sign your full name on the lines marked with a red check."

Randolph found a pen and offered it to Bart who reluctantly took the pen. He wasn't about to sign anything without knowing exactly what it was.

Randolph suddenly stood up and said, "Wait just a minute. I will need my secretary to witness your signature and notarize these documents."

Randolph buzzed his secretary and said, "Please come to my office, and bring your notary book and official seal."

"Right away," the secretary said.

"While we wait for your secretary, I'd like to use the restroom because I drank a lot of coffee before I came," Bart said and then thought, *How dumb does Randolph think I am? It's the bait and switch ploy. I need to call Carol and tell her what's happening.*

"It is just down the hallway on your left." Randolph said.

Leaving Randolph's office, Bart walked down the hallway and entered the restroom. He immediately got out his cell phone and speed dialed Carol's number at the Neuroscience Institute.

He waited five rings and was ready to leave a voice mail when she came on the line.

"Hello," Carol said, sounding cheery after seeing Bart's name on her caller ID.

"As mom probably told you, I met Randy-Dandy today at his office supposedly to talk about going to a Padres' game. Mom says he's trying to be a better father so I agreed. Now I'm sure he's up to no-good."

"So what happened?" Carol asked.

"He wants me to sign some documents that transfer my trust to another bank, supposedly because I'll get better returns. There's six pages of legal documents and understanding legalese is not my strong suit."

"Absolutely don't sign anything you haven't read," Carol said, trying to sound calm but worried Randy-Dandy was doing something devious. "Instead, tell him to give you the documents so you can have a financial adviser give you a second opinion. If the documents are only about transferring funds, Randy-Dandy will gladly give them to you for review. But, if he refuses to give you the documents, you can be sure he's working some scam," Carol said.

"I'm sure this is some sort of scam and there's going to be screaming and shouting because Randy-Dandy never gives up easily," Bard said, feeling strong, confident, and ready for a fight.

Bart walked back to Randolph's office and seeing the door half open, walked in. Randolph was seated behind the desk with his attractive secretary standing on his left. Both were smiling broadly, as if welcoming a long lost friend.

After Bart sat down, Randolph handed him a pen and said, "As soon as you complete signing these documents, we can finalize our plans for the Padres game," Randolph said in a pleasant voice.

Randolph handed the first document to Bart. "Just sign your full name on the lines marked with a red check."

Instead, he picked up the documents and briefly looked at six single-spaced pages of endless legalese. Putting the pages back down, Bart looked up and said, "I think I better take these documents and have them checked by someone more familiar with financial legalese,"

"Oh, there is no need for that. As you know, I am an expert in financial dealings. Besides, I have even asked one of our partners to check for any errors or irregularities. Everything is absolutely correct and legal," Randolph said and then added, "Perhaps it would help if I explained the nature of these documents and remove any doubts you might be harboring."

"I don't need any more explanations. I know these documents transfer my trust fund to another bank, but I would feel better if someone else checked them out," Bart said and then thought about what Carol had said. *If Randy-Dandy doesn't want to hand over the documents for review, he must be working some scam.*

Randolph said, "I am sorry you will not take my professional advice, for which clients pay seven hundred dollars an hour. I drew up these documents as a favor to your mother. Unlike you, she was smart enough to follow my expert advice."

"I do appreciate your advice, but I think the transfer documents should be checked over," Bart said in a firm voice, knowing being stubborn was sometimes as important as being smart.

Bart stood and as he was leaving Randolph's office he thought, *Randolph was never going to take me to a Padres game or make any effort to be a better stepfather. I'll need Carol's help to figure out what Randy-Dandy is trying to pull off.*

Randolph knew if Bart had the transfer documents reviewed it would become clear he had appointed himself sole manager, eliminating oversight from the bank's financial officer. This major change would raise ethical and legal questions as well as bring down the wrath of Marjorie and Carol. *But no matter,* Randolph thought. *As soon as Bart leaves, I will call Jerry and make plans to use the vinegar-approach. It will certainly work but will result in many tears, but that can't be helped.*

As Bart closed Randolph's door he thought of something he had often done as a child when he played a game called spy-on-Randy-Dandy. He would secretly stand with his ear on Randolph's office door and listen to Randolph's phone conversations. He could hear almost everything being said because Randolph's phone voice was unusually loud.

Bart closed the door and checked the long corridor. Seeing no one, he flattened his ear against Randolph's door. If anyone did appear in the corridor, he would immediately bend down and pretend to tie his running shoe. Bart knew from Randolph's expression he would probably get right on the phone to complain to his mother about his bad behavior. As Bart had thought, it was only seconds before he heard Randolph voice, but he wasn't talking to his mother.

"Hi Jerry, this is Mr. Stranger. I hope you remember me."

There was a pause as Randolph listened to a reply from the person on the other end.

"Yes, I'm well. I'm calling because I have a big favor to ask."

Then a few seconds of silence before he heard Randolph say, "I am having a problem with my stepson, and I need to teach him a lesson. I was hoping you could use some of your former police contacts and arrange for Bart to be—"

Just then Bart had to stand back from Randolph's door as the secretary started coming down the corridor. She was looking at some folders in her arms and hadn't yet noticed Bart. Bart bent down and pretended to tie this running shoe, just in case she happened to look up and see him.

He got on the elevator and thought, *I need to call Carol and tell her what I heard Randolph say to someone named "Jerry." I'll bet he's got something really dirty planned."*

CHAPTER 4

As Bart was riding the elevator, Randolph was in the middle of explaining to Jerry what needed to be done.

"I am having a big problem with my stepson, and I could use your help," Randolph said. "I've just learned my stepson is using illegal drugs, which in the past usually involved marijuana. But this time I am really worried because he may doing meth, which you and I know quickly results in a dangerous habit."

"Yes, I do know," Jerry said. "Meth destroyed the marriage of my favorite nephew, and there was nothing I could do to prevent it. So I'll be more than willing to help you save you stepson from that drug."

"I have tried everything, but my stepson simply will not listen. I am at wits, end and believe I need to take more drastic action. I was hoping one of the detectives you still know could pay my stepson a visit. I am sure the detectives will find a stash of illegal drugs hidden in his house, certainly some marijuana, which I know Bart uses. You can claim a reliable snitch tipped you off so the detectives will have sufficient cause to get a search warrant for his rented house. I sincerely regret having to take such drastic action, but everything else I have tried has failed to deter his drug usage. I am hoping his being arrested and spending time in jail will stop him for further drug use. As you know, sometime tough love is necessary, even though that is very hard for me to do."

"Sure, I understand. All I need is your stepson's physical description and the address of his house," Jerry said.

"He is in his middle twenties, has longish blonde hair, nice looking, about six feet tall, a hundred and seventy pounds, athletic build, and blue eyes. His first name is Bartholomew or Bart, and he kept the last name of his biological father, which is Whatting. He has an old, red, rusting jeep he usually parks in the driveway at his rented home at 9511 Cable Street, in Pacific beach," Randolph said.

"There shouldn't be any problems," Jerry said.

"Today is Wednesday, so I wonder if your detective friend could arrest my stepson sometime on Friday. If Bart is arrested on Friday, he will have to spend the weekend in a common jail cell with all the other undesirables, all of who are awaiting arraignments on Monday. That should give my stepson a good scare and time to think about mending his ways," Randolph said.

"I know how hard this decision must have been for you, and I just wish I had done more to help my nephew get off meth. I know being arrested and put in a cell with a bunch of druggies, drunks, and gang members should scare your stepson plenty and make him think twice about using drugs, especially meth," Jerry said

"Oh Jerry, there is one more favor I would ask of you. I would very much appreciate your not mentioning my phone call to anyone. Let's keep this favor between us. I had promised my wife that I would not report my stepson's drug use to the police. But now I see that it is my last resort to get my stepson off drugs and put him back on the straight and narrow," Randolph said, sounding very truthful although he had no evidence Bart used any illegal drugs.

"No problem," said Jerry. "And you can trust me that I won't tell anyone." Randolph took Jerry at his word, not knowing Jerry had a mouth bigger than a hippo and, after a few drinks, would gladly reveal all his secrets.

"Thank you very much," Randolph said. "And Jerry, if you need any future legal help, it will be on the house, as they say."

"I'll call my detective friend today so he can get the search warrant and be ready to make the arrest on Friday," Jerry said, adding, "Thanks for the offer of free legal services. My ex is aching to stick her greedy fingers into my retirement checks."

Randolph hung up the phone and was so pleased with how his plans were working he was grinning like an axe murderer in a horror movie. He was thinking there would be some collateral damage, but it could not be helped. Marjorie will be grief stricken and surely get a migraine. Carol will be angry, but there is really nothing she can do. Bart might end up with a criminal record and even some jail time, all of which he could have avoided by signing the transfer documents. But Bart always was a stubborn kid.

Randolph had known the first step in his vinegar approach, having Bart arrested, would be a little tricky. But his story about Bart using meth had worked like a charm and convinced Jerry to call one of his detective friends to arrest Bart. The second step would be a slam-dunk, since Bart's arrest, with or without a conviction, would automatically trigger the malfeasance clause and give him sole control of Bart's trust. Neither Marjorie nor Carol could do anything to challenge or subvert the malfeasance clause, since it had been written into Bart's trust.

Randolph knew it would be his fatherly duty to be Bart's lawyer and make the best possible defense. He would tell Bart it would be best to make a deal with the prosecution because if his case went to trial, he had no chance of being acquitted. The prosecution would portray him as a rich, spoiled kid with a big trust fund, and the jury will undoubtedly find him guilty. But if he pleads guilty to some minor offence, his sentence would likely be only probation or community service. Marjorie and Carol would be thankful and grateful he got Bart off so easily. Best of all, he would not need to tell anyone the malfeasance clause had been triggered, and Bart's money would then be his money. That would be his secret.

Randolph called his secretary.

"Yes?" the secretary answered.

"I was thinking about celebrating tonight," Randolph said.

"Sounds like a great evening, and I already know what we can have for dessert," the secretary said as her cheeks reddened.

"How about eight o'clock?" Randolph said, already thinking about the dessert.

"Perfect," the secretary, said, already thinking about wearing the sheer white teddy and matching panties.

Randolph had to be very careful when meeting his mistress because of another stipulation the now-deceased Norman had put in the prenuptial agreement. Norman had not been able to dissuade Marjorie from marrying Randolph, but he wanted to make sure he was faithful to her. Norman put in a somewhat unusual stipulation essentially stating if Randolph were ever caught cheating on Marjorie, it would be sufficient grounds for a divorce. Randolph had cleverly rented an oceanfront condo in a fictitious company's name that could never be traced to him. And besides, Marjorie never questioned him about working late at the office or taking endless business trips. She trusted him and never for a moment thought he might be having an affair.

* * * *

As Randolph was arranging to meet his mistress, Bart was entering the lobby. He went to a quiet corner and speed dialed Carol's number.

"Hello," Carol said.

"It's me. Everything happened just like you said. Randy refused to let me take the documents so he must be up to no good," Bart said.

"I suggest you come to my lab immediately and tell me all," Carol said.

CHAPTER 5

La Jolla is a posh northern suburb of San Diego where the median price of a single-family home was 1,500,000 dollars. On its hilly borders were powerhouse research institutions such as the world-renowned Salk Institute, named for Jonas Salk, who had developed the polio vaccine; the Scripps Institution of Oceanography, best known for recording humpback whales' low frequency sounds; the Neuroscience Institute, where Carol and other researchers studied how brains cells communicate and create thoughts and emotions; and the newest addition, the Stem Cell Research Center, whose goal was to use these cells to cure diseases and repair body organs.

In the same general area were about a half-dozen well-financed pharmaceutical laboratories hoping to discover the next block-buster drug that would help people lose weight, sleep better at night, fight depression, or according to the latest rumor, grow hair on bald heads. This rumor seemed so far fetched that researchers at the Neuroscience Institute had started an office pool to correctly guess the date the baldness lab went bust.

About thirty minutes after phoning Carol, Bart drove into the parking lot of the Neuroscience Institute. Getting out of his rusty jeep, he walked through the Institute's doors and checked in with Hattie, the receptionist. She was actually very nice but always looked like she was sucking on a lemon. No one was allowed to wander around the Institute without getting a visitor's pass from Hattie.

"Whom do you wish to see?" Hattie asked, looking up and pushing her big glasses back on her nose, a nervous habit.

"Hi. I'm here to see Dr. Carol Whatting. I'm her brother, Bart, and she's expecting me."

Hattie stared at Bart and remembered him from previous visits. She didn't much like him because she believed anyone that cute could not be trusted.

"Just a moment while I phone to get Dr. Whatting's approval," Hattie said, using Carol's official title.

Hattie had taken a liking to Carol, who was often the target of snide comments like, *I wonder who she thinks she is with a Ph.D. brain in a Playboy body.* Carol was a natural beauty whose face and body made women jealous and stopped men in their tracks. Even though Carol always dressed down, wore no makeup, and never flirted or flaunted her looks, she attracted men like moths to a bright flame. Each man considered her a real challenge and believed he would prove to be the *one* she was looking for.

"Hello, Dr. Whatting. I have a Bart Whatting here to see you. Does he have your approval to enter the laboratory?" Hattie asked, glancing at Bart like he was a stray dog.

"Hattie listened to Carol's answer and then hung up her phone.

Hattie handed Bart a temporary identification pass and asked, "Do you know the way to Dr. Whatting's lab?"

"I know the way," Bart said.

"Just be sure to return the ID pass," Hattie harrumphed.

Bart clipped on his ID pass and walked down the corridor toward Carol's small office, which was located near the back of the first floor. Her office had one small window that overlooked an aging eucalyptus tree, which constantly shed its bark, like an old dog losing its hair. The more senior researchers merited larger offices on higher floors with views of the blue Pacific Ocean.

Bart walked down the corridor and knew Carol could help him figure out what Randy-Dandy was up to. Like Bart, Carol had kept their real father's last name, much to the annoyance of Randy-Dandy. Carol excelled in everything she did, from sports to academics, which might have made Bart jealous but instead made him love her all the more. Carol had always looked out and tried to protect him when he continually got into trouble with Randy.

Bart stopped in front of Carol's office door and knocked once and then twice, the secret code they had used as kids.

"Come in," Carol said in a cherry voice at hearing the secret code.

"How's my favorite cowgirl?" Bart asked as he looked into Carol's incredible green eyes that sparkled like emerald water in a tropical lagoon on a sunny day.

"Be careful, little brother. You know I don't like being called a cowgirl," Carol said in a stern tone, pretending to be angry but actually liking it.

"I just think it's really neat for someone to be a serious neuroscientist on weekdays and then suddenly turn into a stunning cowgirl and go country-western dancing on Saturday nights," Bart said, giving an appreciative smile.

Carol had to smile back because that's exactly what happened. Almost every Saturday night she put on alluring makeup, dressed in relatively sexy outfits, and drove to the Red Bull Saloon in eastern San Diego. She would dance to country-western music all night long and leave all her cares behind. As with everything else she did, she was an excellent dancer.

"I suppose you're going dancing this Saturday with you know who," Bart said.

"Yes, indeed," Carol said. She grinned for a moment, and then turned serious. "But right now you need to tell me about your meeting with Randy."

Bart said, "Everything was fine until I asked Randy to give me the transfer documents so someone else could look them over. He refused and insisted I take his expert advice and sign them right now. I followed your advice, refused to sign and made a beeline to his door."

"I'll bet Randy was fuming," Carol said.

"I'm sure he was and knew first thing he'd get on the phone and call mom to complain about my rotten, stubborn behavior. So like when I was a kid and spied on Randy, I stopped outside and put my ear to his door. Sure enough, I heard him talking on the phone. But he wasn't talking to mom but someone named 'Jerry.' I could hear Randy saying that he was having a problem with his stepson, namely me, and needed to teach me a lesson. He asked if Jerry could arrange for his police friends to do something. That's all I heard because his secretary was coming down the corridor, and I had to leave. So, I didn't get to hear what the police were supposed to arrange, but I don't think it was to give me a birthday party."

"No, I'm sure it wasn't a birthday party," Carol said. Then she sat back in her chair and closed her eyes.

Bart said nothing and just waited. He knew when Carol closed her eyes her brain was going a million miles a minute.

After what seemed like an hour, Carol opened her eyes.

Thinking out loud, Carol said, "Randy arranges for you to come to his office to talk about going to a Padres' game. Then sneaks in an offer to double your returns by transferring your trust to another bank. Seems like a reasonable suggestion until he refuses to allow your transfer documents to be checked over by someone else. Why would he do that? Perhaps those documents he wanted you to sign do more than just transfer your money. What might that be? Randy always has schemes in the works. If one of his schemes had failed, he'd be in financial trouble and needs money to cover his loss. I'm guessing something in those documents give Randy a chance to raid your trust."

"That bastard," Bart said. "I'd shoot him before he gets one cent of my trust."

Carol seemed not to have noticed Bart's outburst and thought out loud, "So, what business venture recently collapsed that Randy might have invested in. Mom always said that he liked to invest in long shots with hopes of making a big killing. That was too risky for her but she'd let him do it as long as it didn't involve her money."

Since they were kids, Carol had been a genius at figuring out what Randy might do.

Carol had been absent-mindedly playing with an index card that had been lying on her desk. She happened to glance at the card and smiled at seeing the date she had entered in the current office pool. All she had to do was correctly guess the date when the neighboring Chinese pharmaceutical company would fold. The Chinese company had claimed to cure baldness with stem cell injections. The Institute's researchers, who were studying stem cells, knew curing baldness might be possible but not anytime soon.

"Ah-ha! That's it," she said and held up the index card. "The Chinese pharmaceutical company with the baldness cure did go bust and my guess was only a week off. I remember because Helen, my assistant, had the closest guess and won a boat trip to see the migrating whales."

"So you think Randy was one of the investors in the long-shot Chinese company?" Bart asked.

"I'm almost positive he was. The pitch to cure baldness with stem cells is a real long-shot and sounded so good he couldn't resist the chance to make millions.," Carol said.

"By why doesn't he just ask mom for the money?" Bart asked.

"Mom would never have given him money for risky investments. Randy would have had to do some dubious financial dealings to get the money. Now that he's probably lost millions, he doesn't want mom to know anything about it," Carol said.

"So what does this have to do with transferring my trust fund to another bank?" Bart asked. "The documents Randy wanted you to sign must have done more than just transfer your trust. They must have given him access to your trust and a chance to rob it ," Carol said and nodded to herself.

"So what do you think Randy will do next?" Bart asked, knowing Randy never gave up.

"I guessing Randy has something more up his sleeve. Something that explains why as soon as you left his office, Randy calls this guy Jerry, and asks for a big favor that involves the police doing something to you. And we both know, the police are not giving you a birthday party," Carol said.

"Let me call my friend and get his advice," Carol said.

"Does your friend happen to be called Bad Billy?" Bart asked.

Smiling, Carol said, "You like saying that name, don't you?"

23

Carol knew only strangers used the name "Bad Billy." She, along with his friends called him just plain, Billy. She also called him other names. When she and Billy were alone, she sometime called him "Honey," which made him wince slightly. And in the dark of night when they were lying next to each other, she called him "Lovey." He would not say anything in return but instead plant a gentle kiss on her sensitive neck, sending shivers through her body.

"I have to admit Bad Billy is a great name, and if I were half as tough, I'd make people call me Bad Bart."

"Well you're not half as tough, so stick with just plain Bart," Carol said and smiled.

"What I have trouble understanding is how a neuroscientist can fall for a private detective named Bad Billy. It's like a cactus making it with a rose, a boxer dating a ballet dancer, a drummer having eyes for a—"

"That's about enough," Carol interrupted. "For your information, it's well known opposites attract."

"Well, don't forget, I'm your biggest fan and firmly believe for every sensitive cowgirl there is a mighty private detective dressed in black leather waiting to sweep—"

"I get the picture," Carol again interrupted.

She had to laugh. She and Bad Billy were opposites in some ways, but in other ways they were so alike it made her cheeks turn red-hot.

"Wow! I made you blush. Do you want to tell me about it?" Bart asked and chuckled.

Ignoring Bart's question, Carol picked up her iPhone and speed dialed Billy.

As Carol waited for Billy to answer, she thought about how she had almost given up trying to find a special person. But then, in one of the strangest places on the planet, she had seen Bad Billy dancing in the Red Bull Saloon. He was tall, handsome, dressed all in black leather with a body made of steely muscle. He had a white feather tucked into the band of a black cowboy hat, which partially hid his ebony eyes. He looked magnificent, wild, and totally confident. Her instant attraction was so strong and so surprising that she had unconsciously held her breath and stared dumbfounded. She heard a primitive voice inside her whisper, *he's the one.* And when he finally asked her to dance, she felt as if she were acting out a romantic fantasy.

"Bad Billy at your service," came a friendly voice that stopped Carol's reverie and made her focus on why she had called.

CHAPTER 6

— — —

"I'm so glad you weren't busy," Carol said, her voice a little tense. "Bart just came back from an ominous meeting with Randy, our stepfather, and we need your advice and help."

"Tell me what happened, and I'll do whatever I can," Billy said, sensing the worry in Carol's tone.

Carol repeated what Bart had told her and had to wait only seconds for Billy's reply. She was constantly impressed at how fast Billy could process information.

"Here's how I see it," Billy said. "Randy needs a bucket full of money, and the bucket happens to be Bart's trust fund. The piece I'm missing is what happened to made Randy desperate enough to try raiding Bart's trust?"

"I'm guessing he couldn't resist investing millions in a Chinese company rumored to have found a cure for baldness, which as the local paper explained, was a gigantic hoax. From what my mom told me, Randy doesn't have millions, so he must have gotten a large loan, which needs to be paid back," Carol said,

"You may be right because I've received phone calls from two frantic investors, each of whom had lost about two million in the Chinese hoax. The investors wanted me to find the crooks and do whatever necessary, legal or not, to get their money back. I told them there was no chance of recovering their money since the crooks were safely back in China, laughing all the way to their banks," Billy said.

"What worries me most was Randy asking this guy 'Jerry,' to contact his police friends and arrange to do something to Bart," Carol said, feeling as protective of Bart as a mother grizzly bear watching her cubs.

"I've been involved in several cases involving trust disputes. Ugly things can happen because people setting up trusts often add conditions to prevent beneficiaries from wasting or squandering the money on drugs and partying. I'm guessing Randy added some condition, such as if Bart

25

did something criminal or were arrested, the overseer would be able to take control of the trust. And in this case, I'm guessing the overseer is none other than Randy."

"So you think Randy's next step is to arrange for Bart to be arrested for some criminal activity?" Carol asked with such anger in her voice it made Billy cringe.

"That's my best guess. But knowing how the police operate, it'll take at least three or four days to arrange for Bart's arrest, which will probably involve getting a warrant to search his house for any kind of illegal drugs. In any case, we need to get Bart out of San Diego as quickly as possible," Billy said.

"What do your mean, *get Bart out of San Diego*?" Carol asked, feeling both worried and anxious.

"If Bart isn't around, he can't be arrested. So the safest thing is to get him out of town. I know Randy uses a private investigator named Matthew Moore, whose specialty is finding people who do not want to be found. So you need to find Bart a hiding place where no one would think of looking. Can't be in Mexico or near the ocean because they know Bart's an avid surfer, and that's where Moore would search first," Billy said.

"So just how do I find Bart a safe hideout where no one would think of looking?" Carol asked.

"That should be easy since everyone says you have a brilliant brain," Billy said, with a mischievous tone in his voice.

"Thanks for all you confidence," Carol said.

She laughed, liking when Billy was being playful.

"This is Wednesday, so I think the police will wait until after the weekend to do anything. That gives Bart a few days to pack. He should try to leave on Saturday, but absolutely no later than Sunday. Be sure neither you nor Bart tells anyone where he's going, and that includes your mother, friends, and even me, unless I ask. And you'll need to arrange a way to communicate with Bart at his new location. Remember, phone calls and emails are easily traceable." Billy said.

"I'll get on the web and start looking for Bart's distant hideout," Carol said, wondering how one finds a hideout.

"In the meantime, I'll try to find out more about the mysterious guy named Jerry," Billy said.

"Many thanks for your help and good advice," Carol said, feeling relieved that Billy came up with a plan to keep Bart safe.

"Well, my services don't come cheap, so there's the matter of payment," Billy said with a smile in his voice.

"And what's that?" Carol asked though she already knew.

"Since Bart will probably be leaving on Saturday morning, how about meeting at the Red Bull Saloon for a Saturday night of dancing?" Billy asked.

"Great idea," Carol said.

She smiled as she imagined dancing across the floor in Billy's arms.

"What time should we meet?" Carol asked.

"Band always starts at nine o'clock," Billy said.

"Yes, OK, and try not to be late," Carol said, already thinking about what she would wear.

Billy had to bite his tongue and not say something sarcastic because Carol was the one who was always late, while he was always on time.

After Carol clicked off her phone, she turned to Bart, who was biting his nails, a childish habit he did when stressed.

"As they say, there is some good news and some bad," Carol said.

"Bad news first, so I have something to look forward to," Bart said.

"The bad news is Billy thinks Randy asked Jerry to arrange for the police to arrest you for—"

"Have me arrested?" Bart interrupted. "I can't believe it. But why?"

"Billy thinks Randy probably added a condition to your trust, such as if you did something criminal or were arrested, Randy would get greater control over your trust and be able to take out money for his own needs," Carol said.

"Oh, no he won't," Bart said. "I'd shoot him before he could spend a dime. I'll cut off his head and nail it to the front of my surfboard. I'll make him—"

"I get the picture," Carol interrupted. "But remember Randy is both super clever and sneaky, and he'll do whatever it takes to get what he wants. And right now, what he wants is your trust money."

"OK. What's the good news?" Bart asked.

"The good news is the police will need several days to set this up and probably won't do anything until after this weekend. That's just enough time for you to pack and for me to find a hideaway as far from San Diego as possible," Carol said.

"That's the good news? I have a few days to get out of San Diego. You must be kidding. Leave San Diego? No way! No how!" Bart shouted.

"If you don't want to be arrested, you'll have to leave San Diego. Besides, it's probably for only a short time, and you'll be back before you know," Carol said, trying to be reassuring although she had no idea of how long Bart might have to stay away.

"Having a few days to pack and leave San Diego is the worst good news

I've ever heard," Bart said, sounding like someone being told he was lucky to lose only one leg.

"Billy said that you should leave on Saturday, but no later than Sunday," Carol said.

"I don't want to leave you, mom, my friends and especially not my girlfriend, Anna. And beside, where will I go?" Bart asked, looking as sad as a droopy-faced hound dog.

"Don't worry, I'll find a safe place," Carol said, although at the moment she had no idea where that might be.

"But what do I tell people?" Bart asked.

"Just tell everyone you're going up the coast to Silicon Valley to work with some computer whiz. All your friends will think it perfectly normal, since they know you've been working on a big computer project," Carol said.

"I don't know if I can get everything packed in just a few days. How about if I leave some time next week?" Bart asked.

"Absolutely, positively not. Billy said that you must leave no later than Sunday. Do you promise to do that?" Carol said.

"Yes, I promise," Bart said.

"Now tell me the kind of place you'll need," Carol said.

"Obviously I need someplace rent free cause Randy will cut off my allowance and cancel my credit card. I have my pride and don't want to be a moocher supported by you. I can't ask mom for money since I don't want to explain that I have to leave town because her husband is trying to have me arrested. But I can offer to pay for room and board by using my computer skills. Finally I'll need a place with a good broadband connection so I can easily get on the web," Bart said.

"There's one more problem," Carol said. "You'll need a place that'll trust you enough to keep your real name secret but that will also let you stay under a fake name, which will make finding you doubly difficult."

"Good luck, cause there's no place like that," Bart said, hoping he might yet be able to stay in San Diego and hideout with one of his surfer friends.

"Don't worry, I'll have most of Thursday to work on a solution. Come by any time after seven," Carol said.

She gave Bart a big reassuring smile.

"OK. I may seem a little grouchy, but I want to thank you for all your help," Bart said as he smiled back.

Then he got up, walked over to Carol, and gave her a big, big hug and whispered in her ear, "Thanks for saving my life."

Bart left Carol's office, walked down the hall, and returned his pass to Hattie. As he stepped out the Institute's front door, he looked up at the sky and saw the colorful hang-gliders soaring high above the blue Pacific Ocean. He had often watched these brave individual hold large nylon wings above their heads, run down a well-worn dirt path behind the Institute, and literally leap off a three hundred foot high cliff. Windy updrafts from the cliff allowed the hang-gliders to soar high above the white-capped waves. The hang-gliders flew in wide graceful turns, looking like prehistoric birds with colorful, thirty-foot wide wingspans.

"I feel like hang-gliding all the way to some deserted island. Provided it had a broadband connection and good waves for surfing.

CHAPTER 7

It was a little after seven on Thursday evening when Bart parked his rusty jeep in front of Carol's condo. Walking to the door, he rang the bell using their secret code.

Carol opened the door, saw Bart's sad face, and gave him a sympathetic hug.

"You know I don't want to leave, but I guess I haven't got a choice," he said.

He looked into Carol's green eyes, hoping she'd say he didn't have to go after all.

But instead she said, "I wish things were different, but you do have to leave San Diego, sooner the better. If you stay, you're certain to be arrested."

He said nothing, knowing she was right. He didn't have a choice but he promised someday he would get even with Randy-Dandy.

"Do want something to drink?" she asked.

"Maybe a beer," he said.

She went to the kitchen and got him a beer.

Coming back, she handed him the beer and said, "I've spent hours on the web and think I've found the perfect hideout."

"With a place to surf?" he said in a hopeful tone.

"No surfing," she said.

"I found a great place for you. It's very secluded, in the middle of a forest that's at least two thousand miles from San Diego. It's someplace no one would ever think of looking. I called and talked to the person in charge of the facility. At first he said it wasn't possible and too risky to take in a complete stranger. But then I told him I was currently an Assistant Professor at the Neuroscience Institute in La Jolla and also your sister. I also explained that you were a junior at UCSD in good standing, and your specialty was artificial intelligence. He said that he was impressed and agreed to at least meet you and then decide if you could stay," Carol said.

"But it's hard to believe anyone would take me in just because I have some computer skills," Bart said.

"The person in charge said that he was willing to take a chance on you because his organization has run into a serious problem and your computer skills might help solve an unexpected problem. That means you'll be able to work off your room and board with your computer skills."

"That's sort of good news, but I'm getting a little nervous when you talk about my staying at a facility. I hope it's not a prison someplace in the high desert."

"No, far from it. It's actually a monastery."

"Now I know you're kidding. You want me to stay in a monastery?"

"Think about it. Who would ever think of looking for you in a monastery? It's the perfect hiding place. Secluded, private, safe, and no one would recognize you wearing a monastic habit.

"That's all true, but you're forgetting one critical element."

"And what's that."

"Don't monks promise to be celibate?"

"The Abbot did say you would have to follow all their monastic rules, which includes being celibate."

"Being celibate. No sex. Are you kidding?"

"Don't fret. It won't be for long, and with Anna gone, you won't be tempted. And just think how great sex will be when you get out."

"Except for the celibacy, it sounds like a real adventure," Bart said. .

"I also told the Abbot you were on summer break and would return to UCSD in the fall. I explained you had a serious disagreement with your stepfather, who was in financial difficulty and might arrange to have you arrested to gain control of your trust fund. At the moment, you needed a safe hideaway until your stepfather's threats blow over and you could safely return to San Diego. I gave the Abbot your real name but asked he keep it secret since your stepfather has a very long and powerful reach and would certainly be sending his private investigator to look for you."

"But does the monastery have a broadband connection to the Internet so I can quickly access and download large amount of data?"

"It just so happens the monastery has broadband service because it has a research program to collect and make digital copies of icons, illustrated medieval manuscripts, and religious images from around the world."

"Well, that's great news," he said.

He reached out, gave her another big thank-you hug and said, "You're the greatest sister in the universe."

His compliment made her smile and she hugged him back.

"I gave the Abbot the number of my supervisor if he wanted to verify my position or obtain a personal or professional reference. I also gave him my cell number and said he could call if he had any other questions, since you would be leaving San Diego very soon."

"Yes, very soon. As you've probably guessed, I can't wait to become a celibate monk."

They both laughed.

"There's just one more problem we need to talk about," she said is such a professional voice it made him cringe.

"Oh no. Please. I can't deal with anymore problems," he said, putting his hands on his head as if were falling apart.

"It's not a big problem, but it's something we need to talk about," she said.

He took another long pull from his bottle of beer, and wiped away a few drips on his chin.

"I'm ready."

"The Abbot remarked how Californians are known for using all kinds of illegal drugs, and he wanted to make sure you did not bring or would use any illegal drugs while you stayed in the monastery. I promised you would neither bring nor use any illegal drugs while staying in the monastery," she said and looked him in the eye, waiting for his agreement.

OK. You know I smoke a little marijuana now and then, have a few beers, but no hard drugs. Never coke or meth. And from this day forth I promise not to use any illegal drugs. Never, ever again while staying at the monastery."

"Finally," she said. "I'm going to give you three envelopes. The first explains the problem you are having with your stepfather, your need for a safe hideout, and your status as a student at UCSD, and my official title and research appointment at the Neuroscience Institute. I sealed the envelope and wrote my name across the back flap to show it is authentic and has not been tampered with. This letter proves who you are, so hand it to the Abbot when you get there."

He took the envelope and noticed she had written her signature across the back flap so any attempt to open it would be noticed.

"It's a great letter, and I will do my best to make a great impression," he said.

"This second envelope contains four thousand dollars for traveling and other expenses. I would like to have given you more, but my mortgage and taxes eats up most of my paycheck. As you know, grandfather had left me a small trust but I used most of it to pay for my college and graduate education and make a down payment on this cond."

"Don't worry, I'll get by. Remember, grandfather also left me a small trust to pay for my education and I've saved some of it. I once told him my dream was to start a high-tech company to explore artificial intelligence. He was kind and generous and left me large nest egg so use, but not until I turn thirty. If Randolph was after my trust, he must be was gunning for my nest egg."

"One more thing," Carol said. "Bad Billy said to either drive or take a bus to Minnesota so your name won't appear on any national passenger list, which Randy's private investigator will surely check. Billy also advised leaving your old jeep next to your house in Ocean Beach. If Randy's investigator drives by to check on you, he'll see your jeep and think you're still in town. Beside, I seriously doubt if your old jeep would even take you half way to where you're headed."

Bart took the thick envelope and said, "Many thanks for the money."

"And here's the third envelope," Said. "It contains the address, description, Google map, and an interesting twelve page history of the monastery. I want you to know all about the monastery so you'll make a good impression," she said.

"I'll memorize every word and may even learn a few words of Latin so I'll fit right in."

"And I want you to promise to stay at the monastery until Billy agrees it's save for you to return."

"I promise," he said.

He looked into her stunning green eyes, reached out to hold both her hands, and said, "I don't know what I'd do without you. You've been looking out for me my whole life. I don't know how I'll ever show my appreciation or repay you."

Carol was surprised to see a tear rolling down his check.

"Just come back, safe and sound," she said and then added, "And remember to be celibate."

They both had to laugh.

"And one last thing. Don't contact me by phone or email. Use snail mail and send it to my friend Helen's address or leave a text message and I will call you back on her phone. I'm sure Randy's private investigator will do whatever it takes to track you down, including hacking into my emails and phone calls. I think that about covers everything, unless you have some questions," she said.

"I don't have any questions about the monastery but I did something really dumb and need your help to make it right," Bart said. He felt beads of sweat forming on his forehead and tried to calm down with a long swig of beer.

CHAPTER 8

▬ ▬ ▬

"It's about Anna. I said something that made her so mad she packed up her things and moved out. I don't blame her because I did shoot off my big mouth. But now I want to make it right," he said as a pained expression spread across his face like a dark cloud passing over the sun.

Jokingly, Carol said, "You do have a big mouth."

"We were living together so happily and then I spoiled it."

"Before we get into the details, I've always been curious how you and Anna met, Carol said.

"I guess I've never told you. It was one of those chance meeting. I was surfing off Dog's Beach in OB and the big waves had brought out more surfers than usual. I was getting ready to catch a big wave when someone crashed into me. I was about to yell at the person for not being more careful when I noticed the person happened to be wearing an eye-catching bikini that barely covered her sexy body. She quickly apologized but I just wanted to find some excuse to meet her. I think I said something dumb like we better head for the beach to check for cuts and bruises. And so we did. She had eyes as blue as the ocean and we hit it off. After about six months I asked her to move in with me. She agreed and we got along really well except for one thing," Bart said and then paused because in retrospect, the one thing was really all his fault.

Carol waited for Bart to continue and finally asked, "So what's the one thing?"

"It's all my fault. Attending highly ranked UCSD and majoring in Computer Science gave me a big head. I didn't bother to give Anna the credit or respect she needed because she was majoring in Theatre at the University of San Diego, the small private Catholic college up on the hill."

Bart's forehead was showing beads of sweat and he was fidgeting like a little kid needing to go to the bathroom.

"This is hard for me to talk about because it makes me out to be a big jerk. I really do need another beer," Bart said.

Carol went to the kitchen and got a beer for Bart and one for her.

After a big swig, Bart continued. "One morning when we were both reading the morning paper and drinking coffee, Anna offered to read me her horoscope. Without thinking I said that horoscopes were stupid and didn't know how anybody could believe in them. She said that horoscopes were fun and often true and accused me of being narrow-minded and pig-headed. I made a stupid reply like 'people who believed in horoscopes don't even have a mind—'"

"You actually said that?" Carol interrupted, wondering how Bart could have made such a dumb and hurtful remark.

"I know, I know. It was dumb, stupid and made Anna cry. She said that I must not love or respect her if I could say such cruel and hurtful things. Then without saying another word, she packed up her things and left. She had a real temper and slammed the rickety screen door so hard it almost fell apart. I followed her out the door, all the time begging her to stay. She gave me a hateful look, got in her car, and drove away. And I haven't heard from her since," Bart said, his sad eyes begging Carol for help.

"Didn't you try to stop her?" Carol asked.

"I did try. All the time she was packing I was saying I was sorry and let's talk but she just kept shaking her head 'no no, no,' and I could see her eyes filling with hurt and tears," Bart said, making a huge effort to find back his own tears.

"Well, I agree with Anna. You were being narrow-minded and pig-headed. A lot of people read and believe in horoscopes, and what's wrong with that?" Carol asked, adding, "Sometimes for fun, I even read mine."

"It's not just about her believing in horoscopes. Anna has some other things I don't agree with. She believes fate plays a big role in our lives, and I think we have a lot of control over what happens. She believes each of us has a certain destiny, and I think we each create our own destiny. She believes happiness depends on developing our inner selves, and I think happiness comes from developing effective strategies to cope with stress. And probably what bothers me most is her thinking it's better to make major decisions using our hearts instead of our heads," Bart said.

He let out a big sigh, having finally aired all his grievances.

"It's apparent you and Anna have different view points and ways of expressing yourselves. And, being a typical male, you decided your point of view is right and hers is wrong," Carol said, thinking about having similar problems with some of her professional male colleagues.

"Well, I'm more fact and science based and think new-wave concepts like fate, destiny, inner self, and using one's heart are unproven fads," Bart said, starting to feel defensive and uncomfortable.

35

"Has it occurred to you Anna's use of words, like *fate* and *destiny*, may be another way of talking about genetic and environmental influences, which you probably prefer? Or her term *inner self* may refer to our powerful, emotional, animal brain, scientifically known as the limbic system. And neuroscientists would agree with Anna that emotions play a big role in making decisions. For example, individuals with brain damage to certain emotional areas find it next to impossible to make decisions, even something as simple as deciding what to order from a menu," Carol said.

"When you put it that way, I can see I was a bigger fool than I thought. So, what can I do to patch things up?"

"First, I suggest you be a little less pig-headed and a little more open-minded. Second, try listening to and understanding Anna's point of view, rather than criticizing and rejecting it out of hand. Third, remember each of you has a different perspective and use different words to explain similar events and happenings. Although these differences will sometimes cause disagreements, they will also make your lives more interesting," Carol said.

"Although I hate to admit it, I guess I was being narrow-minded and pig-headed. I'll try listening more and criticizing less. Now she's gone I keep remembering all the things I really like about here. She's affectionate, enthusiastic, appreciative, loving, interesting, and did I mention very sexy?" Bart said, feeling like an enormous weight had been lifted from his shoulders.

"I'm glad I could help, because I like Anna, although I think she could have done much, much better," Carol said.

She began to laugh as she gently poked Bart in the ribs.

"You better not tell her that," Bart said jokingly.

Bart gave Carol a double high five and said, "Here's to fate and destiny."

★★★

By the time Bart left Carol's condo it was after nine. Driving away in his topless jeep, Bart thought, *I've got to straighten out things with Anna, and I'm not leaving San Diego until I do that. As soon as I get home I'll call and tell her I'm very sorry for being so narrow-minded and saying such dumb things. I'll ask her to forgive me and come back as soon as possible. I'll tell her our destiny is to be together.*

Arriving back at his house in OB, he retrieved the house key from under the cactus pot, went inside, and put Carol's three envelopes on the coffee table. The first thing he wanted to do was call Anna and make things right. He got out his iPhone, speed dialed her number, and listened to five rings before it went to her voice mail.

"Hi, it's me. I'm sorry for being so pig-headed. Please come back. I miss you. Call as soon as you can." Then he paused for a second before saying something that almost killed him dead, "I...I...I think I love you."

He clicked off his iPhone and was surprised at what he had said. He didn't know what had come over him, but it felt right and left a warm feeling. What he needed now was to walk along the ocean and think of what he'd say when Anna called back. He grabbed his windbreaker, put his iPhone in the pocket, and headed out the door.

As he was walking down Newport Avenue, the main street of OB, he almost ran into Tall Sally, who had hurried out of a dimly lit side street.

"You look very thoughtful tonight," Tall Sally said, noticing Bart's expression. "Must be some gigantic bee buzzing in your head?"

"I was just thinking of how I can make up with my girlfriend," Bart said.

"Oh, that's easy. You hold her in your arms, look into her eyes, and tell her you can't live without her. Before she can reply, give her tender butterfly kisses on her forehead and cheeks and loving kisses on her lips," Sally said.

"That sounds like great advice," Bart said,

"And to put some icing on the cake, offer to give her a massage, because a woman likes to feel tender, loving hands caressing her body," Sally said, quickly adding, "It's too bad men mostly use their hands to hold a baseball bat, catch a football, or grab a boob or a butt."

"I think she'd like massage," Bart said, although he had never before given a woman a massage.

"Well, if you need some practice or tips on giving a massage, I'd be glad to help.," Sally said being a professional masseuse.

As they walked down Newport Avenue, Bart noticed every man doing a double take as Tall Sally went by. She was strutting like a fashion model, exaggerating the movements of her sexy butt. She was wearing six-inch high, red platform shoes, short, white shorts, and a skimpy, red bikini top that showcased her considerable physical attributes. Her shiny, raven black hair hung down to the top of her bare, tanned shoulders, and she had a large, white pearl in her belly button. In real life Sally was actually quite short, probably five foot two or three. She had gotten her nickname, Tall Sally, when she rebelled against wearing ugly flip-flops and switched to wearing six-inch high platform shoes whenever she appeared in public.

Bart watched Tall Sally jay walk across the street to the GET IT ON store, which sold sandals made out of used tires, multicolored bongs in unusual shapes, t-shirts with risqué slogans, and Sally's favorites, scented incense and oils for every purpose. As Tall Sally crossed the street, cars in both lanes came to screeching stops and blew their horns in appreciation. She smiled, waved, and rewarded her fans with a little shake of her sexy butt.

***

Reaching the ocean, Bart noticed the tide was coming in. He took off his running shoes, tied them together and hung them over his shoulder. He rolled up his pants to his knees and, like a kid, followed the edge of the surf as it went out and then ran backwards as it came in, trying not to get his pants wet, which he always did.

Bart was standing on the beach getting ready to follow the surf out when he had an eerie feeling someone was standing behind him. He slowly turned around and suddenly his eyes got as big as saucers.

"You look like you've just seen a ghost," said the person standing in the shadows. "I first stopped by your house, but when you weren't there, I remembered you liked walking along the beach at night. And here you are."

"Oh! Anna! I was just thinking about you. I'm so glad to see you."

He held out his arms to welcome her. But when she stepped out the shadows into the bright streetlight, what he saw made his blood boil. Her face covered with ugly, red-purple bruises.

"Oh my god. Anna, who did that to your face?"

Then she was in his arms, crying so hard he could feel her body shaking. He gently rubbed her back, waiting for her tears to stop.

After a short time, Anna stepped back, wiped the tears from her bruised cheeks, took a couple deep breaths, and then said, "After I left you place I drove to Los Angeles and starting looking for some job in film. At one party I met a guy named Tony Koole. He said that he was a movie producer and was looking for someone to star in his new film. He suggested I come to his Burbank studio for a screen test. I was so impressed to have met a movie producer and get a screen test I agreed immediately. The next day, I went to his studio, and he asked me to put on a bikini because it was going to be a surfing movie. A few days after the screen test, he called and said my screen test turned out very good and invited me to his home to discuss a film contract."

Anna paused, fighting to hold back her tears.

"Take your time," Bart said.

He gently kissed her forehead.

"When I drove up to his big mansion in Beverly Hills I was even more impressed and thought how lucky I was to have met such a successful film producer."

Anna paused again. She closed her eyes and took several deep breaths. When she opened her eyes, they were full of pain.

"Tony proudly announced he produced very lucrative porn films, and with my looks and body I was certain to have a great career and make a pile of money. But before offering me a contract, he had this policy of first trying out the merchandise."

"That bastard. I'll break every bone in his body," Bart said, meaning every word.

"But it gets worse," Anna said. "I called him a stupid asshole and said I would never be in a porn film. When I got up to leave, he came over and put his hairy hands on my shoulders. He held me and said he was a great lover, knew some amazing positions, and would give me a night to remember."

Anna took several more deep breaths to stop the angry shivers spreading down her body.

"That's when I went berserk, and most of what happened next is just a blur. I vaguely remember scratching his face and feeling him punching me. At some point he must have seen blood on my fingernails and realized it was his. He grabbed my hands, pushed me back, and shouted I would never get any job in L.A. When he headed for the bathroom to check his face, all I wanted to do was get out of there."

Bart pulled Anna closer and said, "You've been through a lot, and I'm worried about the damage to your face. Should we go to an emergency room?"

"No need. My face looks bad, but I've already checked, and there are no cuts. And if you think my face looks bad, you should see Tony's," Anna said, trying to make a little joke and forcing a tiny smile.

"I hope that bastard has scars for the rest of his sorry life," Bart said, smiling at the thought.

"But I'm afraid there's more bad news," Anna said, her faced all pinched up.

"Did he do something else to you?" Bart asked and his eyes narrowed.

"No, I did something else to him."

"I hope it hurt him bad," Bart said.

He watched as Anna bent down and picked up an expensive looking briefcase that had been lying in shadows behind her. She held up the briefcase, as if showing off a well-earned trophy.

"I wanted to do something to make Tony pay for treating me like merchandise. When he went to check his bleeding face in the bathroom, I looked around for something to break or take. I saw the end of an expensive looking briefcase partly hidden behind a coffee table. Without thinking, I just grabbed the case and ran."

"What was in the case?" Bart asked, knowing it had to be trouble.

"I first drove around L.A. until I was miles from his house," Ann said. "Then I stopped on a street near a light and opened the case. When I saw what it was, I was so scared. I got on I-5 and drove straight to your house, because I knew you would know what to do."

"Let's see what's in the case," Bart said.

Anna let Bart hold the case while she opened it and turned it around so he could see the contents. Bart did a double take at seeing three large plastic bags full of white powder. It didn't take a genius to know he was looking at a fortune in cocaine. He glanced up at Anna, who looked as proud as Olympic winner.

"Losing this pile of cocaine is what that porn bastard deserved," Anna said with considerable bravado in her voice.

Bart stared at the contents and said, "Tony's going to do anything to get this back."

"I just wanted to do something to get even," Anna said in a pleading voice as more tears began running down her bruised cheeks.

"Does he know you might come to San Diego?" Bart asked, feeling like he was being sucked into a whirling tornado.

"Maybe," she said. "I once bragged how I had a great boyfriend in San Diego and how your stepfather was a big time lawyer."

"Do you think he'll come looking for you here?" Bart asked.

"Tony has two big, dumb goons, Ratty and Mousy, who I saw at his studio. Everyone warned me to stay clear of them, because they'd sooner snap your neck then say hello. I think Tony and his goons will come looking for me in San Diego," Anna said.

Bart drew Anna close and gave her a warm hug.

He whispered in her ear, "Somehow we'll get through this."

She gave him a little squeeze to show she agreed.

Bart thought, *But what are we going to do?*

CHAPTER 9

— — —

It was almost noon on Friday when detective Mossback drove the unmarked police car down West Point Loma Boulevard and headed for Ocean Beach. His partner, Jomore, was sitting in the passenger seat chewing his favorite cough drops, which made as much noise as a horse crunching raw carrots.

"What's the druggie's name?" Detective Mossback asked.

Jomore finished crunching cough drops long enough to say, "Kid's name is Bartholomew Whatting."

"Any problems getting the search warrant?" Mossback asked.

"No problems. The judge signed the search warrant this morning, so we can arrest this jerk when he's eating lunch, take him downtown, and book him," Jomore said.

"This better be a good tip, because our last one in OB was a total bust, and the captain reamed our asses for a week." Mossback said.

"Don't worry. My friend Jerry promised this tip came from a very reliable source we are supposed to keep secret. Believe it or not, the source was the kid's stepfather, supposedly a lawyer named Mr. Stranger. Apparently Bart is into drugs, and the big-time lawyer wants to put Bart in jail for a few days and scare him straight. I'm hoping all goes well so I can get an early start for a weekend of gambling," Mossback said.

"Which ones of the neighboring Indian casinos are your favorites?" Jomore asked.

"I like Harrah's Rincon because it has a hotel spa where my wife gets glamorous while I gamble and enjoy free drinks. Then we eat at the forty-foot buffet. Later, we'll work off the mucho calories dancing to disco music in the lounge," Mossback said.

"I see you've found the secret to a good marriage," Jomore said. He laughed so hard he started coughing, so he took two more cough drops, which he chewed so hard the noises drove Mossback crazy.

"Stopped chewing, or I'll make you walk," Mossback said as he turned left on Cable, which was heavily parked on both sides with older cars and motorcycles.

"This druggie lives a few blocks down, on the right side of Cable. I'll let you out at the end of his block so you can walk around and cover the back in case he runs," Mossback said, adding, "I'll bet you twenty he runs."

"That's a safe bet 'cause there's three things we know for sure. First, he'll run. Second, he'll deny his name is Bartholomew. Third, he'll say he was just visiting and doesn't live there," Jomore said. Then he asked, "How do we know if he's home?"

"Jerry said if there's an old jeep in the driveway, druggie Bart is home," Mossback said.

"Why do I always have to cover the back?" Jomore asked. "For just once I'd like to play Bruce Willis and swagger through the front door with a gun in my hand."

Mossback had to laugh because Jomore could no more pass for Bruce Willis than a poodle could pass for a bulldog.

As they drove past Bart's house, they saw an old jeep in the driveway.

"He's home," Mossback said. "I'll let you out at the corner. When you get around in back of the house, beep my cell phone."

Jomore got out of the car, hitched up his pants over his potbelly, and checked the gun in his shoulder holster. Then he found the back alley and walked to the fourth house from the end, which was Bart's house. He checked out the screen door in the back and then waited for Mossback to go in the front door.

Mossback did a U-turn and deliberately parked behind Bart's jeep to block any chance of escape.

When Mossback's phone beeped he got out of the car, took the warrant Jomore had left on the passenger seat, and walked up to the front door, which was an old screen door. He looked through the screen door but couldn't see anyone.

"San Diego Police," Mossback shouted. "We have a warrant to search your premises."

Mossback got no reply. He tried the screen door, which was unlocked. As he entered, he heard running sounds and yelled, "Watch the back door."

Jomore saw the back door fly open, and someone he figured was Bart came running out.

"Police! Stop and get down on your belly and put your hands behind your back," Jomore yelled, getting ready to tackle the person if he didn't stop.

But the person stopped, looked at the detective, and then got down on the ground, putting his hands behind his back.

"Just hold it right there," Jomore said. As he was putting on the jip tie, Mossback came running out of the house and saw the person now lying on the ground.

"See, I told you he'd run, so you own me twenty bucks," Jomore said, holding out his hand.

"I'll write you a check later," Mossback said, then he helped the person to his feet.

"Why are you cuffing me?" the person asked. "I didn't do anything."

"Well, let's go inside and see what we can find," Jomore said.

Mossback and Jomore marched the person back inside the small house and made him sit in one of the two rickety kitchen chairs.

Mossback put on his serious face, stared hard, and said, "Bart, you're in a lot of trouble."

"My name's not Bart, and I don't live here."

Jomore looked at Mossback and said, "I told you he'd deny everything, so looks like you owe me another twenty bucks."

"Don't hold your breath," Mossback said.

Jomore looked squarely at the person and said, "Well, let's look at the evidence. You match Bartholomew Whatting's physical description, you live in his house, and your jeep is in his driveway."

Mossback chimed in, "If it looks like a duck and walks like a duck and quacks like a duck, then you must be Bartholomew Whatting. Based on all the evidence, we'll keep things simple and just call your, Bart."

"Time to do some searching. I'll start in his bedroom," Jomore said as he put on his latex gloves and headed for Bart's bedroom.

Mossback remained standing in front of Bart, "I hear your stepfather is a big shot lawyer and I'm sure he told you to deny everything if you're ever arrested." Mossback added, "I don't suppose you have a driver's license?"

"No, I lost it couple weeks ago, and my name's not Bart, and my father isn't a lawyer. He works in the meat department at the big Vons grocery store on Garnet Street. And I don't live here. I was just hanging out overnight."

"Yeah, right. Do you know how many times I've heard that particular song and dance? You just sit while we wait to see what my partner finds in your bedroom."

A few minutes later Jomore came out of the bedroom carrying an expensive looking briefcase. He stopped at the kitchen table and held up the case for all to admire.

"Now look what I found tucked way under the bed. Are you going to tell me this isn't your briefcase?" Jomore asked.

"That's not my case, and that's the honest truth."

"I like hearing the honest truth. Now let's see what's in this pretty briefcase," Jomore said, having already looked inside.

He opened the case to reveal three plastic bags filled with white powder.

"That looks like cocaine," Mossback said. He smiled because this was turning into a very good bust, almost as good as winning big playing slot machines.

Jomore reached inside the case with his gloved hand and lifted out one of the plastic bags filled with white power. He carefully opened the Ziploc bag, pinched a tiny bit of the powder between two fingers, and tasted it.

"It looks and tastes just like cocaine," Jomore said. He had tasted a lot of cocaine and knew a lab test would prove him right. "Now I suppose you're going to say this isn't your briefcase?"

"It's not mine. I never saw it before. Really, that's not my case. My father works at Vons. I don't live here, and that's not my jeep. You've got it all wrong."

"I see you're doing just like your stepfather would advise, denying everything," Mossback said. "But let me tell you the honest truth. So far you have lied about everything. But don't worry, you'll have a chance to think about all those lies as you spend the weekend in jail with some not-so-good cell mates."

"I'm not talking any more."

"You're doing exactly as your stepfather would advise," Mossback said. Then he began reading Bart his rights.

"Now, let's give our new friend a ride downtown," Mossback said.

Mossback led the hand-tied Bart out the door while Jomore followed, carrying the briefcase in a big plastic bag.

Mossback got in the passenger seat and set the case of cocaine on his lap. Jomore put Bart in the back seat and then got in the driver's seat. Starting up the unmarked Ford, he headed for the high-rise jail in downtown San Diego, about a fifteen-minute drive if the traffic was light.

Once at the jail, the detectives turned Bart over to an officer who booked, fingerprinted, and finally led him to a cell.

"I'd hate to spend the weekend in a jail cell filled drunks, muggers, and major assholes arrested over the weekend. Not a nice crowd," Mossback said as they were getting ready to leave the jail.

"He must really hate his stepfather not to want to call and ask for his help," Jomore said.

"Do you think he suspects his stepfather turned him in?" Jomore asked.

"I don't know, but it's a clean bust, and that's what counts. And remember, Jerry said to keep our mouths shut about the stepfather tipping us off," Mossback said.

"If you ask me, the stepfather sounds like a real jerk to turn in his own stepson," said Jomore.

"I'll tell you what I would do if I were this guy. I'd get me a really good lawyer who wasn't my stepfather," Mossback said.

"Well there's nothing more for us to do here. I told Jerry I'd call and tell him how the drug bust went, and then I'm picking up the missus and taking off for a weekend of gambling," Mossback said.

CHAPTER 10

— — —

"Hello," said the retired police officer, Jerry Gosling.

"It's me," Mossback said.

"How'd the drug bust go?" Jerry asked.

"Like a dream," Mossback said. "The kid was home and tried to run, but we had planned he would and caught him as he came out the back door. We would have been happy to discover some meth but were really surprised to find an expensive briefcase filled with three large bags of cocaine, street value in the millions. So Bart faces serious charges and will be going away for a long time. As expected, he lied about everything, even claimed his father was a meat cutter at the Vons Grocery. We booked him, and he'll spend the weekend in jail, just like his stepfather wanted."

"Are you sure the kid is Bart Whatting?" Jerry asked.

"Absolutely. He matched your physical description, his jeep was parked in the driveway, and we found two utility bills addressed to Bart Whatting. Slam dunk," Mossback said.

"Sounds good to me. I'll give his stepfather a call and ask if he ever worked as a meat cutter at Vons," Jerry said, chuckling.

"Thanks for the tip. I'm going to celebrate Bart's big arrest with a weekend of gambling," Mossback said.

"You deserve it, and I hope you have good luck at the craps table," Jerry said.

After saying goodbye to Mossback, Jerry dialed Mr. Stranger's number to give him the good news.

"Stranger, Foremore, and Long," answered the secretary with the perfect makeup.

"Hi, this is Jerry Gosling and I'm calling Mr. Stranger regarding a personal matter we had discussed earlier."

"Just a moment," the secretary said. She buzzed Mr. Stranger's office, spoke for a few seconds, and then forwarded Jerry's call.

"Hi Jerry," Mr. Stranger said. "I am glad you called. What exactly happened today with my stepson?"

"My detective friends had no trouble getting a warrant, since their tip had come from a very reliable source. When they went to serve the warrant, Bart tried to escape by running out the back door, but one of the detectives was waiting and caught him."

"What did they find?" Mr. Stranger asked, hoping the detectives had found enough drugs to make a felony arrest.

"I think you'll be very surprised. No marijuana as you suspected, but instead they found an expensive briefcase containing three bags of cocaine, with a street value in the millions," Jerry said.

"I must admit I am surprised. Apparently Bart has gone off the deep end and become a drug courier. It is fortunate I intervened now and put a stop to future drug dealing. As I told you earlier, Bart had rejected all my help and excellent advice," Mr. Stranger said, trying not to sound pleased that Bart would be charged with a felony that guaranteed serious jail time.

"But you know what kids are like today. You give them good advice, and they roll their eyes like you don't know what you're talking about," Jerry said.

"Did the detectives book Bart in the downtown jail?" Mr. Stranger asked.

"Yes they did. Bart will have the weekend to think about his future. He'll be arraigned on Monday, probably around noon."

"The very least I can do as his stepfather is act as Bart's lawyer and attend his arraignment on Monday," Mr. Stranger said.

"By the way," Jerry said. "Bart told the detectives that his stepfather was a meat cutter at Von's grocery store."

"I am not surprised," Mr. Stranger said. "As I told you earlier, Bart enjoys scoffing at me and disregarding my advice every chance he gets. However, because he is in considerable trouble, I will overlook his lack of respect, fulfill my duty as his stepfather, and agree to be his lawyer."

"Kids will be kids," Jerry sympathized. "When do they ever grow up?"

"You can see now why I took the rather drastic step of having Bart arrested. It was my last chance to bring Bart to his senses and motivate him to become a responsible adult," Mr. Stranger said in a smug voice.

"Thank you very much for all your help," Mr. Stranger said. "And remember Jerry, if you need any legal advice in the future, it will be on the house."

Jerry hung up the phone and began thinking, *Jomore and Mossback will have five or six beers and brag about a great cocaine bust all because of a tip from the kid's own stepfather. At some point the shit will hit the fan and blow into Mr. Stranger's face when his kid finds out his stepfather had tipped off the police.*

When Randolph hung up the phone, he could not stop gloating. Everything was going according to his well-laid plan. Bart's arrest and certain conviction would automatically trigger the malfeasance clause, which meant he would gain sole control of Bart's trust fund. But now he had a few more phone calls to make and several more lies to tell.

Randolph first called the jail and asked for the officer on duty, who answered on the tenth ring.

"This is Mr. Randolph Stranger, attorney at law. I understand my stepson Bartholomew Whatting has recently been taken to your jail and booked. I will be acting as his lawyer and wonder if you can tell me when he will be arraigned," Mr. Stranger asked.

"Let me check," said the officer, who looked at the booking sheet.

"Yes, a Mr. Bartholomew Whatting was booked this afternoon and charged with possession of cocaine," the officer said. "He will jailed over the weekend and be arraigned on Monday, probably after lunch since the judge usually takes the suspects in alphabetical order."

"Thank you," Randolph said and hung up.

For several minutes, Randolph thought about the next two phone calls and the convincing lies he needed to tell.

He speed dialed Marjorie's number and waited for her to answer.

"Hello," she said in a soft voice.

"I'm afraid I have some very disturbing news," Randolph said in the professional, somewhat unfriendly tone he used when giving clients bad news.

"Does it have to do with Bart? Has something happened to him?" Marjorie asked, knowing it had to be Bart because Carol never got into any trouble.

"Yes, I am afraid it does concern Bart," Randolph said. "I was just informed that Bart has been arrested for having a briefcase filled with cocaine. The possession of that much cocaine is a very serious felony and carries a stiff penalty."

Randolph could hear Marjorie's sudden gasp of alarm.

"Bart would never do that. There must be some mistake," Marjorie said.

"There is no mistake. I just spoke to the arresting detective who said he had acted on a reliable tip from an undercover agent working in the beach area," Randolph lied.

"No, it has to be a mistake. Bart is not a drug dealer," Marjorie said as she started to cry, which infuriated Randolph because he believed crying was a sign of weakness.

"Marjorie, please get control of yourself. Bart is presently booked into the downtown jail, and he will be arraigned on Monday. Of course, I will be his lawyer, attend his arraignment, and try to arrange for his bail," Randolph said.

"I can't believe any of this. Bart's not a cocaine dealer. He told me he's tried a little marijuana, and I truly believe that's all he's done," Marjorie said, her words muffled by her sobbing.

"I am sorry to say Bart has apparently has lied to you, since the detectives found him with a briefcase full of cocaine, which is irrefutable evidence of his drug activities," Randolph said, thinking he might be acting a bit harsh and deciding to soften his approach.

"Of course, I promise you I will go to any length to help him in his time of need," Randolph added. He sounded so sincere he almost believed himself.

Marjorie made an effort to gain some control by taking several deep breaths. "As soon as I change out of my gardening clothes, I am going to the jail to see Bart, talk to him, and find out what happened," Marjorie said, sounding determined and no longer sobbing.

"I am sorry, Marjorie, but that will not be possible," Randolph said in a firm voice. If you were to talk or visit Bart it would be automatically recorded, and the prosecution could use anything he might say to you. When I talk to Bart, everything he says to me is confidential because it is covered by the lawyer-client privilege," Randolph said.

Marjorie said in a discouraged voice. "Then you must do something to bail Bart out of jail today."

"I cannot bail Bart out until after he is arraigned on Monday. But as Bart's lawyer, I can meet with Bart this weekend and begin arrangements to post bail for him on Monday," Randolph said.

But Randolph had no intention of meeting with Bart until his arraignment on Monday. Making Bart spend the weekend in a cell crammed with misfits would be small punishment for his refusing to sign the documents he had prepared to transfer his trust.

"As soon as we finish, I will call Carol," Randolph added, feeling like all the dominos were dropping into place.

"Yes, please call Carol. And after that, please go immediately to the jail and talk to Bart. I'm sure he's worried and scared," Marjorie said and then added, "When will he be arraigned?"

"Sometime Monday afternoon," Randolph said. "You and Carol

can meet me at the courthouse about twelve-thirty and we can go in together."

As he ended the call with Marjorie, Randolph thought about his appearance in court. He would wear his charcoal mohair suit with black pinstripes and a light gray shirt that made him look very officious and very good on television. He would have his secretary anonymously tip off the media about the stepson of a prominent lawyer having been arrested for possession of cocaine. That kind of juicy story would get the media out in force and to ask questions and televise his remarks from the steps of the courthouse, which he considered his very own pulpit.

As Randolph dialed Carol's number he was thinking about how he would give her the news.

"Hello," Carol said. Her tone was very suspicious because she had recognized Randy-Dandy's number, and he rarely, if ever, called her laboratory.

"I am sorry to bother you at the laboratory, but I have some very unfortunate news about Bart," Randolph said.

Carol was too shocked to say anything and tried to brace herself for the bad news.

"This afternoon I was very much surprised when a detective called my office and informed me that, acting on a reliable tip, he and his partner had arrested Bart for possessing a briefcase containing three bags of cocaine," Randolph said.

This news was so unexpected and so awful that Carol's whole body trembled, and she almost dropped the phone.

Randolph heard only Carol's rapid breathing and continued.

"As I said, Bart has been arrested and charged with possessing and selling illegal drugs, which is a felony. He has been booked into the downtown jail and will be arraigned after lunch on Monday."

"When can I see Bart?" Carol asked.

"As I explained to Marjorie, if you were to talk to Bart now, your conversation would be recorded, and the prosecution could use anything Bart said to you. However, as soon as we finish talking, I will immediately go to the jail and talk to Bart, and I will begin plans to bail him out after his arraignment," Randolph lied. He smiled at the image of Bart spending a weekend in jail with all the other drunks and crazies arrested over the weekend.

Carol was biting her tongue to keep from saying anything that would trigger her stepfather's temper and make things even worse for Bart.

Play it cool, she said to herself as she gathered her wits, and then she spoke in the subservient tone she knew Randolph loved. "I'm glad you are going to defend Bart, and I just wondered if there were anything I could do to help?"

"Actually, yes, there are two things that you can do. The first is not to speak to the press, who are sure to get wind of Bart's arrest. Just refer them to me because I know how to deal with them. The second thing is for you and your mother to attend Bart's arraignment on Monday, probably around noon. It is critically important for the judge, the press, and potential jurors to see us all together and to realize that Bart has the full support of his loving family. Just remember, I will do everything in my power and use all my connections to give Bart the very best defense," Randolph said.

"I will pick mom up so we can arrive together and in plenty of time for Bart's arraignment," Carol said.

"That's fine," Randolph said. "I will meet you both at the courthouse steps at twelve-thirty."

"OK, we'll meet you there," Carol said and heard Randolph hang up without saying a polite goodbye.

Randolph was not sure how much money was in Bart's trust, but he figured it was about two million. *Not bad pay for a day's work*, he said to himself. He reasoned that it merited a celebration.

He pushed one of the buttons on his phone console.

"Yes, Mr. Stranger," answered the secretary with the perfect makeup.

"Tonight, same place, same time," was all Randolph said.

"Perfect," was all the secretary said.

* * * *

While Randolph was making plans with his secretary, Carol had dialed Billy and was waiting for him to answer.

"Hello," Billy said in a happy tone, seeing it was Carol.

"Something terrible, really terrible, has happened to Bart," Carol said.

"Just tell me what happened," Billy said.

Carol's words came rushing out. "Randolph just called and said that Bart was arrested by detectives who had found a briefcase full of cocaine in his house. I can't believe it. Randolph said that detectives were tipped off. And the worst part is Randolph said he was going to be Bart's lawyer. What should we do?"

CHAPTER 11

− − −

It was Monday morning. Randolph had finished showering, shaving, and combing his slightly graying hair straight back to give him a distinguished look. He stood before the full-length bathroom mirror to admire his six-foot two-inch, muscular frame, broad shoulders, and flat stomach. For someone almost fifty, he had a youthful, attractive appearance that allowed him to easily pass for forty.

He walked into his closet that was as large as a studio apartment. He selected a European cut, Armani, charcoal grey mohair suit with ultra-thin, black pinstripes, a dark maroon, Hermès tie, and its matching pocket square. He chose a light gray, silk shirt with a matte finish so it would not reflect the bright camera lights of the television crews. Finally he picked out a pair of elegantly shaped, black half boots, which added another inch to his already tall stature and further guaranteed he would tower above most people.

When Randolph finished dressing, he returned to the full-length mirror for a final inspection. He smiled at his reflection and paraphrased the words of the wicked witch in the movie *Sleeping Beauty*. "Mirror, mirror on the wall, who is the best looking lawyer of them all?" And then he pointed at his own reflection in answer to his question.

Truth be told, Randolph *was* very handsome, but it was not only his Hollywood looks that made him stand out in a crowd. It was his ability to project a feeling of power, strength, and confidence, which males secretly resented and females appreciated, swarming around him like bees to a flower's sweet nectar.

He left his bedroom, which was next to Marjorie's, walked down the stairs, and found her having coffee on the covered patio facing the endless expanse of blue ocean waves.

"I must leave now so I can stop at my office before going to Bart's arrangement," Randolph said.

"I just cannot believe this is happening," Marjorie said, vowing to be strong and not start crying.

"Just be sure you and Carol meet me at the courthouse around twelve-thirty. That will allow me time to make a brief statement to the press before we go to Bart's arraignment, probably around one o'clock, unless the judge has a long lunch."

As Randolph drove his silver-gray Bentley Mulsanne to his office, he thought about what he would discuss with the press.

I will say Bart is a responsible citizen who has been wrongly arrested. I will question and cast doubt on police procedures. The presence of Marjorie and Caroline at my side will make a very good impression, especially if there are tears in their eyes, which is something I should mention to them.

Randolph practiced his short speech, noting which words needed to be emphasized and where to pause. He would look directly into the camera, giving the impression he was individually talking to each viewer, some of who might someday be in the jury.

When he got to his office, he picked up Bart's file and then buzzed his secretary.

"Did you alert the press corps?" Randolph asked.

His secretary with the perfect makeup said, "I anonymously called all four local TV stations, plus reporters for the San Diego Union-Tribune and Los Angeles Times. I passed along the tip that Bart Whatting had been arrested on Friday for possession of cocaine and was to be arraigned Monday, around one o'clock. I added Bart would be represented by his stepfather, Mr. Randolph Stranger of the law firm Stranger, Foremore, and Long."

"Are you absolutely sure the reporters knew that Bart Whatting was my stepson?" Randolph asked, angry that both Bart and Carol had kept the name of their biological father when he had married their mother.

"I carefully explained Bart Whatting had retained the name of his biological father but would be represented by Mr. Randolph Stranger, his stepfather," the secretary said, and checked her makeup in a small mirror at the side of her computer.

"Did you make the calls from pay phones?" Randolph asked.

"As you instructed, I made all the calls from several different pay phones in the Fashion Valley Mall, so none can be traced to your office or even to your building," the secretary replied, thinking about applying a little more coloring to highlight her cheek bones.

"Very good," Randolph said before hanging up his phone. It was not every day the stepson of a prominent lawyer is arrested for cocaine possession. Such news should draw a big crowd of news people and spectators, which always brings out his best.

* * * *

As Randolph was talking to his secretary, Carol had been on the phone with Billy.

"Randolph told me Bart's arraignment would be around one o'clock, so Marjorie and I are planning to meet him at the bottom of the courthouse stairs around twelve-thirty. Randolph wants mom and me to be there to show our support for Bart," Carol said.

"I feel I'm much to blame," Billy said. "I was so sure Randolph would need at least a couple days to arrange Bart's arrest. I have to admit, Randolph is a very clever bastard."

"You had no way of knowing Randolph could or would act so quickly," Carol said.

"It seems pretty clear Jerry's favor for Randolph was to tip off the police and get them moving quickly. But I can't figure where all that cocaine came from, unless the police took it from their evidence room and planted it in Bart's house," Billy said.

"There's no way in hell Bart could get millions of dollars worth of cocaine. There's something awfully screwy going on," Carol said. She reluctantly added, "There's one more thing. I think it would be better if you wore normal clothes when you come to the arraignment, not your usual black leathers. I want you to be my secret agent, invisible and anonymous."

"Don't worry. I will be totally anonymous, since I plan to come in drag," Billy said with a smile.

"I can't wait to see Bad Billy in drag," Carol said. They both laughed, easing some of their tension over Bart's arrest.

"I know you asked me to pick up Helen and bring her to Bart's arraignment. Will she be waiting for me at your Condo?" Billy asked.

Helen was Carol's research assistant, best friend, and would turn into a fighting bulldog when hearing people make cruel or snide remarks about Carol's Ph.D. brain in a Playboy's body. When Helen had heard about Bart's arrest, she wanted to provide moral support by being at Bart's arraignment.

"Helen will be waiting for you at my condo. And thanks for picking her up," Carol said.

"I plan to stow my motorcycle and pick up Helen in my truck, provided

I can clean it up and get out all the junk," Billy said. Then added, "See you at the courthouse."

After Carol closed her cell phone, Helen said, "I couldn't help overhearing some of your conversation, and I can't believe anyone is called *Bad Billy*, except in movies. Is this person for real, and what's this about not wearing his black leathers and coming in drag?"

"Billy is for real, and he's like no one you've ever met. His friends call him Billy. But jealous types or enemies call him *Bad Billy*, but never to his face. I first met him at a country-western dance place called the Red Bull Saloon in east San Diego County," Carol said.

"How did you ever find that place?" Helen asked.

""When I first arrived at the Neuroscience Institute, I wanted so badly to prove my worth, I spent all my time doing research. One day I must have looked particularly haggard, and Judy, a secretary I knew and liked, said that I needed to have some fun. She told me how a bunch of them went country-western dancing at the Red Bull Saloon in rural east San Diego County. She guaranteed it would be a unique experience and told me to get into the mood and buy a cowboy hat and cowboy boots," Carol said, grinning from ear to ear.

"You actually bought a cowboy hat and boots?" Helen asked.

"I did, and one Saturday night I met the group at the Red Bull Saloon. And as promised, it was a unique experience. Most of the people were dressed in cowboy attire, there was a live country band, and it was a hoot," Carol said.

"So how does Billy come into the picture?" Helen asked.

"As I watched other dancers, my eyes happened to meet those of a tall, attractive man dressed all in black. Our eyes held for several seconds, and I felt some emotion stir inside, like when I was a teenager and saw a really cute guy."

"This sounds like the beginning of a romance novel," Helen said.

"It gets better," Carol said. "When the next dance started, he came over, touched the brim of his cowboy hat in a friendly gesture, said that his name was Billy, and asked me to dance. He was a great dancer, and each time our bodies accidentally touched there were magical sparks, and I wondered what was happening," Carol said, feeling her face get hot.

"I like to dance, but I'm not sure if I would dance with anybody called *Bad Billy*. What kind of guy is he?" Helen asked.

"I must admit, he's hard to describe," Carol said. "Let me put it this way. Imagine you're driving through a barren desert, seeing nothing but miles and miles of burning sand and blazing sun. Then suddenly you see a solitary, tall cactus that's surviving and flourishing with no help from anything or anybody. That cactus is a stand-in for Billy, prickles and all."

Carol laughed at how accurate the image really was.

"But nobody can be that strong and independent," Helen said.

"Billy is like an endangered species, the last of the mountain men, and a hell of a dancer. You're in for a real treat," Carol said, thinking about dancing with Bad Billy's strong arms around her.

"But how did he get that silly name, *Bad Billy*?" Helen asked.

"There are a lot of stories, but I'll just tell you one. Billy was camping in the mountains, and he woke one morning to see an extra-large rattlesnake coiled in the middle of his sleeping bag, its tongue moving and flicking the air about a foot from his face. Billy simply remained motionless and stared back into the snake's eyes. Some say the standoff went on for minutes, some say hours. In the end, Billy stared the snake down, and it slithered away. When the snake had gone, Billy grabbed his hunting knife, followed the snake, and killed it because he thought it might bite others campers. He cut off the snake's big rattle and hung it on his truck's inside rearview mirror as reminder to never blink at adversity."

Helen stood there with her mouth partly open, trying to decide if Carol was telling the truth or putting her on, especially the part about never blinking at adversity. That was something a Zen master might say, not somebody dressed in black leather, riding a motorcycle.

Carol saw Helen's disbelieving expression and said, "It's all true, and there are dozens more hair-raising stories just like that."

"If I didn't know you were a respected neuroscientist who didn't take hallucinogenic drugs, I'd say you're having me on, big time," Helen said.

"I know it's hard to believe. But when Billy picks you up, check out the snake's rattle hanging from his rearview mirror," Carol said.

As Carol went off to finish dressing, she thought about Bart spending the weekend in a cell filled with drunks, muggers, and stoned-out druggies. She said to herself, *I'll never forgive Randolph for how he's treated Bart.*

CHAPTER 12

——— ——— ———

When Randolph wished to make an especially good impression, he always hired a uniformed chauffer to drive his expensive Bentley Mulsanne, whose custom interior was upholstered in soft, white leather. The chauffer stopped at the foot of the courthouse stairs, got out, and went around to open Randolph's door. A large group of TV and newspaper reporters had already gathered at the steps and began shouting questions as Randolph exited the car.

He stopped, smiled at the news people, gestured for quiet, and said in his commanding, professional voice, "Please, no questions now. I will make a statement in a few minutes."

Then the chauffer walked a short distance to Marjorie's car, which Carol had parked at the bottom of the courthouse steps. The chauffer opened the passenger side door, and Randolph, who had followed the chauffer, stepped forward and graciously extended his arm to help Marjorie out of her car. She was so nervous she stumbled a little as she stepped up to the sidewalk. She was dressed in a somber, dark gray, long-sleeved dress and black pumps, and she wore no jewelry. Her eyes looked red and puffy from crying, and her whole faced showed the effects of too little sleep.

Carol exited on the driver's side and came around to give her keys to the chauffer, who would take care of parking Marjorie's car. Carol was wearing a dark gray blouse under a light gray pant's suit, black pumps, and only enough makeup to hide the dark, sleepless circles under her eyes. Even so, Carol's natural beauty caught the eyes of several cameramen. They made sure she was featured in the shot showing the threesome gathered at the bottom of the courthouse stairs.

When they were all together, Randolph began walking up the dozen or so courthouse steps, with Marjorie holding on to his right arm. Carol walked on Randolph's left side and resolutely refused to hold Randolph's offered arm. At the top of the steps, Randolph turned and led Marjorie and Carol a short distance to a bank of microphones the media had placed on the wide terrace near the courthouse's entrance. Randolph positioned Marjorie on his right and Carol on his left while the press and TV cameramen bunched up in front of them. Randolph was pleased to see tears in Marjorie's eyes but disappointed with the angry look he received when he quietly suggested to Carol that a few tears would be appropriate.

Randolph scanned the group of boisterous reporters who were continually shouting questions. He also noticed a large crowd of spectators who had come for the show. He raised both his hands for silence, which took several long minutes. While he waited for silence, he imagined the headline on the evening news:

PROMINENT LAWYER DEFENDS STEPSON ARRESTED IN COCAINE SEIZURE

Randolph thought, *For a defense lawyer, any press was good press.*

When the crowd of reporters finally went silent, Randolph looked directly into the TV cameras and began speaking.

"Today, I stand before you not only as Bart's lawyer, but also as his loving and concerned stepfather. Speaking in my role as his stepfather, I will admit to being biased, but that is normal for any father who is proud of his son. Bart is currently a college student at the University of California, San Diego campus. He has a long list of academic accomplishments to prove he is an intelligent young man with a sterling character and history of behaving responsibly. Speaking in my role as Bart's lawyer, I can categorically state he has never been involved in, or accused of any criminal activity. In fact the only thing he's ever been guilty of is the occasional parking violation; tickets that most of us have received."

He paused to give reporters a chance to laugh, because they had all received their share of parking tickets. Then he raised his head high and continued.

"Because of Bart's unblemished academic and public records, I find it impossible to believe he can be a perfect, law-abiding citizen one day and suddenly turn into a big-time cocaine dealer the next day. I know and trust my stepson, and I can assure you that he is not like Dr. Jekyll, the respected surgeon, turning into Mr. Hyde, the notorious murderer."

Again he paused as reporters smiled at the Jekyll/Hyde reference, which he knew would be the sound bite featured on all the radio and TV news programs. Then Randolph looked directly into the TV cameras and spoke with great sincerity.

"I think it is obvious that, in Bart's case, the police have arrested the wrong person. As you are all aware, it is not uncommon in drug arrests to discover the so-called anonymous tip was questionable, or the search warrant was obtained illegally, or the evidence was tainted or even planted.

Accordingly, I am absolutely convinced of Bart's innocence, as are his loving mother and sister standing at my sides. I will do all in my power to see that justice is done, which means clearing Bart of all charges. I will defer all further questions until after my stepson's arraignment."

Randolph was delighted to hear reporters buzzing about the unlikelihood of Bart being a Jekyll-Hyde personality and the good possibility that police had either planted the cocaine or arrested the wrong person. Randolph's plan was very clever and very simple. He would publicly proclaim Bart's innocence, at the same time, he would ensure that his stepson was convicted of a felony and sent to jail.

Randolph turned away from the microphones and reporters and began walking toward the courthouse doors with Marjorie and Carol in his wake.

* * * *

As Randolph's threesome move forward, so did the group of reporters and curious spectators, including Billy and Helen.

Helen had felt a little embarrassed standing next to Billy, who was wearing hand-me-down men's clothes from a thrift shop. He was standing with hunched shoulders to better blend into the crowd.

Seeing her uncomfortable expression, Billy had explained, "Carol told me to be anonymous, so I'm playing the role."

"Well, I must say you are very convincing," Helen said.

"We better keep moving," was all Bad Billy said.

He and Helen entered the courthouse and got into one of the two security lines that led to the metal detectors. Billy saw Randolph, Marjorie, and Carol waiting in the other line, with about ten people in front of them.

* * * *

Suddenly an alarm went off, and it's piercing, wailing sound grew louder and louder as it echoed off the big room's marble walls. The jarring sound lasted for almost a minute as people began screaming and trying to run, but there was nowhere to go since the all the doors had automatically closed and locked when the alarm went off. In desperation, many were falling to the floor and curling into protective fetal positions. When the alarm finally stopped, there was a dreadful silence, like the quiet after a violent storm.

Then someone shouted, "He's got a gun!"

Someone screamed, "He's going to shoot!"

People were yelling, "Get down!"

More shouting, "He's pointing the gun!"

A woman screamed, "He's a terrorist!"

Billy stood tall, breathing normally, heart rate in the low fifties, ready to act. He saw one security guard restraining a gray-haired man. A second guard was holding the arm of the gray-haired man so his gun was pointed at the ceiling.

"You damn fools. It's not loaded." The gray-haired man's angry words carried above the din of the crowd.

But his words had no effect on the two guards who continued to restrain the gray-haired man and keep his gun pointed at the ceiling.

"I'm Judge Kramer," said the angry gray-haired man with the gun. "I've got a permit to carry a gun. Get your hands off me, or I'll have you all arrested!"

People had heard bits and pieces of Judge Kramer's words, and comments began to fly around the room.

"It's a judge with a loaded gun!"

"He's going to arrest somebody?"

Then someone was speaking through a megaphone.

"This is security. There is no danger. Please, everyone calm down. There has been a mistake. An officer of the court neglected to tell security about an unloaded gun in his briefcase. Let me repeat. No one is in danger. Please, remain in line. As soon as everyone has calmed down, we will continue the security procedure and get you all on your way. Thank you for your patience."

"It's Judge Kramer all right," one of the guards said. "He pulled the same thing about six months ago when I was on duty. We warned him against bringing a gun into the courthouse, but he's semi-retired and getting forgetful. He only comes in now and then when another judge gets sick."

"Thank god he never loads the gun. The way he waves it around, he's bound to accidentally pull the trigger," a second guard said.

A third guard was running a wand up and down Judge Kramer's body, checking for other weapons. Judge Kramer was very annoyed by having to submit to this examination and kept moving about, refusing to hold out his arms like a common criminal. He was not the least embarrassed by his stupid action since, after all, the guards were paid to find guns, even unloaded ones. Finally the guards let Judge Kramer go, and his final words were, "I hope you guys had a good time playing John Wayne."

"The old judge is really off his rocker today. I've never heard of John Wayne," one of the younger guards said.

"We need to check out the metal detectors because both of them were overturned in all the shoving," another guard said.

It took an additional fifteen minutes for the security guards to reposition the metal detectors, check their sensitivity, and declare them functional. The security guards seemed to be taking forever as they positioned, checked, and rechecked the metal detectors.

Randolph was still tenth in line and kept looking at his watch and worrying about being late for the arraignment and the possibility of the judge appointing another attorney to handle Bart's case. He was shifting from foot to foot, watching the guards, who seemed to be in no hurry, and feeling his irritation grow. Finally, he bolted out of line like a racehorse leaving the starting gate and pushed his way forward until he was face to face with the guard standing at the metal detector.

"I must be allowed through the detector immediately because my stepson is being arraigned in room five-oh-two at this very minute," Randolph said, staring daggers at the guard.

"If you do not allow me and my family through the metal detector in the next five seconds, I will have you fired," Randolph threatened.

The guard was mildly amused by Randolph's demands and threats. But the guard knew exactly how to deal with pompous big shots who were accustomed to always getting their ways.

"Please sir, step back in line and wait your turn. Everyone's in a hurry, and we'll get you through the metal detector as quickly as possible," the guard said in a slightly condescending voice.

"Apparently you do not understand. I am a prominent lawyer, and it is very important that I get to my stepson's arraignment on time," Randolph shouted.

The guard turned, faced the crowd, and asked in a loud but friendly voice, "How many of you are lawyers and have important and immediate business in the courthouse?"

Randolph saw almost everyone in both lines raising their hands, even the reporters, who were pretending to be lawyers.

The guard tried to hide his smirk as he spoke to Randolph. "As you can see, everybody's in a hurry, and just like you, they all have some place to be. So let me say this again. Please return to your line and wait your turn."

As Randolph was walking back to his place in line, the guard silently signaled to another guard holding the hand wand, nodded, and pointed at Randolph.

The guard with the hand wand nodded back, indicating he would pull this asshole aside and give him a time-consuming individual search. The guards exchanged smiles. They knew exactly how to deal with big asshole lawyers who believed they had the God-given, unalienable right to always receive preferential treatment.

Chapter 13

▬ ▬ ▬

The security guard with the megaphone made another announcement. "We are going to sound the alarm one more time to make sure it is properly reset. This is only a test."

The piercing alarm sounded once, very briefly, but caused many of those waiting in line to cringe and duck, as if something terrible would follow. The jarring sound caused Helen to again wrap her arms around Billy and hold on tight. She hated guns, and loud noises, and being stuck in crowds, and all she could think about was how good it felt to hang on to Billy, who made her feel so safe and secure.

Finally the two security lines began moving, but very slowly as the guards opened and examined each and every briefcase. When Randolph went through the metal detector, the guard secretly set off the metal detector's alarm, which meant Randolph had to step aside to be individually examined with the hand wand. During his individual security check, Randolph's face was blood red, his lips were pressed hard together, his eyes narrowed and turned dark, and his one desire was to smash this obnoxious guard in his big, fat, ugly face.

Marjorie and Carol had followed Randolph through the mental detector. They had no problems and were waiting near the sidewall as the guard scanned Randolph's body with the hand metal detector and then insisted on going through his briefcase, picking up and examining each item. It was almost ten more minutes before Randolph was allowed to go, and by then his muscles were as tightly strung as the strings on a guitar. Randolph motioned Marjorie and Carol to follow him as he headed for the elevators, where a big crowd was waiting because only one of the six elevators was working. They had all been automatically turned off by the security alert, and there was now a problem turning them back on.

"It will be quicker if we walk up to the fifth floor," Randolph said as he led Marjorie and Carol to the south stairway.

By then Billy and Helen had passed through the metal detector and were not far behind Randolph's group as they hurried up the staircase. He hated to be late, which was very unprofessional and usually elicited the judge's wrath. When he finally reached the fifth floor, he pulled the door handle but found the door had been automatically locked by the security alert. He began pounding on the door and shouting.

"Open this door. Open this door, immediately!"

After almost a minute of pounding and shouting, an overweight security guard finally heard the noise, walked over to the door, and peered through the bullet proof glass at Randolph's face, which was so contorted by anger that it looked like an ugly Halloween mask.

The guard leisurely sorted through his keys while Randolph continued to pound and shout. The guard tried several keys before one worked. At the sound of the lock turning, Randolph pushed the door open so forcefully that it knocked the guard into the wall.

"Hey, watch it buddy. I can have you arrested for pushing me around," said the guard, who never took any guff from a civilian.

Hearing the surly guard's warning was the last straw. Something snapped and crackled inside Randolph head. He stuck his face two inches from the guards and yelled.

"Go fuck yourself!"

Both Marjorie and Carol were so surprised they stopped in their tracks and stared at each. Never before had either one heard Randolph use the "F" word in public. Randolph always made a point to avoid vulgarities and maintain a very professional public image.

Randolph hurried Marjorie and Carol down the corridor and into room five-oh-two. Soon after, Billy and Helen entered room five-oh-two, looked around, and found seats near the

As Randolph hurried toward the front of the room, he briefly glanced at a young man with longish blond hair, wearing the regulation-orange prisoner's jumpsuit already seated at the defense table. He knew it must be Bart. Next to him was another man, dressed in a suit, most likely a court-appointed lawyer whom the judge had assigned because of Randolph's late arrival.

Randolph went through the gate that separated the court officials from the spectators, faced the judge and said, "Your honor, I apologize for being late. I was unavoidably delayed at security when an alarm went off. My name is Mr. Randolph Stranger, and I am here to represent my stepson, Bart Whatting, who is seated in front of you. There will be no need for a court-appointed lawyer."

"I will dismiss the court-appointed lawyer, and I presume you are familiar with this case, since it is your own stepson," Judge Kramer said.

"Yes, I am familiar with the case," Randolph said.

He proceeded to open the gate, walk over and take his place at the defense table.

After Randolph sat down, he turned to talk to the seated person in the orange jump suit. What Randolph saw rendered him speechless and his eyes dilated as if seeing a ghost.

Judge Kramer noticed Randolph fixedly staring at his stepson and asked, "Are you ready to proceed?"

Randolph stood up, pointed a finger at the young man with longish, blonde hair and said in a commanding voice, "This is not my stepson."

Judge Kramer seemed confused and asked, "How can that be?"

Randolph remained standing and said, "Although there is some superficial resemblance, this is not my stepson. The court officers have obviously make a serious mistake and brought in the wrong prisoner."

Judge Kramer told the prisoner in the orange jumpsuit to rise. Then he asked, "Are you Bart Whatting?"

The young man in the orange jumpsuit looked at the judge and said, "Nope. Everyone calls me Toady, because I hop 'round from place to place."

The courtroom filled with laughter, and Judge Kramer banged his gavel, as he liked to do, until the laugher ceased.

"We will take a ten minute recess so the court officers can determine if they brought in the wrong prisoner," Judge Kramer said.

When Judge Kramer had left the courtroom the media went wild. They were all talking at once as they tried to figure out exactly what had happened.

Ten minutes late Judge Kramer came back in and the bailiff shouted, "All rise. The honorable Judge Kramer presiding."

Judge Kramer took his seat, graveled the news people and spectators into silence, and said, "I will tolerate no further outbursts in my courtroom."

Then Judge Kramer turned and asked the court officer, "Is this the man arrested by the police and identified as Bart Whatting?"

"Yes," the court officer said. "But apparently the police make a mistake in identification."

Judge Kramer looked down at the defendant and asked, "What is your real name?"

"Joey Grumpus," the young man said. "I told the police I wasn't anyone named Bart something. They didn't believe me. They said I looked like Bart, was in his house, his jeep was outside, so I must be Bart. I even told them my father was a meat cutter at Vons, and they laughed and said my stepfather father was a big-time lawyer. Don't I wish."

"What were you doing in Bart Whatting's house?" the Judge asked.

"People call me Toady 'cause I hop around to crash at vacant places in Ocean Beach. Well, I see this guy and his chick coming out a house with some luggage and watch them leave. After they're gone I try the door, and it's not locked. I go inside, make myself at home, even find some food. I'm thinking I hit a gold mine. The next day I'm sitting around, having some coffee, and somebody yells, 'POLICE!' I run out the back door, get caught, and they say my name is Bart somebody. Then the police find a case full of cocaine under the bed. I've never seen it before. I don't have any money, much less a credit card, or even a driver's license, so I can't prove nothin'. And what's the use of calling a lawyer, cause the first words out of their mouth is about money I don't have. But I'll tell you this much, judge. It's no fun spending a weekend in jail with a lot of jerks pissing and puking, and the food's bad too. I don't think that's fair, and I'm thinking I should sue somebody for being arrested for the wrong guy."

Toady finished talking, scratched his head, and then added, "Judge, who'd you think I should sue?"

The courtroom filled with laughter. Judge Kramer shook his head in disbelief since this had never happened before. He saw the news people were talking on the cells phones while the spectators were laughing as they pointed at the misidentified prison.

This is too much, Judge Kramer said to himself. He banged his gavel several times and said, "Take this man into custody until his identity is firmly established as well as his involvement with the case of cocaine the police confiscated. We'll take another ten minute break." Then he wearily got up, shook his head as if not believing what had happened and retired to his chamber.

,Some of remaining reporters were shouting questions at Mr. Stranger, who made no reply. Other news people were on their cell phones, telling their editors about the wrongful arrest of Toady and questioning how a case of cocaine ended up in the home of Bart Whatting, stepson of Mr. Stranger.

Randolph remained standing at the empty defense table, avoiding Carol and Marjorie until he thought of a way to come out of this situation a winner, which he was accustomed to doing.

It is actually very simple, he thought as a sly smiled crossed his face. *I will turn the situation around and sue the police for falsely arresting Joey Grumpus. That will make me look like a defender of the down and out and generate good press. Eventually I will agree to a huge settlement and get at least forty percent of Joey's money. When it is all over, nobody will care or even remember the name Bart Whatting. They will only remember that*

I fought and won for Joey the underdog. And I will explain to Marjorie and Carol I could not visit Bart in his cell over the weekend because one of my important clients had a legal emergency, and I had to spend the entire weekend resolving his problem.

Then his face brightened even more as he thought about the police finding cocaine in Bart's house. *The police will issue an all points bulletin for Bart's arrest on charges of drug possession. As soon as I get back to my office, I will call my own private investigator and instruct him to find Bart as quickly as possible, spare no effort or expense. The sooner Bart is found, the sooner the malfeasance clause takes effect, and the sooner his trust money comes under my control. In the end I always come out a winner.*

When Marjorie had seen the person in the orange jumpsuit turn his head sideways to face Randolph, she had stopped breathing. She had to admit from the back, the person had looked like Bart, having the same blond hair and body build. But as soon as she saw the person's face, she knew it wasn't Bart's and had instinctively clapped her hands like a little kid who had won a prize. But then Marjorie's joyful clapping stopped and her face turned red with anger. She remembered Randolph promising to visit Bart on Friday, find out what happened, and see if Bart needed anything. But Randolph never did.

He lied to me, she said to herself, and for the first time in their marriage, she wondered what else he might have lied about.

Big tears began rolling down Marjorie's cheeks. Some were happy tears because Bart hadn't been arrested. But some were sad tears because her husband had lied to her. Then she remembered Carol saying a private detective with some strange name like Wild Billy was going to meet them at the arraignment. Perhaps this detective could sort all this out because Marjorie wasn't sure what to do next.

Carol was overjoyed to find out Randolph's plan to have Bart arrested had failed, and he had gotten safely away. But Carol was extremely worried detectives had found a briefcase full of cocaine under Bart's bed. *Where did the cocaine come from? Bart would now be in even more danger since both the police and Randolph would be looking for him.*

She didn't know who would find Bart first and felt a cold shiver spread through her body as she remembered Billy's words, *Randolph is a clever bastard.*

Chapter 14

It was Tuesday morning. Anna and Bart were drinking coffee as they sat in the kitchen of a doublewide trailer in Fallbrook. It was a small rural community just fifteen miles from the always-busy I-15 freeway and about thirty miles north of San Diego. Anna's mother had inherited the trailer from her parents who had preferred living in the country with not a neighbor in sight. Anna's mother periodically used the trailer to escape the noisy, complicated world and enjoy the peaceful rural setting with no blaring TV or radio. Anna knew the trailer was currently empty and figured it was a safe to hang out and rest up.

After Anna's unexpected arrival in San Diego on Friday night with a stolen briefcase full of cocaine, they had spent hours discussing what to do. They decided it was best to get out of San Diego sooner than later since mobsters were on her trail and police might well be on his. They had finally left very late Friday night and were much too tired to begin a long cross-country trip to Carol's chosen hideout.

As Carol had advised, he had left his jeep parked next to his rented house in case the detectives came to check on him. They had put his few things into the back of the minivan Anna's mother give her. The van was older but Anna said it had been reliable and they could even sleep in it if needed. The third row of seats had been folded down and he had put his stuff next to the two suitcases she had brought back from her L.A. misadventure. He had noticed the middle seat was occupied by six stuffed animals, which Anna had said were her trusty friends and went where she did.

"I feel better now we're out of San Diego but I can't stop worrying about what Tony and his goons are doing. Do you think they'll find my mom and question her about where I might be staying? Anna asked.

"I'm guessing they'll do anything and everything to get their cocaine back, including questioning your mom about where you might have gone. I'm also worried about what Randolph might have planned for me. Now that we're rested up, I think we'll be safer if we get out of the San Diego area," Bart said.

"I agree," Anna said. "Let's start packing and hit the road."

It was late morning when they left the Fallbrook area, got on I-15 North, headed towards L.A. and eventually Las Vegas, about eight hours away.

As soon as Bart was on the interstate he said, "Only two thousand more miles to go."

"Piece of cake. My six trusty friends in the middle seat and I always enjoy a nice drive in the country."

The sun was almost overhead as they bypassed Los Angeles and reached the killer incline going from sea level to the top of the Cajon pass, almost 4000 feet high. They passed a number of cars parked on the side of the road, their hoods up and radiators steaming. The aging minivan slowed to forty-five miles per hour but kept on chugging to the top of the pass without overheating. Ahead of them lay endless miles of mostly barren high desert, except for various kinds of cacti and real tumbleweeds that periodically blew across the highway.

After two more hours of driving, he saw the sign for Bartow, CA. He tooted the horn several times to wake Anna, who wasn't exactly snoring but was making strange sniffing, snuffling sounds.

She opened her eyes, looked around, and asked, "What's all the tooting about?"

"We're about to make a rest stop in Bartow."

"Thank god. I really need to pee."

"That's makes two of us."

"I've got to admire people who can live smack dab in the middle of the desert and have to put up with tourists either impatient to get to Vegas or depressed going back broke to L.A." she said.

"If heaven were filled with every kind of fast-food place, it would be called Barstow," he said.

He took the Barstow exit and turned right on Main Street. They passed a tall, thirty-foot-high, outdoor thermometer, which already registered 101 degrees Fahrenheit and would probably hit 120 by late afternoon.

"Where do you want to stop?" he asked.

"How about a Denny's restaurant? It's got clean restrooms, and its menu has pictures of all the items so you can see what you're going to get before you get it," she chuckled.

"Any you know what they say about Denny's. No one decides to go to Denny's, but that's were everybody ends up."

"That more than true," she said, and they both laughed.

He pulled into the Denny's lot and parked. They got out of the van, stretched, rubbed their sore butts, and walked inside. The hostess gave them a booth, and in a few minutes the waitress came by and gave them menus.

"I'm going to order the meal with the best picture," she said, studying each colored photo.

"How about the Ultimate Omelette, which is not only misspelled but also trademarked," he said.

"Anything misspelled and trademarked gets my vote," she said, liking its especially big color photo.

After ordering, they went to the restrooms and came back looking much relieved. They were tired, hungry, and spoke very little until the coffee arrived.

"Hey, this is good coffee," she said.

"I'll need at least two cups before I turn into a human being."

"How much further to Vegas?" she asked.

"About three or four hours if the van doesn't overheat in the desert or wander off the road. The steering so lose it's like driving a drunken elephant."

The waitress brought their food, and they hungrily gobbled it down without saying more than, 'Pass the ketchup.'

At last, she pushed away her plate and said, "What they say about ketchup is true."

"And what do they say?" he asked, playing along.

"There's this guy on public radio who claims ketchup is a mellowing agent. I must admit I do feel mellower after using lots of ketchup," she said.

"I have a hard time knowing when you serious or kidding."

"Me too," she said and gave him a big smile.

They got up and walked over to the cashier. As he paid the bill, she went over to a large rack of free brochures. She picked up the one titled *WHAT TO SEE AND DO IN VEGAS.*

After he had paid the bill, she asked, "Can you give me a few bucks to buy the Los Angeles Times?"

She had her own money but wanted Bart to notice what she was doing.

When they got back into the minivan, he asked, "Why buy the Times? It wouldn't have any news about where we're going."

"But you haven't told me where we're going."

"Here's the deal. If you can guess the state, I'll give you a two-hour massage, which Tall Sally said is every woman's dream."

He smiled as he thought about roaming his hands over her sexy curvy body and touching places that made her shiver with delight.

"Tall Sally speaks the truth," she said. She smiled as she imagined his hands caressing her body.

"I'm not great at geography, so I'm guessing Wyoming, Iowa, or Mississippi."

"Nope, not even close. So no message."

"That's not fair," she said, giving him the finger.

"I love your amazing ability to express your true feelings."

She said, "I've noticed you're using the 'l' word more and more, so perhaps there is hope for you yet."

"I'm trying."

"Now, *I'll* make *you* a deal. When you've said that particular four letter word a certain number of times, you'll win a two-hour massage."

"I like that deal, but you haven't said how many times I need to say that particular word."

"Well, just keep saying it, and I'll tell you when you win."

"That's a very tricky deal."

"I'm a very tricky person."

"And that's why I love you."

They both laughed.

"You know how smart and clever Carol is, but this time I think she outdid herself. She found an unusual hideout where neither Randolph nor his detective would ever think to look. I'm going to hideout in a monastery, surrounded by a forest in the middle of Minnesota."

"Yikes. It's certainly someplace no one would ever look. So are you going to become a monk, wear a habit, and pray night and day?"

"That's sort of the idea, but I'm not sure about praying night and day."

"And what about me? I know I can't stay with you in a monastery."

"I'm sorry. Carol had arranged this place when you were still in L.A. I had no idea when you might be coming back or even if you were. Then all hell broke loose, and we both decided it was best to get out of San Diego as quickly as possible."

Now big tears were running down her cheeks.

"So where am I going to stay, and what am I going to do while you're praying in a monastery?" she asked between sobs.

"Everything got bad so fast I just thought the best plan was for us to save our butts by leaving San Diego."

"Well, you have a place to put you butt, but I don't," she said and more tears flowed down her cheeks.

"I know. Let's call Carol, tell her the situation and ask her to find you a place. We'll be on the road for a while, and I'm sure she can arrange someplace for you to stay."

"OK," she said, wiping the tears from her checks.

"Perhaps a nunnery would do."

"You're the biggest jerk in the world," she said. Again she gave him the finger.

"Just remember, I love all your fingers."

They both laughed.

"Just to be safe, you better use your iPhone so there's no record of me calling."

"What's Carol's number?"

She dialed and switched the iPhone to speaker mode.

CHAPTER 15

— — —

Carol was in her office studying computer printouts of brain wave activity when her cell phone rang. She didn't recognize the number but thought she had better answer since it might be Bart calling from a different phone.

"Hello," Carol said.

"Hi, it's Anna, and I'm here with Bart. The phone's in speaker mode so we can both hear and talk to you. Believe it or not, we're sitting in a Denny's parking lot in Barstow."

"Oh Anna, it's good to hear from you and doubly good the two of you are back together. The last time I talked to Bart, he told me how much he missed you, and loved you, and badly wanted you back."

"That nice to hear," Anna said smiling at Bart.

"But I am surprised to hear you're with Bart in Barstow," Carol said.

"I'll give you the short version," Bart said. "Anna unexpectedly showed up in San Diego after a porn producer named Tony Koole treated her badly. They had a big fight, and she got revenge by stealing a briefcase that happened to be filled with cocaine. Tony Koole and his two goons were hot on her trail, so I put the cocaine under my bed for them to find. Since we both had really good reasons to leave San Diego, we left together and are now on they way to my secret hideout."

"Thank God for that," Carol said.

She proceeded to tell them how detectives had come by his house around noon Friday and arrested an intruder named Toady, whom they mistook for Bart. The detectives found and took the briefcase full of cocaine.

"Seems like we left San Diego just in time," Bart said with relief in his voice.

"That's true," Carol said. "But finding the cocaine under your bed is a big problem for you. The police are investigating whether Toady was a drug mule, but at some point the police may put out your photo and an all points bulletin for your arrest. I suggest the first chance you get to change your appearance. The easiest way would be to shave your head. You can also grow a beard and even wear fake glasses. Actually it's good Anna is with you because the police will be looking for a single male with longish blonde hair. In any case I suggest you try to drive straight through."

Bart said, "We're planning to stop in Vegas tonight so we can celebrate a little before I have to enter the monastery. Before we leave, Anna can shave my head and I'll start growing a beard.'

"Good plan. But I'm guessing you called because of some problem," Carol said.

"You're right. There is a problem. Anna's going to need a safe place to stay while the mobsters are looking for her and I'm hiding in the monastery. I wondered if you knew anyone in Minnesota with whom she could stay," Bart said.

There were a few seconds of silence before Carol said, "I actually know a researcher in Minneapolis. Her name is Michele. We went to graduate school together and see each other at research conferences. She has a position at the Veterans Hospital on the outskirts of Minneapolis. She lives in a cottage on one of the neighboring lakes and recently told me she was thinking about getting a roommate."

"Oh, that's wonderful news," Anna chimed in. "I've been so worried about where I'd stay."

"I had suggested a nunnery," Bart said. "And that's when she gave me the finger."

They all had to laugh.

Anna said, "Please tell Michele I'm neat, a pretty good cook, and will try to get a job as quickly as I can. I've given up trying to be an actor and am hoping to get into theatre production, perhaps as a gofer or stagehand."

"What a coincidence," Carol said. "Michele and I are both theatre buffs. I brag about the more traditional Shakespearian plays at the Old Globe in San Diego, and she boasts about the more daring plays at the Guthrie Theatre in Minneapolis. Michele may know some theatre people and be able to point you in the right direction."

The minivan was filled with Anna's happy shrieks.

"Thank you, thank you, thank you," Anna shouted as joyful tears rolled down her checks.

"Here's Michele's phone number and address. I'll call and tell her all about you, and I'm sure you'll like each other," Carol said.

"You are the best sister in the world," Bart said.

"Glad I could help," Carol said. "I'll also call the Abbot and tell him to expect you in the next few days. And I just thought of something else. I'm sure Anna will need some spending money, so give her at least half of the traveling money I gave you. I'll send you more if needed. And remember, don't either of you use credit cards."

"OK." Bart said.

"And thanks a million, billion, zillion," Anna said.

After they all said their goodbyes, Anna said, "I wish I had a sister like Carol."

Bart said, "She always comes to my rescue."

Then he put the minivan in drive, got back on Main Street and found the entrance to I-15.

"Next stop, Vegas," he said.

* * * *

As he drove, she busied herself looking through the L.A. Times for something that was about to shake things up.

"I found just what I was looking for," Anna said as she held up a torn piece or newspaper as if it were a trophy.

"So what did you find?" he asked.

"It's my horoscope. I thought I would read it to you," she said, turning to see the shock register on his face, as if he had just seen a ghost.

He was so surprised and dumbfounded he momentarily let the van wander into the neighboring lane, which thankfully was empty. He hated horoscopes but had enough sense to know she was testing him. In his head he heard Carol's advice about being less pig-headed and more opened-minded.

"I'm ready to listen," he said in a reasonable tone, but he nervously shifting around in his seat as if there were ants in his pants.

Holding up the torn piece, she began reading in a cheery voice, "Be adventurous and brave. Visit new and interesting places. Focus on enjoying things you normally might overlook. Follow your heart and discover new experiences. This is your day to ask intriguing questions."

When she finished reading, she looked over to see his reaction.

He was looking straight ahead, pretending to be totally involved in driving while actually trying to be open-minded. Finally he turned to her, smiled, and said in a kindly voice, "Sounds interesting."

"That's what I thought. Especially the part about being bold and brave and asking intriguing questions."

He had no way to know her horoscope didn't exactly say all those things. She had edited her horoscope to give her an excuse to ask one of those intriguing questions running around her brain.

"It just so happens I do have an intriguing question," she said. She made her biggest, bestest smile.

He was wary of her questions, especially an intriguing one. He was pretty sure she was going to ask about his feelings or what he wanted in a relationship, questions that sorely taxed his male brain.

"I'm ready as long as your question is not too intriguing," he said, feeling all his muscles tighten and his mouth grow drier than desert sand.

"Do you remember the lovely voice message you left when I was still in Los Angeles?"

He knew the message she was talking about and said, "Yes, I do, and I meant every word."

"Well, do you remember exactly what you said?"

He fidgeted in his seat, checked all the dash gauges, looked in the rear view mirror, and did everything but open the door and jump out.

"Well, what did you say?" she asked again, very gently.

He knew he could no longer avoid answering. He took a big breath, sucked in his stomach, squared his shoulders, and said, "I think I love you."

"And that was such a nice message I kept it on my iPhone."

He knew women used the "l" word at least a hundred times a day when talking about clothes, shoes, movies, friends, makeup, and things to do. But like most males, he early on learned saying that particular word meant making a gigantic commitment, which was to avoided at all costs. As his favorite cartoon philosopher, Popeye, might have said, "Love turns strong men into jelly."

"What I want to ask about is the meaning of the word *think*," she said.

"All right," he said, feeling as is he had fallen into pit of quicksand and was sinking fast.

"When someone says, 'I think I'll go to college,' 'think I'll buy a car,' 'think I'll go on a trip,' or 'think I'm pregnant,' it usually means *maybe*," she said.

"My god, Anna, are you pregnant?" he asked, glancing over to see if she was serious.

"No. I just wanted to point out when someone says *I think*, it usually means *maybe*."

"That's probably true," he agreed, knowing full well where she was going but not knowing what he would do when she got there.

"So here's my intriguing question. When you said, 'I think I love you,' did you mean *maybe* I love you?"

He felt completely exposed, as if standing under a million-watt floodlight. He was breathing much too fast, feeling sweat forming under his arms, and knowing there was no place to run and hide. Using all his courage, he turned toward her and said in a clear voice, "I love you." And quickly added, "No maybes about it."

"And I love you," she replied, bending over to plant a kiss on his check.

He had been unconsciously holding his breathe and now let out a big sigh.

"Now, that wasn't so difficult. Was it?"

"A little difficult, but I'll live," he said and they both laughed.

But in the depths of his male soul he knew it was one of the hardest things he had ever done. Harder even than surfing a death-defying, ten-story-high, hundred-foot wave.

"How far are we from Vegas?" she asked.

"Let's see. San Diego to Vegas is about eight hours, and Barstow was about half way. I'm guessing we're about three hours away."

"Well, my horoscope said to discover new and exciting things, so that's what we should do in Vegas, especially since that may be our last night together for some time," she said as she looked through the brochure *WHAT TO SEE AND DO IN VEGAS.*

"Now you're talking. Our last night together has got to be exciting, with plenty of romance and sex," he said, but then he remembered Anna's bruises. "How's your face doing? Is it painful?"

"The swelling is mostly gone, and it only hurts when I laugh."

That made them both laugh.

"I'll plan something bold, exciting, and sexy," she said.

After spending the next half hour reading the brochure about Vegas, she said, "Here's what I'm thinking. For starters, we can get a nice room at the Venetian hotel, which has special rates for newlyweds."

"But we're not newlyweds," he blurted out.

"Don't worry. They won't know. I've got a big collection of rings of all sizes, so we can have fun pretending. We'll get free champagne, a fruit bowl, and free room service with a choice of entrees. We'll sleep like royalty and build up our energy for a night to remember. So no hanky-panky till later," she said.

"I must admit, I'm really looking forward to our nightly adventure and you-know-what. Once I get to the monastery, I'll have to be celibate, unless I can sneak out now and then to visit you in Minneapolis."

"Celibacy sucks!" she exclaimed.

"Well, we still have tonight."

"Here's my idea for our special night. In downtown Vegas there's a nightly super-extravaganza on Fremont Street. Several blocks are completely covered with a ninety-foot-high canopy that is filled with thousands of lights and speakers to create a light and sound show to blow you away. We'll park under the canopy, open the van's big moon roof, lay on the air mattress, and watch the show."

"Sounds good, but something is missing," he said because she hadn't said anything about doing sexy stuff.

"Well, there's a little more. The light-and-sound show will stimulate and heighten our visual and auditory senses. Then I'll unbutton and take off your shirt and play with your nipples and then you can reciprocate."

"That's more like it, especially the reciprocating part."

"We can touch and kiss, but only from the waist up," she said.

He looked disappointed and said, "What about the good things from the waist down?"

"That's for later. The sounds and lights along with our touching and kissing will be incredible foreplay and make us aroused and ready for round two. When the show is over, we'll need to put our tops back on so we look respectable for our drive to the Bellagio Hotel."

"But one of my appendages may be so super excited it will hit the steering wheel and make driving dangerous."

"Dream on, big boy," she said.

"So, when do we get to the exciting places below the waist?"

"The Bellagio Hotel is supposed to have acres of water fountains lit up at night and programmed to dance to music. We'll park on the street, illegally if we have to since local police are usually kind to out of state visitors. We'll open the side door, and watch the musical, mysterious water dance. As the fountains soar into the night skies, we can talk and touch and tell each other about what will happen when the fountains stop."

"Maybe we should skip the fountains," he said.

"Remember, it's our last night, so we need to make it last. When the fountains stop, we'll close the side door, put down the middle seat, open the moon roof, turn on Pandora, select Sarah McLachlan's romantic sounds, and slowly undress each other. Being naked, we can touch and kiss each other's favorite places. Then we can join together for an unbelievable sexual adventure of pure pleasure. As the song says, our love will lift us higher than we've ever been before," she said.

"But I'm already excited. How about pulling over for a quickie?"

"I can't have sex with my six fuzzy friends watching."

"I don't know if you're serious or just putting me on."

"Both."

"I hate to admit it, but your horoscope was right on the mark," he said, his smile as bright as the sun at high noon.

"So, do you now believe in horoscopes?" she asked.

"You've turned me into a firm believer," he said. He thought Carol was right. It was much better being open-minded rather than pig-headed.

She put her hand on the obvious bulge in his jean, gently pressed down and said, "Just remember, anticipation is very close to the real thing."

CHAPTER 16

— — —

After an unbelievable night of kissing, touching, loving, and indulging in sexual pleasures, they came back to their hotel, totally spent. They undressed and took a shower together. They took turns lathering each other with scented soap and then took turns drying each other with big, fluffy towels. Finally, they got into the king size bed, nestled together like two spoons, and fell asleep with smiles on their faces.

The alarm went off at eight o'clock, and he reached over to turn it off. They didn't get up till nine, and each needed two cups of coffee before engaging in semi-intelligent conversation.

"Last night was the best birthday present I've ever gotten," Anna said.

"But it's wasn't your birthday."

"So what? I can declare a birthday whenever I like, and yesterday was my best ever," she said.

"All right. I too declare last night was my best birthday ever. And even more, I declare you're the best lover ever, even though you certainly do need a lot of foreplay."

She gave him a fake hit on his shoulder and then bent over to whisper in his ear, "And you're the best lover ever, even if you don't need any foreplay."

They laughed and gave each other high fives.

"I guess it's time for the big head shaving," Bart said.

"I never shaved anyone's head before so you can be my guinea pig," she said.

"Thanks a lot," he said and they headed for the bathroom.

First she used scissors to cut off most of his longish blonde hair. Then she patted a generous amount of shaving cream over the remaining stubble.

"Don't worry. I'll just pretend I'm shaving my legs," Anna said and began moving the safety razor across his skull.

Bart had closed his eyes and said through partly clenched teeth, "Please be careful you don't nick me cause I think there may be bumps from my years of surfing."

"Stop worrying," Anna said. "I'll be finished before you know it."

After about five minutes Anna finished and washed off the remaining shaving cream.

"Take a look. I personally think shaved heads are sexy."

Bart turned and looked into the mirror. For just a second, he didn't recognize himself.

"Carol was right," he said. "Going bald is a pretty good disguise."

Anna began to fondle and kiss the top of his head. "Do you think we have time for a quickie?" she asked.

"What a dumb question?"

They jumped into the king size bed and had a long quickie.

"Well I guess we need to get dressed, pack up and hit the road. If we take turns we can drive straight though like Carol suggested. At that rate, I think we'll make it to the monastery in about twenty four hours, give or take a few hours for pee stops and dining at Denny's," he said.

They repacked their suitcases and took the elevator down to the lobby. Walking out of the hotel they marveled at the multicolored, patterned mosaics on the floor and the red and gold paintings of Venetian splendor covering the ceiling.

"It's like being in a movie set," she said.

"It's wonderfully fake, but I think I've had my fill of make believe," he said.

They went to the parking garage, found their very plain-Jane minivan, and put their luggage in the back.

"I'll take the first turn and drive till I'm beat," he said.

"Good plan. By then it will be dark. I like driving at night, looking at all the stars, and making wishes on the falling ones."

He got into the driver's seat, and before Anna got into the passenger seat, she opened the sliding side door and rearranged her six fuzzy friends so the two sitting in the middle now got the choice window seats.

He drove out of Vegas and got back on I-15 North.

"It'll be dark when we get to Salt Lake City. We can stop there, eat some good Mormon food, and you can take over driving."

"What's good Mormon food?"

"I thought you knew. It's anything from the Denny's menu."

They both laughed.

She put in the first audiobook CD and settled back to listen to one of her favorite authors, Elmore Leonard, whose likeable, flawed characters tried to make it in a world filled with loads of bad luck.

"I like good-ole Elmore," he said.

She paused the CD and asked, "Do you want to talk or listen?"

"Did you know I bought an Elmore doll that moves its arms and talks in a weird voice?"

"You dope, that's a tickle-me-El*mo* doll."

"Just wanted to see if you were paying attention."

She stuck out her tongue and said, "No more interruptions, please."

Over the next day they took turns driving, listening to audiobooks, and taking turns sleeping in the back of the minivan.

After driving through Utah, Wyoming, and South Dakota, they finally reached central Minnesota, coming in on I-90. He turned north on I-35, and then north again to take I-94, which mostly bypassed the Minneapolis/ St. Paul area, the biggest cities in the state.

"We're about two hours from the monastery. We should get there sometime around midnight," he said.

Normally she would be doing the night driving, but he was too nervous to sleep. He felt better driving, which helped keep his mind off the fact he was actually going to hide out in a monastery.

When they reached St. Cloud, a fairly big city that bordered the Mississippi river, he said, "Only twenty more miles to go."

Anna was feeling sad and exhausted since they had been driving for over twenty-four hours. She had tried to put on a happy face but suddenly she started to cry, and big tears were running down her checks as if a dam had sprung a leak.

"What's wrong?" he asked but knew the answer before she answered. He reached over to gently touch her face. "It's going to be all right. All right for both of us, you'll see."

"I'm sorry for being so emotional," she said between sobs. "It's just, I'm so overtired. I don't want to drop you off just when we're on a loving streak."

"You'll be all right," he repeated. "After you drop me off, you can stay the night and rest up at one of the motels in St. Cloud before driving to Minneapolis. You've already called Michele, and she said she was looking forward to your staying with her. She even said she had some good contacts at the Guthrie theatre."

"I know. Michele sounded so friendly and helpful. But I hate goodbyes and wonder when I'll see you again."

"Maybe I'll be able to sneak away, and we could meet in St. Cloud, which is only twenty miles from the monastery."

"I hope that's possible. If not, perhaps I could dress up like a nun and meet you in the monastery. We could hide in the forest, rip off our respective habits, and engage in some rip-roaring hanky-panky," she said.

The thought of doing that made them both laugh.

"I'll have my cell phone so you can call me. I'll also have my computer so we can use Skype to talk, and you can see me in a monastic habit."

The thought of him in a religious habit made her smile.

"Beside, you'll be very busy. Didn't Michele mention there are classes at the Guthrie in all aspects of theatre production?"

"She did, and I'm thinking about taking classes in set design and lighting effects."

"You'd be good at both since you have a great eye for color and design."

"But how long will you have to stay in the monastery?"

"I really don't know. It depends on whether the police issue a bulletin for my arrest, or if Randolph's private detective finds me, or if Bad Billy discovers a way to get me off the hook. In any case, I'll be safe in the monastery, and you'll be safe at Michele. Tony Koole doesn't know about her, and besides, the police have his cocaine so he has no reason to come looking for you."

"Staying at Michele's is a big relief, and she sounded so nice when we talked. She told me my room has some stuffed animals she had as a girl, and I told her about the one's I'm bringing, and we had a great giggle. I think we'll have lots in common."

"Well, I'll have plenty of time to pray for your success as a set designer," he said.

"Thanks a lot. I still can't imagine a surfer dude like you turning into monk."

"Well, it's certainly a big change. No more partying, texting, socializing, drinking, working on my Facebook page, or having any worldly concerns. It'll be a complete and unbelievable change, but I'm willing to give it my best shot."

"Bart the monk. Perhaps they'll make it into a movie."

And she laughed a little harder than he did.

"There's Exit one-fifty-six. That's the one for the monastery," he said. He checked his watch. It was a little after midnight, and he would soon be changing into a monk, sort of like a modern Cinderella.

He turned off on Exit 156, followed it around and under I-94 until he came to a stop sign. One sign pointed right and indicated it was eight miles to Pinetree, one of the small towns near one of the 10,000 lakes. Another sign pointed left, indicating it was seven miles to the St. Francis Monastery.

He turned left and drove along a narrow, paved road that had no shoulders. The minivan's headlights lit up tall trees and thick bushes that lined the road. The trees' branches had grown over the road to form an overhanging canopy that let in fragments of light from the half moon.

"This seems a little creepy, like driving through a haunted forest," she said.

Neither spoke as the curvy road led them deep inside the silent forest.

Suddenly she shrieked, and her arm shot out to point at two big glowing eyes reflected in the van's high beams.

"It's only a deer," he said.

Then just as quickly, the glowing eyes vanished as whatever it was vanished into the brush.

"This place is plenty scary," she said and added, "If this were a Disneyland ride, it would be called *the Haunted Monastery*."

"Why don't you turn on the radio and get some soothing music?" he said.

She fiddled with the radio, but the only station she could get featured a preacher called Father Dreadforth. He was talking about the Rapture, when the good Lord Jesus Christ would come, surrounded in brilliant, flashing lights, and take them all to heaven. He reminded his listeners to send in their donations, and he would pray so they would be in the group going to heaven with the Lord Jesus.

"That guy is frightening me," she said as she turned off the radio and stared straight ahead. Her eyes grew big like saucers as she imagined some fearful beast leaping out of the dark forest and talking them all to a fiery hell.

After a few more miles, the forest ended, and they emerged into in a large clearing. In the light from the half moon he could just make out a group of buildings on the right and a much larger and newer looking structure on the left. He saw a sign that read VISITORS, and they continued on till he came to a small parking area. He stopped in front of a building with a single yellow light above a door with a sign that read PLEASE REGISTER HERE.

"I'm not getting out of this car," she said, her face drawn and pale, as if expecting to see a ghost.

"Why don't you come in for a minute? Maybe get a coffee or a coke."

"This is a scary place, and I'm not getting out of the car," she said, looking around with quick head jerks, like a wary rabbit watching for a fox.

"How about a last kiss," he said.

She nodded and relaxed a little as he pulled her to him.

Their lips touched and at first they kissed gently. But as they realized this might by their last kiss for some time, they kissed harder and moaned with pleasure. Neither wanted to stop. Finally Bart pulled back, held her head in his hands and whispered, "I love you."

"And I love you," she whispered back.

They looked into each other's eyes, which were filled with love and joy, and knew nothing more needed to be said.

He got out of the van, walked to the back, opened the door, and grabbed his suitcase and box of computer stuff. He carried his things to the sidewalk, set them down, and walked back to the van.

She had scooted over to the driver's side and had rolled down the window.

He stood near her open window, touched his hand to his heart, and gestured as if he was giving his heart to her.

In turn she touched her heart and gestured as if handing her heart to him.

Then he reached out, and they held hands for several seconds, feeling their two loving hearts joining together as one.

There were tears in their eyes as they both silently mouthed, "I'll miss you."

Then he stepped back and watched as she started the van. Before she took off, she threw him a last kiss. As he did the same, she turned and started driving away. Her eyes were so filled with tears she had trouble seeing. She drove carefully as streaks of moonlight came through the overhanging trees and made everything appear surreal.

As he saw the van's taillights disappear into the forest he thought, *I really do love her.*

Then he picked up his suitcase and the box of computer stuff and walked toward the door lit by a single yellow light. On the side of the door was a small, neat sign written by someone skilled in calligraphy: PLEASE RING FOR ADMITTANCE.

He pushed the button, felt his heart pounding as he heard a faint ringing inside.

CHAPTER 17

— — —

He was getting ready to press the bell again when the door opened and a soft voice said, "I am Brother James. Come in and tell me how I may help you?"

"My name is Bart Whatting, from San Diego. I hope the abbot told you I was coming. I apologize for arriving so late and looking so ratty because I haven't shaved or showered in a while. When I get cleaned up, I look like a nice, God-fearing person."

"Welcome to the St. Francis Monastery. The abbot had told me to expect a surfer dude from San Diego," Brother James said, adding, "I do like your t-shirt."

On Bart's t-shirt was the picture of a mouse dressed in a yellow, Superman-like costume with a red cape. The mouse's right arm was raised as if ready to battle evil forces. His name, Mighty Mouse, was spelled out below in big, red letters.

"Mighty Mouse was my boy-time hero, and my sister gives me a t-shirt like this every Christmas. When I face a big challenge, like driving two thousand miles cross-country, I wear my Mighty Mouse t-shirt."

"You might need to wear it every day under your habit, because being a monk is a big challenge. Also, you can tell your sister, whom I talked to several times, your Might Mouse t-shirt made a memorable first impression."

"I'll tell her, because she made me promise to do just that."

"I am sorry to say, we happen to be a bit crowded tonight because of visiting monks, so I'll have to put you in our storage room, which does have a nice spare bed."

"That would be fine," Bart said, grateful for any room with a bed.

"Just follow me," Brother James said, and Bart did.

Brother James had an ancient face, as creased and cracked as the bark on a hundred-year-old oak tree. His habit was dark brown, almost black, with a hood in back and a white, braided rope belt around his waist. He stood straight and tall and insisted on carrying Bart's heavy suitcase, which he lifted as if it were a feather pillow.

Bart had to walk fast to keep up with Brother James, who silently led the way down several long dimly lit corridors whose walls were made of old-looking, red brick. On some of the walls hung religious paintings and beautifully illustrated religious manuscripts.

In the middle of a long corridor, Brother James stopped at a door labeled Visitor's bathroom.

"I am afraid you will have to use this bathroom because the storage room does not have one. The visitor's bathroom does have a great shower, which I am tempted to use every now and then," Brother James said in his soft voice.

A short distance further on, Brother James stopped in front of an oaken door, took out a ring of old-fashioned keys, searched until he found a large bronze one, and used it to open the door.

"This is one of the few doors in the monastery that is kept locked, because some of the things in here are old, fragile, or valuable, and should not be unnecessarily touched or moved."

"I certainly won't touch anything. I just want to sleep and sleep."

Brother James opened the door and flicked on an overhead bulb that barely gave off more light then a candle.

Bart followed Brother James into a large room and noticed the high ceiling, the tall candleholders stacked against one wall, another wall almost completely covered with illustrated manuscripts. There was an upper window that allowed in enough moonlight to partially show a dark drape covering something stored against the back wall.

"The bed is over here," Brother James said and walked over to turn on a small dim light on a table near the bed. Next he went to the high window and opened it half way to let in a nice breeze filled with a woody smell.

"Sometimes this room gets a little stuffy, so the breeze will help. There are towels, soap, and a toothbrush on that table over there. We always have them ready for overflow guests."

"Thank you very much," Bart said. "I'm dog tired. I wonder if it's possible to sleep in and perhaps see the abbot later today?"

"We monks are early risers, but for visitors like you we make exceptions. I will come and get you at 10:00, which is as late as any *God-fearing* person should sleep," said Brother James, nodding at his little joke.

Bart smiled and said, "Ten o'clock it is."

"Don't worry about missing breakfast, which is served at seven, because I'll bring you coffee and some of our famous homemade dark bread. Then I'll take you to meet Abbot Aloysius. He's a wonderful, holy man with a magnificent beard a good sense of humor. People from California would probably call him a *cool dude*."

Brother James smiled at his little joke, but his smile was almost lost in his wrinkly face.

"That would be great," Bart said, liking Brother James and his dry sense of humor. "I wonder if you would do me one more favor?"

Bart opened up his suitcase, dug under a shirt, and found the envelope he was looking for.

"Would you give this envelope to your abbot so he'll know I'm really who I say I am?"

Brother James took the envelope and read aloud the return address printed in the upper left hand corner.

"Dr. Carol Whatting, Assistant Professor, Neuroscience Institute, La Jolla, California."

"Whatting, Whatting. Seems I've heard that name before," Brother James said, looking at Bart with smiling eyes.

"She's my sister, and also a good, God-fearing person like me."

"I did not realize there were so many God-fearing people in California," Brother James said. He paused, looked up at the ceiling, and added, "In the winter when the snow is deep and it's minus twenty degrees outside, I am sorely tempted to head for California. I know the good Lord wants me to suffer for my sins, but getting through a Minnesota winter can seem like cruel and unusual punishment."

Bart had to laugh, and Brother James joined in with a few chuckles of his own.

"I'll see you around ten AM," Brother James said. Then he nodded, turned off the overhead bulb, and left the room, soundlessly closing the door.

Bart kicked off his flip-flops and undressed. Naked, he climbed naked under the cool sheets, turned off the table light, and closed his eyes. It was silent and peaceful, and within a few minutes he was sound asleep.

Bart had probably been asleep for several hours when he was awakened by strange noises coming from the forest outside the opened window. Still half asleep, Bart had trouble opening his eyes and figuring out where he was. As Bart looked around, he saw something that sent shivers through his body.

Moonlight coming through the window partially lit up something along the back wall. Bart took in a quick breath and tried to focus his sleepy eyes. Bart could barely make out what appeared to be the body of a man, almost naked, except for a loincloth. The man's arms were outstretched like one of those demented creatures in a horror movie. The man's face and chest were covered with blood, and he seemed to be looking right at Bart. Bart reached over, fumbled with the table light, and finally turned it on. In the dim light he saw a man's bloodied face, and as Bart nervously fidgeted around, he had the impression the bloody-faced man was moving.

Bart was shaking my head, trying to focus, and wondering if he were in the middle of a bad dream or if some scary person were about to attack me. Bart closed his eyes, shook his head, and opened his eyes.

Bart saw that the almost naked man, face and chest covered in blood, was not a real person, but a life-size statue of Jesus Christ, hanging on a cross. The life-like statue, probably carried in some religious ceremony, had been stored against the back wall, and a gust of breeze from the window must have dislodged the drape. From his early religious upbringing, Bart knew he was looking at a crucifix, but never before had he been so close to a life-size version. Then Bart vaguely remembered having seen a dark drape covering something along the back wall when he first entered the storage room.

Bart waited several minutes for his breathing to slow. Bart knew he wouldn't be able to go back to sleep with Jesus staring at him, so he got up, realized he was naked, and felt embarrassed standing like that in front of a crucifix. Automatically he covered his private parts with one hand. Walking to the back wall, he picked up the dark cloth with his other hand and draped it over the crucifix.

Then Bart climbed back into bed, turned off the light, and tried to think of peaceful images. Bart imagined a monastery full of panda bears and started counting them. He was soon sleeping soundly.

The next thing Bart knew, someone was knocking on the door, but he was in the kind of deep sleep that, try as he might, he couldn't wake up. As if climbing out of a dark hole, Bart slowly regained consciousness and finally opened his eyes. Sitting up, he looked around the room and saw the drape over the life-size crucifix. He shivered and finally said, "Just a minute." Getting got out of bed, he hurriedly put on his cut-off jeans and Mighty Mouse t-shirt, and said, "Come in."

The door opened and in came smiling Brother James with a tray that held a pot of great smelling coffee, a pitcher of what looked like real cream, two thick pieces of dark bread, and two small bowels filled with what looked like real butter and homemade jam.

"Twelve o'clock noon, and all is well," Brother James said, sounding like a watchman on a ship.

"I thought you were coming at ten."

"Not to worry," Brother James said. "You looked so tired last night that I felt charitable and gave you an extra two hours. Have some coffee and try our homemade bread with real butter and strawberry jam, my personal favorites. Use the restroom down the hall to shave and shower, and I'll come back for you in an hour. One more thing, best to wear long pants and a real shirt when you meet the abbot, because we are monks are sticklers for fashion."

Brother James smiled, gave a sly wink, and went out, silently closing the door behind him.

Bart showered, shaved, put on long pants, and chose a clean denim shirt. Then he drank three cups of coffee loaded with real cream and ate two pieces of delicious, dark bread slathered with real butter and strawberry jam.

"This place might not be so bad after all," Bart said out loud. While he was waiting for Brother James, he noticed how quiet and peaceful the monastery was. There were no traffic sounds, no weird rings tones, no people talking loudly on cell phones, no radios blasting, no sirens, no one yelling, no nothing. The monastery was a different world and made him remember and appreciate the song lyrics about the sound of silence and the easy peaceful feeling.

When Bart heard a knock on my door, he checked his watch to see it was one o'clock.

"Come in," Bart said, trying to sound wide-awake.

Brother James entered, glanced at the empty tray, and said, "Seems you enjoyed the breakfast. We monks do not use real cream or butter, too fattening and bad for our hearts. We only serve those treats to visitors."

"It was fantastic, and I think I'll keep being a visitor so I get the treats."

"Dream on, Mighty Mouse," Brother James said and chuckled.

"As you can see, I'm wearing long pants and a long-sleeved shirt and prepared to meet my maker. Oh, I mean, Abbot Aloysius."

They both laughed and Bart was surprised when Brother James gave him a high five.

"Well, let's be off."

Bart followed Brother James down several long corridors whose walls were of old brick and hung with many beautiful illustrated medieval manuscripts.

Brother James stopped in front of a greatly enlarged, illustrated, colorful manuscript and explained, "We have a team of three monks who have a grant to visit monasteries around the world and take digital photos of their illustrated manuscripts. Back in medieval times, most monasteries had gifted monks who hand-illustrated holy texts with colorful symbols, animals, flowers, saints, and heavenly beings."

"This one's incredible," Bart said, admiring the bright yellow flowers, multicolored birds, and several red and gold monsters.

"This is one I actually did," Brother James said.

"Dream on Might Mouse," Bart said.

"You are quick-witted for a surfer dude," he said, giving Bart a sly smile.

They walked in silence until they arrived at a plain, polished oak door with a small sign in beautiful calligraphy that said ABBOT ALOYSIUS, ST. FRANCIS MONASTERY.

"I've never meet an abbot before, so what do I call him?"

"The proper address is 'Most Holy Person and Master of the Universe'," Brother James said in a solemn voice.

Then he looked at Bart and smiled so big Bart could almost see his wisdom teeth.

"That was a small joke. Actually, everyone just calls him 'abbot'," Brother James said and knocked once.

Chapter 18

‒ ‒ ‒

"Come in," said a friendly voice.

Brother James opened the door and Bart followed him inside.

Getting up from a plain, polished oak desk was Abbot Aloysius, barely five foot four and 115 pounds. Like Brother James, he was wearing a floor-length, brown wool habit tied around his waist with a coarsely braided, white rope belt. As he walked over to shake hands, Bart couldn't help noticing he was wearing very colorful running shoes that looked as incongruous as a woman in an evening dress wearing hiking boots.

As he shook Bart's hand he said, "I can see you are surprised by my colorful running shoes."

"They do seem a little out of place."

"God has granted me a special dispensation to wear running shoes because my feet are so old, sore, and boney. Once a year I spend an afternoon with a sports catalogue, choosing a new pair of running shoes designed to make me look like I am very hip," the abbot said, grinning from ear to ear.

"Well, Brother James told me you were a cool dude, and your running shoes prove it. Please don't think I being disrespectful, but in California, calling someone a *cool dude* is a great compliment," Bart said.

The abbot smiled and pulled up his habit to proudly display his running shoes, which had red, blue, and white stripes, like something a hip-hopper might wear.

For good measure the abbot surprisingly did a little jig, and everyone had to laugh.

"I have only two vices," the abbot said, "and one is wearing colorful running shoes."

In the pause that followed Bart knew it was his cue to ask, "So, if I may be so bold, what's your second vice?"

"I thought you would never ask," the abbot said and held out his perfectly groomed white beard, which Bart guessed must be almost two feet long and looked as soft and shiny as a silk scarf.

"This is my second vice," the abbot said, slowly stroking his beard.

"I admit to shampooing and conditioning my beard every Monday and Friday, but never on Sunday, which, of course, is the Lord's Day."

Bart laughed again and so did Brother James, who had heard this joke many times. The abbot used humor to put his guests at ease and create a friendly atmosphere, which it certainly did.

"It is time for me to leave so you two can discuss more weighty matters," Brother James said. He bowed slightly to the abbot, gave me a tiny smile, and left the room, silently closing the sturdy, oaken door behind him.

"Brother James is the official keeper of monastic secrets and never repeats anything he hears in this office, which includes my bad jokes and comments about my beard. He is also my official letter reader, since my eyes no longer like small print. This morning he read me your sister's letter, confirming you are who you say you are," the abbot said.

When Bart looked into the abbot's eyes, he noticed a whitish tinge, the first sign of cataracts, and knew why he needed an official reader.

The abbot turned, walked behind his desk, and sat down in a high-backed office chair that make him look even smaller, like a scene from Alice in Wonderland.

"Please have a seat," the abbot said, adjusting his beard so it flowed down his chest and rested neatly in his lap.

Bart sat down in a plain, oak chair and was very thankful for its soft cushion since his butt was still sore from days of sitting and driving.

"Just yesterday, your sister, Carol, called. She told me the disturbing news about how your stepfather tried to have you arrested and police finding a briefcase full of cocaine under your bed."

"I hope she explained I had nothing to do with the cocaine," Bart said in a panicky voice.

"Yes, she did, but she also said finding the cocaine gives the police good reason to look for you in earnest."

"That's true, but I am hoping they won't put out my photo and issue an all points bulletin for my arrest."

"I will pray the police do not," the abbot said and grinned. Then he added, "I told Carol you would be welcome to hide away in our monastery. She thanked me and said that a stay in our monastery would give you an opportunity to do penance for all your past sins."

"Did she really say that last part, about doing penance for my sins?" Bart asked.

"I cannot tell a lie. I added that last part about doing penance for your sins because it was something a person in my position should say to a surfer dude from California," the abbot said, smiling like a mischievous little boy who had just gotten away with something.

Bart was continually surprised by the abbot's friendly manner and wry sense of humor. He certainly did not fit his stereotype of an abbot, whom Bart figured would be a sour, dour, serious, standoffish, big-bellied, humorless person with a crucifix in his belt.

"I had a nice talk with your sister, but now I would like to hear the whole story from the horse's mouth, so to speak," the abbot said, leaning forward in his chair.

Bart told the abbot everything about his feud with his stepfather, Anna's fight with porn producer Tony Koole, her sudden appearance in San Diego with a briefcase full of cocaine, and the need for their sudden departure. When Bart finished his story, the abbot sat back, absentmindedly stroking his beard, as if petting the family cat.

The abbot asked, "But where is Anna now?"

"She's staying in Minneapolis with a friend of Carol's. When it's safe, we plan on going back to San Diego. Anna is not only smart and clever but also helping me be more open-minded and less pig-headed."

The abbot nodded his head and said, "That is a hard lesson to learn, and I wish Anna would come and teach that lesson to some of our monks."

Then he leaned forward, his face tight with concern and said, "There is one more question I must ask, and you must answer truthfully or your stay in our monastery will be cut short. Do you have any cocaine in your possession?"

Bart looked directly into the abbot's eyes and hoped he could see he was telling the truth. "I didn't take any cocaine out of the case or bring any along. The truth is I tried it once many years ago and haven't used it since."

The abbot was quiet for at least ten seconds, his eyes closed.

Bart had been holding his breath until he heard the abbot say, "Because of my failing eyesight, I have learned to be a very good listener. A person's voice can be just as revealing as looking into a person's eyes. You sounded sincere and I believe you."

"Thank you for trusting me," Bart said as he felt his breathing return to normal.

The abbot shifted in his chair and said, "As long as you are in the monastery, you will have to follow our strict rules regarding obedience and celibacy, both of which might prove difficult for a free-living surfer dude from California."

"Yes, I cannot tell a lie. Celibacy will be difficult, but I have already explained that to Anna, and she grudgingly agreed to stay away so I won't be tempted."

"That is a good start," the abbot said, adding, "How much do you know about our Catholic faith?"

"Actually, my parents were Catholic, and my sister and I were both baptized and raised as Catholics. I even remember when I was seven years old I made my first confession, which was plenty scary. To this day I remember walking into the dark confessional and telling my sins. I told the priest I had disobeyed my mother, twice. I had promised her not to swallow watermelon seeds, which might grow in my stomach, but I did, and they didn't grow. And I had promised mom not to feed my dog peanut butter, which always gave him bad runs. Well my dog and I loved to sit on the porch and eat peanut butter, one spoonful for me and one for him. As expected, my dog got really bad runs and ruined one of my mother's favorite rugs. I even remember the penance the priest gave me, which was to say three Hail Marys and to always obey my mother. And then two weeks later I made my first communion."

"I like the part about you and your dog eating peanut butter. So, are still a practicing Catholic?" the abbot asked.

"When I was nine, my father, who had had some kind of undiagnosed congenital heart defect, had a fatal heart attack. His death was totally unexpected and changed my mother forever. She cried for days and told us kids we would no longer go to church or pray to a God who could be so cruel and uncaring as to take away her loving husband and leave us kids fatherless."

"I am very sorry to hear about your father's death and understand how tragedies can change people's lives. Did your mother ever come back to the Catholic Church?" the abbot asked.

"No she didn't. She believed as long as people knew right from wrong and didn't harm others, there was no need to believe in God. Naturally, Carol and I followed suit, and our beliefs in God and religions faded away."

"Have you ever thought of coming back to the Catholic faith?" the abbot asked in a tone that expressed genuine concern.

"As a child it was easy for me to believe in the wonderful story of how a virgin girl gave birth to baby Jesus in a manger, how Jesus was crucified to get rid of our sins and three days later ascended to heaven. I liked how Jesus could work miracles and walk on water. When I began taking swimming lessons, I fervently prayed Jesus would let me walk on water so I could impress my childhood friends," Bart said, remembering the many times he stood on the end of the dock, closed his eyes, said a prayer, opened his eyes, stepped off the off the dock and sank to the bottom.

"What happened to change your mind and stop being a Catholic?" the abbot asked.

"In high school I got interested in science, which emphasized gathering facts and experimentally testing theories. I realized religious beliefs could neither be tested nor proven and must be accepted on faith alone. I found I could not make that leap of faith and accept the supernatural beliefs the Catholic Church preached."

"I understand your dilemma. But as you may know, many people of all ages come to our retreats every month, make the leap of faith, accept our beliefs, ask to be baptized and become practicing Catholics. In addition, I personally know many scientists who have taken the leap of faith and have no difficulty accepting supernatural beliefs," the abbot said.

"I know that's true because I also know some very religious scientists. All I can say is while I'm in the monastery, I will try to keep an open mind, study your beliefs, and observe your life of prayer and worship."

"That is a good approach, and I look forward to having many more discussions about God and the Catholic Church. My only concern is when you decide to make a leap of faith, just be sure it is not off the top of our one hundred foot bell tower," the abbot said and smiled.

"God certainly gave you a wonderful sense humor."

"I believe having a good sense of humor is almost as good as being able to walk on water," the abbot said, and they both laughed.

Then the abbot started to nervously twirl his beard and looked up at the ceiling as if communing with God. Finally he placed his boney hands on the desk and looked at me through slightly milky eyes.

"Several weeks ago, we encountered a serious problem and have been praying for a solution. Then out of the blue, your sister calls and asks if you could hide out in our monastery because your stepfather wishes you harm. Of course, I was very puzzled and asked how she happened to choose our monastery. She said that she had been looking for a secluded place, far from San Diego, someplace your stepfather would never think of looking. And after much searching on the web, she decided a monastery fit all the requirements. Because our monastery was the only one with access to the supercomputer in San Diego, she chose the St. Francis Monastery. I was hesitant at first, but she mentioned you were a genius at finding solutions to problems by using something called algorithms, which I knew nothing about. She said that algorithms were computer programs that sort of mimic how humans think and are the reason computers can beat humans at chess, checkers, some TV game show called 'Jeopardy', and can match people on dating services," the abbot said, stroked his beard several times and asked, "Do you think computers could be programmed to preach sermons?"

"I think that's possible but I don't think people would want to hear computers taking about God. However, you can now spend $1.99 and download a computer application called *Confession*, which claims to help Catholics examine their consciences and get them ready for confession."

The abbot was so flabbergasted he stopped playing with his beard and stared openmouthed. Finally he said, "Unbelievable. Too bad this application was not available when you were getting ready to make your first confession."

They both had to laugh, and the abbot laughed the loudest.

"But I have gotten off the track. I was telling you how our monastery was facing a devastating problem when Carol calls unexpectedly from California and says you and your computer are great at solving things. As she and I talked, it became crystal clear God had answered our prayers and had arranged for you to come to our monastery and help solve our problem," the abbot said. He held out his hands, palms up, as if to say, *that is obviously the reason you are sitting in my office.*

Bart vigorously shook his head in disagreement and was about to argue, but the abbot held up his hand and gestured for him to be silent.

"Our monastery was established by immigrant monks from Germany one hundred and fifty years ago. In all that time, how often has a surfer dude from California, who is not a practicing Catholic but is a computer whiz, come to hide out in our monastery?"

CHAPTER 19

— — —

Bart knew the abbot's question was rhetorical, but wanting to be polite, he asked, "How many?"

"In one hundred and fifty years, there has been only one person, and at the moment, that individual happens to be sitting across from me," the abbot said, and his raised eyebrows emphasized this rare event.

"Unusual things do happen," Bart said but realized that was a poor explanation.

"For just a moment, think about all the unusual events that had to happen in a certain order so you would come to our monastery. First, Carol told me your stepfather suffered a recent financial setback that motivated him to do you harm. Second, your sister searches the web for a safe, secluded hideout. Third, she finds and selects the St. Francis Monastery because it happens to be the only one with access to the supercomputer in San Diego. Fourth, Anna unexpectedly arrives in San Diego with a case of stolen cocaine and some mobsters close behind. Fifth, you both decide to leave San Diego the night before the police come to arrest you. Sixth, you arrive at the exact time our monastery is in the middle of a financial crisis. Seventh, you happen to have great computer skills and are an expert at solving problems," the abbot said. He spread out his arms to emphasize this unbelievable series of events.

"Okay. I admit a lot of things transpired, but coincidences do happen."

"I might agree if your arrival at our monastery at this particular time involved one or two, but certainly not seven coincidences. No, my good surfer dude, I am certain God heard our prayers and sent you to us in our time of need," the abbot said. He pointed at Bart and nodded to confirm his conclusion.

"I still find it hard to believe God answered your prayers and deliberately arranged these seven events."

"Oh ye of little faith. Just remember God does act in mysterious ways that far exceed our limited human reasoning, as well as all your computer's algorithms," the abbot said. He chuckled, grabbed the end of his beard, and pointed it at me, as if to say, *coincidences be damned.*

Before Bart could argue further, the abbot said, "Now that we have settled how you got here, let me explain the problem God sent you to solve. One of our wealthy benefactors had promised to donate seven hundred thousand dollars to fund the building of a new Exorcism Center, which had outgrown its current location. The benefactor said that he had to make minor changes regarding distribution of monies, but in the meantime, we should find a general contractor and sign contracts to begin construction before the first snow comes. And, all of that we did."

The abbot paused, his face had turned gray and his shoulders had sagged. "But just days before our benefactor could visit his lawyer's office to sign the final papers, he had a stroke, went into a coma, and died four days later."

"Oh my God, that's terrible," Bart said.

Then Bart realized he probably shouldn't have used the name of God so causally, but thankfully, the abbot seemed not to notice and went on.

"About two weeks after his funeral, a lawyer, who has been hired by his three grown children to oversee their father's estate, called to say no donation would be forthcoming since the revised papers had not been finalized. Even though we had had a verbal contract and perhaps could have sued for payment, I felt it was not the proper action to take. According to the contract we signed with the construction company, we needed to make a down payment of three hundred thousand dollars, which is due in three weeks, or pay a penalty of one hundred thousand dollars to cancel the entire contract."

The abbot stopped talking and took several deep breaths, as if trying to regain his strength.

"We have a modest income from a variety of sources, which include selling homemade bread to local supermarkets, reprinting illustrated medieval manuscripts, publishing religious greeting cards and books, and operating our Exorcism Center. Our income is sufficient to cover living and maintenance expenses for our thirty-three monks. We have only a small cash reserve and cannot possibly make the large payments spelled out in the construction contract," the abbot said. He sighed, as if all hope was leaving his body.

"I wish I could help, but I know very little about financial matters," Bart said.

"You do not need to know about financial problem but rather a way to convert some of our assets into real money. We are not looking for a financial expert since we do not have any money to invest, and we do not want to get into a bigger hole by borrowing money we might not be able to repay. Instead, we need someone to come up with creative ways to use our assets, and finding creative solutions is something Carol guaranteed you would do," the abbot said.

It was Bart's turn to be flabbergasted. Bart was pretty sure no algorithm would solve this problem, but when he looked into the abbot's saintly face and saw his hopeful expression, he couldn't bear the thought of disappointing him.

The abbot said, "We do have some valuable assets that you could use. We have almost twenty-five hundred acres of old forest and five hundred more acres of beautiful wetlands. You only need to find a way to turn these assets into real money, without of course, cutting down the trees or destroying the wetlands."

"Let me get this straight. You have valuable trees, but they cannot be cut down and sold as lumber, and valuable wetlands that cannot be turned into golf courses or divided into lots for second homes," Bart said, knowing the abbot was asking for a miracle.

"I admit those are reasonable solutions, except we cannot destroy the beautiful land God gave us. But with a little more thought, I am sure you will come up with better solutions. Just remember, if Jesus could feed hundreds with a few loafs of bread, how difficult can it be for you to turn forests and wetlands into cash?" the abbot asked, looking very pleased with himself.

"I know my way around the web, I can even develop complex algorithms to help computer's solve problems, but I don't have the slightest idea how to turn untouchable forests and wetlands into hard cash," Bart said, trying to wiggle out of the abbot's impossible request.

"Just be thankful I didn't ask you to turn lead into gold, which even I know is impossible," the abbot said. Bart could see a little smile in his milky eyes.

"I can only promise to try."

"There are some things I can do to help," the abbot said. "While you are working on our problem, I will free you from all manual labor, give you a private room, allow you to use your cell phone, grant you a dispensation from attending early morning prayers so you can sleep in after a hard night's work, and even give you full access to the web, which Carol mentioned was something you really needed to complete you project. And of course, once you solve our problem, you can continue to remain in our monastery until it is safe to return to San Diego."

"Now I know why you're the abbot," Bart said, laughing at the shrewd way the abbot had manipulated him into doing exactly what the abbot wanted by giving him exactly what he wanted.

"You have a deal. I'll do my best to find some way to turn your trees and wetlands into money, without destroying them. I don't believe in miracles, but if I can pull this off, it'll be a small miracle," Bart said.

Bart got up and reached out to shake the abbot's hand before he realized how discourteous that was.

"Whoops," Bart said. "We don't need to shake, because if I can't trust an abbot, who can I trust?"

But the abbot was already on his feet, smiling. He grabbed and shook Bart's hand.

"It's a deal," the abbot said.

They were shaking hands as vigorously as two long-lost friends when the abbot said five of the most terrifying words in the English language.

"There's just one more thing."

Those words made Bart stop shaking the abbot's hand, which he dropped like a hot potato. He even backed up several steps.

"I would like to know one more thing, and I realize this might be very personal," the abbot said.

"I'll tell you anything," Bart said, "no matter how personal."

"What is the name of the novel you are teaching the computer to write?" the abbot asked.

Bart felt so relieved that he started laughing and the abbot soon joined in.

"*The Grizzly Bear and the Rabbit*," Bart said. "It's a children's book about a grizzly bear teaching a rabbit to be more courageous and in turn the rabbit teaches the bear be more sympathetic. So far the computer has only written one chapter, which reads as if written by someone barely literate. As you might guess, I'll need to develop much better algorithms."

"What I don't understand is how you're going to get a computer to do the writing," the abbot said, looking genuinely interested as he squinted to get me into better focus.

"That's another story," Bart said. "Perhaps better told over a glass of wine."

"All right. That is a deal. Every now and then a generous person gives me some very good wine, so I will save a bottle for our next discussion and ask Brother James to join us. He knows a lot about rabbits, and I know much about grizzly bears," the abbot said.

Before Bart could ask how the abbot knew about grizzly bears, there was a knock on the door.

"Come in," the abbot said.

The door opened, and Brother James walked as silently as a cat.

"I have just made a very interesting deal with Bart, so make sure he is well-fed and housed," the abbot said.

Brother James looked at me and only nodded. But in that look Bart knew he and the abbot had concocted this whole deal early that morning. Bart could stay in the monastery and even get some perks while working on turning the monastery's untouchable assets into hard, cold cash.

"Perhaps now is a good time to show Bart around the monastery. I think he will be most interested in seeing the forest and the wetlands. And it would be nice if you could find better accommodations than the storeroom, since he may be with us for a considerable time," the abbot said.

"I want to thank you for your kind hospitality and offering me a once-in-a lifetime deal," Bart said to the abbot.

"Do not worry," the abbot said, "I will pray for your success. And remember, God acts in mysterious ways."

Brother James and Bart left the abbot's office and began walking down one of the long, silent corridors.

"You were certainly right about the abbot. He's the coolest dude I've ever met," Bart said.

"That he is," Brother James said. "People tend to underestimate the abbot because he's so friendly and gentle. But the abbot is like cold steel wrapped in soft velvet. Today you saw his velvet side, but if you ever lie or cross him, you'll see his cold steel side, something to avoid at all costs. "

Bart knew Brother James was giving him a polite warning that any deal he made with the abbot had better be taken very seriously.

"Let me show you around," said Brother James.

"I'd like that," Bart said.

Bart couldn't help thinking how easy it would be to ask his mother for money since she could practically buy the entire monastery and never miss the money. The problem was she always consulted his stepfather about financial matters, which means he would learn of Bart's hiding place and come after him like a wolf chasing a rabbit. But Bart really didn't want to ask his mother for money because Bart had had made a deal with the abbot. Bart had his pride and wanted to save the monastery on his own terms. If all else failed, Bart would ask his mother to bail out the monastery, but first he wanted a chance to give it his best shot. Bart remembered a bible quote that his grandfather often used: *Pride goeth before the fall.* But in this case, Bart would rather fall on his ass than not try at all.

As they turned a corner, they passed several other monks, who nodded and smiled. Brother James introduced Bart as a "probational candidate," and they all said they would pray for his success.

"When you become a monk, you'll need to pick a new name, a saint's name," Brother James said.

"Actually, I thought about that on the trip here," Bart said.

"And what did you decide?" Brother James asked.

"I've always liked the story of Paul, who had to be knocked off his horse before he agreed to be on God's side," Bart said.

"Well, that's certainly the worst rendition of Paul's conversion I've ever heard, but nevertheless, it is true," Brother James said.

"So when I become a monk, I'll be Brother Paul," Bart said, and he smiled to himself because never in his wildest dreams had he thought about becoming a monk.

They were walking down a long, silent corridor when Brother James turned to Bart and said, "Can I ask a personal favor?"

"Anything, anything at all," Bart said. "You've been so kind to me that I'd give you the shirt of my back."

"That's exactly what I was about to ask. I wondered if I could borrow your Mighty Mouse T-shirt?"

Bart burst out laughing. "You can't be serious," I said

"I'm very serious," Brother James said.

"Of course you can," Bart said. "But why and where would you wear it?"

"Every Saturday afternoon I help the other brothers replace candles in the church for Sunday Mass. We all wear regular work clothes—pants and shirt—so our habits don't get tangled up in things. I would be a big hit wearing a Mighty Mouse T-shirt," Brother James said, smiling like a little kid asking for a new tricycle.

"As soon as we get back to my storeroom, I'll give you the Mighty Mouse T-shirt," Bart said. "But you had better wash it first, because I lived in it for several days."

"I can see you're very easy to make deals with," Brother James said. "I'll be interested to hear more about the deal you made with the abbot."

"You better pray long and hard I can pull that one off," Bart said.

"As soon as you get your things from the storeroom, I'll take you to your new accommodations, which has a private bathroom, nice desk, and a spectacular view of the forest and the wetlands," Bother James said.

Bart just hoped his new accommodations didn't have any large crucifixes that came out at night.

As they walked in silence toward the storeroom, Bart couldn't help worrying about his safety. Although Bart was hiding in a monastery, there were people itching to track him down. First, there was his stepfather, who would go to any lengths to find him. Second, there was the police, who might soon put out an all-points bulletin for his arrest. Third, there was a dark horse in the name of Tony Koole, who might be looking for revenge at any cost.

Bart figured he was safe in the monastery for a short time, but he knew one of these three would eventually find him. He just didn't know which one to bet on.

Chapter 20

– – –

About a week after Bart's arrival at the St. Francis Monastery, three gangster-types walked into the lobby of a fifty-two-story, glass tower that housed the offices of the prestigious law firm Stranger, Foremore & Long.

"What d'ya think of all those fishes?" Ratty asked as he stopped to stare at the tons of colored fish swimming in the enormous aquarium that stretched across most of the lobby.

"I'd like to put couple shots in that tank and watch it break up so everything pours out and floods the people and makes them run and scream," said Mousy, who saw most things in terms of how much damage and violence he could do. And Mousy could do a lot of damage because he had the strength that comes with the massive body of a weight lifter and, for good measure, always carried a gun in a special holster fitted under his left arm. Mousy carried the same kind of gun that his all-time hero, Clint Eastwood, had used in all his "Dirty Harry" movies. Mousy bragged about knowing how many people Clint killed—well over 100—and remembering Clint's best line—"Go ahead muddafucker. Make my day, or I'll shoot you in the ass." Of course, that wasn't what Clint had said, but no one was about to correct Mousy, which would be like telling a rhino to think twice before charging.

"Hey, shitheads. Listen up, and listen up good, cause I'm not going to say this again. I don't want to hear another word from either of you while we're in this building. I'll do all the talking, so you two keep your mouths shut tight," said their boss, Tony Koole. He was dressed in a shiny, silver sport coat over a black, turtleneck sweater, set off with flashy, double gold chains that were too much glitz, but that was Tony.

Ratty, who was wearing an avocado green sport coat, looked at Tony and nodded his big head several times to indicate he heard and wouldn't say another word. Ratty had gotten his nickname because he had the annoying habit of twitching his face like a hungry rat and sniffing loudly through a nose mostly plugged from being broken too many times.

Unlike Ratty, Mousy did not nod his head in agreement. He hated being called a shithead or being told to shut up. He flexed and rippled his many layers of chest muscles, and with about as much grace as an eighteen-wheeled truck making a tight turn, Mousy turned to face his boss.

Mousy had teeny eyes that were almost hidden under big, bushy eyebrows, so Tony had difficulty knowing if Mousy was trying to stare him down. Mousy wasn't into staring, which he considered a kid's game, but he knew exactly how to piss off his boss. He didn't say any words out loud, but instead he silently and slowly mouthed the words, "Yes, Boss," using the kind of exaggerated lip movements that chimps are so good at.

"Goddamn it, Mousy, I've told you a million times not to mouth words with your big lips. It's disgusting and disrespecting," said Tony, whose favorite expression was a well-practiced scowl, which had about as much effect on Mousy as an ant telling an elephant to watch it's step.

Mousy liked the money he was paid for being Tony's bodyguard, but he considered Tony a dumb ass, little prick whose claim to fame was a porn business he got after his fat father kicked the bucket from too much snorting and too much screwing. Mousy was getting tired of putting up with Tony's crap. He knew one day he'd shoot Tony in the ass to show what a pain he was. Then for good measure he'd shoot Tony in the head to destroy what little brains he had. Mousy figured that some times the only good solution was to shoot things.

Tony Koole, followed by Ratty and Mousy, walked through the lobby and stopped in front of the elevator that served only the top floors. Tony nodded at Ratty, who punched the "up" button about a dozen times, believing the more the punches, the faster the elevator came. Tony had told Ratty a hundred times to punch the button only once, but Ratty liked punching things, big or small. While Ratty was busy punching the elevator's "up" button, Mousy had positioned his 280 pounds of muscle in the area directly in front of the elevator to make sure nobody else could get on.

After a short wait, there was a ding, and the elevator door opened. A few people got out and Ratty immediately got on, followed by Tony, followed by Mousy, who stopped, turned, and stood only inches inside the elevator's open door to block anyone else from getting on. About a dozen people had been waiting for the elevator but none had the courage to say, "excuse me," and try to edge by Mousy, who looked especially large and threatening in his burnt orange sport coat.

Ratty started punching the elevator button for the 52nd floor and was still punching it when the door closed. Tony made it a point to never ride the elevator with strangers, because in his specialized business, he couldn't afford to take chances.

The three of them rode up in silence, except for Ratty making sniffing sounds and every now and then punching the 52nd floor button to make sure that's where they were going. With his back to Tony, Mousy was looking at his reflection in the polished brass elevator door and silently mouthing, "asshole," which was what he thought of Tony for calling him a shithead and telling him to shut up. Tony couldn't see what Mousy was silently saying since Tony saw only Mousy's back, which was as big as a garage door.

The elevator stopped on the 52nd floor, and the door opened. Mousy got out first, looked around, saw nothing suspicious, and nodded at Tony. Tony got out, followed by Ratty. With Tony in front and Ratty and Mousy in back, the three hoodlums walked on the deep maroon carpeting and stopped in front of the frosted, double glass doors. Tony read aloud the lettering on the door.

"Stranger, Foremore and Long," he said. "This is going to be fun."

Mousy pushed then held open the right glass door while Ratty pushed then held open the left door so Tony could walk through the middle like he was a Saudi crown prince entering his palace.

Mousy and Ratty followed behind Tony, who walked up to the front of the secretary's ebony desk, which was surrounded with a waist-high, chrome enclosure to keep clients from getting too close and personal.

"I'm here to see Mr. Stranger," Tony said.

"Do you have an appointment?" asked the secretary with the perfect makeup. She thought the smaller man doing the talking looked atrocious in his out-of-fashion, shiny, silver sport coat, black turtleneck, and gold chains. She tried not to stare at the two weight-lifting monsters, one wearing an ugly, avocado, loosely-fitted sport coat and the other a hideous, orange one, which could only have come from the clothes rack in a 99 cent store.

"I'm afraid my secretary neglected to arrange an appointment. Just tell Mr. Stranger that Tony Koole, that's Koole with a K at the beginning and an E on the end, is here to see him."

"I am afraid that Mr. Stranger is very busy today," the secretary said.

"I'm also very busy today and do not like to be kept waiting. Tell Mr. Stranger I've come to see him about something his son stole from me. The sooner Mr. Stranger sees me, the sooner I'm gone, and with no harm done," Tony said. His mouth was fixed into a horrible smile while his eyes turned into two black marbles.

The secretary's body became rigid as she realized Tony Koole was some kind of hoodlum, potentially a very dangerous one, who had brought two monsters big enough to snap someone's neck like it was a pencil.

For several seconds she was too frightened to speak and just stared at Tony.

"Wha'cha looking at?" Tony asked.

Finally the secretary said in a strangled voice, "Please have a seat, and I will tell Mr. Stranger that you are waiting to see him.

She waited for the three men to sit down and wondered if the beautiful designer chairs would crash under the weight of the two huge monsters. She punched a button on the phone console and began talking on her headset with Mr. Stranger.

"Crappy chairs," Ratty said in a loud grumble, already forgetting Tony's warning to say nothing. Mousy made matters worse by glancing at Tony and using exaggerated lip movements to silently mouth, "crappy coffee." Mouthing words pissed off Tony more than anything, because he never knew what Mousy was saying but was sure it was totally disrespectful.

"One more word out of either of you, and you walk back to L.A.," said Tony, making a point to scowl first at Ratty, who nodded agreeably, and then at Mousy, who raised his shoulders and spread his hands as if to say he hadn't said nutting, so what's the big deal.

Tony watched the secretary talk into her headset for several minutes. Then she looked up and said, "Mr. Stranger will see you shortly."

"While we're waiting, my friends and I would really appreciate some coffee, with cream and sugar," said Tony, who could be friendly, if needed.

"Of course," said the secretary, who pushed another button and spoke softly into her headset.

In a few minutes, an assistant brought out a silver tray with three tiny cups of very hot coffee with cream and sugar, and set the tray on the coffee table in front of Tony.

"Thank you," said Tony, who was very courteous, just as long as he got his way.

The coffee cups were so small neither Ratty nor Mousy could get their thumbs through the elegant handles. They had to cradle the cups in their big hands, but the cups were very hot, so they had to shift the cups from hand to hand to avoid getting burned.

The secretary smiled to herself as she watched the two giant thugs switching the hot cups from hand to hand. She hadn't like the way they treated her so she told the assistant to use their smallest cups and make the coffee especially hot.

After a short time, the secretary talked into her headset, looked up, and said, "Mr. Stranger will see you now. His office is at the end of this hallway." She pointed to the hallway on her left.

All three got up, but only Tony walked over to the secretary's desk. Tony stopped, leaned forward a little so he could size up her face, boobs, and body.

"You're a real looker, and with that face and those boobs I could make you into a movie star. I'm not only a film agent but also a film producer, and I can guarantee you a starting role in my next porn film," Tony said as he leered, and grinned, and pointedly stared at her boobs.

The secretary gasped, her checks turned bright red, and her hands were trembling so badly she put them on her knees. She had never been treated or spoken to like this, and her anger gave her the courage to speak out.

"I find your offer disgusting, and you are beyond despicable," the secretary said.

Tony saw the secretary's face turn red, and watched her eyes blaze with fury, and found all this very arousing, and that gave him an idea. In making a deal with Mr. Stranger, he would insist on getting a night with this tight-assed secretary. He would show her a trick or two, and she would thank him in the end.

"Well, if you change your mind, here's my card. I guarantee you'll be making three times what you're getting her and having a hell of lot more fun to boot."

Tony held out his card, which was black with neon pink lettering that read, "True Sex Inc." She made no movement to take his card, so Tony dropped it on her desk.

"You could make a lot of money, tons of money with your kinds of boobs," Tony said and gave one last smile to show that down deep he was a nice guy who really did appreciate and like women, especially ones with big knockers.

Tony Koole turned and walked down the hallway, followed by his two scary goons.

"She really did have great tits," Ratty said as he walked, and at the same time he rotated his hands like he was feeling cantaloupes.

Tony reached Mr. Stranger's office, read the sign on the door, and opened it without knocking. He walked into the office, followed by Ratty and then Mousy, who walked in last because Tony had given him the dumb job of closing doors and keeping others out. Mousy hated shutting doors after Tony and closed the office door more loudly than needed while silently mouthing, "asshole," and smiling broadly.

While Tony Koole had been kept waiting, Randolph had done a Google search as well as talked to a Hollywood lawyer, who summarized Tony Koole as being street smart, arrogant, mob-connected, and involved in illegal drugs. Randolph neither rose nor offered to shake hands with this glitzy man or his two ugly bodyguards dressed in fruit-colored sport coats.

I know exactly how to handle these kind of people, Randolph thought. But little did he know what he was in for.

CHAPTER 21

"My name is Tony Koole, that's Koole with a K at the beginning and E at the end. I'm a Hollywood film agent as well as a film producer and distributor. I hate to just barge in like this, but I've got serious business to discuss and hope we can make a mutually satisfactory deal," Tony said, not bothering to shake hands. He moved one of the chairs closer to Randolph's desk, sat down, adjusted the crease in his slacks, and sat back like he was king for the day.

Ratty and Mousy remained standing, one on each side of Tony, like two menacing warriors guarding their general.

"I have a very busy schedule today, so let us get right to the point of why you are here," Randolph said, showing no reaction to Tony's impertinence or the bodyguards who were scowling because they had to stand while Tony got to sit.

"It's like this. I found out some dumb San Diego detectives arrested a homeless guy thinking it was your stepson. During the arrest, the detectives found a briefcase full of cocaine hidden under his bed. It turns out that your stepson's girlfriend stole the cocaine from me. Since your stepson and his girlfriend have both disappeared, I'm holding you personally responsible for my loss. It's a two million dollar loss," Tony said. Like his last name demanded, he was trying to be very cool.

"That certainly is a remarkable story, Mr. Koole. The problem is I have no way of knowing whose cocaine was found under my stepson's bed. Furthermore, you have no way to prove the cocaine was, in fact, yours. Finally, I am certainly not liable for your loss, which is something you will have to take up with the police," Randolph said, using his all-business voice and deliberately staring at Tony Koole.

Tony didn't like being stared at or told to take a hike and ask the police to return his cocaine. Tony's face was turning hot, and he was tempted to tell Ratty to punch this smart lawyer in the face. But first he would try to make a deal and if needed, any punching would come later. Tony stared back with narrowed eyes and bent his head forward like a snake ready to strike.

"From what I've heard on the street, they say you're a bright lawyer, but you're sounding like a dumb shit whose head is screwed on backwards," Tony said, still keeping his cool. "I know your kid hid my cocaine under his bed and let the police waltz in and take it. So I'm out two million and came to make a deal with you. My best advice is you do just that, or my two large friends will work you over, and you don't want that. Believe me, you don't want that," Tony said, opening his hands like a used-car dealer trying to convince a customer to buy a crappy used car.

Randolph had never been threatened before and was sure Tony would turn his goons lose, if necessary. He could not go to the police since it would be his word against Tony's. Tony would certainly deny having any knowledge of the cocaine or threatening Randolph's life. But Randolph knew how get out of tight situations and make deals, and that is what he needed to do now.

"I want to repeat, I have no way of knowing if you are in fact the owner of the cocaine or simply claiming to be the owner and trying to shake me down," Randolph said, using the authoritarian tone of a attorney.

"Don't give me any shit. That was my coke, and I can prove it."

Tony turned his head toward Mousy and barked, "Show this dumb prick the proof it was my coke."

Mousy knew what that meant. He reached inside his loosely hanging, avocado-green sport coat and brought out his Clint Eastwood gun. It was a .44 Magnum, to which Mousy had added a pearl handle, which he thought gave it a certain class, not realizing the pearl handle would have make Clint drop dead. Mousy bunched his bushy eyebrows, focused his tiny eyes, grinned, and pointed the Magnum's long barrel at Randolph's heart.

Randolph rocked back in his chair but made a conscious effort to keep the shock off his face, which would be a sure sign of weakness. He knew this situation demanded immediate action and reached for the phone to call security and have these vicious hoodlums extricated from his office.

Tony had given each of his bodyguards a different job. Mousy was to close doors, point his gun, and keep people away from Tony. Ratty's job was beating up people or stopping them from doing stupid things like reaching for a phone or hidden gun. Just as Randolph's manicured fingers were about to pick up his phone, Ratty stepped forward, grasped Randolph's hand, and squeezed like a vise.

"Ratty can to turn your fingers into mushy tootsie rolls, so listen up. Ratty is your proof the coke was mine, so you better think about coming up with the two million," Tony said, smiling broadly at how everything was going like he wanted.

"Please tell your bodyguard to release my hand. I will neither call security nor reach for a gun, because I do not keep one in my office," Randolph lied. He kept a compact, semi-automatic 9mm Glock mounted just below his middle desk drawer. He had purchased the gun after a disgruntled client shot one of his colleagues. He had practiced with the Glock and become a very good shot. If he got the chance, he would surreptitiously reach under the middle drawer, grab his Glock, and turn the tables on these dumb goons.

Tony was pleased to see how easily Randolph had given in, but that's how all these high-priced pricks were, all talk and no action. A tiny smile creased Tony's pockmarked face, and he said, "Okay Ratty, let his hand go, but if he tries anything, anything at all, you know what to do."

Ratty nodded his agreement and gave one last hard squeeze before he let go of Randolph's hand. Ratty stood close by and if needed, would punch Randolph in the face, which was one of Ratty's favorite activities.

"What I still do not know is how the case of cocaine happened to end up under the bed in my stepson's house?" Randolph asked. He was flexing the fingers in his right hand and hoping they were not damaged.

"How it got there ain't important. The only thing you got to know is your stepson got his hands on my two million dollars of coke. He hid it under his bed, went looking for a buyer, but the police got there first," Tony said, making up the story as he went along cause he wasn't going to tell how that dumb broad, Anna, stole it from right under his nose. He'd deal with her later, after he got this big-talking lawyer to pay the two million.

"Since you say my stepson was responsible for allowing the police to abscond with your cocaine, why are you harassing me, instead of dealing directly with my stepson?" asked Randolph.

He already knew the answer, because for the last two weeks, his own private detective had not been able to find Bart, who seemed to have vanished from the face of the earth. Randolph was asking these questions to stall for time. He needed sufficient feeling to return to his right hand, so if given the chance, he could grab and shoot the Glock.

"It's simple. I couldn't find your stepson, who must be scared shitless and hiding someplace, but you're easy to find, name's on the door," said Tony, who laughed like he had just explained a big mystery to a little kid. "And besides, you're the one with money, so either we make a deal or somebody gets hurt, and that somebody is you." Tony liked to make threats and watch people squirm almost as much as he liked to screw, which reminded him of the secretary whose tight ass would be part of any deal.

Randolph had managed to move his right hand to the edge of the desk, and some feeling had returned to his fingers, but it was not enough to reach in, grab the gun, and pull the trigger.

"It would be impossible for me to recover your cocaine from the police, since cocaine is an illegal drug and the police do not return illegal drugs to the general public," Randolph said, stalling for time.

"Boy, you're really a bright lawyer to figure out that walking into a police station and asking for a case of cocaine is a stupid thing to do," said Tony, laughing so hard he almost doubled over.

Ratty was laughing too because he laughed when Tony did, but Mousy never laughed at anything Tony said because Tony never said anything funny. Mousy stood silently, keeping his .44 Magnum pointed at Randolph, wishing he could shoot this sucker so they could go and have lunch.

"If the police won't give me back my coke, what's left for you to do?" asked Tony, who was smirking because he knew what was left to do, and he knew Randolph knew what was left to do, but he wanted to make this big shot say it.

"You expect me to cover the cost of your lost cocaine and reimburse you for two million dollars," Randolph said. He had managed to move his right hand to the chair's armrest, almost out of the bodyguard's sight and only six inches from the middle desk drawer.

"Bingo. You got that right," said Tony, nodding and smiling like a windup toy clown.

"But suppose I inform the police that porn king Tony Koole admitted to being the owner of the case of illegal cocaine," Randolph said. He had an idea of how to outfox these three idiots.

"Most lawyers are stupid, but you're dumb to boot. You tell the police one fucking word about me and the next day Mousy shoots you dead," Tony said, his face turning as hard and ugly as a used manhole cover.

"Let me punch him around a little before Mousy shoots him," said Ratty.

"I told you to shut your mouth," Tony said.

"Just wanting to be helpful," Ratty said.

"Not one more word outta your mouth," Tony said as he gave Ratty a scowl that could have made a dog run for cover.

Ratty nodded, although he thought Tony owed him the chance to punch this guy around, especially if Mousy was going to shoot him anyway.

"I've got another idea," Tony said.

"I am listening," Randolph said.

"It's well known by all the people I talked to that your wife's loaded, big time. I even heard she's got so much money she gives you a little on the side, to help pay for extras, like your mistress," Tony said, breaking into a mocking smile that showed off the gold fillings in his back teeth.

Randolph sat bolt upright, because if any one told Marjorie about his mistress, it would create enormous difficulties.

CHAPTER 22

— — —

At hearing the word *mistress* Randolph's face turned bright red, and he clenched his fists. He was so angry he momentarily forgot about the big bodyguards and the gun pointing at his heart and started to rise out of his chair. But Randolph managed to rise only a few inches before Ratty's powerful hand landed on his shoulder, shoved him back down, held him there, and squeezed so hard the pain made him cringe.

"I see you're a little touchy about getting money from your lovey-dovey wife so you can afford to keep screwing your lovey-dovey mistress," Tony said. He had only guessed Randolph had a mistress—all these high-priced big shots had them—but now he knew he had guessed right. He thought about how he would use this info.

"I wasn't sure about your mistress until I saw your face turn redder than a baboon's ass, and you looked like you were about to crap in our pants. But, don't worry. I won't tell anyone, provided we make this deal," Tony said.

Tony didn't like anything about Randolph, especially how he talked like he had a dictionary for a brain. When this was all over, Tony decided he'd get this jerk where it hurt. He would anonymously tip off the wife about Randolph having a mistress and then sit back to watch what happened when the shit hit the fan.

For the first time, Randolph was worried. If Marjorie ever found out about his mistress, the result would be catastrophic. Marjorie's father had so disliked and mistrusted Randolph that he had added a stipulation to their prenuptial agreement: if it were ever proven that Randolph was unfaithful, such behavior would be grounds for immediate divorce proceeding as well as void any 50-50 split of assets so Randolph would get nothing. A divorce was something Randolph had to avoid at any cost since it would end his chances of ever gaining control over Marjorie's vast fortune, his main reason for marrying her. However, Randolph had been very discreet and was positive no one else but Tony knew of his mistress. Randolph now would have to make sure Tony never had a chance to tell his wife or anyone else about his mistress.

Randolph made himself calm down and then said, "It is well-known my wife is very wealthy, but according to our prenuptial agreement, her inherited fortune is administered by a bank regent, and I have no say in its distribution. If you decide to approach her directly and ask for two million dollars, you would not receive a cent because the bank administrator would never approve that kind of transaction and would immediately notify the police of our unusual request. The only reason I am willing to deal with you is because one of your goons wants to shoot me and the other wants to beat me, both of which I would like to avoid."

"So let's start dealing before I run out of patience and maybe tell Ratty to punch you face until it looks like hamburger or maybe let Mousy put a couple of .44 slugs into you sorry knees so you'll never walk straight," Tony said, his voice rising to a higher pitch, which happened when he got irritated about things not going his way.

Only half listening to Tony's wild threats, Randolph was making a plan to solve his two big problems, which were paying Tony two millions dollars and preventing anyone from telling Marjorie about his mistress. His plan would mix truth and lies and be somewhat complicated, so Tony's tiny brain could never figure out what was true or a lie.

"Let me spell out the problem about withdrawing or transferring large amounts of cash in today's world. Recent concerns over national security and funding terrorist activities have made it virtually impossible for anyone to walk into a bank and withdraw large amounts of cash. So if I walked into my bank and asked for one or two million in cash, sooner or later the FBI would be in my office asking where that money went. When I told them I gave the money to you, they would snoop around your film operation. And I will bet the FBI would discover that you were using your porn film operation to launder profits from selling illegal drugs," Randolph said.

"What the fuck you talking about me laundering drug money?" said Tony, and his face turned red hot and his hands balled into tight fists just like Randolph had done when Tony accused him of having a mistress.

"I was just discussing a hypothetical situation. I was not saying or implying that was what you were doing," said Randolph, delighted to see from Tony's reaction that he had guessed right about Tony's porn business being used to launder drug profits. Now he knew Tony also had a big secret to hide and that should make him more amenable and eager to accept Randolph's plan.

"You better watch you mouth, or I'll tell Mousy to shoot it full of hypothetical lead," Tony said, smiling at his own joke.

"Let me punch him first," said Ratty, who every time he heard anything about shooting, thought about first doing some punching.

"For the last time, shut the fuck up about punching," said Tony.

Randolph said nothing for about ten seconds because he wanted Tony to have time to think about what would happen if the FBI discovered his laundering operation.

"So, okay. I'm listening, but you better be offering some good faith money up front, or it's all over for you," threatened Tony, trying to talk and act like he was back in charge.

"I will agree to a good faith payment. Our law firm keeps a certain amount of cash in our vault that anyone of the partners can use in an emergency. I can pay you a hundred thousand now that will give me time to come up with the remainder in three weeks," Randolph said.

"Are you kidding me? Nothing less than two hundred thousand right now, and maybe I let you pay the rest in a few weeks," Tony countered.

Randolph had banked on Tony making a counter offer, which meant Tony was ready to close the deal.

"Let us split the difference. I will pay you a hundred and fifty thousand now, and in three weeks I will make a balloon payment to cover the balance," said Randolph.

Talking about money was something Tony liked to do, and suddenly— and out of nowhere—came a whole new idea for big money, and it was one of the best ideas he'd ever had. He'd moan a little but eventually agree for Randolph to pay the $150,000 now and the rest in three weeks. And during the next three weeks, he'd get Jesús, his drug connection in Tijuana, to contact some professional kidnappers, which in Mexico was big business. As soon as Randolph paid the entire two million, he'd have a Mexican gang kidnap him, and then he'd send a large ransom note to his wealthy wife, since she's the one with all the money. Tony was thinking how smart he was and how much money he was going to make.

"All right. You pay a hundred and fifty thousand now and rest in three week. If you don't, you're dead," Tony said, crossing his arms and looking very stern. He added, "But before Mousy shoots you, I'll give Ratty a chance to beat you to a bloody mess, which he's very good at."

"Beat him dead," Ratty said and his face lit up.

"Shut the fuck up!" Tony yelled, then added, "So we have a deal. A hundred and fifty thousand now and the rest in three weeks. Just remember. If you don't have the rest when we come back you're a dead man."

"All right. We have a deal. I will need to get my partners' verbal approvals and then I will come back with a hundred and fifty thousand in cash," Randolph said.

Getting up, he left his office and walked down to the firm's vault. He would talk to his partners later but now he just wanted those goons and their guns out of his office. The firm usually kept about 300,000 dollars in the vault for emergencies. He could replace the money before the partners knew it was missing by skimming money from Marjorie's accounts. He opened the vault and counted out one hundred and fifty thousand dollars. He put the piles of one hundred dollars bills in two large FedEx boxes and walked back to his office.

Returning to his office, Randolph put the two FedEx boxes on his desk and asked, "Do you want to count it?"

"Nah. I trust you because you know what'll happened if it not all there," Tony said.

"You'll be good and dead," Ratty said.

"Shut the fuck up," Tony said to Ratty.

Tony narrowed his eyes to give Randolph his best gangster stare and then said, "Nice doing business with ya. We'll be back in three weeks for the rest of the cash. I'll even call ahead to make an appointment and make sure you're here."

Randolph nodded and almost smiled because he knew Tony would not be walking around three weeks.

Tony got up and said, "I hope you don't mind me calling your secretary for a date and me telling her that you had said it was okay."

"I am very sorry Tony, but that request is way out of bounds, and I think you know that," Randolph said, thinking how having a date with Tony Koole would be like going out with a gorilla.

"No harm in asking," Tony said, who planned to call the tight-ass secretary and tell her that Randolph suggested they get together for a drink—sooner the better—or she would be fired.

Tony and his two oversized goons had no sooner left his office then Randolph was phoning Matthew Moore, his private investigator, to arrange the second part of his plan.

"Hi Matthew, I have a very important task for you," Randolph said.

"You know I'm working full time trying to find Bart," Matthew said, sounding annoyed at being assigned another job.

"This is very important and will require only a few minutes of your time. I want you to call Oscar Gonzales, who is the head of a big Tijuana drug cartel. He was a former client of mine and owes me a big favor for settling one of his cases. Ask Oscar to have one of his professionals meet and talk to Tony Koole and his two goons. Tony should be easy to find. He has a porn studio in Los Angles. Oscar will know what to say and I will make it worth his time. Tell Oscar it is very important to arrange the meeting in the next two weeks."

"All right," said Matthew, who was paid handsomely to follow Mr. Stranger's orders and ask no questions.

As Randolph hung up the phone he was thinking, *Once Oscar eliminates Tony Koole and his goons, I'll be home free and also prevent Tony from ever telling Marjorie about my mistress. Not bad. Two birds with one stone.*

Randolph was confident Oscar would agree to eliminate Tony Koole since that was one of Oscar's specialties. Oscar had recently been linked to a number of executions, including the Tijuana police chief, who had been asking too many questions; the editor of the Tijuana newspaper, who had been writing accusatory articles; and five police officers, who had reportedly killed five of Oscar's drug dealers. The bodies of the five police officers were individually wrapped in sheets and thrown off the back of a truck in front of the police station in broad daylight. As they say on the street, Oscar has big *cojones* and could eliminate Tony Koole as easy as swatting a fly.

Randolph walked over and sat down in his favorite Eames leather chair that was positioned by the window so he could look at the beautiful San Diego harbor and watch the classy boats sailing by. He could not help but smile as he thought over what had just transpired. Tony Koole and his two goons, none with an IQ higher than the freeway speed limit, had marched into his office and tried to extort two million dollars. Tony Koole had no idea he was dealing with someone a hundred times cleverer and smarter.

Randolph reached for the phone on the coffee table next to his chair, punched one number, and when the phone was answered he said, "Tonight, same time, same place."

"Yes," said the secretary with the perfect makeup.

Randolph smiled as he hung up the phone and silently repeated one of his favorite sayings, "To the victor belongs the spoils."

CHAPTER 23

— — —

Although it was Saturday afternoon, Carol was in her laboratory at the Neuroscience Institute reviewing the latest batch of computer printouts. She was making steady progress in recording and analyzing brainwaves to detect if people were lying when answering questions. She was up against stiff competition from researchers across the country, but these recent results were encouraging. She closed her tired eyes, massaged her forehead, and hoped the slight pain she felt in her right temple did not signal an impending headache. She was ready to call it a day when her phone rang. She tensed, fearing it was bad news about Bart. She picked up the phone and tentatively said, "Hello."

"Hi, it's Helen. I know you're getting ready to leave, but I wondered if I could stop by for a few minutes. Tonight I have a date with a new guy I found on the web, and I need some girl-talk."

"Come on by. I've just finished reviewing some printouts, and I need a break. I would love some girl-talk."

"I'll be right over," Helen said. She too had been catching up on work this Saturday afternoon.

After a few minutes, there was a soft knock on the door, and Carol said, "Come in."

Helen walked in and said, "I'm glad you're still her, because I really do need your advice."

"I'll try to help," Carol said, "But first we need some refreshments."

Walking to the noisy fridge, Carol jerked open the door and dug out two bottles of green tea from among layers of ice."

"My offer stands. I'll clean your fridge for a thousands dollars," Helen said, and they both laughed.

"Before we start our girl-talk, let me tell you the good news. The recent printouts look promising, which mean we're making progress on finding a brainwave lie detector that is one hundred percent accurate," Carol said.

"That is great news. I guess we need to thank Bart for helping us develop the algorithms to better analyze brainwave activity," Helen said.

"Here's to Bart," Carol said as she and Helen clinked their bottles of green tea. They took big swigs. "But I don't want to think about research any more today. Let's do something more enjoyable and discuss the men in our lives."

"Well I did like you said and went on the web dating site to look around, and I think I may have found a really good possibility," Helen said, her face all smiles. "His name is Steve. He's nice looking, intelligent, likes my kind of music, reads best-sellers like me, and, amazingly, works in a pharmaceutical lab just down the road."

"So far so good," Carol said encouragingly.

"We made a date to meet tonight, but I need your advice because my recent attempts at dating have been disappointing," Helen said as her smile slowly turned into a frown. "My problem is, men seem to like me at first because I'm a good audience. I ask questions, am genuinely interested in what they say, and laugh at their jokes—even bad ones," Helen said.

"Well, you seem to be doing all the right things," Carol said.

"But I keep discovering men would much rather be the center of attention and don't show equal interest or ask questions about what I do and think. And if I happen to disagree with something they've said, they get grumpy and treat me like my opinions don't matter."

"I know exactly what you're talking about, because I have a similar problem with some of my male colleagues. They don't respect me as a fellow researcher, can't take their eyes off my body, and constantly disregard my opinions," Carol said, her voice rising in anger. She couldn't help remembering when a prominent male researcher had refused to give her a position in his lab, saying women were only interested in getting married and having children.

"Well, I'm sure of one thing," Helen said in a very determined voice. "I want men to treat me like an equal and not like a submissive, little mouse. I know it's a cliché, but I want a man to respect and value me, and that includes both my body and my brain."

"I don't think that's asking too much," Carol said. "You may have to date a lot of jerks, but someday, somewhere, you'll find a man who values and respects all of you, mind and body. As one of my former college roommate always said, 'don't stop looking till you dead.'"

"How can you be so sure I will find that special someone?" Helen asked.

"Because I'd been looking longer than you, dating a lot of jerks, and had almost given up trying to find Mr. Right. But then I finally found Billy. He is respectful, values all of me, and treats me like an equal. So I am confident there are good men out there, and you just need to keep looking and not get discouraged. And from what you've told me about Steve, he just may be the one you're looking for," Carol said.

"If Steve doesn't work out, perhaps you can ask Billy if he has a brother," Helen said, and they both giggled.

"Just remember to be yourself. You're really cute, smart, likable, and full of energy, and Steve would have to be a first-class jerk not to see that. And if he has any questions about your sterling qualifications, tell him to call me," Carol said. She gave Helen a high five, and they both laughed.

"But that's enough about me and my dating problems. I can't wait to hear what happened when you went to Billy's place last weekend," Helen said, learning forward, her eyes big with interest.

As Carol thought about her weekend with Billy, her eyes began to sparkle like sun shinning through emeralds.

"When Billy asked me to spend a long weekend together, something we hadn't done before, I was really excited. I thought this meant he was getting serious about our relationship and thinking of us as a couple. Over the last many months, we have spent nights at each other's place but not a long weekend together."

"I think inviting you over for a long weekend means he's getting serious," Helen said.

"Billy has a secluded A-frame in rural East County. It overlooks a beautiful lake and has a back yard filled with pine and oak trees. There's no one else within miles. No city lights. No traffic sounds. Just birds singing and wind blowing through the trees. Being there with him makes me feel like we're the only two people in the entire universe." Carol eyes had a dreamy look.

"Sounds like the perfect place to spend a long weekend with someone you care about," Helen said in a wistful voice, hoping a romantic long weekend was in her future.

"Billy told me to bring a bikini for swimming in the lake and soaking in his outdoor hot tub, causal clothes for exploring Mount Palomar, and a warm jacket for late-night walking along the lakeshore. Then almost as an afterthought he said I might want to bring some sexy things to wear at our candlelight dinner on Saturday night." Carol paused as a red tint was coloring her cheeks and a heat wave was traveling down her body.

"Don't stop now," Helen said.

"I arrived Friday evening, just in time to watch the sunset and sip margaritas. That night we watched a movie, ate popcorn, and petted like a couple of teenagers. We went hiking Saturday afternoon around Mount

Palomar, and when it got dark, went got back to his place. He suggested we shower and hinted that I might want to change into the sexy things items I had brought. When I came out of the bedroom, there were dozens of candles giving the living room a warm glow. I had put on a white, lacy teddy, silky, white bra, white thong, silver hoop earrings, and a pair of white, knee-length, cashmere socks."

"Wow! All I can say is you must have looked spectacular," Helen said.

"Billy had changed into a sexy, black, silk T-shirt and black shorts that showed off his great body. We sat across from each other at his dining room table, stared at each other bodies, nibbled on appetizers, and drank some wine. After dinner, he put on soft, romantic music, and we started slow dancing in the warm candlelight. Then between songs, he surprised me by slowly taking off one piece of clothing at a time. After taking off an item, he would touch and kiss the area. Then we would dance a little more, and he would take off another piece, and before I knew it, I was wearing nothing at all."

"Wow! I can't wait to see the movie!" Helen almost shouted. She was happy for Carol, but at the same time she couldn't help feeling a little envious.

"As you might guess, it was an incredibly exciting weekend, and you can probably understand why I think Billy is my Mr. Right."

"I certainly can," Helen said, raising her hand for another high five.

"But I'm a little worried about what's going to happen to our relationship. Some of Billy's former girlfriends, who I happened to meet at the Red Bull Saloon, were only too eager to warn me Billy doesn't stay very long with the same person."

"Oh, they're just jealous. Billy will surely realize how much you have to offer and never want to move on to anyone else," Helen said.

"I sure hope so," Carol said, closing her eyes and fighting away the first sign of tears. She knew she was falling in love with someone who prided himself on being independent and self-sufficient, but so did she. She was willing and ready to make a commitment and hoped Billy felt the same way.

"If he doesn't have the brains to appreciate you, I'll bang him on the head until he does," Helen said. She made pounding gestures until they were both laughing.

"I've been telling my mother how well things are going with Billy, and she wants to meet him and take us all to dinner. I know my mother will really like him, and I'm doubly sure he'll like her. I told Billy about my mother wanting to meet him, and I thought he would be pleased, but he seemed a little hesitant. He said that we could discuss it when we meet for dancing tonight at the Red Bull. I just hope he agrees to meet my mother." Carol closed her eyes and thought how wonderful it was to be falling in love with Billy.

"I'm sure he will, especially after your incredible weekend together." Helen nodded repeatedly to make her point.

"I sure hope so," Carol said.

CHAPTER 24

— ▬ —

Billy was sitting on the balcony of his A-frame cottage in East County. It was late afternoon, and normally he would be enjoying a cold bottle of Dos Equis beer, watching the sunset on Lake Cuyamaca, and listening to country music. Instead, worries had made his forehead look like a washboard, and his muscles were pulled tighter than guitar strings. All his thoughts were on what to tell Carol. *I've got to explain I'm not ready to meet her mother. But what if she doesn't understand, and we get into a big fight?*

Billy looked at Mighty Mo, a 25-pound coon cat sitting on a comfortable, beat-up cushion across from him. Like most pet owners who live alone, he had gotten into the habit of talking to this giant cat. Mo would look at him with big, unblinking eyes and flick his pointed ears back and forth, as if following his every word. Now and then Mo would make low, growling purrs, as if giving reassurance and indicating agreement.

"Everything was great until a couple days ago," Billy said to Mo. "That's when Carol said her mother wanted to meet me. A siren went off in my head, because meeting someone's mother sends a message. I'll admit I'm serious about Carol, but I don't want to be pushed into making a commitment."

The thought of making a commitment sent shivers through Billy's body. He suddenly stood up and began pacing the balcony. Mo's eyes closely tracked Billy's every step and turn, as if watching a squirrel scurrying across the forest floor.

"I've worked all my life to become independent and self-sufficient. Making a commitment means giving up my independence, and that scares me half to death."

Billy stopped pacing, stood at the balcony's rail, and stared at the lake. He couldn't help thinking about the long, hard road he had traveled to become his own man and develop a successful career.

As a young boy he had been abandoned by his drugged-out mother and forced to endure foster homes run by adults more concerned about making money than giving support, love, or encouragement. He had been sent to public schools in some of the worst neighborhoods, where he was constantly pressured into joining gangs, which he refused because he was done taking orders or being bullied. At first he suffered a lot of beatings, but being clever, quick, and muscular for his age, he gradually developed into a very good street fighter. Eventually the gangs and bullies left him alone, but that meant he had few friends and became something of a loner. He put all his energy into studying, knowing his one chance to get out of his crummy foster home and make something of himself was to earn grades good enough to get a scholarship to college.

He worked very hard in college, not only getting grades good enough to make the Dean's List every semester but also developing the kind of confidence and self-assurance that made him independent and self-reliant. No one could hurt him. After college he worked for six years with an experienced private detective, who taught him the trade and later sold him the practice when he retired.

His former boss had told him the importance of developing a hard-nosed, tough reputation, because that's what people looked for in a private detective. He had played the role, acting as mean and tough as a pit bull and developing his nickname, Bad Billy. He also had a completely different side he rarely showed, because it might be mistaken for weakness. When he was with Carol, he could be as warm and loving as cuddly puppy. Loving Carol was wonderful, but at the same time it made him feel vulnerable because it threatened his independence.

He stopped pacing when he noticed the sun had set and the sky was darkening. There was just time enough to feed Mo, grab a quick meal, shower, and dress. As he was leaving his second floor balcony and walking down the stairs, he was thinking, *I just need a little more time before I'm ready to make a commitment and meet Carol's mother. I just hope Carol understands.*

Seeing Billy head for the stairs, Mo got up, stretched and followed Billy down the stars and into the kitchen. Billy picked up Mo's large food bowl, filled it with tuna-in-spring water, and set it down on the floor. Billy made himself a burnt grilled-cheese sandwich and ate it while talking to Mo.

"She's got a temper almost as quick and hot as mine. What happens if she doesn't understand why I need more time. Or thinks I was only leading her on? The truth is I didn't lead her on. I really do like her."

Billy walked up the stairs to the master bedroom, followed closely by Mo, who thought it was time for an after dinner nap. Once in the bedroom, Mo jumped onto his favorite chair and curled up. He was soon asleep, dreaming about hunting varmints in the forest and bringing Billy a present.

After showering and dressing, Billy selected a black cowboy from the hat rack and stuck a white feather into its band. He went back downstairs, through the kitchen, and into attached garage. He put his cowboy hat into the motorcycle's left saddlebag and put on his helmet. He opened the door and rolled out his black and chrome Harley, a mean-looking model called *Fat Boy*. He closed the door, got on the Fat Boy, started the motor. He let it throb and growl for a few seconds. Then he took off in a load roar that echoed across the lake and startled sleepy birds into flight.

Billy was wearing black leather pants, a black leather jacket, and a black helmet with a gray visor. The night was dark, and his black attire made it seem like a phantom was riding the Harley. Within seconds he was speeding down the road with the twin mufflers roaring like a pride of hungry lions. He passed Lake Cuyamaca, wound around the base of Palomar Mountain, and turned onto the two-lane, curvy County Road 67. The wide, Marathon racing tires kept the Harley glued to the road. He carved through each turn by leaning over so far his knees almost touched the road.

Fifteen minutes later, he was turning into the parking lot of the Red Bull Saloon. He parked in a small area near the entrance that was reserved for bikers. High above the entrance hung a giant bull's face outlined in red neon lights with flashing yellow neon horns, but only one horn was working. Billy had been coming to the Red Bull Saloon as religiously as someone attending every Sunday church service.

After parking his bike, he removed his helmet and strapped it to the handlebars. Then he reached into the right saddlebag, took out a soft chamois, and wiped the road dust from his black cowboy boots with silver tips. Putting away the chamois, he reached into the left saddlebag. He got out his black cowboy hat and adjusted the white feather in its band. He swept back his longish, black hair and put on his cowboy hat. The hat's wide brim shadowed his handsome face and hid his dark probing eyes.

The Red Bull Saloon's parking lot was quickly filling with people coming from all over San Diego and East County. They were mostly city folk who enjoyed dressing up in western garb for a night of dancing, drinking, hooting, and hoping this was the night they met that special person.

As a favor to Billy, the bikers who arrived early always saved a prime parking spot near the entrance for Carol, who was always late. Billy was now standing at the front of the prime parking spot. His looks, stance, and attitude warned away anyone dumb enough to try parking in Carol's spot.

Unlike rock and roll bands that started whenever they damned well pleased, the Country Casanovas started at exactly 9:00. Billy could hear the band begin playing a familiar George Strait song, which was a slow two-step so the dancers could warm up. Just as the band finished the song, Billy saw Carol's red, Miata convertible turning into the parking lot. As she drove into her saved spot, Billy heard her car's stereo blasting out Paul Simon's rhythmic song *Diamonds on the Soles of Her Shoes*. Billy knew Carol always dressed down at the Institute, but when she went dancing, she always wore something spectacular.

He opened her door, stepped back, and watched her get out of the car. She was wearing fitted, soft, white leather slacks with a thin, black belt accented with sparkly rhinestones and a white, silk blouse with black pearl buttons down the front. Over her white blouse and slacks, she wore a stunning black, mesh, silk vest that hung open and almost reached her knees. When she moved, the silk vest clung to her body and highlighted her wondrous curves. On her feet were white leather cowboy boots tipped in black chrome. Her golden hair, which at work was locked in a tight bun, hung down freely and brushed her shoulders as she moved. Finally, she reached behind the driver's seat, picked up a white cowboy hat whose black band held a white feather tipped in black, put it on, and said, "I'm ready to dance."

"My God, you're beyond beautiful," Billy said, and he motioned for her to turn around so he could admire every part of her.

"Thank you," Carol said. "I appreciate your compliment."

After Carol finished turning around to show her outfit to Billy, the remaining bikers smiled and applauded. Carol smiled back, bowed, and threw them a kiss.

Billy extended his arm, which Carol took and gave a loving squeeze. Hand in hand they walked to the entrance and went through the swinging doors, one painted green and one red. People developed superstitions about which colored door to push open, depending on previous success in meeting Mr. or Ms. Right. When Billy and Carol entered, the doorman, who had a secret crush on Carol, said, "There's never no cover for you. Just walk on in and enjoy the music."

"Well thank you," Carol said and gave him a peck on his check. The doorman's face colored like it had turned into a gigantic strawberry.

As Billy went by, he tucked a twenty-dollar bill into the doorman's hand and smiled a big thank you. They walked over to the side of the dance floor and sat down on two empty bar stools in a relatively quiet corner.

The saloon advertised having the biggest wooden dance floor in southern California, the best live country-western bands, five beers on tap, and five kinds of margaritas—strawberry being the most popular. An especially big and lively crowd showed up every Saturday night, and a well-muscled security force, wearing black T-shirts emblazoned with red bulls spouting yellow horns, made sure no one took booze onto the highly polished dance floor, which was as smooth and slick as an ice skating ring.

The Country Casanovas liked Carol, and when they saw her enter, they began playing one of her favorite songs, Fire on the Mountain, which starts slowly but gradually speeds up. The couples started out doing the relatively slow two-step, circling the outer part of the floor and making a human merry-go-round. Billy thought the slow two-step a little boring and took Carol just inside the crowded circle of dancers, where there was more room to move. Billy led Carol in a non-traditional, double-time step, and they flew around the floor, passing all the other dancers. The slower, more traditional two-steppers gave Billy and Carol disapproving looks and mumbled about them showing off or not knowing how to dance.

As the band steadily increased it's beat, the dancers were forced to move faster and faster, until they were circling the outer part of floor like a merry-go-round out of control. When the band was playing the fastest beat, Billy led Carol to a small space, completely deserted, in the very center of the floor. Unlike the whirlwind of dancers racing around the floor, Billy and Carol had slowed down by dancing to every other beat. They were doing slow spins, elegant twirls, and synchronized, over-the-head spirals. Carol's long hair flowed like strands of gold, and her black, silk vest clung to her body and highlighted her lovely curves. Together they looked like two beautifully carved figurines slowly rotating with grace and elegance on top of an antique music box.

When the music stopped, Billy and Carol remained standing in the center of the floor, bathed in red, blue, and green colored lights from the overhead, rotating crystal ball.

"It's so exciting to fly around the floor at the start and then do slow romantic spins at the end. I wish we could dance like that forever," Carol said, her sparkly green eyes filled with love.

"Dancing with you is even better than riding my Harley," Billy said and laughed. He bent down to kiss her, and when the tips of their tongues touched, an electric current passed between them.

Marge had paused from her waitressing duties to watch Billy and Carol dance. She had a big crush on Billy and was thinking, *I only wish it was me he was holding and kissing. And taking home tonight.*

When her shift ended later that night, Marge would get plenty of offers to dance. She had a sexy body and the kind of friendly attitude that made every man men believe she was especially interested in him. When she was dancing, she sometimes closed her eyes and pretended she was dancing with Billy. She knew Billy's reputation of moving on, so she would wait her turn and prayed it would come soon.

Just then the band began playing a funky electric slide, and dozens of line dancers were filling the floor. Billy took Carol's hand and led her back to their stools, where it was quieter and they would be able to talk.

As they walked to their stools Carol was thinking, *this is going to be a great night for dancing and will get even better when he agrees to meet my mother.*

When they reached their stools, Billy was thinking, *I'll tell her I really do care about her but need a little more time before I'm ready to meet her mother.*

CHAPTER 25

Carol sat down on her stool while Billy stood in front of her. "We need to talk about my meeting your mother."

Carol felt excited and was all smiles as she looked into Billy's eyes. Meeting her mother would be a sign he was committed to their relationship, something she wanted more than anything. It would also mean she didn't have to fear the ugly rumors about Billy always moving on to another woman.

But what she saw in Billy's eyes made her abruptly sit back, as if punched in the chest. Billy's eyes were filled with sadness, and she knew something terrible was coming, like hearing a thunderclap and knowing lightening was about to strike. She had the sudden urge to run away and hide, but fear kept her seated, as if she were paralyzed.

"You know I really like you, and god knows our dancing and sex are incredible. But meeting someone's mother usually means a couple is committed and halfway to getting married. Right now I just don't want that kind of pressure. I've been an independent cuss my whole life and need time to change my way of thinking. I'd like to meet your mother at some point, but not quite yet."

"You say you *really* like me. But what does that mean?" Carol shot back in anger. "Apparently you don't like me enough to meet my mother because it's suggest we're a serious couple. So what am I to you? Just a good time? Are you getting ready to move on? Look for greener pastures? I didn't want to believe the ugly rumors about your never staying long with any woman. But now I see the rumors were true. You really fooled me. You're not Bad Billy. You're Bastard Billy."

She felt betrayed by someone she loved. Someone she thought loved her. Tears were streaming down her checks. Her sparkling green eyes had turned cold and steely. Her beautiful face had twisted into an ugly scowl. She crossed her arms tight across her chest, as if trying to protect herself from an evil monster.

Seeing the fury in Carol's face made Billy automatically step back and raise his hands in apology. "You've got it all wrong. I really care about you. I'm not moving on. I'm only saying I need more time. I want—"

"After our wonderful weekend, I thought we had something special. I was sure you'd agree to meet my mother to show you're serious about us. But no, I was wrong. That was too much to expect of you. You like using women and then moving on to somebody new. I hate you!" she shouted, not caring if anybody heard.

Before he had a chance to reply, she abruptly turned and walked away. She made an effort to hold her head high. She wasn't much of a drinker but badly needed one now. She brushed away her tears and headed for the bar. *I'll show you, Bastard Billy. I'll treat you like you've treated me. I'll see how you like being thrown on the trash heap."*

When the bartender came over, Carol said in a sharp voice, "Double shot of tequila. Extra Añejo."

The bartender gave Carol a look because that stuff cost seven dollars a shot. But when he saw the fierce look on her face, he asked no questions. He put a double shot glass on the bar and filled it to the brim with the expensive gold liquid.

With trembling hand, Carol raised the shot glass to her lips and emptied the glass in two big gulps. The golden liquor went down smoothly and gave her a warm feeling. As she put down the shot glass she happened to see her face in the big mirror on the back wall. She didn't like what she saw. Her face was drawn, and her eyes were narrow and filled with hate. She realized booze wasn't the answer, and besides, she wasn't much of a drinker. *Now's not the time to get drunk. Now's the time to get even and give Bastard Billy a taste of his own medicine.*

She threw some money on the bar and began walking back to the dance floor, planning her next step.

While Billy and Carol were having a heated exchange, Marge had come to the bar and given Hank, the bartender, her order: three strawberry margaritas and three mugs of locally brewed beer. While she waited for Hank to fill her order, she happened to glance up and see Carol standing alone at the end of the bar, holding an empty shot glass. Marge thought, *That's not like Carol. She never drinks the hard stuff. Maybe they had a big fight. I hate to take advantage of somebody's back luck, but maybe this will be my chance to dance with Bad Billy.*

"Don't say anything," Hank said as he filled Marge's drink order. "From that goo-goo, gaga look in your eyes and that dumb smile on your face, I know you're thinking about Bad Billy. *Please Bad Billy, dance with me. Oh, please Bad Billy, take me in your arms. Hold me. Kiss me till I'm numb,*"

Hank said. He was smirking at his rather good imitation of Marge's piteous, pleading voice.

"You don't have enough brains to know what I'm thinking, and you're the biggest jerk I know, and I know a lot of them," Marge said, furious at hearing Hank's jeering words and mocking tone.

"Let me tell you about Bad Billy," Hank said. "Some think he's part Mexican, because he's swarthy looking with slick black hair. Some think he's part American Indian, because he's got such creepy cheekbones and scary eyes. But here's the truth. Bad Billy is just some brownish colored, illegal alien who snuck across the border, rides a twenty-thousand-dollar Harley, and dances like he's got a pole up his ass. Besides that, nobody likes him."

"Yeah, and if you had Billy's muscular, trim body, rugged, handsome face, great cheek bones, and sexy dark eyes, you'd be king of the mountain and not some second-rate, dumb-ass bartender pouring drinks to a bunch of drunks in a fake cowboy saloon," Marge shot back with a triumphant look on her face, proud of how she had put down poor Hank.

Hank hated Bad Billy more than anybody or anything. Hank had the misfortune of being secretly in love with Marge, who paid him no mind, made fun of him, and put him down to boot. Hank was sick and tired of hearing Marge brag about Bad Billy's looks. His dancing and romancing skills. He wished Marge would give him just a little understanding and one ounce of encouragement.

"I'll tell you another thing," Hank said, now letting his anger run wild. "How do you suppose he got the nickname *Bad* Billy?" Was it because he's a nice guy? Helps old ladies cross the street? Volunteers for the Salvation Army? Not on your life. He's a shit-kicking, no good, brainless biker, who sells dirty drugs. How any woman could fall for such a jerk is way beyond stupid. He's a total asshole, and don't you forget it," Hank finished, proud of his total destruction of Bad Billy.

"Your description of that jerk is totally accurate, and I couldn't agree with you more," said a voice that Hank knew too well.

Hank glanced to his right and was horrified to see Bad Billy standing there and smiling—actually smiling—at him. Hank's face turned as pale as a dead person, and fear froze his hand on the open tap. Beer was pouring out, overflowing the mug, running over the bar and drenching Hank's fine, $300 cowboy boots, which were his pride and joy.

Hank had been so intent on convincing Marge that Bad Billy was the biggest, ugliest jerk in the world, he hadn't noticed Bad Billy standing off to the side, waiting to order a beer.

"Hi yah, Bad Billy. Uh, what'll you have? Just talking about you.

Nothing serious. Just putting Marge on. She can't take a joke. You know how women are. Always making up stuff and hoping for the impossible," Hank blabbered.

"You better turn off that tap before you're knee deep in beer. I'll be back in a few minutes, so you'll have time to clean up this mess and pour me mug of Amber Lager," Billy said.

Then Billy nodded at Hank, smiled at Marge, and walked off to use the men's room.

Chapter 26

— — —

His real name was Jack Johnson, but he hated that wimpy name and always used his nickname, Slash. He was in the Red Bull's men's room, standing at a urinal, ranting about women being devils. In the neighboring urinal stood Cecil, who had come in right before Slash. Cecil hated listening to Slash's rude and despicable comments about women.

"After a few drinks, women let their hair down and get flirty. But at the end of the night, when it's time to put out, they say goodnight and leave you holding your dick. If it wasn't for what's between their legs, I'd never talk to any of those she-devils. But there is one woman worth talking to. Do ya know the one?" Slash asked, giving Cecil a raunchy grin.

Cecil said nothing because he was raised in a God-fearing, Christian home where people did bathroom things in private and certainly never talked while doing them. He wanted to zip up and walk away but had to stay put. When Slash was talking to you, it wasn't smart to walk away.

"Her name's Carol, and she's supposed to be Bad Billy's woman. But that doesn't scare me, because I'm tougher, smarter, and very handy with a knife. I'm going to persuade Bad Billy's woman to leave with me and let the good times roll. What do yah think?" Slash asked, turning to look at Cecil and make sure he was listening.

Cecil reluctantly nodded his head but said nothing. He thought Slash was pure evil. And having to listen to his crude comment made him so tense he couldn't pee a single drop. All he could do was stand there, hold his thing, and wait for Slash to finish. When Slash finally finished, Cecil pretended he had peed and followed him to the sink. Cecil was too upset to do anything more. He'd come back later so he could pee in private.

"I've got a plan," Slash said as he finished washing his hands.

Cecil had heard rumors about how Slash operated. He'd wait till the dancing ended, pick out the drunkest woman, and sweet-talk her into going for a ride. There were rumors about Slash getting rough, but women were too afraid to accuse Slash of that.

"I'm gonna tell her how great she looks and ask her to dance. Between dances I'll ask questions about her work, and if she likes pizza, and what movies she's seen. I'll be so nice and polite, she'll trust me and agree to taking a ride around Lake Jennings," Slash said, nodding at his sure-fire plan.

Cecil said nothing but busily lathered his hands with enough foamy soap for five people. Then he turned on the water and vigorously started washing, being careful to avoid making eye contact or offering Slash any verbal encouragement.

"And then," Slash said, looking into the mirror and leering from ear to ear, "when the truck stops, it'll be wham, bam, thank you ma'am."

Cecil was washing his hands and thinking Slash was an evil monster.

"And here's the best part," Slash said as he looked in the mirror and adjusted his cowboy hat. "Carol might get angry at first, but then she'll beg me to do it again and again, 'cause the one thing I really know how to do is please women, since I have all the equipment to do a very fine job."

Cecil knew he had to say something, so he muttered something unintelligible, which Slash took for approval. After Slash left, Cecil thought, *I hope God strikes him dead and sends him straight to hell.*

As a good Christian, Cecil rarely wished anyone ill tidings, but he wanted Slash to be punished severely for his terrible sins. Cecil dried his hands and grabbed another towel to open the door. Cecil knew Slash made fun of him for being such a religious person, but he didn't care. God had given him the talent to be a great line dancer and his instructional video on YouTube got millions of hits. He always made an effort to dance next to Slash, who was an okay waltzer or two-stepper but line-danced like a three-legged mule.

Shortly after Slash and Cecil had left the restroom, one of the stall doors opened and a man came out. He walked to the sink, washed his hands, and looked into the mirror. He adjusted the white feather in his black cowboy hat, turned, and walked out the door. His jaw was set, and his eyes were narrowed and black as coal. He had overheard Slash's plan for Carol.

While Slash had been talking to Cecil in the men's room, Carol had walked over to the edge of the dance floor and was waiting to dance. She'd planned to dance with someone attractive and make Billy jealous. *Two can play the game,* she thought. *See how he likes being rejected.*

Carol was glancing around, looking for an attractive dancing partner. Suddenly, standing before her was a good-looking man: six foot two, muscular, perfectly tanned, with longish, blonde hair, brilliant, blue eyes, and a sensational smile.

"Man oh man, you look so good I could eat you, leather boots, hat, and all," Slash said. Then he laughed because he thought he had said something funny. He looked Carol up and down a few times, trying to see if she was wearing a bra.

"My name's Slash. What's yours?" he asked, giving her a big, friendly smile and showing off his blue eyes, which he knew women loved.

"Carol," she said, trying not to stare at his blue eyes. She had heard stories about Slash and usually avoided him like the plague, even though many women thought he was the sexiest stud for miles around. She had always rejected him when Slash had asked her to dance, but the double shot of tequila and her hatred of Bastard Billy were giving her second thoughts. *If I dance with Slash, it will make Bastard Billy really jealous, and that's what he deserves.*

Carol nodded and headed for the dance floor with Slash right behind. The band was playing a country waltz, and she loved waltzing best of all the dances. Slash was a good waltzer and smoothly led Carol around the floor. She was surprised Slash made no attempt to bring her close and rub her body, which many men tried to do. They glided around the dance floor, turning and whirling like professional ice skaters. Several times she noticed Bastard Billy dancing on the opposite side of the floor. She made a point to look into Slash's blue eyes to make Billy even more jealous.

When the waltz ended, Slash said, "Jesus, Carol, you're the best damn looker and dancer in the whole world. Would you like to dance some more?"

They danced some more, and all the time Slash was the perfect gentleman, continually giving her compliments and never once bringing her in close to feel her body. All the dancing increased her heart rate and made the tequila run through her brain. She felt a little woozy and wished she hadn't drunk a double shot. She was in no condition to drive and thought about letting let Slash take her home. *Leaving with Slash would really send a message and make Bastard Billy's eyes pop out of his head.*

Slash had watched every movement of Carol's sexy body. *I've got to get her in my truck*, he thought, and a horrible grin spread across his face.

"I'm getting a little tired, and maybe I've had a little too much to drink," Carol said, knowing Slash would eagerly volunteer to drive her home.

"You do look a little tired," Slash said. "Perhaps I could drive you home, especially if you're feeling the booze."

"I think I better accept your offer. I don't think I'm in any condition to drive. I'll ask the doorman to watch my car," Carol said.

"Okay, let's go," Slash said, holding out his arm for Carol.

Carol put her arm around his, and they started walking toward the exit. Just before they went through the swinging doors, she deliberately turned and looked back. At the edge of the dance floor stood Bastard Billy. For an instant their eyes met, and then he quickly turned away.

You got what you deserved, she thought. She was both angry and sad over how the evening ended. She loved Billy, but he had treated her badly, and she was fighting back her tears.

Seeing Carol leave with Slash made Billy's blood boil and his fists clench as if readying for a fight. *I can't believe she's leaving with Slash. Well if that's what she wants, so be it.*

Slash led Carol to his big, red, four-wheel-drive pickup truck. It had a row of six halogen lights on top of the extra large cab, double chrome shock absorbers that raised the truck several feet off the ground, and enormous, ribbed tires with the name *Devil Truck* stenciled in raised, white letters along the sides of the tires. Slash was very proud of his specially outfitted truck, which also had a small refrigerator filled with cans of beer behind the front seat.

"Here we are," Slash said, using the key fob to unlock the passenger-side door. "Just put one foot on the chrome rail and step right in."

Carol was having second thoughts about getting into Slash's truck because she had heard rumors about his conquests. But he had been such a perfect gentleman, and besides, she had a can of pepper spray in her purse. She put one foot on the chrome rail and stepped up into the cab. Closing her door, Slash walked around to the driver's door and got inside.

He started the big, 5.7 liter, 390 horsepower, Hemi V-8 and let it rumble. Reaching behind the seat he took two large cans of beer from the fridge. He opened both and handed one to Carol.

"Have a beer. I'm sure you're hot from dancing, and a cold beer is just the thing for cooling off," Slash said.

Carol *was* hot, and a cold beer *did* sound good. *Just a couple sips,* she thought. "You probably don't know where I live," she said. "Just turn left when you leave the parking lot."

"Oh, that's okay. It's such a beautiful night, I thought you might enjoy a short drive around Lake Jennings. It's only a few miles down the road, off Highway sixty seven. I'm sure you'll love it," Slash said, thinking of all the things he'd do to Carol. He felt himself getting hard.

"I'd rather just go home," Carol said.

"The lake is really close, and it's a beautiful, restful spot. We'll just drive around, drink some cold beer and listen to some music. Then I'll drive you home," Slash said.

"Alright," Carol said, stifling stifled a yawn. *Driving around the lake does sound relaxing, and it might help me stop thinking about Bastard Billy.*

She took a few sips of beer, which tasted cold and refreshing. Then she put the can of beer in the cup holder and casually reached into her purse. She wanted to make doubly sure the pepper spray was within easy reach. Even though Slash had been a gentleman on the dance floor, she wasn't taking any chances. She'd use the spray at the slightest provocation.

CHAPTER 27

Slash turned right as he drove out of the parking lot, and he headed down Highway 67 to the Lake Jennings Regional Park. He got off on Mapleview Street and drove a short distance to the lake's concession area. At this time of night the concession area was closed and the gate across the road was locked. Slash stopped the truck, got out, and walked over to the padlocked gate. From his key ring he found the one he had stolen long ago and opened the gate. He pushed the gate open, got back into his truck, and drove through with his headlights off because he knew this road very well and there was a full moon to light his way. He didn't bother to close the gate, because at this time of the night, nobody would try to enter the park.

He drove about a mile around the lake until he reached Siesta Cove, which he called his sex spot. He backed his truck under an enormous Canary Island Date Palm tree, whose low hanging, twenty-foot-long fronds practically hid the truck. The whole area around the lake was completely deserted, so no one would interfere with what he had planned.

Carol had taken a sip of beer and was enjoying the view through the truck's open window. The lake was bathed in moonlight and looked as pretty and peaceful as if she looking at beautiful painting.

Suddenly, in one quick motion, Slash grabbed and held both her arms and while using one of his muscular legs to pin down her feet. His attack was so quick and unexpected she didn't have time to grab her pepper spray. Her adrenal gland kicked in, and she struggled and bucked like a wild bronco, but Slash's brute force held her tight, like a fly trapped in a spider's web. She screamed in panic, and tears of fear rolled her checks.

"I like the screaming. It makes me hard. But there's no one within miles to hear you," Slash said, leaning very close to her ear.

She felt his hot breath on the side of her face and kept screaming, but all it did was make Slash breathe faster and get more excited.

"Where's Bad Billy when you really need him?" Slash asked. He laughed close by her ear, sounding like the devil himself.

"Stop it! Stop it!" Carol shouted.

"No! No!" Slash answered. "I've only just begun. I've got big plans for your lovely body."

Then he raised both her arms over her head, tied them together, and held them tight with a rope he had taped to the back of her seat. This left Carol sitting in a vulnerable position with her blouse pulled tight and showing off her breasts. Slash had done this trick many times with other women, and the whole maneuver took only seconds.

"No use listening for Bad Billy to come to your rescue, 'cause we could hear the loud roar of his motorcycle a mile way. It's just you and me, honey pie, and I've got great plans for us," Slash said.

Carol screamed again and again, but that only excited Slash. He licked her neck and ran his hand over her breasts. "I can't wait to rip off your blouse."

Then he opened the glove box and took out two ropes. In turn he tied each of her legs to the opposite sides of her seat, leaving her even more vulnerable to his future advances. Then he reclined her seat until she was almost lying flat.

"The best is yet to come," Slash said, giving her his best lecherous smile.

Carol's heart was banging against her chest, and she was breathing in rapid gulps, but there was no way out of this nightmare. She was disgusted with what she had done. She had planned to use Slash to get back at Bad Billy, and instead Slash had planned to use her for his pleasure. She had been so intent on making Billy jealous she had disregarded all the rumors about Slash abusing women. Slash had played the perfect gentleman to gain her trust and persuade her to leave with him. She had foolishly trusted him and let herself fall headlong into Slash's trap.

"So, what'll we do next?" Slash asked. "I know what. I'll give you two choices, and you can pick one. Doesn't that sound fair?"

"Please Slash, just let me go. I won't tell anyone. Please," Carol begged. Her eyes were filled with tears.

But Slash continued as if he hadn't heard her.

"Here's your two choices. I can cut off you blouse and play with your sexy titties, or I can cut off you slacks and play with your snatch. Gotta get you ready for the big event."

"You're a sick fuck!" Carol shouted, unable to take any more. She wasn't going to make a choice. She'd wait for her chance to knee him in the balls, or bite his cock, or spit in his face if he tried to kiss her.

"My, my, what bad words for a fine girl like you. I guess I'll have to make the choice for you. I'll flip a coin. Heads its titties, and tails it's snatch.

I'm pretty good at this game, 'cause I've had a lot of practice," Slash said as he got out a quarter, tossed it in the air, and caught it.

"Well, guess what. It's heads, so I win," Slash said. He laughed, thinking he had said something funny.

He reached into the opened glove box and brought out a six-inch switchblade. He clicked it open and moved the shiny blade back and forth in front of Carol's eyes, like a cobra moving it's raised head from side to side before striking.

Carol wasn't going to scream, because she knew it only excited him. Instead, she made her face go blank, showing no emotion, and made her body relax, going limp like a rag doll.

Slash was disappointed by her lack of emotion, because he liked his women to scream and shout and fight back. That's what made him stay hard.

"Maybe I'll first cut your beautiful face a little, first the right cheek and then the left. Or maybe I'll cut one of your titties. How'd you like that?" Slash said.

He was getting so excited that a line of drool came down the side of his mouth. He gave his evil smile, bent down, licked her neck, and whispered in her ear.

"I've been waiting a long time to see your cute titties."

Slash raised the switchblade to begin cutting Carol's blouse. Suddenly the driver's door was pulled open. A hand reached in, grabbed Slash's hair, and pulled his head back. At almost the same time, another hand reached over and grabbed his arm holding the knife.

"What the fuck!" Slash yelled as he was dragged out of the truck and tossed on the ground.

Carol heard a lot of yelling and struggling, and then it stopped, and the night was quiet. Carol tensed, not knowing what would happen next, hoping she would not see Slash's face grinning at her.

Then her door was opened, and she saw Billy's face. She cried with relief. "Oh thank you, thank you," she kept repeating.

Billy cut her ropes, helped her out of the truck, and held her tightly in his strong arms.

"You're safe now. Don't cry. Slash can't hurt you anymore," Billy said.

"Oh my God. I was so scared. I thought he was going to cut and rape me," Carol said. Big tears came down her cheeks.

"It's okay. You're safe," Billy repeated. "Did he hurt you?"

"No, I'm alright. I was such a fool. I was so angry. I wanted to hurt you, make you jealous by leaving with him. Will you ever forgive me?"

"Only if you forgive me for being a fool about your mother. I do want to meet her, and sooner the better," he said as he bent down to kiss her.

They kissed a very long time, neither one wanting to stop. At last he pulled back and said, "I don't know how I could have been so dumb. Loving you is the best thing that's ever happened to me."

"And I'm so sorry for calling you *Bastard* Billy. From now on, you're *Beautiful* Billy."

They kissed again, first sweetly, then passionately, as loving energy flowed between them like a mighty river.

Then Carol pulled back so she could see his face and gaze into his loving eyes. "How did you know to follow me, and why didn't I hear your motorcycle?" she asked.

"When I saw you leave with Slash, I knew it was a big mistake, because he's a psycho. I couldn't follow you on my noisy motorcycle, so I borrowed the doorman's Prius, which runs on batteries and is totally quiet. I followed Slash's pickup but had to stay way back because there was almost no traffic. I didn't want him to think I was following him. When I got to Lake Jennings, I saw the concession gate open and drove through. I didn't see his headlights or hear his truck, so I figured I'd better get out and walk. Then I saw the front of his truck under the tree, and you know the rest."

There was more hugging and tender kissing.

It suddenly occurred to Carol she hadn't heard a peep from Slash.

"What happened to him?" she asked.

"Come along, and I'll show you."

They walked to the front of the truck, and Carol almost shouted for joy. Slash was lying on his stomach, gagged with his own shirt, his hands and feet bound with zip ties so he couldn't move.

She wanted to kick him in the balls, but his feet were bound together. Instead, she kicked him twice in the ribs, grabbed his hair, and pushed his face into the dirt.

"I'm giving you two choices," she said. "I'll flip a coin, and heads means I use your switch-blade to cut off your cock, and tails means I cut off your balls."

Slash was lying on his stomach and turned his head just enough to see Carol pretending to flip a coin.

"Sorry, Slash, it's heads. Say goodbye to your cock."

Billy handed Slash's knife to Carol, who bent over and started cutting. Billy held Slash down as he struggled and tried to holler, but the gag muffled his sounds.

"How you doing, Slash? Like getting some of your own medicine? Like being tied up and cut?" Carol asked.

When she finished, she held up what she had cut off and showed it to Billy.

"A little ragged along the edges but not a bad job," Billy said.

"I know it's a little ragged, but it's the best I could do with all his struggling," she said.

Then Carol gave Slash one last kick in his ribs and said, "Hope you don't bleed to death before help arrives."

She and Billy walked to the Prius, got in, and drove quietly around Lake Jennings. They turned east on Highway 67 and headed for the Red Bull.

"I'll return the Prius to the doorman. You can get your car, and I'll ride my Harley. I'm hoping you'll follow me to my A-Frame so we can spend the night together."

"That's a great idea," she said.

"I must say you certainly put the fear of God into Slash when you took his knife and began cutting. I really didn't think you would do it," Billy said.

"I couldn't resist," Carol said, "Not after what he did to me."

"It will be quite a spectacle when they find Slash tomorrow," Billy said.

"I tried really hard not to nick his ass when I cut away the butt part of his Levis. But my unconscious desires got in the way, and I think I nicked him a time or two. He won't do much sitting for the next few days, and I'd like to hear him explain what happened."

"I think you should take that ragged piece of Slash's Levis and hang it on the rearview mirror of your car. It'll remind you to be ready for any adversity, just like the snake rattle I have in my truck."

"No way. I never want to be reminded of anything to do with Slash. And to make sure he never seeks revenge, I used my iPhone to take a picture of his bare ass mooning the moon. I also took a photo of his face when he turned his head after I gave him that last kick. If he tries to get back on me, I'll threaten to put the picture of his face and his bare ass on the web for the whole world to see. That would be so embarrassing he could never live it down," Carol said.

"When I was tying Slash to the bumper, I warned him stay away from the Red Bull. I also said if I ever heard about his giving any woman a bad time, I would break every bone in his body," Billy said. From the tone in his voice, Carol knew he meant every word.

"I thought about reporting him to the police for what he tried to do. But I had been dumb enough to drink and voluntarily go for a ride in his truck. I'm sure a trial would come down to he-said and she-said kind of testimony and I'm not sure he'd be convicted of anything. And then I nicked his butt pretty good so I might be accused of causing him bodily harm. I think your warning of breaking every bone in his body and my threat of putting his bare butt on the web will keep him away from the Red Bull Saloon or taking advantage of women. I also have to worry about career. Some of my male colleagues at the Institute don't respect me now and would make my life miserable if any of this stupid affair became public," Carol said. "My only regret is I didn't kick him in the balls."

"It's not too late for that. We can go back. I'll untie him and spread his legs so you can kick him where it really hurts."

"Right now I want to forget about Slash and think about us. I want to personally thank you for not only rescuing me but also for agreeing to meet my mother.

"Can you be a bit more specific about how you'll thank me?" Billy asked.

Carol snuggled closer and whispered the specifics in his ear.

"Really! You want to do that?" Billy said in mock horror. They both laughed.

"I love you," she whispered in his ear.

"I love you," he whispered in her ear.

Less than an hour later, as a dozen beeswax candles glowed in Billy's bedroom, they made love until they were exhausted. So much had happened that neither was ready to sleep. Instead, they put on big, fluffy bathrobes and cuddled on the balcony. The moon shimmed on the lake and the soft night breeze mixed hints of pine and sage with the candles' sweet honey perfume.

CHAPTER 28

▬ ▬ ▬

Pinetree, Minnesota was a small farming community of 534 friendly and hard-working folks, who rose when the sun came up, ate supper before it set, and were asleep long before the 10 o'clock news. The most popular place in Pinetree was Betty's Beer & Eats. It was filled with locals needing social contact, farmers done with chores, and a few tourists headed north to see a tiny stream that was the beginning of the Mississippi River.

Tonight the menu at Betty's featured Polish sausage and sauerkraut sprinkled with brown sugar, blood-red head-cheese, new baby potatoes in cream sauce, locally caught sunfish fried in butter and fresh-picked sweet corn, and hot strawberry-rhubarb upside down cake topped with homemade vanilla ice cream.

The back half of Betty's was filled with happy eaters, many overweight and proud of it. The front half was crowded with patrons drinking real beer, not that Lite crap, and ordering shots of Jim Beam on the side. The drinkers had arranged their chairs to look out the bar's extra-wide picture window. They gossiped about people coming and going on Main Street, which was all of six blocks long, with a Catholic church on one end and a Lutheran church on the other. After the third or fourth round of drinks, they tired of gossiping and got into fierce arguments like whether walleyes were the best tasting fish, are northern pike were the trickiest to catch, or if muskies bit best on live bait.

"Hey, look at that," Dick shouted as a strange car slowly drove by the bar's extra-wide picture window. Dick was one of the retired farmers who had moved to the "big city" of Pinetree but wasn't all that happy with his new life. He had auctioned off everything but his favorite tractor, which now sat in his back yard, covered with an old canvas and slowly rusting away. People worried about Dick, because after a night of drinking he would go home, uncover his tractor, and sit in the seat until the mosquitoes got too bad.

"I don't see anything," said Widow Gerty, whose hair was dyed jet black to show she was available and looking for husband number three, her lucky number. She hadn't seen anything because the strange car had driven farther down Main Street,.

"There it's again," Dick said, pointing at the unusual car parking right in front of the extra-wide picture window.

"It look's like a baby whale with four tires," said Herman, who regularly watched nature channels. He was able to make the strange, low whale sounds, which he sometimes did in church during a dull sermon.

The unusual car happened to be a long, black, beautifully rounded, and perfectly restored 1950 step-down Hudson. And from the side, it did resemble a baby whale on wheels.

"It looks like a car a bishop or the pope might drive!" yelled Clem, who was hard of hearing and didn't know he was shouting.

"The pope doesn't drive his own car," said Carolyn, who prided herself on knowing such things.

"Somebody's getting out," Dick said. Standing up, he pulled his pants over his fat stomach, and waddled closer to the window.

As Dick watched, a tall man in a black suit with a religious collar got out of the car and walked toward the bar. Dick noticed he was wearing a black patch over his left eye. As the man reached the middle of the picture window, he stopped, nodded, and smiled at the patrons looking out. Dick's mouth opened wide, not believing what he was seeing. On the man's black eye patch was a shiny silver cross.

"There's a silver cross on his eye patch," Dick said in a loud whisper, afraid he might be seeing a ghost.

"Oh my God, it's him!" Gerty shrieked, absolutely sure she was looking at the Grim Reaper, who was using a disguise and coming for her.

"Now I've seen everything," Tony said. Ironically, he had in fact seen very little, having never ventured more than fifty miles from Pinetree.

"God Almighty, looks like he's coming in," said Abner, whose poorly-fitted false teeth clicked so badly no one was quite sure what he said.

The tall man wearing a black eye patch adorned with a silver cross opened the door and walked into Betty's Bar & Eats. Frightened beyond their wits, all the Catholics made the sign of the cross while all the Protestants reached for their glasses and drank deeply.

For the first time in as long as anyone could remember, the bar was eerily quiet, except for Abner nervously clicking his poorly-fitted false teeth like a cricket looking for a mate.

Then the stranger addressed the crowd.

"Hello, my name is Father Dreadforth. Some of you may have heard my voice on the radio. I have a late night religious program that is very popular in these parts. Perhaps I can buy you all a drink," he said, knowing these folks appreciated a free drink almost as much as a getting a good place in heaven.

With the offer of a free drink ringing in their ears, all the patrons started talking; it sounded like a flock of chickens about to be fed.

"I heard you on the radio but never saw you in person."

"I like your preaching."

"Thanks for the free drinks."

"I once sent you five dollars."

"Make mine a double shot of the good stuff."

"Do you think the rapture is coming soon?"

And so forth and so on until the patrons were busy drinking and trying not to stare at the silver cross on Father Dreadforth's black eye patch.

"I was wondering if any of you could tell me where Jim and Harry live? They are good friends of mine, and I would like to stop by and see how they are doing," Father Dreadforth said.

"Oh sure," said Betty, the owner and sometime bartender. She was built like a 200-pound, round bale of hay with arms and legs, and she knew where every one of the town's 534 people lived.

"I know a shortcut," said Dick, hoping his directions would earn him another free drink.

Father Dreadforth was a good judge of people and turned to Betty for directions.

"Just drive down to the end of town, turn right at the Catholic church, look for the first dirt road, turn left, and it's the second house on the block. Can't miss it, because it's the one that badly needs painting," Betty said.

"Needs more than paint," Dick said, angry with Betty for always taking over.

"Well, thanks very much for the directions. Hope you all have a pleasant evening, and I encourage you to tune into my religious program, eight hundred on the AM radio dial. And do not forget, the good Lord said that gentleness, self-control, and generosity—especially making donations—are the keys to heaven. Galatians, five twenty-three."

That was not exactly what Galatians said, but no matter, Father Dreadforth often edited scriptural sayings to fit his needs. He had learned people were impressed and listened more closely when hearing someone quote line and verse, true or not.

Before leaving, Father Dreadforth handed Betty two folded twenty-dollar bills that quickly disappeared into one of her large, calloused hands.

"This is for the drinks, and keep whatever is left for your tip," Father Dreadforth said.

The regulars strained to see how much money Father Dreadforth had passed to Betty, hoping there might be enough for another round of free drinks.

"Thank you very much. You're very generous," Betty said. She smiled for the first time that day. No one in this cheap town ever tipped, which was considered throwing away hard-earned money for no good reason.

As Father Dreadforth left the bar, got into his car, and drove away, Gerty's eyes filled with tears of joy. She was so thankful he hadn't been the Grim Reaper. Now she could continue her search for a third husband.

* * * *

"I have never been to Jim and Harry's home in Pinetree," Father Dreadforth said to Bart, now known as Brother Paul. "But tonight I need a great favor and thought it best if I asked them face to face, so they would be unlikely to refuse."

Father Dreadforth and Brother Paul were engaged in what was best described as a "pseudo-religious" activity, which is what had brought them into Pinetree, about ten miles east of the St. Francis Monastery. Abbot Aloysius allowed Brother Paul to periodically leave the Monastery and explore the surrounding areas, provided he was under Father Dreadforth's supervision.

Father Dreadforth neither lived in a monastery nor had taken the vow of poverty. He was the respected pastor of St. Mary's Church in St. Cloud, which provided a modest stipend but not enough to meet his expensive tastes. He had spent a small fortune restoring the 1950 step-down Hudson, chosen because it looked like the car a bishop or the pope would own and clearly signaled the owner was someone important. He bought fine, European, tailored suits because they added to his physical presence, gambled in sunny Las Vegas to escape Minnesota's freezing winters, and lived in an expensive, three-story house located on the banks of the Mississippi River. At this point in his life he could no more survive on his modest parish income than a pot-bellied pig could survive on eating two carrots a day.

It was quite by chance that Father Dreadforth met Brother Paul in the monastery's library. Abbot Aloysius had charged Brother Paul with organizing and upgrading the monastery's aging web site, which along with selling dark, many-grained, homemade bread, also sold copies of gloriously illustrated medieval manuscripts. Back in the Middle Ages, monks had labored to add imaginative beasts, colorful birds, religious symbols, and mystical signs to religious texts. The St. Francis Monastery had received a grant to visit European Monasteries and digitize these priceless medieval manuscripts to both preserve them and make them available to the general public.

For some time, Father Dreadforth had been purchasing copies of these manuscripts from the monastery's web site. He would bless manuscripts and give one to each person who sent in a donation of twenty-five dollars. For a donation of fifty dollars, he would send a blessed manuscript mounted in a special, gold frame—painted gold, not real gold. Father Dreadforth's philosophy of giving something to get something increased his donations by almost fifty percent. Because of the ever-increasing number of manuscripts Father Dreadforth was purchasing, he had asked Brother Paul for a discount. Brother Paul, with the abbot's agreement, gave Father Dreadforth a twenty percent discount, and they soon became good friends.

But unfortunately, as more money came in, more money went out, and Father Dreadforth's debts edged forever upward. He earnestly prayed for financial help, and one night his prayers were answered. God had come to him in a dream and given him a wonderful idea.

"We are almost there," Father Dreadforth said as he turned onto the dirt road.

"I'm curious. How did you happen to meet Jim and Harry?" Brother Paul asked.

"On my radio program, I tell listeners to write in and tell me about their problems, and I will pray for their deliverance. I received this sad letter from Jim and Harry about their parents working in a silo and dying after breathing the deadly, odorless gas produced by fermenting silage. Jim described how they had sold the farm but ended up with little money because they were much in debt. They had moved to town, rented a rundown house, and were doing menial tasks to barely get by. About the same time, God had just given me an idea for a special project, and I thought Jim and Harry would be the perfect ones to carry it out. I asked them to come to my house and told them what they needed to do and how much they would be paid. They were more than willing, and as I explained to you, the project has become very lucrative."

"That looks like their house," Brother Paul said as he pointed to a weather-beaten structure.

Father Dreadforth parked on the side of the road. Then they both got out and walked to the front door. As Father Dreadforth knocked on the door, the loud music was suddenly turned down. Opening the door, Harry said, "Hey, Father Dreadforth. Nice to see yah."

Father Dreadforth had become accustomed to seeing Harry's completely shaved head, which must have had sent shockwaves through conservative Pinetree. *Only old men were supposed to be bald, so what had dim-witted Harry been thinking!?* But Harry didn't care one bit. He had seen tough basketball players with shaved heads on TV, and he thought it was very cool. Now Harry was thinking about getting a tattoo.

"Come on in," Harry said. He gave them a big smile and shouted, "Hey Jim, look what the old cat dragged in."

Harry had no idea it was disrespectful to refer to a monk as something the old cat dragged in. But he had often heard his grandma say something like that, and what was good enough for granny was good enough for him.

Father Dreadforth had to chuckle. He knew Harry was big-hearted but lacked a few brain parts and hadn't meant to be rude.

"Hi Father," Jim said, coming from the back kitchen. "We're always happy to see you, but I'm surprised you took the trouble coming here."

"One of the reasons I came was to introduce my new partner, Brother Paul. He will be helping with distribution, advertising, and related tasks," Father Dreadforth said.

Jim and Harry nodded and smiled. Each shook hands with Brother Paul.

After some friendly chitchat, Father Dreadforth said, "The other reason I came was to ask for a big favor."

As Father Dreadforth described the favor, Harry's brow furled, and he shifted from foot to foot, as if standing on a hot plate.

"No problem," Jim said, "You've done so much for us, we'll gladly do any favor for you."

Harry reluctantly nodded, but if it had been up to him, he wouldn't have agreed. He didn't like going to the special project place at night, when bad things might happen.

As they were driving away, Brother Paul said, "Jim seemed happy to do the favor, but Harry looked most uncomfortable."

"Oh, that is Harry. He is afraid of the dark, but Jim will pull him through," Father Dreadforth said.

"Aren't you afraid Jim or Harry might accidentally talk or brag about what they're doing and all the money they're making?" Brother Paul asked.

"No need to worry. I put the fear of God into them. I made them promise on their immortal souls not to say a word. If people ask what they are doing, I told them to say they are growing organic tomatoes for the monastery, which as you know, is partly true," Father Dreadforth said, smiling.

The special project had grown very profitable and required almost all Father's Dreadforth's time. He knew he needed a partner, someone he could trust beyond a shadow of a doubt. That person turned out to be Brother Paul, whose job would be to develop a computer program to keep track of expenses and contacts, as well as process payments through PayPal. Brother Paul had agreed to become Father Dreadforth's partner only after being reassured that the project would be kept secret and that he could back out at any time.

Even so, Brother Paul had felt a little guilty about becoming Father Dreadforth's partner because no one at the monastery, not even the abbot, knew about the project. . He had promised Carol not to get involved in anything the least bit wicked as long as he was staying at the St. Francis Monastery. But he needed to earn money, both for his own needs as well as to send some to Anna, who still hadn't found a job and was hurting financially. He couldn't ask his mother for money because he had told her he was doing a college exchange program and taking classes at the Sorbonne University in Paris. And he couldn't keep asking Carol for money because he had his pride, and he wanted to show her he could take the initiative and solve his own problems. In any case, there was much money to be made, and if he weren't getting it, Father Dreadforth would find someone else. When he had questioned Father Dreadforth about the moral aspects of the project, Father had reassured him with a quote from scripture. "Work willingly at whatever you do, as though you were working for the Lord. Colossians, three twenty-four." And that forever ended any discussion of moral issues.

As they were driving back to the St. Francis Monastery, Brother Paul asked, "What time do you think Jim and Harry will finish their work?"

"I told them to meet me in St. Cloud around nine tonight," Father Dreadforth said. Then he added in a worrisome tone, "If all goes according to plan."

CHAPTER 29

— — —

"This isn't a favor. It's downright suicide. It's fun coming here in the daytime to pick tomatoes but not when it's dark. How many times did granny warn us about devils hiding in these woods and coming out at night?" asked Harry, who believed granny's stories about devils as surely as he believed in God.

"I don't want to hear anything about devils," Jim said as he tightly held the shaking steering wheel of the battered 1971 Dodge Power Wagon, which his grandfather had left him. He had left the paved road that went to the monastery and turned onto a narrow, bumpy, seldom used, dirt track. This track snaked through some of the rarely visited 3000 acres of woods and wetlands surrounding the St. Francis Monastery's. The truck rattled, rumbled, and groaned as its huge, knobby, all-terrain tires and extra-low gear helped it plow through muddy potholes and crush thick, overgrown brush.

"Granny said when lightening strikes trees, they die. When they turn black, they are favorite hiding places for black devils. That makes the devils hard to see, except for their red, beady eyes. If dummies like us to get too close, a devil will jump out from behind the black tree, crawl inside your body, and grab your soul. Then it's the pits," Harry said, nervously rubbing his newly shaved head.

The deeper they drove in the forest, the scarier it got, as moonlight filtering through the tall trees created eerie shadows. And even worse, every time the old truck hit a bump, the headlights bobbed and made the trees seem to jump, like giant monsters doing some weird dance. Harry was getting that creepy feeling he got when watching a scary movie, knowing something really bad was about to happen.

"We have to do this, because Father got a rush order and needed us to get some stuff and deliver it to the usual place no later than nine tonight," Jim said.

Unlike Harry, Jim didn't much believe devils lived in the forest. But he usually didn't drive into the monastery's forest at night because it meant listening to Harry complaining and repeating granny's stories about devils waiting to get jump inside and steal their souls.

The more nervous Harry got, the more he rubbed his shaved head and the redder it got. "This makes no sense. If I had brains, I'd stayed home so a devil won't get me. And this junk truck is shaking all my bones lose."

Jim had enough of Harry's complaining and hit the big button in the middle of the steering wheel. There was a monstrous blast from the air horn grandpa had mounted on the roof to greet the big eighteen wheelers going by.

"Say anything bad about this truck or another word about devils, and I'll blast you again," Jim said, knowing Harry hated loud noises.

But the air horn blast just made Harry mad, and he wasn't going sit quiet like some dummy. "Even the pope believes in devils, and that's a fact," Harry said, and he nodded to himself, knowing nobody could doubt the pope.

Harry remembered seeing the pope on TV and was surprised the pope wore a tall hat like the cat in his favorite Dr. Seuss book, *Cat in the Hat*. But Harry didn't blame the pope for copying the cat's hat, because it was a great hat.

"I want you to shut up for the rest of this trip. Not another word about anything. Not about my truck, and especially not about devils," Jim yelled.

Jim felt a little guilty for yelling at Harry, who was younger and not all that bright, despite his big heart. When they were growing up, Jim had protected Harry from town bullies and gossips that made fun of Harry's ways of thinking and talking.

"Yeah, so that's it. Now you tell me to shut up, just like Sister Margaret did in Catholic grade school when I asked why I had to give my lunch money to baptize pagan babies in Africa," Harry said.

"Not another word about pagan babies. Just watch for the big, dead tree that marks our turn off," Jim said.

"I'm sure fat Sister Margaret spent my money on sugar donuts," Harry said. "But I got even. I lit a votive candle so she'd end up in hell."

Jim did his best to cope with Harry's outbursts about devils, popes, and pagan babies. He had been able to keep Harry from telling people about the candle he lit to punish Sister Margaret, but he hadn't been able to stop Harry from shaving his head. In Pinetree it was like walking around town in the nude. Vicious gossip spread like a wild fire through a dry forest.

"Did you see Harry's shaved head?" the town barber had complained. "He thinks he's too good for one of my haircuts."

"It's not your fault, I heard that Harry uses all kinds of drugs and that makes him do strange things."

"Not only takes them, he gives them to his dog, too!"

"He does?"

"He does. The poor dog don't always raise his leg when he pees, so he must be drugged."

Harry had been quiet for the last five minutes, but when the truck hit a huge pothole, his head hit the top of the truck, and he started talking as if a switch had been turned on. "I can hear granny's warnings plain as day about black trees turning into magnets that attract devils."

"NO MORE!" Jim shouted. "I don't want to hear another word about granny's devils. Just sit quietly and watch for the big oak tree with the broken branch that marks our turn off to the tomato patch."

"You do what you want, but I'm going to watch out for dead, black trees hiding devils with red eyes," Harry said in a very determined voice.

Jim decided to try a friendly approach. "If you don't say anymore about devils, I'll buy you a super duper iPad after Father Dreadforth pays us tonight."

The thought of getting an iPad really got Harry's attention because he wanted one more than anything, even a pony. He almost stuck his head out the window to make sure Jim didn't come close to a black tree and a devil got him before he had a chance to get an iPad. But looking for black trees in the dark forest was proving difficult and made the hair stand up on his arms.

"Don't pay any attention to black trees," Jim said, trying to be reassuring. "Black trees are just dead trees and not hiding places for devils."

But Harry was beginning to see black trees everywhere, and his nerves were starting to tingle and twitch. Even so, he might have remained silent, but hearing Jim say that word—*devils*—set him off.

"Granny said people from all over the world came to the monastery to be cured of devils. Monks waved crucifixes, sprinkled holy water, and even prayed in Latin to make the devils leave. Devils only speak Latin."

Jim grimaced and said in an exasperated voice, "I don't care what granny said, devils don't speak Latin."

"Ah hah," Harry said. "The only thing I learned in catechism class was that devils speak Latin, just like priests."

Jim threw up his hands in disgust, and the truck almost went into the ditch. "You didn't learn that in catechism class," he said.

But Harry was on a roll and wasn't going to be stopped by facts. "Granny said a devil shouts Latin curses, shrieks, and even squeals like a stuck pig when it leaves the person. And it's a known fact devils didn't go back to hell but hide in the forest and wait for their next victims."

Suddenly, Harry was shrieking, wailing, and shouting Latin words he had learned as an altar boy. Jim grimaced but couldn't take his hands off the steering wheel to cover his ears. After what seemed like hours, Harry wore himself out and stopped trying to imitate the sounds a devil might make. Harry had never heard the sounds a devil make sounds but was pretty sure his sounds were true to life.

Jim thought Harry might have shouted himself hoarse, but the silence lasted only minutes.

"And here's the best part," Harry said, smiling because he liked telling this part best of all. "Devils fly out of a person and leave gray smudges on the church's ceiling. And granny said no matter how hard monks try, they can't wash away the devil's evil smudges."

Jim knew it never paid to argue with Harry, but for the hundredth time, Harry had gone too far.

"The smudges on the ceiling of the old St. Francis church were not caused by devils! They were caused by water stains from a leaky roof!"

"Oh yeah," Harry said. "That might be what you and all the Lutherans and pagans say, but not granny. She said an old monk who never lied swore the smudgy marks on the church's ceiling were made by fleeing devils. And I saw the marks, and so did you. And why do you think the monks built a whole new church?"

Before Jim could answer, the headlights lit up a big oak tree with a broken branch.

"There's the tree," he said, making a sharp right turn. "We're almost there."

Harry had been energized by his devil sounds and had one last argument to make.

"And what about those teenagers who went to drink and party in the forest? They saw red devils' eyes of devils staring out from behind the black trees and barely escaped with their lives. They promised never to go back. Not for all the tea in China!"

Then something bad occurred to Harry, and he asked, "Do you think devils ever hide behind tomato plants?"

"Devils don't like tomatoes," was all Jim said.

Chapter 30

Jim drove out of the dense forest and entered an open meadow bordering a spring-fed lake used for irrigating the tomatoes and other vegetation if there wasn't enough rain. He stopped the truck near the tomato patch, where the headlights illuminated row after row of six-foot-high, carefully-staked Big Boy tomato plants. Jim had tried growing other kinds of tomato plants, such as Celebrity Hybrid, Better Boy, Hall of Fame, Big Girl, and even Tomato Sweet Tangerine—a golden tomato that his grandma always insulted by saying, "if it's not red, it's not a tomato." But the winner was always Big Boy, which was sweet, juicy, and big enough so one slice could cover an entire burger.

Nobody besides Jim and Harry visited this tomato patch because it was deep in the virgin forest and almost impossible to reach. The monks didn't have any reason to visit the tomato patch since almost every week during the growing season Jim and Harry would bring baskets of Big Boys to the Abbey's kitchen. The monks truly appreciated their donation and the flavor of homegrown tomatoes.

But if any visitors had come and looked closely at the plants, they would have noticed that every third or fourth plant was tall like a Big Boy tomato plant and green like a Big Boy tomato plant, but no tomatoes hung from its vine. Instead, these tomato-less plants were full of large buds, which if rubbed between one's fingers, would leave a sticky residue that gave off a sweet odor. Under Father Dreadforth's clever planning, Jim and Harry's tomato patch had actually become the perfect cover for growing their especially potent marijuana plants. These had been grown from seeds Father Dreadforth had obtained from a friend in Vancouver, home of some of the best marijuana in North America.

"There's no place like St. Christopher's place," Harry said and looked fondly at the big marijuana plants. He couldn't wait to smoke a little.

Harry had named the tomato-marijuana farm in honor of his favorite childhood saint, St. Christopher. He figured since St. Christopher had kept the marijuana farm safe, it proved he was a true saint—even though he had recently been told that the Pope had taken St. Christopher's name off the list of saints. Besides, he reasoned, what did the pope know about St. Christopher, who lived long before the pope was even born?

"I've got to take my hat off to Father for coming up with this idea," Jim said, remembering when Father Dreadforth had told them how people in California grew marijuana plants using the natural cover provided by state and national forests. "What better place to hide a marijuana farm then in a legitimate tomato patch in the middle of St. Francis Monastery's forest?"

"I think it was neat that Father Dreadforth blessed the entire lake so we could use holy water for the marijuana and tomato plants," Harry said.

"How about his thinking up the name BRM for our marijuana plants?" Jim asked.

"I keep forgetting what that stands for," Harry said.

"BRM stand for *Blessed, Religious Marijuana*. Father Dreadforth tells all his customers it's the only marijuana in the world grown with holy water, and thus it's guaranteed to give users a truly blessed and powerful high," Jim said.

They both laughed.

"I can swear to that," Harry said.

"Well, let's get to work," Jim said.

Jim would pick about forty large marijuana buds while Harry picked six cartons of Big Boy tomatoes. When they were done, they would treat themselves by smoking some of this fantastic grass and snacking on the chocolate-covered raisins, honey-roasted mixed nuts, malted milk balls, and gummy bears stashed under truck's front seat.

"Let's have a joint now," Harry said, which is what he always said when they arrived.

"Not until we're finished," replied a very determined Jim.

Jim and Harry put on their boots and turned on their special headbands with bright lights so they could see what they were doing. Normally they only came to the tomato-marijuana patch in the daytime, but Father Dreadforth said a good client had decided, on the spur of the moment, to throw a party on Saint George Lake, near St. Cloud, and he needed the marijuana later that very evening.

While Jim was gathering the marijuana buds, he was thinking once again about their ultimate fantasy. They would use the money to escape the freezing cold winters and nasty, gossiping busybodies in Pinetree. They would buy a little cottage on one of the good fishing, bass-filled lakes in central Florida, where they could fish every day and never have to wear scratchy wool underwear.

"I'm almost done," shouted Harry, even though he had only filled two of six cartons.

Jim knew that Harry wasn't even close to being done, but as always, Harry was anxious to get to the good part: smoking some BRM.

"Keep picking tomatoes so we have enough to cover the marijuana buds and sell a bunch to the big St. Cloud supermarket," Jim said.

The manager of the supermarket couldn't get enough of Jim and Harry's Big Boy tomatoes. He advertised them as "organically grown by local monks," and they usually sold out in one day.

Father Dreadforth had come up with the idea of transporting the marijuana at the bottom of the tomato bushels, and it had worked well. They had only been stopped once by Sergeant Tom, the part-time cop in Pinetree. He had recognized Jim's truck and stopped him for no good reason other than Tom believed people who didn't go regularly to church, like Jim and Harry, had to be up to no good. But Tom saw had seen nothing but tomatoes in the back of Jim's truck, so he would had let them go—but not before, after taking some Big Boys for his supper.

"OK, Harry, let's pack it in," Jim said as he started walking back to the truck. He could see Harry's light bobbing up and down as he ran back to the truck, carrying the last carton of tomatoes.

When Jim got back to the truck, he divided the forty or so marijuana buds into five separate piles and put each pile into a double zip-top bag to lock in its sweet smell. He put the marijuana bags into the bottoms of two bushel baskets and filled the tops with tomatoes. He tied down the two marijuana baskets at the front of the truck's bed and placed the rest of the cartons containing only tomatoes nearer the back. The newly-picked tomatoes gave off a fresh, flavorful odor that would mask any smell from the marijuana that might seep through the zip-lock bags. As he closed the tailgate he noticed its latch was getting pretty rusty, and he hoped it would last a few more trips before he had to replace it.

While Jim had been busy packing and securing the cartons of marijuana and tomatoes in the truck, Harry was gleefully rolling a large joint and shouting at Jim to finish loading the truck. "Hurry up before the sun comes up!" It was another of his grandma's favorite sayings. Actually, grandma had said, "Hurry up before the sun goes down," but Harry was not a slave to details.

At last, Jim got the bag of goodies from under his truck seat. Harry spread a tarp on the ground, and they sat, lit up a big joint of BMR, and began smoking.

"Did I tell you the sad story of the horny moose in Vermont?" Harry said, eating about one malted milk ball a second and trying to talk in between smoking, chewing, and swallowing.

"Oh please, not the one about someone video taping a horny moose humping a VW bug," Jim pleaded, having heard that story almost ever time Harry smoked.

"No, it's a horny *moose*, not a horny *mouse*." In his drug-altered state, Harry had misheard Jim's response. "Even I know the difference between a big, horny moose and a tiny, horny mouse."

Harry's marijuana-soaked brain conjured up the image of a tiny, horny mouse trying to screw a VW bug, and he laughed so hard tears ran down his checks.

After about an hour of smoking, snacking, and Harry singing a verse or two of his favorite songs, Jim said, "We gotta go so we can meet Father Dreadforth around 9:00 at the twenty-four- hour Perkins in St. Cloud."

"What's your plan?" Harry asked, because granny had told him to always have a plan. But Harry wasn't good at making plans, much preferring to take short cuts that seemed a more interesting way to go and never minded getting lost.

Even though the route was a bit complicated and he had smoked a bit, Jim could rattle off the roads because he had taken them so many times. "When we come out of the old forest trail, we'll get on County Road 75, take that to Interstate 94, go north 'til we reach Highway 23, get off on Highway 23, which takes us into St. Cloud, and then we'll head to the all-night Perkins on Sixth Avenue."

"Wait just a minute," Harry said. "I know a shortcut to save time. We should—"

"We're not taking any of your short cuts," Jim said in a very stern voice, knowing Harry had no more sense of direction than a blind skunk high on marijuana.

Chapter 31

— — —

About the time Jim and Harry were smoking their joint and snacking on goodies, Sergeant Tom was finishing his first beer. He was sitting in front of his TV, watching an old black-and-white movie, and swatting mosquitoes that had come in through holes in his patched screens. His one-bedroom house was on the outskirts of Pinetree and far enough away that nobody complained about his grass never being cut or the rusty, old refrigerator standing in his front yard. Tom had been hired to patrol several of the neighboring small towns, since none could afford a full-time cop. Tom often did his patrolling late at night when tourists were coming from the twin cites of Minneapolis and St. Paul and speeding to northern Minnesota to catch the big muskies in Leech Lake.

Sergeant Tom wore a hearing aid in his left ear that might or might not have a functioning battery and glasses whose frame was patched in the middle with black electrical tape. He wore a blue shirt, which on the right side the word POLICE had been stenciled in large white letters. On the left side were three fake military medals that he had bought at a garage sale because he thought they would give him a very official look.

"We'll take a nice drive tonight," Tom said to Orlando, his pet tabby cat, who closely resembled the smiling Cheshire Cat in the Alice in Wonderland movie.

Tom didn't like drinking alone, so he always poured some of his beer into Orlando's water dish, which made Orlando smile from ear to fuzzy ear.

"Meow, meow," Orlando purred, wanting a little more beer.

"You've had enough," Tom said as he finished his beer. He got up and pinned on his badge, grabbed his baton, and got his shotgun, which wasn't loaded but was good for scaring people. He grabbed a bag of dried tuna bits for Orlando's midnight snack and carried everything outside. He opened the passenger door, put most of the stuff on the floor of his 1966, four-door Ford Galaxy. Its black and white paint had faded, but the siren worked most of the time, and a red light mounted on top lit up and sometimes even spun around. Orlando had followed him outside and jumped up on the passenger seat when Tom had opened the door.

He backed out his driveway and drove two blocks on a dirt road before turning right and getting on Pinetree's paved Main Street, which was actually County Road 75. He drove out of town with his headlights on high beam so he could see better, because he had trouble seeing at night.

He drove at a steady 65 mph so if anyone passed him, he could issue a ticket. He drove about 10 miles until he reached the point where County Road 75 ran along the northern boundary of the monastery's 3000-acre forest. Tom found his secret hiding spot that was near the beginning of an old trail into the woods that almost no one used. He backed in until the car was almost hidden by brush, but the spot still gave him a pretty good view of County Road 75. Without realizing, Sergeant Tom had backed his police car into the forest trail that Jim and Harry were now diving down to reach County Road 75.

"Yep, I'll write a bunch of tickets tonight, so I'll be able to take Claire out this weekend for dinner of butter-fried sun fish at the Horseshoe lake Pavilion," Tom said to Orlando, who added an occasional, "meow, meow," as he sniffed at the bag of dried tuna bits on the passenger seat.

Although Tom's faded Galaxy police car didn't look like much, it had a specially rebuilt motor and could hit a 110 mph and catch any speeder in no time. Tom liked to ticket city slickers who came off Interstate 94 and sped down County Road 75 on their way to one of the 10,000 lakes. He gave speeding city slickers a choice of paying in cash or coming back the next day to pay the fine at the county clerk's office in Pinetree. Most everybody grumbled but paid in cash, half of which Tom kept for himself because the small towns he worked for barely paid enough to buy Orlando dried tuna bits.

Tom settled down to wait for speedsters and his other favorite targets: cars with one headlight or a broken taillight. He opened his second beer, poured a little into Orlando's water bowl on the floor, and tuned the car radio to his favorite late-night program. He had to crank up the volume because he was hard of hearing. Father Dreadforth's deep voice came booming out of the car's speaker as if God himself were speaking directly to him.

"I know many of you listening may have money problems, health worries, personal concerns, lost a loved one, or just plain feel life is not worth living. Well, I'm here to tell you Jesus Christ is watching over every single one of you, and he will take care of you. Remember, God so loved each of you that he gave his only son so that you do not perish but can enjoy eternal life, John 3:36. Let your hearts be filled with hope because there are many signs the rapture is coming soon. And when it does, Jesus Christ will reappear on earth in a blaze of lights with angels singing and personally take you into heaven. I will pray for you and make sure you have a place at the front of line when the rapture comes. Do not put off sending your donations, because the devil is always roaming about and seeking to steal your soul and take you to hell, 1 Peter 5:8. Those of you sending in twenty-five dollars will receive a beautifully illustrated medieval manuscript personally blessed with holy water from the Pope himself. Those of you sending in fifty or more dollars will receive two blessed manuscripts in special gold frames suitable for hanging. Remember to send in your donations, for as it says in Matthew 6:33, those who are generous shall have all things given to them."

As Tom got older, there were very few things he believed in, but one sure thing was the rapture: the second coming of Jesus Christ. His friend Claire, in Pinetree, had been keeping track of the signs and said that the rapture could happen any day now.

"If I catch a speeder tonight, I'm going to send half the money to Father Dreadforth so I get a place in front of the line for the rapture," Tom said. He finished his second beer and reached down to rub Orlando's soft thick fur.

Orlando purred, finishing the beer in his water bowel and looking very contented.

Tom was feeling a little tired, so he took off his glasses, laid them on the dash board, put his head back on the seat and thought he'd rest a little before catching his first speedster.

"How much further to Highway 75?" Harry asked. He needed to pee but wasn't about to walk around these woods in the dark and find himself standing next to one of those devils with their big, red eyes.

"Couple more turns and we can get off this old trail and get on County Road 75," Jim said.

His driving skills were not as sharp after smoking pot, and he missed seeing a fallen log at the side of the road. The right front tire hit the log and jolted Jim, and as he tried to get control of the wobbling truck, his left hand accidentally hit the air horn button in the middle of the steering wheel. A horrendous blast split the quiet night, as loud and frightening as a lion's night-time roar in the vast African plains.

The sound of the air horn jolted Sergeant Tom, who had been snoozing in his police car not more than twenty feet away. He recognized that sound and knew only huge, eighteen-wheel trucks had air horns, but they didn't drive through the woods. To see what was happening, he tried turning around in his seat to look out the back window, but the steering wheel was in the way. He kept jerking his body around, and in the commotion, his left foot accidentally hit the brake pedal several times, which caused the car's red, round brake lights to repeatedly blink on and off.

Besides waking Sergeant Tom, the horn blast startled Harry, who, half-stoned and not thinking so well, sat up and looked around. What he saw caused terror to rush through his body like water thundering over rapids. Not more than twenty feet away, partially hidden by brush, he was sure he had seen devils' round, red eyes blinking at him.

"Devils! Devils!" Harry yelled, his arms and legs flailing about, trying to avoid certain disaster.

"Oh my God!" Jim yelled as he too saw the blinking round red eyes. His half-stoned brain warned that Harry had been right, and he was about to run into a bunch of devils.

Harry was wildly trying to grab the steering wheel and turn the truck away before those devils had a chance to jump into his body and steal his soul and take him to hell.

"Let go of the steering wheel," Jim yelled.

As they each fought to get control over the steering wheel, Jim accidentally hit the air horn switch several more times, and loud blasts rocked the normally silent forest.

The additional loud blasts caused Sergeant Tom's body to jerk some more, and his foot hit the brake pedal several more times, and the car's red, round brake lights blinked again and again.

"Devils right over there," Harry said, convinced the car's red, round, blinking brake lights were actually the eyes of devils, only ten feet away, hiding behind some trees, waiting to get him.

Harry was yelling like a banshee, and his rush of adrenalin gave him the strength of a weight lifter. He momentarily gained control of the steering wheel and was turning the truck sharply to the left. It put them on a collision course with a big oak tree that had been growing for a hundred years, was at least ten feet in diameter, and could easily stop a speeding train.

"Let go, or we'll hit the tree!" Jim shouted.

At the last second, Jim managed to turn the steering wheel just enough to miss the huge oak tree but not enough to miss the back of Tom's police car, which was partially backed into the entrance of the overgrown trail.

The sudden crash to the back of the police car broke the left tail light and knocked Tom's glasses off the dashboard and onto the floor. Orlando was so frightened that he jumped on Tom's shoulder and dug in his claws to hold tight. The sudden pain caused Tom to let out a string of swear words that were so bad he'd have to confess them for sure.

"We hit the devils!" Harry shouted. He was sure all was lost and hell was the next stop.

"Let go of the steering wheel!" Jim yelled. "We're heading for the ditch!"

"We hit the devils!" Harry yelled again, too stoned to know they had only hit the back of Tom's patrol car.

The very idea of actually hitting a pack of devils pushed Harry over the edge. The fear glued his hands to the steering wheel, and he held on like it was his life raft in a raging sea.

With Harry's holding the steering wheel, Jim couldn't turn the Power Wagon and avoid heading straight for the deep ditch that was partially filled with water from the last rainstorm. And even worse, Jim hadn't realized in fighting with Harry that he had pressed the accelerator to the floor and the truck was thundering ahead, like an unstoppable herd of stampeding elephants.

"Get you hands off the wheel," Jim shouted, but Harry's fear made him hold tight, and the truck hit the deep ditch with such force that muddy water splashed the windshield and came through the open side windows, soaking them both.

Hitting the water-filled ditch bounced Harry around, and he finally let go of the steering wheel but kept yelling, "The devils are going to take us to hell!"

When the Power Wagon hit the water-filled ditch it paused for only a second as its powerful motor kept all four huge, knobby tires turning and digging in deep. Although the back tires were slipping on the mud, the front ties managed to find footing in the solid, rocky bank, and the four-thousand-pound truck began to crawl up the steep slope like a rock climber going up the face of a mountain. No other vehicle could have survived driving into the deep, muddy ditch, much less find traction to crawl up the steep bank, but Jim never had any doubts. Grandpa had often told him that nothing could stop the Dodge Power Wagon as long as its wheels were turning.

But at the top of the bank was another obstacle in the form of a sturdy metal guardrail that bordered this section of Interstate 94 and prevented cars from accidentally veering off the road and crashing into the steep ditch. The metal guardrail was designed to stop an average car or even a big SUV but not the tank-like Power Wagon, which had a five-hundred-pound, steel wench welded to its front bumper. Normally the wench's cable was used to pull out the truck if it got stuck, but the wench itself could also function like a battering ram. When the heavy, steel wench struck the metal guardrail there were terrible grinding and screeching sounds as the metal guardrail ruptured and the truck plowed through.

Harry heard the terrible screeching sounds and was sure they were being made by devils. He couldn't bear to look outside and have his worst fears confirmed. Instead, he put his hands over his eyes and shouted, "The devils are right outside,"

Jim laughed and said, "Open your eyes and look around. The devils aren't making those noises. Just the Power Wagon smashing through the guardrail and getting us on Interstate 94. We took sort of a shortcut like you're always talking about."

Jim was smiling, and to show his pride in what his Power Wagon had done, he proudly patted the steering wheel, as if he were patting the butt of his girlfriend. He shifted the transmission into its highest gear and the Power Wagon gradually reached its top speed of 56 miles per hour. He relaxed a little, knowing they could still make their 9:00 o'clock meeting with Father Dreadforth in St. Cloud.

What Jim didn't know was that the jolts and jerks of going through the deep ditch and busting through guardrail had snapped open the rusty latch on Power Wagon's tailgate and turned over several cartons of Big Boy tomatoes. The big red juicy tomatoes were bouncing out of the truck's open tailgate and making a big, slippery, soggy, red mess on the highway.

Chapter 32

Sergeant Tom remembered being awakened by an air horn blast coming out of nowhere and then feeling a loud bang when something hit the back of his police car. He was pretty near-sighted, but his far vision was pretty good. He had watched some kind of truck go by and drive right into the muddy ditch. And then to his amazement, the truck somehow climbed up the impossibly steep bank, broke through a guardrail that would stop a speeding car, and got on Interstate 94.

"I must be dreaming," Tom said, but the pain left by Orlando's sharp claws digging into his shoulder brought him back to his senses. He knew for sure whoever was driving that truck was up to no good, and he'd get them. Nobody crashes into his police car and gets away with it.

Tom could see the truck's tail lights going down Interstate 94 toward St. Cloud, and he took off in such a hurry that he forgot to turn on his siren or the red, flashing light on top of his police car. He was breathing hard as he took the on-ramp to Interstate 94 and saw the truck's taillights in the distance.

"I'll catch those bastards and make them pay big time," Tom said to Orlando, unknowingly repeating words he had heard cops say in the movies.

Orlando was meowing and busily searching the seat for dried tuna bits.

He was slowly gaining on the truck's taillights and noticed his high-beam headlights were showing big, red blotches on the highway.

"What's those red blotches?" Tom asked Orlando. "Is the truck leaking red paint? Not likely."

The answer suddenly came to him, and he shouted, "It's blood! All over the freeway. I'll bet there's a body in the back of that truck, and blood's pouring out all over the road!"

Tom was excited and kept talking out loud, "It'll be my first murder case, and after I arrest those bastards, I'll be famous!"

Tom wondered how to arrest those bastards. He could pull them over, but his shotgun wasn't loaded, and they might shoot him and toss him in back with the other body. He didn't have a cell phone, so couldn't call for help. His best bet was to follow and see where they were going.

What Sergeant Tom didn't know was when the truck had hit the back of his patrol car, it had broken his left taillight.

Unfortunately, the driver of a state highway patrol car going by on the opposite side of Interstate 94 did notice the broken light.

"Tail light out," the taller state trooper said to his partner, glad to have something to do on this boring late night shift.

"It's about time for a little action. Let's get 'em," said the shorter highway patrol trooper in the passenger seat.

"I'll take the next median U-turn and come up on his rear," the taller one said.

At the next median U-turn, marked POLICE ONLY, the state trooper cut across to the opposite side and put his foot to the gas. He began chasing the car with the broken taillight, which just happened to belong to Sergeant Tom.

"I won't use the flashing lights or the bull horn until we're right on the car's tail," the taller trooper said. He wanted to suddenly appear and the scare the shit out of unsuspecting driver.

Tom was keeping far enough back of the murderers' truck so they wouldn't get suspicious of being followed but close enough so he wouldn't lose the truck's taillights.

"What kind of body do you think they're hauling?" Tom asked Orlando, who was busy cleaning himself after having eaten every last dried tuna bit.

"I'll bet it's a woman's body. I'll bet they kidnapped and raped her. Then they got scared, killed her, and were going to bury her body in the forest. But when they accidentally hit my police car, they took off and are looking for another place to dump the body."

Tom kept seeing the red blotches of blood on the highway and was thinking about getting his picture on the TV news. Suddenly his rearview mirror and the back of his car were filled with bright, dazzling, colored lights that whirled around and seemed out of this world.

"What's going on?" Tom asked as he glanced back and was blinded by the whirling colored lights.

As he tried to make sense of the dazzling lights, he remembered something he had heard earlier that night on Father Dreadforth's gospel program. In fact, he could almost repeat Father Dreadforth's exact words, "Jesus Christ will come again, surrounded with dazzling lights."

"Orlando, it's happening," said a very excited Tom, who hadn't been this excited since he thought he had won fifty million dollars in a multi-state lottery—but it turned out he had misread two of the seven numbers.

"It's the rapture!" Tom shouted. "It's happening just like Father Dreadforth said."

Although Tom was happy about being taken into heaven, he wished Jesus had waited another day so he could have seen his photo on TV. How proud his dead wife, Emma, would have been to see her husband heralded as a hero cop on the TV news. Tom was so excited about the rapture he began wandering down the freeway, like someone who had too much to drink.

The state troopers had waited to turn on the bar of flashing red, yellow, and white lights until they were right on Tom's back bumper. But instead of the driver slowing down and pulling over to the side, this driver just going on, and even worse, he was wandering all over the road like a drunk.

"It's time for the bullhorn," the shorter trooper said.

The bullhorn was mounted on the police car's right front fender and pointed directly at the offender's car.

"This is the highway police. Pull over immediately. I repeat, Pull over *now!*" the shorter trooper said, pronouncing each word very dramatically.

Tom's hearing was poor to bad, especially since his hearing aid's battery was almost dead. He could hear the sounds of a booming voice, but he had trouble understanding the exact words. But he didn't care. Tom knew that the powerful voice was surely that of Jesus Christ, who was speaking directly to him. Tom was so excited he kept right on driving and wandering all over the freeway.

"Did you hear that?" Tom asked Orlando. "It's Jesus Christ. He's talking to me."

The short police officer saw the driver was not stopping but continuing to drive erratically. He turned up the volume of the bullhorn and spoke very slowly and distinctly, "Pull over, and get out of your car."

With the raised volume of the bullhorn, Tom understood some of what the Lord was saying, and it sounded like he was being asked to stop so he could be taken to heaven.

Sergeant Tom slowed down, pulled over, and stopped along the side of the road. He was breathing in short quick gasps, and his heart was pounding so hard from all the excitement that he was afraid he might have a stroke before getting into heaven. But before he got out of the car, he reached down and picked Orlando off the floor because he wasn't going to heaven without Orlando.

Although Tom hadn't cried since his wife had died two years ago, the thought of he and Orlando going to heaven caused tears of joy to freely flow from old, dry eyes. He tightly held Orlando in one hand, opened the door with his other hand, and got out of the car. He was immediately blinded and awed by the dazzling, whirling colored lights, just like Father Dreadforth had said the rapture would be. And then he heard Jesus Christ speaking to him again in a loud deep voice, "Put your hands on the roof of the car."

Sergeant Tom was too excited to understand what Jesus was saying. All he could think was being taken into heaven and reunited with Emma, who would make him some of these sticky caramel rolls he so dearly loved. Tom hoped there were microwaves in heaven because he liked to heat up the roll and spread it with butter.

Tom saw a tall person walking out of the dazzling light with one hand outstretched and knew it must be Jesus Christ, reaching out for him. He immediately fell down on his creaky knees and wished he had on his glasses so he could see Jesus' holy face. His wondered whether he had sent Father Dreadforth enough money to get a good place in heaven.

* * * *

Having not the slightest idea of what was happening in back of them, Jim and Harry drove on to St. Cloud and met Father Dreadforth at the all-night Perkins on Sixth Avenue.

"Have any trouble?" Father Dreadforth asked.

Harry was about to tell every last detail of how they were minding their own business and driving through the forest when devils—

"No, no trouble," Jim said as he kicked Harry under the table to signal him to keep his mouth shut.

"Many thanks again for doing this favor. And to show my gratitude, I have added a little extra," Father Dreadforth said as he handed an envelope to Jim.

"Thanks," Jim said. He gave Harry a very dirty look that meant *keep your mouth shut.*

"Well, take your time and finish your late night breakfast. I must be off to meet my client. Whatever money you receive for selling the tomatoes at the supermarket is all yours," Father Dreadforth said.

As Father Dreadforth got up and was walking to the door, Harry was muttering how the devils almost got him and grandma was right and so on and so forth, until he got tired of muttering with no one listening. He

169

gave up and went back to eating his French toast topped with butter, honey, maple syrup, and two scoops of vanilla ice cream.

As Jim finished his four-egg omelet he was thinking how their pot of money was growing steadily and maybe they'd soon have enough to get out of Minnesota before the first snowfall.

CHAPTER 33

— — —

"That fucking Mr. Stranger stopped payment on those goddamn worthless cashier's checks," Tony Koole said, almost shouting, his face turning beet red as he banged his beer bottle on the table. "Nobody, and I mean nobody, fucks with me," Tony added, trying to sound mean but sweating more than a tough guy should.

Tony was sitting in a sleazy strip joint called *El Loco*—roughly translated, it meant "The Crazy"—which was located on a dark alley a couple blocks off of Revolution Avenue, Tijuana's main street. The joint wasn't air conditioned and smelled like beer, sweat, and aftershave. On either side of Tony sat his two bodyguards, Ratty and Mousy, both wearing jackets to cover their pieces and drinking as fast as they could since the beer was on the house. The bodyguards had been paying little attention to Tony's outbursts because they were busy leering at an almost naked stripper on a small stage at the front of the bar. She had long legs and was dancing around a polished chrome pole to the loud, heavy beat of ZZ Top's song, *Jesus just left Chicago*.

"So what do yah want from me?" Oscar asked in accented English.

Oscar Gonzales was head of the biggest drug cartel in all of Baja, a 1000-mile-long peninsula with Tijuana at the top. At the bottom was beautiful Cabo San Lucas, with the Pacific Ocean on one side and the Gulf of Mexico on the other. Along with his gorgeous wife and three children, Oscar lived in a gated, three-story, five-thousand-square-foot mansion with a five-car garage in the hills of Tijuana. He also had a marble-floored getaway mansion with full-length windows on the tip of Cabo San Lucas. That's where he entertained clients and took them fishing for beautiful, prized, silver-blue marlins. Oscar had several marlins mounted and hung in each of his residences.

Around midnight, Oscar had closed down the bar and kicked out all the drinkers. He had agreed to let one of his favorite strippers keep working because she wanted to make extra money and she would make a nice distraction for his new clients. No one knew Oscar actually owned El Loco, which he often used to meet clients he didn't know or trust. Clients who might need to be thrown out if negotiations turned soar. Oscar's new clients were Tony Koole and his two bodyguards, who had arrived promptly at the agreed time of 12:30 a.m. Oscar had a rule about being late: don't be, unless of course you were a beautiful woman.

"How much to kidnap or kill that muddafucker?" Tony asked, partly slurring his words because he had been nervous and already chugged down two bottles of Dos Equis while talking about everything but what he wanted.

At the beginning of any negotiation Oscar kept to another of his rules: first talk about general things, such as how to collect from a deadbeat or the best strategy for betting on professional sports. He found this technique very useful in spotting a client's weakness, such as whether the client was a braggart, a down-and-out liar, or just plain stupid. It was almost 1:30 a.m., and Oscar, a confirmed night owl, was doing his best thinking. He had noticed Tony Koole was slurring his words and beads of sweat were running down his forehead, showing he had been drinking too much and was worried and nervous. This meant Tony badly needed Oscar's help, which also meant Oscar could increase his prices. Oscar had survived the deadly drug wars because he recognized the weaknesses in his enemies, many of whom did not seem to live very long. In fact, during the past year, there had been 172 confirmed drug-related killings in Baja, most of them by Oscar's men.

"As you know, kidnapping and killing can be very costly and dangerous," Oscar said. He took another sip from his bottle of Dos Equis, a very popular beer in Mexico, Texas, and most of California.

Although Oscar appeared to be drinking as much as the others, he was actually only sipping his beer. Each time the waitress had brought more beers for the clients, she had removed Oscar's bottle, whose dark brown color concealed the fact that it was almost full, and had set a new bottle in front of him, which he pretended to drink. As his clients drank themselves into stupidity, Oscar stayed sober so he would be as clever as a wily fox getting ready to break into a coop of plump chickens.

"I know it's going to cost, but *how much* is the question," Tony said, sounding impatient because he was used to being the top dog and didn't like being the beggar at the bottom of the heap.

"Well, that depends on whether you're willing to pay as much as your good friend, Mr. Stranger, who made me an offer a couple days ago that might be of great interest to you," Oscar said, a crafty smile on his pockmarked face, which had a whitish scar running down his left check.

"What did that son-of-a-bitch offer you?" Tony asked, both his hands forming into iron tight fists.

"Stranger offered ten thousand dollars to wipe you off the map and an additional ten thousand to get rid of your two bodyguards," Oscar said. He looked Tony in the eyes, holding that stare for several seconds. He was pleased to see that Tony was first to look away, showing who was boss in these negotiations.

"You're not getting rid of me for a measly ten Gs," barked Ratty, who had suddenly stood up, his huge legs jolting the table and knocking over several bottles of beer. Ratty narrowed his eyes, drew out his big knife, and looked around for somebody to stick, his favorite thing.

About the same time, big Mousy had secretly and silently reached under his jacket and put his hand on his .44 Magnum, ready to shoot anybody who tried to wipe him off the map. He didn't care if somebody did in Tony, whom he hated more than a rabid dog, but nobody was going to touch him.

"Be cool, be cool," Jesús said in a soothing voice and gestured for Ratty and Mousy to calm down. "Nobody's going to kill nobody here, tonight."

Jesús was a friend of Oscar's as well as Tony's drug connection in Tijuana. As a favor to Tony, Jesús had arranged this midnight meeting with Oscar, but only after Tony had promised him a month's supply of uncut coke.

Ratty slowly sat back down and made sniffing sounds because when he got excited he had trouble breathing through his many-times-broken nose.

As Ratty was sitting back down, Mousy heard noises in back of him, and when he looked around, what he saw made him take his hand off his gun and put both hands on the table.

Six men dressed in black seemed to have come out of nowhere. They were standing in front of a black, floor-to-ceiling screen. Three were holding short-stock, automatic shotguns and three held Glocks with long, black silencers. Mousy knew about guns so he sat very still.

"It's OK, everything's cool," Oscar said and nodded at the six men who just as quickly vanished behind the black screen.

"But Tony," Oscar said, using the client's first name, his way of establishing a personal relationship. "You can see I have two offers on the table. If I accept Stranger's and shoot the three of you here and now, I make a quick twenty grand. Not bad, not bad at all."

Oscar paused to let this deadly thought sink into Tony's beer-soaked brain and cause his fear level to soar like a rocket shot into space.

"Or, I can help you kidnap and perhaps kill Stranger for a yet undecided fee, which will be considerable."

Oscar's broke into a big grin, because this was turning out to be a very interesting evening, and he would be a big winner however it turned out.

"Holy Christ! I can't believe it! Muddafucker Stranger hired you to kill me?" Tony asked, shaking his fists in the air, trying to appear braver than he felt.

"Calm down," Jesús said, putting his hand gently on Tony's shoulder. Jesús was smiling to himself because he never liked Tony, who always played the big shot but now had gotten the short straw.

"I'll pay whatever it takes," Tony said, feeling sweat run down his forehead and arm pits and wishing he hadn't drunk so much so he could figure this out.

For the first time that night, Oscar actually took a big swig of beer, knowing he had Tony's balls in a tight vice. Tony would have to agree to whatever Oscar proposed.

"Here's what it'll cost," Oscar said and paused as he made up figures in his head.

"If you want to keep living, it'll cost twenty thousand for the three of you to walk out of this joint," Oscar said and looked at Tony, who reluctantly nodded in agreement because he wanted to walk out and not be carried out.

"If you want my men to help kidnap Stranger in San Diego, that's another twenty," Oscar said, knowing one secret to a successful negotiation was getting the client to agree to each separate demand rather than ask for one large sum. Oscar looked at Tony, who nodded in agreement, still in shock from hearing that Stranger tried to get him killed.

"After the kidnapping, my men will smuggle Stranger into Tijuana and hide him for ten grand a week, with a three week minimum," Oscar said

"OK," was all Tony said, knowing he'd to pay whatever it took to kidnap Stranger.

"We shouldn't have any trouble kidnapping Stranger since we do a lot of that in Baja and are usually very successful. Since my men will be doing all the dirty work, taking all the risks, and paying off the Tijuana's police, my cut of the ransom money will be seventy percent," Oscar finished, looked at Tony, and added, "There's no haggling, take it or leave it."

"Yeah, yeah. OK. I'm fucked either way," Tony said, closing his eyes and hoping this was all a bad dream. He hated to part with so much money, but what choice did he have?

"I'll need sixty thousand up front. Two of my men will follow you back to Los Angeles and pick up the money tonight," Oscar said. "Once I have the sixty thousand, my men will begin planning to kidnap Stranger."

"Sooner the better," Tony said, feeling a little better now, knowing he was going to keep on living but Stranger's days were numbered.

"For the ransom demand, we'll initially ask for five million and perhaps come down to two," Oscar said.

"His wife is loaded, so I figure at least two mil," Tony said, thinking his share would be $600,000, and that was a good payday for anybody.

"After we get the ransom money for Stranger, should we kill him and send his dead body back to San Diego?" Tony asked, hoping they would kill that bastard, Stranger, which is exactly what he deserved.

"Let's see how things develop," Oscar said, thinking he would probably end up killing Tony and his two thugs so he could keep all Stranger's ransom money. After all, he didn't owe Tony anything. He didn't even like him. He did like Stranger, but he didn't trust him. He might have to kill him, too.

Oscar stood up, smiled, and put out his hand. He and Tony shook on the deal.

CHAPTER 34

— — —

It was almost a month since Tony had visited Oscar in Tijuana to discuss killing and kidnapping. During that time Billy had discreetly looked into who had tipped off the police and got Bart arrested. Billy now knew the answer and dreaded having to tell Carol. He was calling Carol on her cell phone because he worried that Matthew Moore, Randolph's private detective, had bugged her landline phone.

"Hello Bad Billy," Carol said, recognizing his number and joking about his name.

"Be careful what you call me, because I'm a really tough guy," Billy said, and they both laughed.

"Do you have any news about who tipped off the police?" Carol asked.

"I've been having beers with some of my friends on the police force and finally hit pay-dirt. Bart's arrest for having a case of cocaine under his bed had most of the department talking and wondering where the tip came from," Billy said.

"I've got a strong feeling it was Randolph," Carol said, "But for mom's sake, I sure hope I'm wrong.

"No, you're right about Randolph. Apparently he had called a former client, a retired detective named Jerry Gosling, who owed him a favor. Gosling drinks too much and has trouble keeping secrets. According to his story, Randolph called and told him Bart was hooked on illegal drugs and getting high on his mother's prescription painkillers. Randolph told him it was important Bart be arrested for something so he could be scared straight and stop using drugs," Billy said.

"My god!" Carol shouted. "Randolph wanted Bart's trust money so badly he wanted Bart arrested on some trumped up drug charge. What will I tell mother?"

"I wouldn't tell her anything just yet," Billy said. "Better to wait until we can explain how Bart got hold of a briefcase full of cocaine."

"Bart already told me how that happened, and it's a bizarre story. It turns out his girlfriend, Anna, had gone to Los Angeles with hopes of being an actress. A guy claiming to be a film producer agreed to give her a screen test. After the test he offered her a role, but it was in a porn movie, and he insisted on first sampling the merchandise. When she refused, there was a violent argument, along with some real fighting and scratching. When the porn guy went to the bathroom to check how badly she had scratched his face, Anna was furious and wanted revenge. She looked around, saw an expensive briefcase, took it, and ran, not knowing what was in it. When she opened it and saw it was full of cocaine, she panicked. Her only thought was driving to San Diego and asking Bart for help. After Bart heard her story, he figured the porn guy and his thugs would soon come to San Diego, because Anna had told them about Bart and his lawyer father. Bart decided the best thing for them to do was leave town quickly. He put the cocaine briefcase under his bed so it wouldn't be noticed if any of his friends came over. But it would be easy to find when the thugs came looking. Unfortunately, the detectives had been tipped off and got there first," Carol said.

"It is so bizarre I'm not sure the police will believe Bart's story, and they're unlikely to believe Anna because she's his girlfriend. And the porn guy and his thugs will deny everything, so that leaves Bart in a really vulnerable position. If the police arrest him now, it will turn into a big mess, so keep Bart hidden away. The best thing would be for me to bring Bart and Anna in voluntarily so they can explain how the briefcase and cocaine got under his bed," Billy said. He added, "In the meantime, I sure hope Bart is safely hidden away.

"Believe it or not, he is hiding in a secluded monastery in the middle of Minnesota," Carol said.

"A monastery? You're a genius. The police or Matthew Moore would never think of looking for Bart in a monastery," Billy said.

"Bart says he's a probationary monk, and the Abbot already has him working on an impossible problem. He didn't tell me what the project was except that it was sort of like the bible story of Jesus turning water into wine," Carol said, and they both had to laugh.

"Can Bart write an algorithm to do that?" Bill asked.

"If anybody can, it's Bart," Carol said, feeling very proud of her brother's computer abilities.

"Now that we know Randolph set up Bart's arrest, I wonder what other dirty deeds he might have done." Billy said.

"I do know he recently moved all of mom's money to a different bank, saying it paid a higher interest. I wonder if that's the real reason." Carol offered.

"I better check out his finances. For all we know, he may have invested some of your mother's money without her knowing and lost it all when the baldness cure turned out to be a hoax. The bank may be calling in his loan, he can't cover the loss, and that's why he's after Bart's trust," Billy said.

"And worse, if Randolph used some of mom's money without her knowledge, he'll be doubly desperate and dangerous," Carol said.

"I agree, and I'll have to be sneaky, something I'm good at. I'm not only bad, I'm sneaky bad," Billy said and laughed. "But seriously, word on the street is Randolph has a lot of enemies, and I'm sure some will be eager to talk about his financial and personal affairs.

"That's a great idea because I know mother always worried about him fooling around. My grandfather never trusted Randolph and made mom insert a clause into their prenuptial agreement that automatically initiates divorce proceeding if Randolph is found to be unfaithful," Carol said, feeling very sorry for her mother.

"I'll discreetly do a little surveillance and find out if he's cheating on your mother."

"By the way, do you know what Mathew Moore has been doing?" Carol asked.

"Mathew's busy questioning Bart's friends about favorite surfing spots. But he hasn't had much success since Bart's friends don't know him or why he looking for Bart. They're sending him on wild goose chases up and down the California coast and Baja peninsula. And more importantly, none of Bart's friends know where Bart is."

"Thank God I found the monastery hideout," Carol said.

"It's too bad your brain lie-detector test isn't up and running so we could use it on Randolph and ask what he's planning," Billy said.

"I'd love to do that, especially now that my most recent data looks very promising. I'm hoping to become the female Sherlock Holmes of the twenty-first century," Carol said, a broad smile lighting up her face.

"I must say I'm a little worried about dating Ms. Holmes and always having to tell the truth," Billy said. He added, "You never did explain how your brain lie-detector works."

"Thanks to Bart's suggestion, I' been using algorithms. Google became famous and wealthy by developing algorithms to search for information, online dating services use them to match people, and programmers use them to beat humans at chess, checkers, backgammon, and Jeopardy. I'm hoping to go a step farther and use algorithms to decide if and when someone is lying," Carol said.

"But what exactly do your algorithms do?" Billy asked

"When a person answer's questions, my test takes detailed pictures of neural activity inside the living human brain. The algorithms will try to pick out brain areas that only become active only when a person is lying. But I'm not the only one doing this kind of research. I'm competing against researchers at high-power places such as Temple University, MIT, UC Irving, University of Texas, and two private companies that are already offering tests at five-hundred dollars a pop. But so far no researchers have nailed down those brain areas specific to lying," Carol said. She let out a big sigh, thinking how much work she had yet to do.

"Why will your test be more accurate than the current one?" Billy asked.

"Unlike the impression you get from movies and television, the current lie-detector test does not really measuring lying. It measures only physiological arousal, such as increased heart rate and breathing, which could result from feeling guilty when you tell a lie. However you can just as easily become physiologically aroused from feeling stressed, nervous, or anxious about taking the test. Since the current lie-detector test cannot tell the difference between arousal caused by lying or from being anxious or stressed, its results are not permitted in most court proceedings. However some corporations and governmental agencies, such as the FBI and CIA, continued to use lie detector tests in hopes of scaring people into being honest or making a confession," Carol finished.

"Wow. If you're successful, a brain lie-detector would have an enormous impact. No longer could criminals, politicians, or big shots in business get away with lying. I can't wait," Billy said.

"It would truly be a brave new world," Carol said.

"But aren't you worried about your algorithms being stolen by the competition? They must be worth more than a gold mine." Billy said.

"Yes, I worry all the time, especially now that I'm having more success. I've sworn Helen, my assistant, to secrecy and would trust her with my life. I do worry about my competition going to great lengths to steal my algorithms. I've planted some fake ones in a secure file on my lab computer. An experienced hacker could eventually break into my secure file and steal the fake algorithms, believing they are the real ones. But As soon as the hacker opens the file, a virus will pop out and disable everything in the computer network. I'm hoping the hacker will believe the virus is a protective device and keep trying to retrieve the fake algorithms. No one but Helen knows the real algorithms are stored in a flash drive I carry with me," Carol said.

"As I've said a million times, you're much smarter than you look."

They both laughed.

"The truth is I've been under a lot of pressure would like to take a few days off. I was thinking and hoping we might spend a long weekend in Cabo, which I know is one of your favorite places."

"Yes it is, but I've only camped there and never stayed at one of the big, expensive resorts, where I'm sure you'd like to stay," Billy said.

"You're right. I'm not much of a camper. But I know a person who knows a person who can get us a great deal. What do you say?" Carol asked.

"I'll leave it in your very capable hands," Billy said, liking the idea of staying at one of the expensive places, if they got a big, big discount. "And don't forget, Red Bull on Saturday night. There's a great new band that adds a little funk to country music."

"Wouldn't miss it for the world," Carol said. She made the sound of a kiss before saying goodbye.

Billy smiled and thought, *sometime life is good. Very, very good.*

CHAPTER 35

— — —

Matthew Moore had been waiting for thirty-five minutes in the reception room for the law offices of Stranger, Foremore, and Long.

"Mr. Stranger will see you now," said the secretary with the perfect makeup.

"Thank you," Matthew Moore said. He got up, walked down the hallway, and knocked on Randolph's door.

"Come in," Randolph said.

As Matthew opened the door and entered the office, he wondered how this meeting would turn out, since he was the messenger of both good and bad news.

"Well, I hope you have good news," Randolph said, motioning Mathew to sit down.

"Actually, I do have some good news," Mathew said. *It's better to start with the good news, since Randolph hates bad news.*

"As you know, I had bugged Carol's phone and added additional hidden microphones in her condo to record conversations she might have on her cell phone. This morning she received a call on her cell phone from someone she called Billy. I only heard her side of the conversation, but I did learn Bart was hiding in a monastery somewhere in Minnesota, but she never mentioned the monastery's name."

"That is great news. All you need to do is call each of the monasteries until you locate where he is hiding," Randolph said. He flashed a big smile, confident his financial worries would soon be over. After Bartholomew was brought back to San Diego and arrested for cocaine possession, Randolph would have complete control of Bartholomew's trust fund.

"There are over twenty different Catholic, Lutheran, Buddhist, and nondenominational monasteries in Minnesota. I have already called eight monasteries, but none would give out any personnel information about their monks, other than telling how many monks were at their monastery," Matthew said, seeing Randolph's facial muscles begin to tighten.

"No problem. It just means you will have to visit each monastery and personally look for Bartholomew," Randolph said.

"It may not be that easy. All the monasteries have a policy of protecting their monks and allowing visitation only from close family members and only with the monk's agreement. Apparently, some families do not approve of their sons joining a monastery and will try almost anything to get them back, including physically removing them against their wills," Matthew said.

Randolph was silent, not liking what he was hearing but quickly thinking of another solution.

"I will give you a notarized letter, describing how Marjorie, Bartholomew's mother, has had a serious stroke that caused complete paralysis and may be life threatening. The letter will say the family is keeping a vigil at Marjorie's bedside and that you, acting as an official agent of the family, need to meet with Bartholomew and ascertain if he wishes to return to San Diego and see his mother before she dies," Randolph said, knowing no monastery would refuse a request that involved a dying mother.

"I am very sorry to hear about Marjorie's stroke," Matthew said.

"No, no, she has not really had a stroke. I just created that sad scenario because it is a very effective way to persuade monks to allow you to meet with Bartholomew," Randolph said, thinking he was much too clever to be outwitted by a bunch of God-loving monks.

Matthew thought, *Randolph would do anything to achieve his ends, but making up a false story about his supposedly dying wife is going too far.*

"I will compose a letter appointing you an agent of our family, have my secretary type the letter on our official law stationary, and finally have her notarize it. You can pick up the letter on your way to the airport."

"All right," Matthew said, hating to be a part of this dirty business.

"Get on the first flight available, go stand-by if you must. I want you in Minnesota as soon as possible so you can start looking for Bartholomew," Randolph said.

"There's one more thing," Matthew said, eager to tell the bad news.

"And what is that?" Randolph asked, mulling over extradition procedures to bring Bartholomew back to San Diego.

"From Carol's part of the conversation, I learned this person, Billy, had been snooping around, talking to detectives. Apparently he heard you were the one who tipped off the police that led to Bart arrest," Matthew said.

Randolph's eyes darkened, and his face turned mean like that of a mad bulldog. He stood up, put his hands on the desk, leaned forward, stared angrily at Matthew, and said in a deadly tone, "That accusation is completely false, and I will sue the person or persons responsible for making such slanderous statements."

I know he's lying but, there's nothing I could do about that, Matthew thought. *I've never liked working for him, and if he didn't pay so well, and if I didn't have two kids in college, I'd quit tomorrow.*

"As it now stands, Carol believes you were responsible for tipping off the police," Matthew said in a calm, even voice, wanting to pour a little more salt into Randolph's open wound.

"I do not want to discuss this accusation any further since it is totally without merit. As soon as you return from finding Bartholomew in Minnesota, I want you to discover who had been telling Carol these outrageous lies. Once I know this person's identity, I will deal with him or her in my own way," Mr. Stranger said, his angry voice betraying his evil intent.

"I better get busy packing and making plane reservations," Matthew said and stood up. He left Mr. Stranger's office, and as he walked down the hallway, he worried about what he would do or say when he finally came face to face with Bart.

* * * *

At the Neuroscience Institute, Helen was on her way to Carol's office. Carol had called earlier and wanted to show her the latest results from the brain lie-detector test, whose accuracy had reached ninety percent, something no other research had achieved. Carol had also said she needed advice on how to deal with a man's pride, meaning Billy. That made Helen wonder about what had happened on Carol and Billy's last week dream trip to Cabo. She was lost in her thought, walking fast and coming around a corner almost ran into Sam.

"Hey girl. Just thinking about you. Why don't you come to my place tonight and show me your algorithms," Sam said. A mocking grin spread across his face making him look like a gargoyle on speed.

"I've asked you a hundred times not to call me '*girl*'," Helen said. She gave him a furious look, but Sam didn't seem to notice. He stood in the middle of the corridor, grinning and blocking her path.

"Oh, I'm so sorry," Sam said, "But calling you 'girl' is just being friendly. It's like when I call Carol 'cowgirl'. Just being friendly. But I really would enjoy seeing your algorithms," he said in a voice loaded with sexual overtones.

"Go to hell," Helen yelled. She was a breath away from slapping his face and erasing his leering grin. But she held back because Sam was responsible

183

for repairing and servicing their lab's computers and complicated technical equipment. That was the only reason other researchers put up with Sam's irritating ways. Most everyone called him 'SS', which he was led to believe stood for 'Super Sam', the super technician. But all the researchers knew better, because SS actually stood for Sleazy Sam, Sick Sam, or Helen's personal favorite: Shitty Sam.

"Looks like someone is having a PMS day," Sam said in a mocking tone. He disliked Helen, who never gave him proper credit for his work, and he was jealous of Carol, whose success was due to luck and definitely not brains. Sam had been pleased when he was contacted by a competing private company and given a chance for some payback. The company offered Sam a lot of money for secretly providing information on the kind of algorithms Carol was developing in her research.

"I don't have time for you today," Helen said, trying to control her anger and turning to walk away.

"Heard the accuracy of your infamous brain lie-detector test is stuck in the low eighties. Maybe it's time to pack it in and leave the tough research to men," Sam said and made another mocking grim.

Helen wasn't normally an aggressive person, but Sam's ugly words and ridiculous grin were too much for her to stomach. She took a few steps forward until she was only inches from his face.

"Well, SS, you heard wrong. Our latest results show our accuracy is in the nineties. So eat your heart out!" she yelled.

She knew better than to brag about their results, but Sam had pushed her too far and she wanted to make him really jealous.

"In the 90s. Well, that's hard to believe. Your competitors are a lot smarter and have more research money, and they only claim accuracy scores in the low eighties," Sam said in a tone indicating she was full of crap.

Helen's anger boiled over and she couldn't stop herself. "Believe what you want. Our accuracy is in the nineties, and let me know if you want a crash course in algorithms."

"A dead cockroach could write better algorithms than the two of you," Sam said, his words coming out with such force that spittle was running down his chin.

Helen knew she had pushed Sam too far and needed to get away before she said even more. Carol had warned her about not trusting Sam because she had found him snooping around their lab and asking far too questions about their research.

Helen quickly turned and almost ran down the hall, not looking back.

Sam's raging anger made his body tremble. *I'll get even, if it's the last thing I do.* He hurried to his office, sat down at his computer, and banged out an encrypted email.

COWGIRL CLAIMS ACCURACY IN 90S. WHAT NEXT?

He hit the send button and waited for an answer.

Forty seconds later he read the encrypted reply.

STEAL COWGIRL'S ALGORITHMS. DO WHATEVER NECESSARY. REPEAT. WHATEVER NECESSARY!

"Yes, indeed," Sam said out loud and added in a low, malicious tone, "Cowgirl, I'm about to stick a hot branding iron up your cute ass."

Sam was chewing on his lower lip as he thought about stealing Carol's algorithms. *She'd shit her panties if she knew when I set up her computer system I had added a secret backdoor into her files.*

Then he sat up straight when he remembered a few years ago when Netflix gave a million dollar prize to group who developed algorithms to better predict movies their customers would like. *Carol's algorithms would surely be worth a million dollars.* Sam began grinning like a chimp finding truck full of bananas.

Helen knew she had to get into a better mood before she met Carol. She knew what medication she needed and stopped at the vending machine. She put in a dollar, made a selection, and watched as a package of Reese's Peanut Butter Cups dropped down. She had been really angry, so it took three cups before she was feeling better.

She knocked on Carol's door and heard the friendly, "Come in."

Helen walked in and saw the happy look on Carol's face.

"I've just looked at our latest results, and it seems our revised algorithms are working," Carol said.

"That's incredible," Helen said. "Are you sure?"

"Here, look at this summary table. Our revised algorithms correctly identified when a subject told a lie about ninety percent of the time. If we can replicate these results with more subjects, we'll really be on to something big," Carol said, her face flushed with excitement, like a little girl who got the doll she had always wanted.

"Our new algorithms turned the computer into a thinking machine that gradually learned from its mistakes, made fewer errors, and was better able to identify the real liars. But before we celebrate, I wanted you to check the results. Maybe I saw what I wanted or made some other mistake," Carol said and handed Helen the summary table.

The room was silent as Carol watched Helen go over the results, line by line, hoping and praying she hadn't made a mistake.

It was almost ten minutes before Helen put down the summary table and looked Carol in the eye.

"I think you did make a mistake," Helen said very seriously.

All the blood suddenly drained from Carol's face. She turned ghostly white and muttered, "Oh no, oh no."

"You did make a mistake," Helen repeated. "It's not the low nineties, it's more like the *middle* nineties."

The smile on Carol's face lit up the room, and she gave Helen a double high five.

"This is really big," Helen said.

"I think we need a celebratory drink," Carol said. She went over and opened the refrigerator's small door, dug around in the snow-coated mess, and managed to pull out two bottles of green tea. She handed a bottle to Helen.

"Here's to us, the two best lie detectors in the world," Carol said and clinked her bottle against Helen's.

"I still can't believe it," Helen said. For a second her face took on a worried look as she remembered her angry conversation with Sam. But then she thought, *what can he possibly do?* Her smile returned.

"Now, tell me about your trip to Cabo," Helen said

CHAPTER 36

— — —

"It's a long story. The trip was fantastic until it came to paying the bill," Carol said.

"I like a long story, especially if there's some sex in it," Helen said and giggled.

"There are some sexy parts," Carol said, her cheeks turning a little pink.

"Then I'm all ears," Helen said.

"I persuaded Billy to spend a long weekend in Cabo. It's one of his favorite places for camping and one of my favorite places for escaping. It's on the very tip of the Baja peninsula, with the Sea of Cortex on one side and Pacific Ocean on the other. There are deserted sandy beaches, towering rocky cliffs, and it's all together very romantic," Carol said and let out a big, happy sigh.

"Enough about geography. I want to hear about the romance part," Helen said and laughed.

"Billy only knew about camp spots, so he told me to select a hotel, but he warned me not to pick anything too expensive. I knew a great tropical resort named Esperanza that my mother and I had once stayed at, and I had always hoped someday I could go there for a romantic interlude.

"Sounds perfect, so what's the problem?" Helen asked.

"Well, Esperanza is exclusive, private, romantic, and expensive. I mentioned going there to mother and that it might be *too* expensive. She said not too worry. It would be her treat," Carol said.

"But I thought Billy warned you to find a place not too expensive," Helen said.

"Well he did, but since mother said it would her treat, I thought Billy would be doubly pleased. We stayed in a private villa with a secluded sundeck and outdoor Jacuzzi overlooking the ocean. The villa was shielded from prying eyes by palm trees and red climbing bougainvilleas, which seemed on fire in the bright sun," Carol said, her emerald eyes glowing with excitement.

"Wow, that's where I want to go if things work out with Steve, and I win the lottery," Helen said and added, "So when do we get to the romancing part?"

"We arrived in the late afternoon, unpacked, and then ordered drinks. I got a pitcher of the resort's special tropical drink, and Billy got a six-pack of Dos Equis. We nuzzled together on our sun deck, kissed a lot, and watched the burnt orange sun slowly drop into the very blue ocean. By the time the sun had set, we were both completely naked," Carol said, making another happy sigh.

"This is the part of the story I like," Helen said.

"That night we had a candle-lit dinner on our patio, and later we walked along the deserted sandy beach until we found a secluded cave in one of the red-rocked cliffs along the ocean. Billy spread our beach blanket, and we had fun taking off each other's clothes. When we were naked again, we went into the ocean, which was warm and soothing, and we began touching each other until we were beyond ready."

"I think beyond ready is a great place to be," Helen said, her own checks turning a little pink.

"I asked Billy if we could wait and have the rest of the fireworks in our bedroom. When I was much younger, I had this fantasy about a dark, handsome man tying me to a bed and making love to me all night long," Carol said as her face was turning brighter pink. "The room just happened to have a king-sized, four-posted bed, topped with a colorful light blue silk canopy."

"I think I know where this is going, and I can't wait," Helen said.

"After I whispered my young-girl fantasy in his ear, he agreed to wait until we got back to our bedroom," Carol said.

"Why do you have all the luck?" Helen said and feigned disappointment.

"Well, we went back to our room, and Billy got the long ties from our soft, terry cloth bathrobes. After I got naked, he tied my arms to the bedposts and then whispered in my ear all the things he planned to do. And then, slowly and tenderly, he did all the wonderful things. By the time he finished, was sure I had died and gone to heaven," Carol said as a dreamy smile crossed her face.

"Well, if that's what heaven is like, I can't wait,' Helen said, then she added, "But, didn't it feel a little strange being tied up?"

"I have to admit, at first I felt a little strange because this had only been a fantasy and I'm not into bondage, but this was so different. Billy was kissing me everywhere, telling me to relax, touching and teasing me with his hands and tongue, whispering sweet things. The sensations were so strong and pleasurable, and all I wanted was to give myself completely, no holding back, no worrying about anything," Carol said.

"Well I have a fantasy of my own I would like to try," Helen said, "And if I ever do, you'll be the first to know. But what I don't understand is how any of this has to do with Billy's pride. It sounds like he was perfect."

"Well, he was perfect, in every way, except when he happened to see the bill. I had told the manager to personally give the bill to me, but some clerk had mistakenly slipped the bill under our door the morning we were leaving. When Billy saw it he went ballistic. The bill for four nights in our private villa overlooking the ocean, with gourmet meals, expensive wines, late night snacks, and my time in the spa came to just over three thousand dollars. Billy said that he could go camping for six months for that much," Carol said, looking very sheepish but knowing it had been worth every penny.

"I have to admit that's a bit much, so I'm not that surprised by Billy's ballistic reaction," Helen said.

"I explained to Billy how mother had wanted to give us a big treat, so it wasn't costing us a penny," Carol said, nodding as if that were a great deal.

"What did Billy say?" Helen asked.

"He got even madder. He said that having my mother pay for their romantic weekend not only hurt his pride but also made him feel like a jerk. It was the first time I've seen Billy get really angry," Carol said, her eyes filled with sadness.

"I can understand how Billy felt," Helen said. "I know he prides himself on being very independent and self-sufficient, so letting your mother pay was like a blow to his gut."

"But my mother has a ton of money, and she wanted to give us a treat. We did have the perfect weekend, so why can't Billy just enjoy it and not make a fuss about where the money came from?" Carol asked.

"Taking money from your wealthy mother threatens Billy's independence, suggests he can't make it on his own, and puts him in the category of being a kept man," Helen said.

"I never thought he might feel that way," Carol said.

"If you promised to discuss all future financial arrangements I think Billy would love you dearly," Helen said.

Carol's face broke into a big smile. "That's a great idea."

"You're a genius when it comes to algorithms, but you're not so great at understanding men. Just remember, men get very angry when their pride is threatened." Helen said.

"I've learned my lesson," Carol said and added, "But the story does have a happy ending. When our plane landed in San Diego, I told Billy it had been the most romantic, thrilling weekend I had ever spent. I held my breath, wondering is he would agree.

"Well, what did he say?" Helen asked.

"He didn't say anything for a long time. My heart sank, and I just stared at the floor. Then he gently raised my head, looked into my eyes, and said their weekend together had been the best time he'd ever had. His words made me so happy I kissed him so hard my lips hurt. I now have hope my big, strong, independent, prideful Billy may be falling in love with me," Carol said, her smile as big and bright as the rising sun.

"I think you may be right," Helen said, and she thought, *they're so different, but yet so good together. I sure hope it works out.*

Just then Carol's cell phone rang, and she automatically tensed. Family and friends knew not to call her cell phone when she was in her lab, unless it was an emergency.

She checked caller ID. She was much relived to see it wasn't Bart, but at the same time worried by the fact that it was her mother who was calling.

"Hi mom. What's happened?" Carol asked. She heard sobbing on the other end.

"Something terrible. Something terrible," her mother repeated between sobs.

"Try to calm down, and tell me what's happened," Carol said.

She heard her mother take several deep breaths. Her sobbing decreased.

"I received an anonymous note in today's mail," her mother sobbed. "The note said Randolph is having an affair with his secretary."

"Oh no," Carol gasped. "Read the note to me."

Between sobs her mother read the note.

"Did some business with your asshole husband. Treated me like crap. Owes me two mil. Probably money he stole from you. Bragged about screwing his secretary with the big tits. That's the God's truth. Stick it to him, 'til he bleeds. He's noting but a big jerk-off. p.s. You should have better."

"Oh mother! This is awful. I'll be right over. I'll try to get hold of Billy so he can help us decide what to do," Carol said, feeling so angry she wanted to take a knife, go to Randolph's office, and shove it deep into his lying heart.

"Yes, please come over. I don't know what to do. Maybe it's a bad joke. I don't want to believe it," her mother said. "I don't want to believe it."

"I'm on my way," Carol said. She heard her mother crying and softly moaning.

Carol clicked off the cell phone and stared into space, too angry to cry.

"What's happened?" Helen asked.

"It's my mother. She got an anonymous tip that Randolph is screwing his secretary and probably embezzling her money," Carol said, her hands forming fists.

"Good God! Do you think it's true?" Helen asked.

Carol though for several seconds and then said, "I do. Yes, I do. I've always suspected Randolph of being a ladies man because he's fired and hired three secretaries in the past five years, all of them sexy with big boobs. And he has very expensive tastes, so I'm not a bit surprised he may be embezzling some of my mother's money."

"So what are you going to do?" Helen asked.

"I'm not sure. I'm going to call Bill and see if he can meet me at mother's house. And why don't you come along, because more brains the better," Carol said.

"I'll be glad to help in any way I can," Helen said.

Carol had dialed Billy's private number and got him right away. "My mother got an anonymous note saying Randolph is cheating on her and stealing her money. Can you drop everything and meet me at my mother's house?"

"I'll be there in twenty minutes," Bill said.

Carol knew this was not going to be easy. Randolph was very, very clever and would deny everything unless they had absolute proof he was having an affair with the secretary and embezzling mother's money. *Leave that to Billy. If anyone can get proof, Billy can.*

CHAPTER 37

— — —

Bart still had trouble thinking of himself as Brother Paul but was gradually learning to respond to his name. He was sitting in his small cell on the third floor of an old monastery building that had been built with hand-made bricks by the founding monks in the early 1900s. He was working at his computer and remembering the words of Abbot Aloysius: *Trust in the Lord to show you the way, and I will pray you see the light and find a solution.* But he wasn't sure he would see the light and find a solution unless God pointed it directly in his face.

Abbot Aloysius had kindly agreed to let him hide away in the monastery, receive free room and board, and even be shielded from prying eyes. All he had to do was pull three-hundred thousand dollars out of thin air, which he knew would be a major miracle.

The abbot's words were playing in his head. *If Jesus could turn a jug of water and a few loafs of bread into enough wine and bread to feed hundreds, you and our computer can certainly find a way to turn the monastery's three thousand acres of virgin forest and wetlands into real money.*

How do I work a miracle? He thought for the hundredth time. *How do I find a pot of gold in the middle of a forest?*

He grumped, got up, and walked over to stare out his window. He needed some help, like God pointing to a spot in the forest with a big sign that read DIG HERE TO FIND GOLD.

He had first thought coming up with $300,000 might be doable, until the abbot had added a stern warning, "You may not cut down a single tree for lumber or destroy wetlands by building a golf course surrounded with luxury condos."

He didn't want to disappoint the abbot, who firmly believed God had heard the monks' prayers and sent him, a surfer dude from San Diego armed only with a computer, to save a monastery in central Minnesota. He had told the abbot if he had any chance of succeeding he needed the peace and quiet of a private room, which was not usual for probationary monks, who always shared a room. He had asked for and gotten a broadband cable connection, an iPhone, and even an iPad, which he used to play games and watch movies late at night when he was thinking about Anna and couldn't sleep.

He happened to glance at the religious wall calendar and see the big, red X, marking his approaching deadline. This month the religious calendar featured a painting of St. Laurence, who was pictured lying on a huge, red-hot frying pan. The story beneath the picture explained St. Lawrence was being tortured for giving all the church's riches to the poor and none to the Roman Prefect. According to the story, after St. Laurence was fried on one side, he asked to be turned over and broiled on his other side, his way of showing his complete and enduring love for Christ. Bart shook his head in awe and disbelief, but he was grateful the abbot hadn't mentioned any kind of torture if he failed to perform the $300,000 miracle.

The more he stared at the big, red X on the calendar, the more his nerves ran wild, as if someone had plugged him into an electrical outlet. The walls of his small cell seemed to be closing in, and he needed some relief. He put on his habit over his t-shirt and jeans, grabbed the book about St. Francis the Abbot had given him, and headed for the cloisters.

* * * *

The cloisters were a medieval structure that monks used for walking and mediating. They featured a rectangular walkway under a covered top with one side formed of open gothic arches. When the monks were not lost in meditation, they could look through the open arches at a center area open to the sky and filled with colored flowers.

The cloisters were one of his favorite places, all peace and quiet, and a chance to enjoy nature, in this case thousands of flowers. In busy San Diego, he had never paid much attention to the flowers, but in the solitude of the monastery, flowers seemed to take on a whole new life. An older brother with a green thumb cared for the flowers and even posted handwritten labels in beautiful calligraphy so dummies like Bart could learn their names. Bart's mother loved flowers and would be amazed and proud of his ability to point out the wisteria bushes with lush, blue trumpet flowers; jasmine vines with tiny, delicate, white, scented blossoms; bright red, pink, and lavender geraniums that glowed in the sunshine; and scrambling sweet peas that gave off the sweetest scent, which the old gardener had told him was the perfume of angels.

When he arrived at the cloisters, about a dozen other monks were already there, walking silently, in single file, leaving space between each monk to give a feeling of privacy. He had asked Brother James why monks always turned to the right as they followed the rectangle path. Brother James said an obscure verse in the Old Testament suggested turning right would lead to heaven, while turning left would lead to hell. But Brother James had a subtle sense of humor and may have been putting Brother Paul on.

As the monks walked down the center of the ten-foot-wide cloisters' pathway, some silently prayed with moving lips, some meditated with half-closed eyes, and others read spiritual books like *Life of Saint Francis of Assisi*. Every so often, a monk might move to the edge of the path, stop, and write down a religious insight or spiritual resolution in his private diary to document his growing relationship with God.

Bart liked walking in the cloisters, which was like being in a silent, peaceful universe, far removed from the stresses and strains of real life. But, he was a total failure when it came to mediating, praying, or having spiritual insights. No matter where his thoughts started, they always turned to a single topic: sex. The more he tried not to think about sex, the more he did. It was like an experiment in psychology he had read about. Students were told to try very hard not to think about a white bear, but the more they tried not to think about a white bear, the more they did. In his case, all he could think of was sex, sex, sex, sex, and more sex.

One minute he'd try thinking about St. Francis' message of being generous, loving your fellow, doing good deeds, and the next minute he'd be imagining putting his hands under Anna's T-shirt, feeling her wonderful breasts and hard nipples, until he was horny enough to hump a wisteria bush. He concluded he was not meant to be celibate, and he literally prayed he could somehow sneak out and meet Anna in neighboring St. Cloud so they could make love. But he had promised the abbot he would remain celibate as long as he was in the monastery, and so he would. Besides, he had grave doubts God would hear, much less answer his prayer to have sex with Anna.

He deliberately got back to reading the book about St. Francis and his amazing 360-degree turnaround. St. Francis went from being the son of a wealthy and privileged merchant to renouncing this comfortable lifestyle and giving away all his possessions. He changed to wearing coarse clothing, going barefoot, and preaching repentance. Bart was reading about how much St. Francis loved animals and nature when, for some unknown reason, an image the monastery's green forests and wetlands flashed in his head.

"I've got it. Go green! Thank you, God!" he shouted in excitement, forgetting for a moment he was breaking the silence of the cloisters. When he looked around, all the other monks in the cloisters were staring and giving him reproaching looks.

He put his head down and bowed, offering a nonverbal apology for his outburst. With head still bowed, he took the first exit out of the cloisters, and literally ran back to his cell, all the while thinking about the monastery's acres of green.

He couldn't help thinking about the answer coming to him while he had been walking in the cloisters, reading about St. Francis. He had an eerie feeling that somehow, someway, the answer might have come from God. He thought, *that's too weird and scary to think about now.*

When he returned to his cell, he took off his wool habit, got on the Web and began searching. Within ten minutes he found what he was looking for and began doing some calculations. When he had all the numbers, he started writing his proposal.

An hour later, he was printing out the proposal, which he had titled *$300,000 Miracle.* Unexpectedly, his cell phone rang. Only three people in the world had this number: the abbot, Father Dreadforth, and his sister, Carol, who would only call if there were an emergency.

"Brother Paul, could you come to my office?" the abbot said in a voice with a serious tone.

"I'll be there in five minutes," Bart said.

Placing his proposal into a folder, Bart put on his habit, and left his cell. As he hurried to the abbot's office, he wondered what had happened.

CHAPTER 38

— — —

Bart knocked on the Abbot's door and waited until he heard him say, "Come in."

As Bart entered the office he saw worry written across the abbot's face.

"I just received a visit from Brother James, who is both our official receptionist and our connection to the outside world," the abbot said, nervously tugging at his beard.

"I know Brother James. He helped me settle in."

"Brother James said that he had just received a phone call from someone named Mr. Mathew Moore, who was trying to reach Bartholomew Whatting from San Diego, California. Mr. Moore said that he believed Bartholomew had recently joined a monastery in Minnesota. It was important Bartholomew be found and informed of a family emergency," the Abbot said.

Hearing the name Mathew Moore made Bart's blood pressure hit the moon. "Matthew Moore is my stepfather's private detective, and I've been told he's very clever. But I know for sure there is no family emergency, because if there were, Carol would have phoned me immediately. And she hasn't called. Randolph has cooked up this family emergency story in an attempt to find me and haul me back to San Diego."

"I presume Randolph is the stepfather you have been avoiding?" the abbot asked.

"He's the very one, and he will go to any length to find me, even faking a family emergency."

"Do not worry. Brother James told Mr. Moore the monastery does not give out personal information about our monks. And, any request for information about a particular monk must be made in writing and sent to the abbot. This process that usually requires from two to three weeks," the abbot said.

"But how did Matthew Moore know I was here? No one knows except Carol, you, and Brother James," Brother Paul said in a strained voice.

"It appears Mr. Moore only knows you are staying at one of the many monasteries in Minnesota. He does not know which specific one."

"At least that's some good news. So what do you think Moore will do next?"

"Every monastery protects the privacy of their monks and will not give out personal information over the phone. The only thing left for Mr. Moore to do is come to Minnesota and visit each monastery. If he is as clever as you say, he might make up his own story. He could say he was thinking about becoming a monk and wondered what the qualifications were. He could ask if he could have a tour of the Monastery, which would give him the opportunity to look for you," the abbot said.

"Wow. You'd make a great private detective," Bart said.

"In many ways, an abbot's job is much like a private detective's. I must observe and be aware of problems monks might be having, make suggestions, and carefully help monks find their pathways to God," the abbot said.

"I can still remember how carefully you treated me in our first meeting. You asked questions and gave suggestions. You didn't criticize or get down on me for no longer being a practicing ."

"You forget to mention I also agreed to pray for your enlightenment," the abbot joked.

"But what'll happen if Moore does come here? What'll you say? I know telling a lie is against your faith."

"If Mr. Moore does come to ask if Bartholomew Whatting is in our monastery, I can honestly say 'no'. That is technically true since your name is now Brother Paul. Only Carol, Brother James, Father Dreadforth, and I know your real name. So for the moment, you are safe," the abbot said.

"How soon do you think Moore will turn up here?"

"That I do not know. But remember Moore will be looking for a longish, blonde-haired Bart. Now that your head is shaved and you're growing a beard, I think Moore will have difficulty recognizing you. Just to be safe, put on a pair of fake glasses. You will be surprised how those simple changes in appearance make recognition very difficult," the abbot said.

"How do know so much about disguises?"

"Every now and then we have to give a probationary monk a disguise so he can take part in our church services and not be recognized by a former romantic partner who might want to cause a scene," the abbot said.

Just be sure your disguise is in place on Sunday, when we have open house and people come to tour the church and hear about our Exorcism Center," the abbot said.

Brother Paul nodded and remembered how before coming to the monastery he had known little about exorcism, except for what he had seen in movies. Out of curiosity, he had attended several of the abbot's lectures on exorcism and found the subject weird and fascinating. The abbot had noticed his attendance and encouraged him to learn about exorcism, since he sometimes needed a backup when his laryngitis flared up. The abbot had encouraged him by saying, "People will like your boyish good looks and appreciate your enthusiasm." Bart had studied up, and after giving one of the lectures, he found he enjoyed doing it. He was amazed at how interested people were in exorcism and how many raised their hands when asked if they believed in devils. He still wasn't sure devils really existed, except of course for Randolph, who met all the qualifications.

"If Brother James had a description of Mr. Moore, he could watch and warn you if Moore did show up," the abbot said.

"I only saw Moore once and only briefly as I walked by when he was talking to Randolph's secretary. I seem to remember he was short, perhaps five-feet-six, with broad shoulders, round face, partly bald and middle-aged. The only thing about him that caught my attention was his suit. He was wearing the kind of thousand-dollar tailored suit that Randolph wears. That surprised me because my stereotype of a private detective is someone wearing casual clothes that won't be noticed."

"Well, except for the suit, your physical description of Mr. Moore fits half the men in the world. I will tell Brother James to watch for a short man in an expensive suit. In any case, if you do happen to see a short man in an expensive suit, just act naturally and go on with your lecture. Mr. Moore will be looking for a blonde, long-haired, beardless youth who does not wear glasses," the abbot said. He gazed at the ceiling for a moment and stroked his beard. "On second thought, perhaps it would be prudent if you did not appear in public and give the lecture on Sunday."

"I was thinking about opting out, but then I'd just sit in my room and worry about Moore. Might he come this Sunday? Maybe next Sunday? Maybe on a weekend? I would worry myself sick. I'd rather keep busy, give the lecture, and trust in my disguise. And besides, I have a secret weapon that will protect me from Moore."

"Pray tell, what is your secret weapon?" the abbot asked.

"It's you, of course. All the monks say you have a direct line to God, so if you pray for my safety, Moore can't get me."

There were two seconds of silence before the abbot's office was filled with laughter.

"Well, that's enough about Mr. Moore," Bart said. "I have something to give you that will knock your socks off, as we surfers say." Then he handed the abbot a file folder labeled in big bold type *$300,000 MIRACLE*.

"What is this?" the abbot asked as he took the proposal and read out loud, "The three-hundred-thousand-dollar miracle?"

"It's my idea for turning the monastery's forest and wetlands into piles of money without cutting down a single tree or destroying one acre of wetlands."

"I can read the big label, but tell me your idea. My aged eyes do not like to read small print."

"I didn't have a clue about how to come up with three-hundred thousand dollars, so I took a walk in the cloisters. As you suggested, I was reading and thinking about the life of St. Francis and how he liked nature and all animals, great and small. Then suddenly an idea came to me. The monastery sits in the middle of a huge nature preserve that might be as valuable as gold."

"You have my complete attention," the abbot said. His old eyes seemed to have gotten bigger and he had even stopped stroking his beard.

"I happened to remember reading about big industries offsetting the effects of their pollution by buying some kind of credits. I searched the web for pollution credits and found they're officially called 'environmental credits'. Big industrial companies get these credits by paying real money to preserve forests and wetlands so they can never be destroyed. The more factories pollute, the more environmental credits they need to buy. And here's the really good news for your monastery. I discovered the going price to buy environmental credits in Stearns county, where your monastery sits, is about eight-thousand dollars an acre. Your monastery has at least one thousand acres that qualify as natural forest and wetlands. If you turn one thousand acres into environmental credits, you're sitting on about eight million dollars," Bart said. He got up and gave the abbot big high-five with both hands.

"You have lifted an enormous weight from my already stooped shoulders. As I told you before, I believe God answered my prayers by sending you all the way from San Diego, California, to help a Minnesota monastery in deep financial trouble. I must admit your solution is spectacular, almost miraculous," the abbot said. A broad smile lit up his wrinkled face, like the sun breaking through dark clouds.

The abbot's words reminded Bart of all the strange events that had occurred and somehow led him to this particular monastery. Then he thought about the answer to the monastery's financial problem suddenly coming to him while walking in the cloisters, thinking about the life of St.

Francis. All these coincidences made him wonder if somehow, someway, he had gotten a little help from someone high above. That was a scary idea, especially since he wasn't yet sure he believed in that someone high above.

While he had been lost in thought, the abbot had gone over to the wall cabinet and come back with two glasses and a bottle of monastic-made apple cider wine.

"Time for a little celebration," the abbot said. He filled the glasses and handed one to Bart. As they started to drink, the office door almost burst open and in came three people dressed in dark blue jackets emblazoned with three large yellow letters: DEA. Behind the three came Brother James, who looked outraged at what was happening.

Bart was frozen with fear, knowing his worst nightmare was about to come true. He had watched enough crime programs on TV to know the letters DEA stood for Drug Enforcement Agency. These DEA agents had somehow found him, and they had come to arrest him for the briefcase full of cocaine found under his bed.

Chapter 39

— — —

The first DEA agent through the door was big, ugly, and had a protruding belly. His jacket was purposely opened wide to show his holstered gun, billy club, and can of pepper spray. Behind him came two other agents: a skinny man and tall woman, both equipped with similar weaponry. Bringing up the rear was Brother James, who looked so angry he might explode.

Brother James approached the abbot and said, "I am very sorry for this intrusion, but these agents insisted on seeing you immediately, without first calling. When I told them you do not see anyone without an appointment, they threatened to arrest me for obstruction of justice."

The abbot did not stand up or try to shake the agents' hands. Instead, he stared at each of the three agents in turn and then said, "I know the initials D-E-A stand for Drug Enforcement Agency. I have no idea why you are here, but I do know you have no excuse for treating Brother James so rudely, bringing lethal weapons into our monastery, or bursting into my office."

"Are you in charge of this monastery?" asked the big, burly agent in an unfriendly tone, obviously trying to intimidate the abbot.

"Actually God is in charge of this monastery. I am simply his agent," the abbot said.

The abbot's surly answer made the big agent's face turn red with anger. He was accustomed to blustering, posturing, and instilling fear, but this small, ancient, bearded man seemed not the least bit intimidated.

"Let me remind you that we are federal agents from the Drug Enforcement Agency and have every right to question you."

"Let *me* remind *you* that you are in God's house and need to show proper respect to me and my monks," the abbot answered. "Unless you do, neither I nor any of my monks will answer any of your questions."

"I'm sorry," said the woman agent, speaking in a reasonable voice, obviously the good cop in this trio. "We don't mean to be rude or disrespectful. We just have a few questions to ask."

"All right," the abbot said. "I will try to answer your questions."

"We have evidence that marijuana is being grown on your premises," the woman agent said.

Bart felt so relieved that the DEA agents had not come to arrest him he almost shook their hands and thanked them.

The abbot said, "If this were April first, I would say your accusation was an April fool's joke. But from your earnest expressions, I can see you are being serious. I can assure you there is no marijuana or any kind of illegal drug being grown on our monastic grounds." The abbot had responded truthfully. He had no way of knowing that under Father Dreadforth's supervision, Jim and Harry had been growing marijuana hidden about the tomato plants. "The only drug we make and use is home-brewed apple cider wine. And, I am sure you know, even Jesus approved of drinking wine. In fact, Brother Paul and I were just having a glass. Perhaps you would like to try some. It is good and refreshing." The abbot pointed to the bottle of cider wine sitting on his desk.

"No, no thank you," the female agent said. "There's no law against brewing apple cider wine for your personal use. We're here because of an unusual tip from a policeman in St. Cloud. He regularly buys organic tomatoes advertised as being grown at this monastery. The policeman swears, pardon my expression, that these are the best tomatoes he has ever eaten. But he noticed ever so often the tomatoes have a lingering sweet smell, much like that of marijuana. Our job is to check out every lead relating to growing marijuana for illegal distribution, no matter how far fetched, and that's why we're here today."

"In fact, we do have two lay persons who grow very good tomatoes on the monastic grounds. They give some of the tomatoes to us and sell the remaining in St. Cloud to cover their costs. But the idea these two lay persons, who are both good catholic boys, or any of our monks are growing marijuana with the tomatoes, is one of the strangest stories I have ever heard." The abbot relaxed in his chair. "I can already hear the monks laughing when I tell them of your accusation."

The three agents looked uncomfortable, shifting back and forth, not know what to say. They had to believe the abbot, who was not a man to tell a lie. But had yet to discover how some organic tomatoes, which the abbot admitted were grown on monastery grounds, carried the faint sweet scent of marijuana.

"I suppose you have already considered the possibility that one or more of the employees at the supermarket, who handle the tomatoes, may have smoked marijuana and in the process, contaminated the tomatoes with the marijuana smell," the abbot said.

"Actually we had considered that possibility and think you may be right. It is likely one or more of the store's employees smoked marijuana and then handled the organic tomatoes, and that left them smelling like marijuana. But you must understand, we needed to visit your monastery and check out any and all possibilities," the female agent said, somewhat apologetically.

"I see, I see," the abbot said. "If you wish to search our grounds or question our monks about growing marijuana, I hereby instruct Brother James to offer our complete cooperation. And if necessary, I will put such permission in writing."

"Oh, that won't be necessary. We just needed to make an official visit to show we had checked out the lead from the officer in St. Cloud. We'll make a report saying you were very cooperative and we found no evidence of your monks growing marijuana. In layman's terms, it means this case is closed," the female agent said and actually smiled a little, relieved this interview was over. She couldn't imagine monks growing marijuana.

The abbot slowly got to his feet, came around from behind his desk, and made it a point to shake each of the agents' hands.

"Oh, Brother James, be sure to give each of these agents a loaf of our famous homemade bread," the abbot said.

"Certainly," Brother James said.

"Thank you very much," the three agents said in unison.

After Brother James and the DEA agents had left, the abbot said, "I find it almost impossible to believe anyone would suspect or believe marijuana was being grown on the monastery's grounds."

Bart nodded in agreement but felt a little bad about the abbot, whom he had grown to like and respect, being left in the dark about Father Dreadforth's marijuana project. But he rationalized that he hadn't been involved in the growing part, which had occurred long before he arrived. Only recently had he become involved in the project and then only in some bookkeeping. He had promised Father Dreadforth to keep the marijuana project secret, and that's what he'd do. He'd tell Father Dreadforth about the DEA agents coming to the monastery and let him decide what to do. He couldn't help remembering Father Dreadforth's words, *No one in his or her right mind would ever believe the preposterous claim the monastery was in the marijuana growing business.*

"You certainly handled those agents very well," Bart said.

"They were no better or worse than some of the cranky monks I have dealt with through the years," the abbot replied.

"I'm sure they won't be back any time soon," Bart said.

"Now that the agents are gone, we can discuss how many acres of our forest or wetlands we should designate for environmental credits," the abbot said, smiling and stroking his beard as if it were a furry cat.

"You can begin by designating a small number of acres for environmental credits to cover the three hundred thousand dollars you owe the contractor. As you need more money, such as a winter trip to Tahiti, you can designate additional."

"Stand behind me, devil, and do not tempt me with a winter trip to Tahiti," the abbot said in a resounding voice, and they both had to laugh.

"Tonight at Vespers I will give special thanks to God for not only sending you here but also for helping you come up with the idea of environmental credits. As you can surely see, God does act in mysterious ways," the abbot said.

"Yes, thank God," Bart echoed. He was still unsure and confused about how much God was involved in all these happenings, if at all; but he had to admit the coincidences were mounting up and suggesting help from a higher source.

"What we need now is a little more cider wine, which I personally know cures a sore throat," the abbot said.

"I can agree to that," said Bart as he got the bottle and refilled their empty glasses. He thought the wine's alcoholic content must be pretty high since he was beginning to feel a nice buzz.

"I will tell you a secret," the abbot said, his face breaking into a sly smile. "I have two vices that cause me considerable guilt and require frequent confessing. The first you already know, which is spending two hundred dollars on exorbitantly flashy running shoes, which pamper my bony feet and put a bounce in my step. The second is drinking apple cider wine, which soothes my laryngitis and helps me forget about my aching muscles. I know I should renounce such worldly pleasures, but I pray daily for God to forgive me my small pleasures."

Then the abbot pulled up his habit a little, stuck out and wiggled both feet to display his latest pair of garishly colored running shoes that would normally be seen on a teenage hip-hopper's feet.

"Don't worry," Bart said. "My computer has a web site for God, and I'll ask him to overlook and forgive all of your guilty pleasures.

"If only it were that easy," the abbot said, and they both laughed.

Chapter 40

— — —

As the abbot had instructed, Brother James gave a loaf of the monastery's famous homemade bread to each DEA agent. The agents reluctantly thanked Brother James for the bread and headed for their big, black, powerful SUV, parked in front of the reception center.

The big, burly agent got into the driver's seat and the female agent settled in the passenger seat, while the skinny male agent was relegated to the back seat. The big agent started the twin-turbo-charged, 550-horsepower motor and put the SUV in drive. Just to be surly, he laid down a little rubber as he started down the monastery's narrow road. He was anxious to get back to the twin cities and watch the Vikings play on national TV. Although he had promised his wife many time to stop betting on sports, he had five hundred bucks riding on the football game. If she found out he was still betting, she would raise holy hell, but he was used to that after 15 years of marriage. And when he won, he always bought her something nice.

After a few minutes of silence, the big agent said, "That abbot may be a man of God, but he's a crafty old bastard, and I don't trust him one bit. I'll bet you a million dollars there's a marijuana farm somewhere on the monastery grounds."

"I thought he was very clever," the woman agent said. "He made us look foolish when he suggested the marijuana smell on the tomatoes came from one of the stocking clerks in the supermarket and not from anyone associated with the monastery."

"That's what I thought all along," said the skinny male agent. He liked to take credit any chance he got, and it drove everyone else nuts. It was one of the reasons he was forced to sit in the back seat.

"You're so full of shit that your stinking up the SUV," said the big agent. "Just remember, you're the jerk who said we should drive over and check out the monastery because you didn't trust monks."

Then the big agent deliberately turned around and gave the skinny agent in the back seat a look that said, "If I weren't driving, I'd bust your head in."

The big agent was very close to his breaking point. He'd been furious at the abbot for showing no respect and making him feel like a jerk. He was angry at his wife's nagging about his betting. He was worried about losing five hundred bucks on the Viking game, a bet he had placed impulsively. His knuckles were turning white from holding the steering wheel so tightly. His anger was eating at him, and he was driving much too fast on the narrow, curvy monastery road.

"Oh, let's not argue anymore about this. I'll write the final report and give all of us credit and that's that," the female agent said, tired of the other two quarreling like four-year olds.

"Slow down, or you'll kill us," warned the skinny agent in the back seat, who liked being an irritating back-seat driver.

"One more word and I'll throw you out," the big agent said as his rising blood pressure made the veins in his forehead pulse with each heartbeat.

He was just coming around a sharp curve when an old, crummy pickup truck seemed to shoot out of an overgrown forest road and turned right in front of the speeding SUV.

"What the hell," the big agent yelled, as he pressed his foot hard on the break pedal. If it weren't for antilock brakes, the SUV would have plowed into the back of the old pickup, which was going about as fast as an aging snail.

The big agent immediately turned on the special flashing headlights and hit the SUV's hidden siren, which wailed like an angry banshee.

The sound made Jim reflexively jerk around and see a huge black SUV with flashing lights right on his back bumper.

"What's happening?" Harry yelled as he turned around to see the looming black SUV. "It's got flashing lights and looks mean, like in the movies."

"Why turn on the siren? What's the deal? I've got every right to drive on this road," Jim said to no one in particular. He hated the sound of a siren because it always meant big trouble.

"Well I'll show them," Harry said and reached over to switch on the air horn that grandpa had put on the old truck as a joke. The air horn's bombastic blast easily trumped the siren's wails, and together they sounded like a jet plane taking off in the middle of a forest.

"Take that," Harry said, as he turned around, smiled, and waved his middle finger at the SUV.

"Can you believe that guy giving me the finger?" the big agent shouted, trying to be heard over the deafening air horn. He was past the breaking point. His face had turned purple-red. He would make someone pay.

The big, black SUV, with siren wailing and lights flashing, pulled alongside the old pickup. The SUV's blacked-out back window lowered, and the female agent gestured for Jim to pull over.

Jim was so mad he might have kept on going, but the SUV was moving closer and forcing him toward the side of the road. Slowly, Jim brought the truck to a stop.

The SUV pulled up in front, across the narrow road, blocking the truck's path, allowing no escape.

"Don't you say a single word," Jim cautioned. "I'll do all the talking. Not a single word out of your mouth. Got it?"

"Why do you get to do all the talking?" Harry asked.

"Because I think faster and better than you," Jim said, trying not to snap at Henry, whose feelings were easily hurt.

Jim was warning Harry to keep his mouth shut when his driver's door was yanked open. Jim saw what looked like an angry bully with a face as red as one of grandma's homegrown monster beets standing there and yelling.

"Get out!" the burly agent screamed. "Now! Put both hands on the side of the truck!"

"So what's the problem?" Jim asked, not wanting to get out of the truck.

"What's the problem? What's the problem? You're the problem! Now get out of the truck," said the burly agent. He had taken out his gun and was pointing it at Jim and Harry.

Jim got out, followed by Harry, who came around to Jim's side of the truck. Then they did as the agent had said and put their hands on the side of the truck.

Jim leaned over and quietly said in Harry's ear, "Don't say a word."

"Which one of you assholes gave me the finger?" the big agent asked, pointing his gun first at Jim and then at Harry.

Jim and Harry were too scared to say anything.

"I'm from the Drug Enforcement Agency, and you're both in a lot of trouble. If you don't cooperate, you'll be in jail for a very long time," the big agent said, looking and sounding like someone over the edge.

Jim and Harry were staring at the gun the agent was pointing and waving in their faces. Jim was afraid, but his stubbornness gave him courage to stand tall. Harry was petrified and trying to fight back tears.

The big agent pointed to the truck bed and almost shouted, "We came to the monastery because we got a tip someone was growing illegal marijuana among the tomatoes. Your truck bed just happens to be loaded with tomatoes, and when I put on the siren, you don't stop. Hiding something under the tomatoes? I'll bet it's marijuana. That's what I'm about to find out." The big agent smiled like a psychopath about to slit someone's throat.

"We growed those tomatoes. We're going to sell them in St. Cloud. Everybody know that's what we do," Harry said, getting back a little spunk as he remembered grandma saying that 'whatever your growed was yours and others better stand back and keep hands off.'

"We don't know nothing about marijuana. We only grow tomatoes," Jim said like he meant it.

"Well we'll see about that. I want you to open the tail gate and start dumping the tomatoes on the ground," the big agent said.

"No. They're our tomatoes, and you can't touch them without a warmmit. No warmmit, no touching, or you're dead,'" Harry said. He had learned a lot about police stuff from listening to rappers.

"He's just kidding," Jim said as he realized Harry had made the big guy so angry his eyes were shooting bullets.

"Did you hear what that jerk said?" the big agent asked as he glanced at the other two agents, who had gotten out of the SUV and were standing behind him. "No warmmit, no touching. That's really cute." Then the big agent turned back and stared into poor Harry's eyes. "You probably meant to say *warrant*. We'll, we don't need a warrant because we've got probable cause. And if anyone ends up dead, it's going to be you."

The big agent walked to the back of Jim's truck, unlocked and dropped the rusty tail gate, and was about to grab a carton filled with big, perfectly ripened, Big Boy tomatoes.

"You touch one of those tomatoes and I'll send the devils on you," Harry said.

"I'm not worried about devils, but maybe you should be," the big agent said.

"Oh please, don't ruin our tomatoes," Jim said in a begging tone. "Each carton is worth about a hundred dollars. That's how we make our living. Growing organic tomatoes, giving some to the monks and selling the rest. We don't know nothing about marijuana."

"Well, we'll see about that," the big agent said.

"Can I talk to you for a minute," the female agent said. She motioned for the big and skinny agents to follow her to the side of the SUV for some privacy. When all three agents had gathered, the female agent said, "That guy may be dumb, but he's right. We do need a warrant to make this search legal because we don't have probable cause. We're on private monastery property and we can't legally search their truck just because it's carrying tomatoes. I don't smell marijuana and don't see any evidence the truck is transporting marijuana. We need to back off and let them go."

The female agent was the expert when it came to legal matters, such as deciding when and if a warrant was needed to conduct a search for illegal drugs.

"Well I don't give a shit about legalities now. I'm pissed off, and I know the abbot was lying through his false teeth. I'm going to make them dump out every carton of tomatoes until I find the marijuana. Then I'm going back to the monastery and rub it in the abbot's face. And don't either of you try to stop me," the big agent said, so furious that he was spitting as he spoke.

The big, red-faced agent turned, walked back to the old pickup, and stopped in front of Jim and Harry, who were standing by the side of their truck.

"I'm going dump out every carton of tomatoes until I find the marijuana. If either of you move an inch, I'll handcuff you to a tree and leave you to die. Just stand and watch. Got it?" the big agent yelled in Harry's face.

"Please, let me pour the tomatoes out of their cartons so they're not damaged and we can still sell them in St. Cloud," Jim begged.

Harry was nodding his agreement.

"One of you gave me the finger, so I'm not doing you jerks any favors," the big agent said. He walked to the back of the truck, grabbed a Big Boy tomato from the first carton, turned, and threw it at a big oak tree across the road.

They all hear a loud *splat* when the tomato, almost as big as a softball, hit the tree. Then the big agent's pent up anger and rage came out, and he went berserk. As fast as he could, he was picking up tomatoes and hurling them across the road at old oak trees, whose trunks were slowly turning bright red from tomato juice. The big agent continued throwing tomatoes until the first carton was empty. He was so furious and out of control that he squashed many of the tomatoes before throwing them, and his hands, shirt, pants, and jacket were stained bright red with tomato juice.

After emptying the first carton of tomatoes, the big agent stopped. He looked at Jim and Harry and said, "If you want to save the rest of your tomatoes, tell me now where you have hidden the marijuana."

"There isn't any marijuana," Jim yelled.

As Harry watched his beloved tomatoes being destroyed by this big bully, some of his courage came back. Before the big agent started throwing tomatoes from the second carton, Harry yelled, "Take this!" and gave the big agent the finger.

"You do it again, and I'll break off that finger and stuff it in your mouth," the big agent roared as he reached into second carton. But instead of throwing tomatoes at the oak tree, he began throwing them at Jim and Harry, whose faces and clothes were soon red and sodden with tomatoes juice. All the time the big agent was laughing like a drugged-out maniac.

The other two DEA agents could do nothing but watch. They knew it would take a dozen of them to stop the big agent, who had totally lost control.

By now the big agent was into the third carton, alternating between throwing tomatoes at Jim Harry and the oak trees. The other two agents had no choice but to stand back and wait for their partner to wear himself out.

There was so much going on that no one noticed the arrival of a large, black car, shaped very much like a baby whale on wheels. The streamlined car had silently pulled up and stopped, hidden completely by the agents' big SUV, which had been parked across the road to block Jim's pickup.

Chapter 41

■ ■ ■

The driver's door of the baby-whale-shaped car opened, and out stepped a man dressed in a black suit, wearing the white collar of a priest. But more noticeable than the white collar was his black eye patch, emblazoned with a silver cross. The man came around the SUV and walked toward Jim and Harry. He stopped in front of them. The tall priest's unexpected appearance in front of Jim and Harry stopped the big agent's hand just he was about ready to hurl another tomato.

"What's going on here?" Father Dreadforth asked in the sudden silence. He used his most commanding voice, the one he used to mesmerize his radio listeners.

The big agent's mouth opened, but no sound came out. The agent's arm, which had been coming forward to throw a tomato, was fixed in place, as if turned to stone. The other two DEA agents, who had been watching the mad, ugly, tomato-hurling show, looked with surprise at the tall man, who had the voice of authority, as well as a silver cross on his black eye patch.

"Holy shit," the skinny male agent said, and then he quickly added, "I've had nothing to do with this. It was all his idea." He pointed at the big agent, who was still holding a tomato.

"Oh no," the female agent said and spread out her arms as if asking for peace and forgiveness.

"Who are you?" the big agent finally managed to say, his face twisted with anger and his hands and clothes red from tomato juice.

Father Dreadforth took his time replying. He looked at the three agents. They were wearing jackets with yellow DEA initials on the right front sides of their jackets. He looked at Jim's truck, whose bed was filled with cartons of tomatoes. The priest was not surprised to see Jim and Harry because he had previously arranged to meet them at the monastery road's turn off.

Without saying anything, Father Dreadforth went over and whispered some instructions in Jim and Harry's ears. Then he reached into his suit coat pocket, brought out his iPhone, and began taking photos of the DEA agents.

Suddenly, Jim and Harry ran over and laid down in front of the big agent's feet and began mugging pained expressions and acting very much like they had been severely beaten.

Father Dreadforth took pictures and a short video of Jim and Harry, whose faces and clothes were red from tomato juice, lying at the feet of the big agent, whose hands and clothes were also red from tomato juice.

"Just give me a minute while I email these photos and a short video to the diocese's attorney in St. Cloud. You can be certain he will be quite amazed and disturbed by what he sees," Father Dreadforth said.

The agents didn't know what to do.

Jim and Harry had gotten up, walked over to stand next to Father Dreadforth. They were smiling broadly, like two children who had just pulled off a prank on the neighborhood bully.

The big agent was slowly returning to his senses, like someone coming out of a coma. He dropped the tomato he had been holding but hadn't yet said a word.

In his commanding voice, Father Dreadforth said, "As I am sure you will agree, the color photos and video I took will clearly show Jim and Harry, beaten and blooded, lying at the feet of an official agent, whose DEA initials can be clearly seen on the right side of his jacket."

The three agents said nothing.

"I assume you do not have a warrant to search this truck or destroy the owner's private property," Father Dreadforth said, knowing the answer.

"They didn't have a warmmit," Harry shouted. "I asked them for one and said touch nothing or you're dead, like in the song, and then that big guy got mad and threatened us and started throwing tomatoes."

"Harry's right," Jim added. "I said I would carefully take out the tomatoes so they won't be damaged, but that big guy started gabbing and throwing tomatoes like he was a mad Frankenstein monster."

"He said he was looking for marijuana, and I said he was crazy, and he said he would break my finger unless I pointed to the marijuana," Harry said. Even Harry knew that this wasn't exactly what happened, but it had some truth to it, and that was good enough for him.

"There was a misunderstanding," the female agent said.

She had been going over what had happened, and it was much worse than a misunderstanding. They were involved in making an illegal search on private property with no probable cause and without a warrant. Furthermore, one agent was involved in deliberately destroying valuable assets—in this case, tomatoes—as well as attacking two men with tomatoes.

And these actions were photographed and video taped and sent to the diocesan attorney, who would assume the two men had been beaten and bloodied by the big agent, at whose feet they had laid. Even though it was only tomato juice, it would look like blood. And it would be the agent's word against the word of a priest as to what happened, and the agents would lose. The agents were in very big trouble.

"This was certainly more than a misunderstanding, as the photos and video will show. However, despite your blatantly illegal actions, I do not want to embarrass the DEA or jeopardize your careers. And as the bible says, forgive people when they do wrong things, Mathew, 6:14. I will forgive the evil you have done to Jim and Harry and allow you to drive away...under the following conditions. Whatever happened here will remain confidential, provided you file no charges or take any further actions against Jim and Harry, two very good friends of mine," Father Dreadforth said. He paused, allowing time for the agents to consider his generous offer of forgiveness. "If instead you chose to press on and file some made-up charges against Jim and Harry, I will give the photos and video I just took to newspapers and TV reporters, as well as post them on the Web. In that case, you will have to explain to the public and to your bosses in Minneapolis, why Jim and Harry were beaten and bloodied for hauling tomatoes to the local market in St. Cloud." Father Dreadforth deliberately made eye contact with each agent.

"There was a misunderstanding," the female agent said, worried this incident might destroy her career in the DEA. "One of our agents let his anger override his sanity and obviously went too far. We are very sorry for what happened and wish to make amends. We accept your generous offer of forgiveness. We will not report what happened, press charges, or make any future arrests. We will leave this premises and no one will ever hear or know what happened."

"In that case, you will be forgiven. But remember, if you ever change your minds and pursue any future actions against Jim and Harry, I have photos and a video I will make public and will destroy your careers. Is that clear?" Father Dreadforth asked, in his commanding tone.

"It is very clear," the female agent said.

"Let me hear from the other two agents," Father Dreadforth demanded.

"It is clear," said the burly agent covered in red tomato juice.

"It is clear," said the skinny agent, who gave his burly colleague a dirty look for having caused this trouble.

Without further adieu, the three agents walked over to their SUV and got in. But this time the female agent got into the driver's seat and the skinny male agent got into the passenger seat. The big male agent, red and sticky from tomato juice, got into the back seat, feeling like he had been shit upon. The female agent started the motor, and pushed the SUV's accelerator to the floor.

No one spoke for several miles, but then the burly agent in the back seat finally said, "That dirty priest bastard planned the whole thing to look like I beat those two kids bloody."

"Forget it," the female agent said. "You were way out of bounds and got what you deserved. Just be careful because if anyone ever sees those photos, our careers will be over."

"I knew we should have never come to the monastery," the skinny male agent in the passenger seat said. Secretly he was overjoyed the big dope had finally got what he deserved and had been put in his place.

Jim, Harry, and Father Dreadforth watched the agents' SUV disappear down the road. They waited a few minutes to make sure the SUV was not coming back.

"Got to thank you for getting rid of those federal agents. For a while I thought we were goners," Jim said.

"Yeah. I liked the way you scared the shit out of them, pardon my language" Harry said.

"I always take care of my friends," Father Dreadforth, said and he checked his watch. "I am sure the agents are on their way to Minneapolis. Let us see what you have in the truck bed."

"OK," Jim said and reached over the side of the truck. He unloaded two cartons of tomatoes that were in at the very front of the truck's bed.

"It's really great stuff. It's the best yet, and I knew that for sure," Harry said and grinned like a young child who just got a wished-for puppy. He always said that it was the "best yet," because for him, it always was.

From the top of each carton, Jim carefully removed several layers of tomatoes, which he would sell later in St. Cloud. Then he took out eight plastic zip-top bags filled with Blessed Religious Marijuana, known to all the local users as BRM.

Father Dreadforth examined each bag before putting it into his specially designed, black leather briefcase that had a large silver cross embossed on its front. When closed, this particular briefcase was designed to be airtight, thus preventing the escape of any telltale sweet marijuana odors. Father Dreadforth was successful at everything he did because he thought of every detail and never left anything to chance.

"I am very concerned about the unexpected arrival of the DEA agents, so we need to be extra careful," Father Dreadforth said. "You need to close down the monastery's marijuana field as soon as possible. Be sure to take away and bury all the remaining marijuana plants so there will be no incriminating evidence if the meddlesome DEA agents decide to return to do a more thorough search. We still have a large supply of potent marijuana seeds to plant next spring".

"I'm afraid we won't be around to plant any seeds next spring," Jim said. "Harry and I have saved our money, and as soon as we clean out the marijuana field and get packed, we're heading for big Lake Okeechobee in southern Florida."

"Oh-choke-bee, Oh-choke-bee, here we come! Catch some bass as big as Aunt Lucy's big ass," Harry shouted and started jumping with his arms and legs going in every direction, like a puppet whose strings got crossed.

Father Dreadforth was not known for displaying much emotion, but even had to smile at Harry's show of unbridled exuberance.

"I know you have been talking about going to Florida for some time," Father Dreadforth said.

"Maybe you can give us some holy water to pour into lake Oh-choke-bee so the bass will be easier to catch," Harry said, believing there was no limit to what a little holy water could do. Then Harry got worried and asked, "Is it OK to swim in holy water?"

"Yes, it is alright to swim in holy water, and it may even make you a better person," Father Dreadforth said, and then he added as his own personal joke, "Just do not try to walk on it."

"I won't. I won't," Harry said and broke into a smile as innocent as that of a two-year old.

"Well, come visit us in Florida," Jim said before he got into his truck. "We'll be staying at one of those small towns around the huge lake, probably Clewiston or Pahokee. We'll let you know."

"Best of Luck," Father Dreadforth said as he handed Jim an envelope stuffed with one hundred dollar bills. "Just remember, the bible says, 'the lord has plans to help you prosper,' Jeremiah, 29:11. I will be sure to send Harry a big bottle of holy water and also pray for your continued success."

Jim put the bulky envelope in his back pocket and smiled as he thought about finally getting out of Minnesota. Never again would he have to struggle through sub-zero winters, sweat through hot-humid summers, or battle monster mosquitoes with stingers like machine guns.

Jim and Harry said their good-byes and Harry gave Father Dreadforth a big hung. Then they got into the old truck, Jim started it, and they headed for St. Cloud to sell the remaining undamaged tomatoes.

Father Dreadforth returned to his 1950 restored Step-down Hudson and drove away to make his last delivery of marijuana. Although he was disappointed the lucrative marijuana project had ended, a favorite verse from Philippians, 4:13, came to mind. He said to himself, *I can do everything through him who gives me strength.* Then he smiled because the good Lord had just sent him an idea for new, interesting project.

CHAPTER 42

— — —

A rather ordinary-looking, middle-aged man was driving his rental Ford Focus down the tree-lined road to the St. Francis Monastery. It was a beautiful sunny Sunday afternoon, and he couldn't help admiring the trees. Their leaves had turned brilliant shades of red and yellow, as if someone had gone wild with a paint gun. He had just rounded a sharp curve when he saw an older car stopped along the side of the road. A young woman was standing near the back of the car, waving her hands in the air, obviously needing help. No sooner did he stop than the young woman was at his open window, bending down to talk.

"My old van died on me. Its fuel gauge no longer works, so I think I must have run out of gas. I drained the battery trying to get it started, and now it's beyond dead. I was wondering if you could give me a ride to the monastery?" the young woman asked, seeming nervous and talking fast.

She didn't like asking a strange man for help, much less getting into his car, something she'd never normally do. But she wanted to get to the monastery for the Sunday tour and thought she was already late.

"No problem. Glad to help. Just hop in we'll be on our way to the monastery," the middle-aged man said and smiled.

"Oh, that's great. Thank you," the young woman said. She paused several seconds to observe the man's smile. She had learned a man could lie with his eyes but not with his smile. She knew when a smile was fake and being used to cover a lie. *This man's got a friendly smile and be could be trusted.* She nodded to herself, went around to the passenger side, got in, and as she sat down, she gave a big sigh of relief.

The man checked the rearview mirror, saw nothing coming, and pulled out.

"Sorry about your car. It's lucky I came along because I think we're at least eight miles from the monastery. That's a long walk, even if the scenery is so spectacular," the man said, happy to have such an attractive young woman to talk to after driving alone for the last 75 miles.

"The leaves are beyond incredible. They remind me of the colored crayons I had as a child. I loved the yellow, red, and orange crayons most. I didn't like the gray, black, or brown ones. I fed them to my dog, who ate them. It turned his teeth funny colors," the young woman said and laughed. She knew she was talking silliness, but she wanted to forget about her car breaking down and almost being late for the tour.

"And what are you going to do at the monastery?" the man asked. "Are you thinking about becoming a monk?"

He laughed, and she joined in because it was an outrageous idea. She wondered how she would look in a monk's habit and if they would make her remove the two earrings in each pierced ear?

"I'm planning to meet someone," she said and added, "What about you?"

"I'm also planning to meet someone," he said. "Who are you planning to meet, if I'm not being too nosey?"

She hesitated for just an instant, wondering how much to tell. For some strange reason she had always found it easy to tell anything and everything to a complete stranger, and so she told him everything.

Over the course of their drive, she found him to be a great listener. Along the way, he had offered some helpful suggestions, but he wasn't pushy, unlike most men who wanted to do all the talking. The miles passed so quickly that before she realized, he was parking the car in the rather crowded visitor's lot.

After he had parked, she turned to him and said, "I want to thank you again for giving me a ride, for listening to me, and especially for all the wonderful advice."

"I was glad to listen, and I hope I was of some help," he said. "Perhaps I'll see you later?"

"That's for certain," she said and smiled.

She was feeling better all around and impulsively stuck out her hand.

He took her hand and gave it a friendly squeeze.

Then they parted and went their separate ways.

* * * *

About the same time the middle-aged man had stopped and offered a ride to the attractive young woman, Abbot Aloysius was sitting in his office, chewing on lozenges to ease his laryngitis and stroking his long, gray, silky beard. He was worrying about what would happen if Mathew Moore showed up for the exorcism lecture and tour. He was wondering if Moore could see through Brother Paul's disguise. He was considering if the prudent thing to do was cancel the lecture and have Brother James conduct the tour. Then his phone rang.

"Hello, this is Abbot Aloysius."

"This is Brother Paul. I wondered if I could drop by for a few minutes and ask for a favor."

"Since you saved our monastery financial ruin, I owe you a hundred favors, provided what you ask is legal, moral, and righteous," the abbot said.

"It's all the above and concerns Mathew Moore."

"I will be waiting for you in my office."

Bart put down the phone and for the hundredth time, looked at himself in the mirror. His head was shaved, his short, blonde beard was dyed dark brown, and he was wearing a pair of large, ugly glasses.

Even I don't recognize me. It's sort of fun to being a wolf in sheep's clothing. But he couldn't completely erase the nagging thought in the back of his head. *If Moore somehow recognizes me, will the abbot come to my rescue?*

He left his monastic cell, hurried to the abbot's office, and knocked on his door.

"Come in," said the abbot, his laryngitis making his voice sound like a sick frog.

Bart went in, stopped in the middle of the room, and made like he was a statue. "Who do you think I am?" he asked.

"If I did not know better, I would think you were Samson himself."

They both laughed, and Bart was grateful for the relief.

"Seriously, if you looked real hard, would you recognize me as Bart?"

"If I looked real hard, I might think you were Delilah," the abbot said.

They both laughed, this time so hard the abbot began coughing and had to chew two lozenges.

"A good laugh is worth a million dollars. But about your favor, am I correct to assume it concerns Mr. Moore?" the abbot asked.

"It does. If Moore does show up and recognizes me, he'll likely call the state police, have me arrested for cocaine possession, and I'll end up in jail." Bart said and wiped the beads of sweat from his forehead.

"That is most likely what will happen," the abbot said and frowned.

"Although Randolph is paying Moore to find me, I'm hoping he's an honest man and would agree to meet with you and me. I'm hoping you'll help me persuade Moore to give me a chance to clear myself. I'm going to ask Moore to take me to Minneapolis and meet with Anna. She'll explain taking the case of cocaine from Tony Koole, not knowing it was full of cocaine, and bringing it to San Diego. I'll explain all I did was put the cocaine under my bed for Tony and his goons to find. I'll ask him to let me and Anna drive back to San Diego. We can't fly because my name would be flagged for having an outstanding arrest warrant. Once back in San Diego, I'll get a good lawyer, anyone but Randolph, to make a statement to the police and clear us of any drug charges."

"I think it is a good plan, but I am concerned about what happens to Moore when Randolph discovers he found you but let you go," the abbot said.

"I thought about that. Perhaps Moore could tell Randolph he didn't find Bart Whatting, which as you said is technically true since he only found Brother Paul. And I know my mother will show her appreciation for Moore's help me by giving him an appropriate reward. It'll probably be the first time a private detective gets paid for not finding someone."

"There is just one more thing," the abbot said.

"And what's that?" Bart asked as he felt his muscles tighten.

"You may be leaving us very soon, and we have not had a chance to discuss how you teach a computer to write a children's book."

"Well, it has been very busy around here, doing miracles and all, but I did do some experimenting. I tried teaching the computer to write religious nursery rhymes, which I thought might be right up your alley. Do you want to hear one?"

"A religious nursery rhyme. That is something I have always longed to hear," the abbot said and grinned.

"All right. Here are two examples, and you better hang on to your beard."

Little Miss Muffet sat in a pulpit
Eating soft scrambled eggs
Suddenly Baby Jesus appeared
Sat down beside her
And took all her sins away."

Bart noticed the smile on the abbot's face as he continued.

"Peter, Peter the ice cream eater
Had a wife but couldn't keep her
Had her baptized by the pope
Now she happily sits around and smokes dope."

"Your computer's algorithms are outrageous," the abbot said. He was laughing so hard he needed to take three lozenges to stop coughing.

"When I get back to San Diego, I'll have my computer write a book of religious nursery rhymes and dedicate the book to you," Bart said.

"Deal," the abbot said. He got up and came around to give Bart a big, friendly hug.

"Well, I better get ready for my lecture," Bart said, stepping back. The abbot's friendly hug had touched him so deeply he was trying hard to hold back his tears. After all these years, he had finally found the father he had been looking for.

CHAPTER 43

On leaving the abbot's office, Bart went back to his cell to dress and go over his lecture. After checking his notes a last time, he put on his brown, somewhat scratchy, wool habit, tied the white knotted-rope belt around his waist, and adjusted the hood so it didn't bunch up and make him look like he had a growth on his back. It was going to be a warm Sunday afternoon, so underneath his robe he wore only briefs and a t-shirt.

He left his cell and began walking to the monastery's Hospitality Hall. As he thought about giving his lecture, he hands got clammy and his mouth turned dry. He always got nervous before speaking in public, but this time he was doubly nervous. *What if Matthew Moore turns up and sees through my disguise?*

He walked to Hospitality Hall and entered through its fifteen-foot-high, wooden door decorated with carvings of angels. Hospitality Hall had once been the monastery's church, built in the late eighteen hundreds by the founding monks. But after a new and larger church was constructed, the old church was deconsecrated. It could now be used for non-religious activities, such as a gathering place for tourists.

Every time he entered the hall, he couldn't help looking up at the gigantic face of Jesus painted on the great dome of the soaring, forty-foot-high ceiling. The face of Jesus was brightly illuminated and seemed magically suspended in space, like the full moon hanging in a night's black sky. Jesus had large, dark eyes that magically seemed to follow him as he moved around the hall. Every time he looked up and saw Jesus' dark, mysterious eyes looking at him, he had to take several deep breaths.

He watched as Hospitality Hall slowly filled with visitors. They had come to hear a lecture on the Exorcism Center, gaze upon the stained glass façade of the new, ultra-modern church, peruse the library's vast collection of illuminated medieval manuscripts, and buy a loaf or two of the monastery's famous homemade multigrain bread.

He walked around Hospitality Hall, introduced himself, and shook hands with the visitors. Between handshakes, he had to dry his clammy hands by wiping them on his forgiving habit. He tried to act naturally while at the same time discreetly searching for anyone resembling Moore, especially anyone short and very well dressed. Most visitors were casually but nicely dressed. As the abbot had said, 'Minnesotans were not show-offs, so a well-dressed man, like Moore, should stand out like a peacock in a flock of chickens.' But so far, no man had been wearing a tailored suit. He just hoped and prayed that Moore had not decided to dress down, knowing that he would stand out in his tailored suit.

Bart glanced up at the large clock on the refurbished brick wall and saw it was time to begin his lecture. He walked to the front of the hall, turned, and faced the group of visitors.

"Would you please take your seats," he said.

The thirty or so visitors, more women than men, began sitting down in handmade, dark-stained oak chairs made comfortable with thick red cushions. Once again Bart casually tried to look at each of the dozen or more men. He felt some relief at seeing no one resembling Mathew Moore.

After everyone was seated, Bart pointed to an impressive, fifteen-foot high, white Carrera marble statue situated in the center of the semi-circle of the visitor's chairs. "You're looking at a statue of St. Michael, who is called an archangel because he was ranked highly by God,". "St. Michael was chosen to be the patron saint of the monastery's Exorcism Center because he led an army of faithful angels in a heavenly battle against rebellious angels. The leader of the rebellious angels was called Satan, or Lucifer, who wanted to be like God and share in his power and glory. St. Michael drove Satan and his rebellious angels, thereafter called devils, into the fires of hell. St. Michael is often portrayed as a mighty warrior, as you see here. He holds a jewel-studded sword in his right hand, a blue shield emblazoned with a white cross in his left, and under his foot is the ugly, horned head of Satan. Many people believe devils do exist, roam the earth, and tempt good people to engage in sinful actions and perform evil deeds. Just out of curiosity, how many of you believe in devils?"

As expected, almost everyone raised his or her hand, and a few even waved their hands back and forth to emphasize their very firm belief in devils, much like people at a concert wave their hands to music.

"Well, just remember that St. Michael, a powerful archangel, is on your side. He is someone you can pray to when tempted by the devil."

Then Bart moved slightly to the right side of the statue and stepped on a hidden floor switch. The lights gradually dimmed until the hall was completely dark. Then four floodlights hidden in the floor around the

223

statue of St. Michael flashed every few seconds, creating the illusion of St. Michael's fully extended, fifteen-foot, silver-tipped wings moving back and forth.

When Bart had first proposed creating this wing illusion, many of the older, more conservative monks thought it totally irreligious and a mockery of St. Michael. But the abbot overrode the conservative monks and told Bart to install the flashing lights, which would get the visitors' attention and fix the powerful image of Saint Michael in their thoughts.

And the abbot had been right because these visitors first sat in awed silence then spontaneously starting clapping as they watched St. Michael's magnificent, fifteen-foot, marble wings appear to move. After a few minutes, Bart stepped on another floor switch, and the flashing lights stopped. A single flood from above came on to put all the attention on him and St. Michael, leaving the rest of the hall dimly light.

"Wow, that was impressive," said a man wearing suspenders over a plaid shirt.

"Never seen anything like that," said a woman in a long, floral print dress.

"Do it again," said someone in the back.

Bart just smiled and waited until the crowd settled down, and then he restarted his lecture.

"The most famous Exorcism Center is located at the Vatican, in Rome. The Vatican center offers a six-month course in exorcising devils and enrolls about one hundred and twenty individuals per year, including priests, lay people, and theology students. The St. Francis Monastery's Exorcism Center offers a similar six-month course with an enrollment of twenty-five to fifty individuals, including monks, brothers, priests, theology students, and interested laity."

"How many exorcisms are done each year?" interrupted a woman at the very front, who was holding a bible in her lap.

"At the Vatican's Exorcism Center, about three hundred individuals go through the exorcism rituals each year. Here at St. Francis, the monks perform fifty to one hundred exorcisms each year, and the number has been steadily increasing."

"How much does each exorcism cost, and how do you set the price for doing what is really God's work that should be done in the name of charity, as preached by your own founder and namesake, St. Francis?" the same woman asked in a belligerent voice.

The abbot had warned Bart that there were usually one or two visitors who for some personal or religious reason made hostile comments.

Bart turned to look at the woman and said in as friendly a tone as he could muster, "There is no fee for an exorcism, for as you so correctly pointed out, it is God's work. Some individuals make donations, but are not required or asked to do so."

"How do you know if someone is possessed?" asked an elderly man in the second row.

Just as he was about to answer, he heard the sound of the main oak door opening and reflexively turned in that direction. There were always one or two visitors who came in late. He watched the visitor enter, walk through the well-lit foyer, and continue on to take a seat in the back of the dimly lit main hall.

What he saw made him hold his breath. The late-arriving visitor was short and wore what seemed to be an expensive, tailored suit. He realized the late-arriving visitor most likely was Matthew Moore. The abbot had told him that if Moore did show up, he should act natural, continue the lecture, and trust in his disguise. He took a couple of deep breaths, faced the seated visitors, and continued his lecture, speaking clearly and slowly to cover his growing fear. "Someone had asked how one decides if someone is possessed," he said and avoided looking where Moore might be sitting.

"This is the most difficult question because there is no absolute test to determine if someone is possessed by a devil. Rather it is a matter of interpreting various signs that suggest demonic possession. According to the Exorcism Center at the Vatican, these signs are diverse and may include a person suddenly developing an aversion to holy water, spiting out the sacred host, blaspheming the cross, swearing repeatedly at priests or nuns, displaying superhuman strength, or suddenly speaking a foreign language. A large part of our course on exorcism involves identifying signs and symptoms that separate devil possession from mental illness."

"This devil stuff sounds just awful. What I want to know is how exactly do you drive out a devil?" asked a woman in a trembling voice, as if she suspected a loved one might be possessed.

"For reasons of privacy I can't go into cases from our Exorcism Center. But I can tell you about a case published by Father Amorth, the well-known Vatican exorcist, who is said to have performed many thousands of exorcisms. He describes a forty-four-year-old woman, the mother of two, who had endured years of pain, had been tested by many doctors and spiritual healers, had attempted suicide, and had experienced several previous exorcisms. Father Amorth explains the devil is a very stubborn enemy, and a possessed person is not usually cured in a single exorcism but may require many exorcisms, over many years. According to Father Amorth, this woman displayed rather typical symptoms of demonic possession, such as experiencing a visceral and utter repulsion of all holy things. As part of the exorcism ritual, Father Amorth wrapped a priest's purple scarf or stole around the woman's shoulders, made the sign of the cross with his finger on her forehead, and began praying while anointing the woman with holy water and oils, all the time demanding that the devil state it's name and be gone from this woman. During the exorcism ritual, the devil fought back and the woman ranted in foreign languages, showed violent and superhuman strength, and could barely be held down. Amorth reported that her devil was finally exorcised and the woman feels strong and is on the road to full recovery."

"That's unbelievable. Is all that stuff really true?" asked the woman with the troubled expression.

"Father Amorth says that his favorite film is The Exorcist, which he says is based on an actual case. It is substantively correct, although the special effects were greatly exaggerated."

"How do we find out more about devil possession and exorcism?" asked a woman in the back who Bart could not clearly see.

"As you leave the hall, feel free to take one of our brochures about the monastery's Exorcism Center. There will also be several monks in the foyer to answer any other questions. It's almost time for Vespers, which is the name for our afternoon religious service when all the monks gather in the church to give praise to God. You are all invited to attend Vespers and see our magnificent church with an entire wall made of stained glass. When the late afternoon sun flows through the glass windows, the interior of the church is filled with hundreds of dazzling rainbows, a spectacular sight that will gladden your hearts." He paused and waited as most of the visitors nodded their heads to indicate they would like to attend Vespers. "During Vespers you will also have a chance to hear the monks singing Gregorian chant, which originated in the Middle Ages and has a very simple, soothing, haunting rhythm. Some say the angels sing in Georgian Chant when praising God in heaven. After the Vespers' service, I encourage you to make the short walk to the monastic library, where you can view the vast collection of beautifully illuminated manuscripts. There were described by a previous visitor as something that will knock your socks off."

Bart waited for the laughter to die down before continuing. "There is coffee, tea, or soft drinks on the table to your right, along with some of the monastery's famous bread, which you can spread with butter, honey, or homemade jams. The Vesper service starts at five o'clock so that gives you about thirty minutes to take a break and enjoy all our homemade goodies. After Vespers you will have time to visit the abbey's library and view the illuminated medieval manuscripts."

He couldn't help thinking about Moore and made himself look around the hall to find him. He looked carefully, checking out each man, but he didn't see any sign of Moore. *He must have left through the door in the back, the part of the Hall that was dimly lit,* Bart thought. He knew that if Moore had decided to leave and call the police it would only take them twenty minutes to come from St. Cloud. He could feel sweat running down his body and smelled the fear coming from every pore. He was trying to decide between running and hiding or turning himself in to Moore when he felt a tug on his sleeve. He slowly turned, knowing he would be looking into Moore's eyes. But it was only Brother James. Bart let out an enormous sigh. Brother James smiled, handed him an envelope, and left without saying a word.

CHAPTER 44

On the front of the sealed envelope he saw a single hand-printed word: BART. His heart began to pound, and he knew his worst nightmare had come true. Moore had somehow seen through his disguise.

But how did he recognize me? Even I didn't know me when I looked into the mirror.

Then it suddenly came to him. His voice. Moore must have recognized his voice, which he hadn't disguised. Randolph had always bragged about secretly recording his clients' conversations. Randolph could have played back their conversation so Moore could recognize his voice during a phone call.

One last time he desperately studied each man in the big hall, which was now brightly lit. But there was no sign of a short man in a well-tailored suit. He looked down at his name on the envelope, torn it open, and with trembling hands pulled out a single piece of folded paper. He unfolded the paper and read the hand-printed message.

WHEN VESPERS BEGIN, MEET ME IN THE CONFESSIONAL ON THE RIGHT SIDE OF THE CHURCH. TELL NO ONE.

He read the note over and over as unanswered questions swirled around in his head like food in a blender. *Why hadn't Moore given me the note? Why did he want a secret meeting in the church? Wasn't he worried I might run? But where would I go? Only one road out of the monastery. He could easily follow me if I took off. But why meet in a confessional and why during Vespers?*

As he remembered from an earlier tour of the church, there were three standard confessionals on the left side of the church. They were all standard: small, dimly lit cubicles with privacy screens to shield the identify of the person doing the confessing. But on the right side of the church was a single confessional with a sign on the door that read BY APPOINTMENT ONLY. This wasn't the standard confessional but rather a relatively large, moderately lit room with two facing comfortable chairs and no privacy screen. Brother James had explained this room was used if someone wanted to confess and then discuss a religious or personal issue in a face-to-face setting. He realized Moore was being clever by not only arranging to meet in complete privacy but at a time when all the monks would be at Vespers and unable to come to his aid.

He folded the note from Moore, put it back into its envelope, and stuck it into his habit's large pocket. For a moment he thought about calling 911 and saying, "I need help. I'm about to be kidnapped from a monastery and arrested for cocaine possession." That sounded so absurd he had to smile, and that helped calm him down.

According to the big clock on the wall, the church bells would start ringing in about ten minutes, summoning everyone to Vespers. Once again he wiped his clammy hands on his all-forgiving wool habit. He needed to distract himself and began wandering around and talking to the visitors, who were gobbling up the goodies as if it were their last meal on earth.

"I enjoyed your lecture," a man said and then took a big bite from a piece of homemade bread overflowing with strawberry jam.

"Thanks. Glad you enjoyed it," was all Bart could say. He kept moving to hide his nervousness.

"Have you ever done an exorcism?" asked a woman in a plain, flowered dress who had stepped into his path. She looked at Bart while trying to lick some golden honey off her fingers.

"No, I haven't," he said and kept going, not wanting to explain he was only a probationary brother who was filling in for the abbot.

Waiting ten minutes seemed like ten hours, but finally the church bells began ringing and signaling it was time for Vespers. It also meant it was time for Bart's dreaded meeting with Moore. His big hope was to persuade Moore to meet in the abbot's office. In order to carry out his plan, he needed the abbot's help and support.

After he went through the plan again in his head—get Moore to hold off informing Randolph so he and Anna could return to San Diego, explain everything to the police, and clear themselves—he thought about all the trouble he was in. He glanced at the stature of St. Michael and silently prayed for help. He hadn't prayed since he was a kid, but right now he needed all the help he could get.

He followed the visitors as they left Hospitality Hall and walked the short distance to the monastery's modern church, whose entire front was made of stained glass windows. They entered through large, black-oak double door carved with faces of many well-known saints. The late afternoon sun was pouring through the stained glass windows, filling the interior with glorious colors that suggested a higher presence.

After the visitors were seated, the organist began playing the famous, majestic organ piece *Bach's Toccata and Fugue in D minor*, which thundered through the church and hinted of God's power. As the organ continued to play, monks filed into the sanctuary, an area close to and facing the altar. They carried lit candles and their hoods were up to show respect for God's presence. Half the monks went to the individual choir stalls on the right side of the altar while the other half went to the left side. After entering the individual choir stalls, the monks placed their candles into holders on top of each stall, creating a glowing light around the altar.

After the last two monks had entered their choir stalls, the organ's thunderous music suddenly stopped, resulting in a silence so absolute it often made visitors hold their collective breath. Then the monks began singing in unaccompanied Gregorian chant, their haunting, heavenly sounds floating through the church like a gentle breeze.

Bart had been standing near the back of the church, partially shielded by the baptismal font and its large, marble statue of St. John, whom the bible says baptized Jesus. When monks began singing and all attention was focused on them, he stepped out from behind the baptismal fountain, and following Moore's instructions, he walked the short distance to the confessional on the right side of the church. He stopped in front of the door with its "By Appointment Only" sign, glanced around to be sure no one was watching, and opened the door. He entered the lit room, expecting Moore would already be there, but the room was empty.

He could barely hear the monks singing and realized the room must have been partly soundproofed to prevent anyone from overhearing private conversations. He made himself sit down in a chair facing the door, but after a few minutes of nervous fidgeting, he got up and paced around the room like a lion in a small cage. When he got tired of pacing, he sat back down and just stared at the doorknob, wondering if Moore would be reasonable or a mean son-of-a-bitch.

After what seemed like several lifetimes, Bart saw the doorknob turn. The door started to open, and Bart knew his worst nightmare was about to come true. He wasn't surprised to see Moore had dressed in a monk's habit with the hood up so his face was concealed. Dressed as a monk and with his hood up, Moore could blend in and freely wander around the monastery, and that's how he must have discovered this very private confessional on the right side of the church.

Moore came into the room, closed the door, and walked forward until he stood directly in front of Bart, who was now standing and nervously waiting. Then Moore slowly pushed back his hood to reveal his face.

"Oh my God!" Bart exclaimed. "Can it really be? Am I dreaming?"

Bart's eyes were dilated to the max, and his mouth opened wide, as if he were seeing a ghost.

"Are you glad to see me?" Anna asked, breaking into a sensuous smile.

"Yes! Yes! Yes! I can't believe it. I was expecting someone else. You can't know how glad I am to see you!"

"My horoscope said to take chances, and so here I am," Anna said.

They both laughed.

"This is bigger than a surprise. It's a miracle," he said, and he felt like pinching himself to make sure he wasn't hallucinating. "I've got a million questions, and I don't know where to start."

"Please, save your questions for later. I have other things on my mind. And by the way, I think your shaved head is very sexy, but I could do without the beard and glasses," Anna said.

"I still can't believe it's really you," he said, taking off his glasses and letting them fall to the floor.

"I know you're a true scientist, so would you like me to prove I'm really Anna?".

"I certainly would," he said, remembering how Anna loved to play games.

"OK. Just sit back down, and I'll prove it's really me," she said.

He sat back down and watched as she slowly began to raise her monk's habit. She was wearing high heels that had made her appear tall enough to be mistaken for Moore. She slowly and teasingly raised her habit to reveal slim ankles, slender calves, and toned thighs. With each successive revelation Bart's heart rate and breathing reached new levels, and there was so much adrenalin pumping out that he feared exploding before seeing her really good stuff.

Anna paused, fixed Bart with a devilish smile, and asked, "Would you like more proof? Or have I convinced you?"

"More proof! More proof! More proof!" he shouted, like an overly excited cheerleader.

"Don't you feel just a little guilty about seeing a naked lady in church?" Anna asked.

"Well, I *am* having bad thoughts, and I hope God forgives me," he said, remembering all those dark nights in his monastic cell when he fantasized about seeing and touching Anna's gorgeous body. And now here she was, standing in front of him in high-definition, 3-D, living color.

She fluttered her eyes and began raising her habit inch-by-inch, revealing more and more, until in one quick over-the-head-motion, took off her habit and let it drop to the floor. She stood completely nude in front of him, showing off her luxurious curves. It was as if Aphrodite, Greek goddess of love and beauty, had suddenly come to life.

"Now it's your turn," Anna said. She bent over and whispered in his ear, "I want to do some very sinful things."

And they did many sinful things, stopping only when he heard the faint sound of people walking past the confessional door, which meant Vespers had ended.

"I can hear people walking by," he said.

"Are you sure we want to stop?" she asked, looking at him with big eyes full of excitement.

"I really, really don't want to stop but, I don't want to frighten some tourist who opens the door by mistake," he said.

They each put on their respective habits. Anna raised her hood to conceal her true identity, making sure her long, light brown, silky hair was completely hidden. If a curious visitor happened to open the confessional's door, he or she would see only two monks, sitting down, apparently having a serious discussion. Hopefully no one would notice that one of them was wearing high heels.

"You had been on my mind, so I checked the abbey's web site and saw that every second and fourth Sunday the monastery had open house. A second Sunday was coming up, so I thought it would be a great chance to see you," Anna said.

"I am so glad you came. Thoughts of you were always on my mind. I couldn't call or email to say how much I missed you because I had promised the abbot to refrain from any and all sexual activities, including contacting or encouraging you to visit. He knew your coming would be a temptation too great for me to resist. Of course, he was absolutely right. I can only guess what the abbot might say if he hears about what we did, but I think he would forgive me this one transgression."

"My lips are sealed, so the abbot will never hear about it from me," Anna said.

"So, how did you know about this confessional?"

"I ran into Brother James when I arrived today and asked him for help. I explained we had driven together to the monastery, and I had dropped you off and gone to live in the twin cities. I said I missed you and wanted to visit and asked if he knew somewhere private we might meet. He said you had done the monastery a great service and would be only too glad to help. He suggested we meet in this confessional during Vespers when all the monks would be in church and no one would see us. I thanked him and then wrote the note he gave you. "

"It was a brilliant idea, and one I'll never forget."

"Judging from your outstanding performance, I think being celibate has made you a far better and harder person," Anna said.

Her comment made them laugh so hard they reflexively covered their mouths to stifle the sound.

"I do have a million questions," he said, trying to decide which one to ask first.

"You're always so full of questions. I wonder how you get through life knowing so few answers," Anna said.

He had to smile at Anna's very clever and funny put-down.

"We have a great relationship. I'm full of questions, and you're full of answers," he said

"So, you think I'm pretty smart to arrange all this. Perhaps even as smart as you?" Anna asked.

"There's no doubt about. You are very smart, perhaps even smarter than me."

"I think I'll write that down and have you sign it, and then I'll put it on the refrigerator door for all to see," Anna said and gave a satisfied look.

"Well, let's start with an easy question. How did you decide to come on this particular Sunday?"

"Of that's easy. My horoscope said to do something that had been on my mind," she said and then added, "I seem to remember since Las Vegas you've become a fan of horoscopes."

"A really big fan," he said, and his face broke into a huge grin.

"But I think the more interesting question is who gave me a ride to the monastery when my car broke down?"

"Well, who did?

CHAPTER 45

— — —

"You'll never believe who it was," Anna said.

"Tell me right now, or you'll be sorry."

"How sorry?" she asked.

"Tell me now or a big red pimple will pop out of the end of your nose." That was the biggest threat he could make since Anna feared pimples even more than big, black, creepy spiders.

"Who's the last person in the world, besides the devil and your stepfather, you'd want to meet?"

He shuddered at naming the person but finally said in almost a whisper, "Matthew Moore."

"And what's so bad about him?"

"Randolph sent him to find me and take me back to San Diego so the police can put me in jail."

"You won't be going to jail," she said and confidently raised her chin.

"That's great news, but how can you be so sure?" he asked.

"I'll tell you why but only after you apologize for saying something that really hurt my feelings."

"What did I say?" he asked, knowing he sometimes shot his mouth off when he should have kept it shut. He also knew Anna's feelings were easily hurt, and she could hold a grudge to the end of time.

"On our trip from San Diego, we were talking about fate, and you said only dummies and know-nothings believed fate affected their lives. I found that remark insulting and disrespectful," she said and lowered her head to emphasize her hurt feelings.

He knew Anna seriously believed fate played a major role in her life. Since there was no way to prove fate did or didn't exist, it had been pompous of him to say otherwise.

"I am sorry and do apologize for running at the mouth and hurting your feelings. I should have known better," he said and looked into Anna's eyes to show he was being sincere.

Anna did not reply immediately but instead stared into his eyes. After a few seconds, she nodded and said, "I know you're being sincere, and I'm glad you're man enough to admit fate often has the answer when science doesn't."

That wasn't quite what he had said, but this wasn't the time to argue over details. Instead he asked, "Who did give you a ride?"

"You already guessed. It was Matthew Moore, who turned out to be a really thoughtful, sympathetic, and understanding person," she said.

"You may think Moore is understanding and sympathetic, but he's here to take me back to San Diego and have me arrested for hiding your cocaine under my bed," he said, his tone more angry than he had intended.

"Don't go blaming me. Hiding the cocaine was your great idea. If it were up to me, I'd have dumped it over the Ocean Beach pier and watched the whales and dolphins have the time of their lives."

"I'm sorry. I don't have any reason to get angry with you. I'm just on edge. I don't know what Moore will do when he finds me."

"Stop your worrying. I have straightened things out with Moore," Anna said and smiled graciously.

"And how exactly did you manage to straighten everything out with Moore?"

"Well, thanks to fate, my car happened to run out of gas just as Moore was driving up behind me. He was kind enough to stop, and he offered to give me a lift to the monastery."

"And then?" Bart asked and gestured for her to go on.

"You know how it's sometimes easier to talk to strangers and tell them all your troubles. Well that's what happened. Before long I was telling Moore everything. Fighting with Tony Koole. Stealing his briefcase. Discovering it was full of cocaine. Panicking and driving to San Diego. Asking for your help. Hiding the cocaine under your bed. Leaving town and coming to the monastery." Anna sighed with relief.

"Did Moore believe you?"

"He said he did, and I believe him because he has honest eyes," she said.

"So what happens next?" he asked, hoping Anna had actually straightened everything out.

"Moore suggested meeting in the abbot's office," she said.

"That's incredible. Just what I wanted to do," he said, but in the back of his mind there rose the frightening thought that this all seemed too easy.

"I told him we could meet in the abbot's office after Vespers since you would be extremely busy during Vespers," she said and grinned from ear to ear.

"You're right about being occupied during Vespers," he said and leaned over to kiss her neck and nibble her ear.

"He was kind enough to give me his cell number and told me to call if you agreed to meet him in the abbot's office."

She reached into her habit's big pocket, pulled out her cell phone, and speed dialed Moore's number.

"Hi, it's Anna. I talked to Bart, and he and I will meet you in the abbot's office in about twenty minutes. Bart wants to thank you for helping us out." Then she listened for a few seconds and clicked off.

"I'm glad you thanked Moore for helping us."

"See, I told you I was good at straightening things out."

She leaned forward and gave him a long, sweet kiss that grew more passionate until he forced himself to draw back.

"I'd love to do this forever, but if we don't stop now we'll miss our meeting with Moore. And I still want to know how you got that habit and how you knew about this private confessional."

"Take a wild guess about who helped me."

"That's easy. You rolled your big eyes, looked helpless, and turned Brother James into your guardian angel," he said.

"Brother James said he was glad to help since you had just saved the monastery from financial ruin," she said and gave a shy smile.

"I need to thank Brother James, and I'll let him keep my favorite Mighty Mouse T-shirt to show my appreciation," he said.

"But the idea to disguise myself in a monk's habit was mine. It suddenly came to me when I saw a habit hanging in the back of the visitor's lounge. I took the habit and went into the adjoining bathroom a woman and came out a monk. I stashed my woman's clothes in a cabinet. Now I better go back to the visitor's lounge. This time I'll go into the bathroom a monk and come back out a woman. Although I must admit, being a monk was truly one of the great experiences of my life," she said.

They both laughed and hugged for a long time.

Finally, Anna stepped back, pulled up the habit's hood to partially conceal her face, and made sure her golden hair was not showing.

He watched her leave first and waited several more minutes before exiting the confessional. He would soon be meeting Moore and wanted to think about what might happen. The church was completely empty and so peaceful. He sat down in one of the back pews and admired the stunning colors coming from the wall of stained glass windows. Then, unexpectedly, a frightening image popped into his head. He saw Randolph grinning and sitting in his big, black leather office chair. Fear washed over him as if he had been hit by a huge ocean wave.

Randolph was paying Moore big bucks to bring him back to San Diego. Meeting in the abbot's office might be a trick. The police might be there, waiting to arrest him. Was he about to make the biggest mistake of his life?

He felt beads of sweat running down his sides. He thought about calling Father Dreadforth and asking for help. Perhaps he could hide out in one of the monastery's outbuildings until dark. Then Dreadforth could pick him up and maybe help him get to Florida and stay with Jim and Harry. He would be safe there for a while, but he'd be on the run and would have to keep looking behind him. *And what about Anna?* He couldn't leave her now.

He took several deep breaths to calm down and think straight. Anna had believed Moore was going to help them, and he trusted in Anna's uncanny ability to judge if someone were telling the truth. More than anything he wanted to straighten everything out. The only solution was to meet with Moore and stop this madness.

He checked his watch, got up, and forced himself to walk to the visitor's lounge. He hoped that either Anna's fate or the abbot's God would help straighten everything out.

CHAPTER 46

— — —

Bart went to the visitor's center and couldn't help fidgeting as he waited for Anna to appear. At long last she came out dressed in her own clothes, looking attractive and hopeful. She immediately came over and whispered in his ear, "Just remember. I straightened everything out. Moore is going to help us."

As Bart and Anna were walking to the abbot's office, he couldn't get rid of the nagging feeling that Moore had lied to Anna and he was walking into a trap.

When he knocked on the abbot's door, he was unconsciously holding his breath.

"Come in," the abbot said through the door.

Bart's muscles tensed as he thought about police waiting to arrest him. Then he slowly opened the door and stepped aside so Anna could enter first. He followed her, and what he saw made his eyes get big and his mouth open wide, as if seeing a vision. In the middle of the room stood the abbot. He was doing a slow, soft-shoe shuffle, holding up his habit to show off his latest pair of racy, colorful running shoes. Watching him was a well-dressed man who Bart assumed must be Mathew Moore.

Without a moment's hesitation, Anna was at the abbot's side, joining in his slow soft-shoe shuffle. They looked like two little kids having a wonderful time. Even Brother James, who had been standing in the background, was smiling and enjoying the performance. The delightfully bizarre scene was like something from *Alice in Wonderland*.

The abbot soon tired and went to sit and rest in his office chair. Matthew Moore walked over and said, "Well, you certainly gave me a run for the money. Should I call you Brother Paul, or do you prefer Bart?"

"I guess I won't be Brother Paul much longer, so Bart is fine."

"Anna's car running out of gas as I was coming by was a fortunate coincidence," Moore continued. "On the drive to the monastery, she explained all that had happened to the both of you. I believe Anna's explanation of what happened and realize neither she nor you have committed any crimes. I've also had a chance to talk with the abbot, and he gave you the highest recommendation. Taking all this into consideration, I will do all in my power to help you and Anna get this mess straightened out. And I must add, it's turned into a big mess. There's not only Randolph, who is roaring mad and anxious to find you, but there is also an outstanding warrant for your arrest for possessing a considerable amount of cocaine."

"Anna told me she'd talked to you and straightened everything out, but it sounded too good to be true. I couldn't help worrying you'd follow Randolph's orders and have me arrested as soon as you found me. But hearing you say you'd be willing to help takes a big, big load off my mind. I'll be forever in you debt," Bart said, sticking out his hand and shaking Moore's hand long and hard.

"See, I told you Mathew's an understanding and sympathetic person and would help us," Anna said and gave Moore a big smile.

Just then the abbot's phone rang, and everyone grew silent. Brother James looked angry because he had told the monk at the reception desk not to forward any calls but instead take messages. The abbot looked unhappy because he did not want to be disturbed until everything had been settled. Bart looked worried because all along he had expected Mathew was setting a trap and the police were calling to say they were at the front desk. Anna was not the least bit concerned because she believed fate and Matthew were both on her side.

The abbot finally said, "It must be a mistake."

But the phone kept ringing, and after the seventh ring, the abbot reluctantly picked up phone. "This is Abbot Aloysius."

The room remained silent, and everyone watched the abbot's expression change from surprise, to alarm, and then worry, all within seconds.

The abbot listened and said only, "Yes, I understand."

Then he handed the phone to Bart and said, "It is your sister, Carol. She wants to talk to you."

Having seen the alarm and worry in the abbot's expression, Bart gingerly took the phone as if it were a red-hot poker.

Bart asked in an anxious tone, "Carol, what's happened?"

"A little while ago mom got a frightening phone call from a man with a thick Mexican accent. The man said his group had kidnapped Randolph and taken him across the border into Tijuana. They would return him unharmed after she paid a three million dollar ransom, not a penny less. If she argued about the amount, they would only raise it. Mom thought it might be a cruel joke and asked to speak to Randolph. Randolph came on the phone and said he was all right. Before he could say any more, the kidnapper came back on. He said she had five days, more than enough time to get the money. It was to be used, unmarked fifty and one-hundred-dollar bills. He'd call back with instructions about where and how to make the exchange. He warned if she told the police or the FBI, she would never see Randolph again. I immediately called Billy and told him about the phone call. He said kidnapping was a big business in Mexico and much of South America. But he was surprised because Mexican gangs rarely come into the U.S. to kidnap American citizens and take them back to Tijuana. He thinks someone in the U.S. must also be involved. This is really hard on mom, so I'm staying with her now. And I don't think it's safe for you to come back to San Diego. Billy checked and there's an outstanding warrant for your arrest," Carol finished.

"This all sounds like a bad movie, but I'm sure Billy will know what to do," Bart said. "I hate to say it, but I think Randolph finally got what he deserved. Right now I'm more worried about how mom is doing," Bart said.

"She's doing all right. She can be tough when needed. Is there anything new at your end?" Carol asked.

"There is, and you'll never believe who showed up today," Bart said.

"Did Mathew Moore finally find you?" Carol asked.

"Yes he did, but what happened next is even more unbelievable," Bart said.

"Don't keep me in suspense. What happened?" Carol asked.

"Matthew happened to run into Anna on the way to the monastery. She told him all that happened, and he's agreed to help Anna and me straighten everything out. It's such great news, and I still am having trouble believing it. He's standing right here, so I'll let you tell him about Randolph's kidnapping," Bart said and handed the phone to Moore.

Moore took the phone and said, "I overheard part of Bart's conversation, something about Randolph's kidnapping."

"I know this may be difficult for you to believe," Carol said. And then filled Moore in about Randolph's kidnapping.

"This is difficult to believe," Moore said after hearing everything.

"I've asked Billy Lightfoot to take charge. He's a good friend of mine, and like you, he's a private detective. Billy thinks Randolph's kidnappers are part of a dangerous Tijuana gang who are in the business of kidnapping wealthy individuals. At this point, Billy told my mom not to call the police or the FBI until we know more."

"I don't know Billy Lightfoot personally, but I know of his well-deserved reputation. I also know his unique nickname, Bad Billy. He's a first-rate private detective, and I'll be glad to assist him in any way I can. I'll try to get a late-night flight out of Minneapolis tonight and hopefully be back in San Diego tomorrow. I agree with Billy to hold off informing the police and FBI until we know more. If you give me your and Billy's cell phone numbers, I'll call as soon as I arrive in San Diego," Mathew said. He wrote down the phone numbers she gave him.

Then Carol asked, "Now that you've found Bart, what are you going to do?" Mathew switched the abbot's phone to speaker mode so everyone in the office could hear his answer.

"I first must say I was reluctant to search for Bart because I believed any caring father should do everything possible to help a son in trouble. Instead, Randolph was looking for Bart so he could be turned over to the police, and I didn't think that was right. I decided that when I found Bart, I would first listen to his side before informing Randolph or the police," Matthew said.

Carol broke in and said, "Both Billy and I think Randolph got involved in a financial deal that went bad. He lost a lot of money, perhaps millions, and needed to cover his loses. He could cover his losses by getting control of Bart's trust fund, which apparently would happen if Bart were arrested and had a criminal record. So it all comes down to money and greed," Carol said.

"I'm only glad I happened to meet Anna, whose car gave out on the way to the monastery. We had a chance to talk, and she explained about impulsively stealing Tony Koole's briefcase, which happened to be full of cocaine and Bart putting it under his bed for the goons to find when they came looking. It turns out I had heard rumors about Tony Koole being a porn producer and having mob connections. I immediately called a detective I know on the San Diego Police Force and asked if any other fingerprints were found on the case besides Bart and Anna's. He said they had also found prints of Tony Koole and his two goons, all of whom have long police records. I told the detective how Anna and Bart had accidentally gotten their hands on the cocaine. He listened and agreed to hold off arresting them until after they had a chance to make their statements. Because of Bart's outstanding warrant, I'd advise he and Anna to drive back to San Diego. I'll arrange for a good lawyer to accompany them to the police station when they make their statements. After the detective gives their statements to the prosecution, I'm sure all changes will be dropped," Matthew said.

Bart had been listening closely to how Matthew would help and got so excited he ran over to Anna, gave her a big hug and kiss, and then lifted her off her feet and swung her around like two little kids having the time of their lives. After Bart put Anna down, he was smiling from ear to ear as he went over to hug both the abbot and Brother James.

Carol heard Bart's shouts of joy in the background and waited a few minutes before saying, "I want to thank you for all your kindness and understanding and helping Bart and Anna clear themselves."

"When I heard their sides of the story, I had no choice but to help," Matthew said. He knew that was the least he could do, especially after bugging Carol's condo to find out where Bart might be hiding. He would make up for doing that dirty deed by now helping Bart and Anna clear themselves of all charges.

"Many, many thanks," Carol said again. "And call me when you get back to San Diego so I can arrange a meeting with mom and Billy."

"Will do," Matthew said. He put down the phone and looked around the abbot's office at all the smiling faces.

The abbot said, "God acts in mysterious and wondrous ways."

"Amen to that," Matthew said. He truly hoped everything would work out.

"Double amen," Bart said. He couldn't help but to wonder if God had added a helping hand.

"Triple amen," Brother James said. He was glad his prayers for Bart's deliverance had been answered.

"A hundred amens," Anna said. She was certain fate had come to their rescue.

Matthew watched everyone celebrate with high fives and couldn't help thinking about the sudden turn of events. He had great difficult believing Randolph had been kidnapped and at some level thought Randolph might have finally gotten the just punishment he deserved. Matthew had never liked doing Randolph's dirty deeds, especially being told to go to Tijuana and meet Oscar Gonzales, a notorious drug dealer and former client who owed Randolph a favor. Mathew was supposed to arrange for Oscar to eliminate Tony Koole and his two goons as soon as possible. But Mathew had never gone to meet Oscar in Tijuana because arranging murders, even of worthless mobsters, was where he drew the line. He couldn't help thinking Koole and his goons might have joined up with Oscar and the three of them had arranged to kidnap Randolph. They certainly knew Randolph's wife was wealthy and able to pay a huge ransom. Both Oscar and Koole were ruthless and they would do anything if the price were right. And three million dollars was certainly the right price for doing a kidnapping.

CHAPTER 47

———

Matthew had taken a midnight out of Minneapolis and arrived in San Diego on Monday morning. Later that day he met with Billy, Carol, and Marjorie and discussed plans to come up with three million dollars by Thursday, when the kidnappers said the exchange would occur.

Anna and Bart had arrived early Tuesday, after 35 hours of nonstop driving, except for eating at fast food places and using their restrooms. They had met with Matthew and his lawyer friend, gone over to the police station, made their statements, and had to wait for the prosecutor to read their statements and consult with the detective handling the case. The detective informed the prosecutor of Tony Koole and his two goons' fingerprints being all over the cocaine-filled brief case and that Bart and Anna had not really done anything criminal, except handle the case. The prosecutor agreed with the detective, dropped all charges against Bart and Anna, and cancelled Bart's outstanding warrant. The prosecutor put out a new warrant for Tony Koole and his two goons, but the detective said he had looked for them and that they were no longer in Los Angeles.

Bart and Anna celebrated by dressing up and going to one of the fanciest restaurants in San Diego, which was a wonderful change from eating greasy fast food and wearing the same clothes for 35 hours. They slept late at Bart's house, had lunch on Ocean Beach Pier, and talked about whether or not Randolph deserved to be kidnapped. When it came time to vote, both raised their hands to signal "yes."

After lunch, Bart and Anna went over to his mom's house to meet Carol, Billy, and Matthew, who were discussing how to deal with Randolph's kidnapping.

"Why haven't the kidnappers called?" Marjorie asked for the hundredth time.

"Don't worry, mom," Carol said. "I'm sure they'll call soon, and we can use the time to discuss some important issues."

Just then the phone rang, and Marjorie anxiously answered it. "Hello," she said. She listened for a moment and then held the phone out.

"Carol, it's for you. It's Helen at your lab. She sounds really upset."

Carol took the phone and asked, "Helen, what's happened?"

"Oh, I know it's a bad time for you, but something terrible has happened. Yesterday, when you told the secretary about not being in today, Sleazy Sam must have overheard. When I walked into our lab a few minutes ago to make sure all the equipment was turned off, I found Sleazy Sam sitting at you computer, holding a flash drive. He looked shocked to see me and tried to cover up by saying you had told him to check your computer for any viruses. I'm sure he had copied something, and it's got to be the new, more accurate algorithms we've just developed for our lie detector. Remember I told you earlier he had quizzed me about our algorithms and I had foolishly bragged about our accuracy being in nineties. I'm sure he's stolen our latest algorithms! Should I call security or the police?"

"Don't call anyone. For sometime I've suspected Sleazy Sam was after our algorithms, especially after you warned me of his interest. Like you, I don't trust him. So I set a trap. I labeled a file *Newest Algorithms*. At first glance the algorithms look very impressive, but they turn out to be pure junk. Apparently Sleazy took the bait, and he'll try to sell the algorithms for a lot of money to one of our commercial competitors. When that competitor finds out the algorithms are junk, Sleazy will have to run for his life. I never leave the real algorithms on my computer. I carry them with me at all times on a flash drive that looks like trinket," said Carol.

"You think of everything," Helen said and let out a big sigh of relief.

"I know we're on the right path, and pretty soon the accuracy of our brain lie detector will be in high nineties. Just image a world where important people will have to tell the truth or else."

"It's mind-boggling," Helen said. "I can't wait to test Steven, my new person, and ask him if he loves me!"

"You just met him, so give him few months before popping the question," Carol said. "I have to go now. We're expecting an important phone call."

"Okay," Helen replied. "Talk to you soon."

As Carol hung up the phone, she noticed everyone was looking at her. She shook her head and said, "Don't ask. Right now we need to discuss some important issues about Randolph."

"What issues?" Marjorie asked, her nerves on edge and the growing pain in her right temple signaled the onset of a migraine headache. Before anyone could answer he question, she made a beeline for her bathroom to get a migraine pill. "I'll be right back," she shouted over her shoulder.

Carol said to the group, "Both Billy and I have critical information about terrible things Randolph's done, and mom needs to hear it."

"I too have some troubling information about Randolph," Matthew said.

They waited in silence and their faces showed the growing tension. In a few minutes, Marjorie came back and sat down. She noticed everyone seemed to be looking at her. "What going on? What did I miss?" she asked.

"Mom, this is going to be difficult for you to hear, but we must discuss some awful things Randolph has done. The first one involves the anonymous note you received about Randolph having a mistress. Do you remember that note?" Carol asked.

"I remember that awful note, and I'm sure it's pure nonsense," Marjorie said, fighting back tears because that note had ripped a hole in her heart.

"I've never heard anything about some anonymous note," Bart said, reaching over to hold his mother's trembling hand.

"Some time ago," Carol began, "Mother received an anonymous note saying that Randolph was having an affair with his secretary. Mom had said she didn't believe it and thought somebody wanted to make trouble for Randolph. I wondered it there were any truth to the accusation and asked Billy to check it out. I've never told mom what Billy learned, but now I think she needs to know. I'll let Billy tell you what he discovered."

Billy said, "After Carol told me about the note, I watched Randolph for several weeks and found that after leaving his building at night, he got into a waiting taxi and went to an expensive-looking condo in Solana Beach. I discovered a dummy corporation in the Cayman Islands owned the condo. The current resident was listed as a 'Miss Murphy,' but that was a fake name. The current resident was actually Randolph's secretary. I have photos of Randolph and his secretary, singly and together, entering and leaving the condo. I think there is no question Randolph was having an affair with his secretary," Billy said. "Carol and I were going to tell you about this earlier but they never seemed to be a good time. But now we both agreed it was time you knew."

Marjorie could no longer hold back her tears. "Oh no. Oh no. How could he?" she said between sobs. "He promised me he was faithful."

"What a cruel bastard!" Bart shouted. He saw his mom in tears and put his hands on her shoulders, gently massaging, showing his love and soothing her pain.

Carol said, "I'm afraid there's more to this story. It turns out grandfather did not like or trust Randolph. He told me about a stipulation he had asked mom to add to the prenuptial agreement. If there were evidence Randolph was unfaithful, she could immediately initiate divorce proceeding and prevent Randolph from making any claims to her money. Randolph took all those precautions to hide his affair because he had a great deal to lose."

The room was silent. Everyone saw the pain in Marjorie's face, watched the tears streaming down her checks, and wanted to say something to comfort her.

Finally Carol said, "I'm so sorry, mom. I put off telling you about Randolph's affair because I know how much it would hurt. We might never have found out except for the anonymous note. And I'm ever sorrier to say there is more ugliness to tell. Again, I'll let Billy fill you in."

"I think we were all puzzled why detectives suddenly showed up at Bart's house with a warrant to search his house for illegal drugs. No judge would issue a warrant unless the police could say they were tipped off by a reputable source. I have some good friends on the police force, and it only took a few beers to learn the tipoff came from the stepfather, a prominent lawyer. In other words, it was Randolph."

"That son-of-a-bitch!" Bart shouted. "I hate him and wouldn't pay ten cents to get him back."

Marjorie had covered her eyes with her hands and was visibly trembling. Then she lowered her hands and said in little more than a whisper, "I remember being so happy when Randolph called to say he wanted to be a better father. He wanted to start by taking Bart to a baseball game. I would never have believed Randolph would do anything so terrible as try to have his stepson arrested." Her soft words came across almost like a shout in the eerily quiet room. Finishing her thought, she finally broke down completely. She was sobbing uncontrollably and making painful sounds, like those of a wounded animal.

Carol came over and sat down next to her mom. She put one arm around her mom's shoulders, pulled her close, and whispered in her ear. "I'm so sorry for how Randolph's treated you and Bart. I'm so sorry."

Then Carol looked over at Billy and nodded.

Billy nodded back and said, "We were also puzzled as to why Randolph wanted Bart arrested. It turns out Randolph got greedy and invested two million dollars in the notorious Chinese Company that claimed to have found a cure for baldness that later proved a hoax. The bank only loaned Randolph the two million dollars because the loan had a responsible, wealth cosigner, whose name was Marjorie."

Everyone heard Marjorie gasp in disbelief. "I never cosigned a loan for two million dollars. I certainly would have remembered a loan for that much. I don't understand why he would steal money from his own wife?"

Then the realization hit her hard, as if being punched in the gut. How many times had Randolph lied to her, stole from her or forged her name on documents. How many times had he said he was working late so he could see his mistress? How could he have arranged to have his own stepson arrested by the police? She had been duped her over and over. But no more! She stopped crying, sat up straighter, and felt her hurt turn into anger.

"Marjorie is right," Billy said. "The bank finally had the loan document examined by a handwriting expert. The expert concluded Marjorie's signature was a very good forgery. After the baldness hoax, Randolph needed to find a way to pay of his two million dollar loan. Apparently he had slipped a stipulation to Bart's trust that if Bart were ever arrested, Randolph would gain complete control of the trust and raid it as needed. That's why Randolph sent Mathew searching for Bart, because the sooner Bart was found, the sooner police could arrest him, and sooner Randolph could start raiding Bart's trust."

"Fucking bastard!" Bart shouted. "I can't believe it. Randolph turns out to be an adulterer, a forger, and an embezzler. He was rotten through and through."

"Billy, are sure about all this?" Marjorie asked, looking stern and in control, like she used to be before marrying Randolph and letting him run things. She was done crying and beginning to feel nothing but contempt for Randolph.

"I wish I could say I had some doubts, but it's all true," Billy said.

"Just when you think it can't get any worse, it does," Matthew said. "I'm afraid I too have something to add to Randolph's growing list of terrible deeds. Tony Koole and his two goons came to see Randolph. They were claiming his stepson, Bart, had let the police take their cocaine worth two million dollars. I'm guessing Randolph was given the choice of either paying the two million or they'd kill him. At that point, Randolph told me to go to Tijuana and meet with Oscar Gonzales, a notorious drug dealer and kidnapper. I was to arrange for Oscar to eliminate, that is, murder Tony and his two goons. I never did meet Oscar because I wasn't going to be involved in anyone's murder. I hate to say it, but Randolph seems to have been a very well-dressed, pure-blooded sociopath."

Everyone was stunned by Randolph's list of repulsive behaviors, and no one knew what to say. The room remained silent for what seemed a long time. While each one was waiting for the other to speak, the phone rang and broke the silence like a stone being thrown a window.

Carol was getting up to answer it when Marjorie stopped her.

"I'll get it," Marjorie insisted. She stood up and walked over to the phone. She knew, as did all the others, the kidnappers had called at last. She picked up the phone and set it on speaker.

"Ju know me?" asked a man with a thick Mexican accent.

"Yes I do," Marjorie said in a calm determined voice. "You're one of the kidnappers."

"Ju got three million?"

There was a long pause.

"Don't fuck me. Ju got it or not?" repeated the kidnapper.

There was another long pause. Then Marjorie put back her shoulders, rose to her full height and said, "I do not have the money."

"Ju had five days. By tomorrow…or else. "

"I am not getting the money tomorrow or ever," she said very slowly and confidently.

"Ju stupid bitch. No money, no Randolph."

Marjorie waited. She gathered her courage and said, "I understand perfectly."

"Dumb bitch. Ju pay up…or else."

Marjorie took a deep breath, let it out, and then said in a clear, controlled voice, "As my son said, Randolph's not worth ten cents."

"Ju crazy. Don't pay. We do bad things to him?"

She was holding the phone tightly. She could never forgive Randolph for lying to her and having Bart arrested and even arranging to have somebody killed. Her anger had turned into hate and disgust. Randolph wasn't worth ten cents. He was a horrible person. He needed a taste of his own medicine.

Then out of nowhere a well-known line popped into her head. It was from her favorite movie. It was said by a character who had had experienced countless lies and deceit and would take no more. She raised her chin and announced, "Frankly, my dear, I don't give a damn."

And then she hung up the phone.

After a moment of absolute shock, everyone was standing and applauding and shouting and laughing. She had said what they all secretly hoped. They had wondered if she had strength to turn her back on Randolph as he had turned his back on his family.

"Mother you were great. Randolph got what he deserved. I'm so proud of you," Carol said.

"I hope the kidnappers cut off his balls," Bart said and gave his mother a big hug.

"You made the right call," Billy said and nodded his head in agreement.

"I admire your strength and courage," Matthew said and gave Marjorie a big reassuring smile.

"You're going to have a great life because fate is surely your best friend," Anna said and hugged Marjorie.

Marjorie knew she could never forgive Randolph for all the horrible things he had done. In the end, she thought Randolph got what he truly deserved. He could the rest of his life with a bunch of rotten kidnappers.

And may they all burn in hell.